W9-APN-480

For the King

ALSO BY CATHERINE DELORS

Mistress of the Revolution

For the King

CATHERINE DELORS

DUTTON

DUTTON
Published by Penguin Group (USA) Inc.
375 Hudson Street, New York, New York 10014, U.S.A.
Penguin Group (Canada), 90 Eglinton Avenue East, Suite 700, Toronto, Ontario M4P 2Y3, Canada
(a division of Pearson Penguin Canada Inc.); Penguin Books Ltd, 80 Strand, London WC2R 0RL,
England; Penguin Group Ireland, 25 St. Stephen's Green, Dublin 2, Ireland (a division of Penguin
Books Ltd); Penguin Group (Australia), 250 Camberwell Road, Camberwell, Victoria 3124, Australia
(a division of Pearson Australia Group Pty Ltd); Penguin Books India Pvt Ltd, 11 Community Centre,
Panchsheel Park, New Delhi–110 017, India; Penguin Group (NZ), 67 Apollo Drive, Rosedale, North
Shore 0632, New Zealand (a division of Pearson New Zealand Ltd); Penguin Books (South Africa)
(Pty) Ltd, 24 Sturdee Avenue, Rosebank, Johannesburg 2196, South Africa

Penguin Books Ltd, Registered Offices: 80 Strand, London WC2R 0RL, England

Published by Dutton, a member of Penguin Group (USA) Inc.

First printing, July 2010
1   3   5   7   9   10   8   6   4   2

 REGISTERED TRADEMARK—MARCA REGISTRADA

LIBRARY OF CONGRESS CATALOGING-IN-PUBLICATION DATA has been applied for.
ISBN 978-0-525-95174-2

Printed in the United States of America

PUBLISHER'S NOTE

For Milette

For the King

From triumph to downfall there is but one step. I have noted that, in the most momentous occasions, mere nothings have always decided the outcome of the greatest events.

NAPOLÉON BONAPARTE, 1797

I

*I*t had been one of the shortest days of the Year Nine of the Republic, the 3rd of the month of Nivose in the revolutionary calendar. The 24th of December 1800, old style. Christmas Eve, as they used to say before the Revolution. Night had long fallen on Rue Nicaise. People were beginning to call it Rue Saint-Nicaise again, for saints were reappearing in everyday language. A few hundred yards away, the lights at the windows of the Palace of the Tuileries glowed dim through the fog.

Passersby, wrapped in coats, hurried home, their workday over. Some, smartly dressed, were going to the houses of friends to celebrate the ancient holiday with a *réveillon*, the traditional Christmas Eve feast. In the Café d'Apollon, patrons were drinking and cheering.

The shops were still open. The glove maker's pregnant wife, her two-year-old boy clutching her skirts with both hands, leaned against her counter. She chatted with her maid, who was peeling carrots and turnips in preparation for the feast. The tailor next door was cutting a piece of fabric laid on his workbench. Across the street, the watchmaker, a magnifying lens to his eye, inserted a spring into a timepiece. Musicians, recognizable by the odd-shaped cases they carried, hurried in the direction of the brightly lit Longueville mansion. They had been hired for a lavish party there.

In spite of the damp chill, people on Rue Nicaise kept their doors and windows open to see the carriage of Napoléon Bonaparte, the First Consul, pass by.

France had been a Republic since 1792. King Louis XVI had been guillotined. General Bonaparte, since seizing power a year ago and becoming the First Consul, had settled in the royal Palace of the Tuileries. He liked to drive around Paris in a carriage drawn by six white horses, accompanied by a guard of soldiers, at the sound of trumpets, drums artillery salvos.

Tonight, however, there would be no such military pomp. The newspapers had announced that the First Consul was simply to attend the première of *The Creation of the World*, by Haydn, at the Opera. It was the most anticipated musical event of the season, and tickets sold for twice the usual price.

Joseph de Limoëlan was well informed of this. He had read and reread all the details in every newspaper, though he did not plan on attending the show. Indeed he was not dressed for an evening at the Opera.

Whip in hand, coarse trousers and a loose jacket disguising his tall, slender frame, he led a horse-drawn cart down the street. A gray tarpaulin came down to the hubs of its wheels. Clouds of mist blew out of the nag's nostrils with each of its breaths. Another man, Pierre de Saint-Régent, also slightly built, his brows knit, walked by the side of the cart, his mouth tight. A third companion, François Carbon, strutted close behind on his short, sturdy legs, and stared at every woman they passed. The three men were dressed in matching blue jackets, coarsely embroidered around the neck in red and white.

Limoëlan stopped the cart in front of the Café d'Apollon. He had surveyed one last time the whole length of the street that afternoon, and determined this was the narrowest spot. But Saint-Régent's frown became more pronounced.

"No, this light won't do at all," he hissed, nodding in the direction of the café. Its windows projected bright yellow rectangles that illuminated this entire stretch of the street.

Limoëlan, without a word, pulled on the horse's bridle. The animal snorted and set forth reluctantly. They moved the cart thirty yards down Rue Nicaise, at the intersection of Rue de Malte. It was darker there, and the other street provided an escape route, should any of them escape.

Limoëlan stopped the cart sideways to impede the flow of traffic. Other drivers pulled on their reins, swerved and cursed at the three men, who ignored the volleys of insults. Each in turn went into the Café d'Apollon and, grim-faced, gulped down in silence mug after mug of wine. Their purpose was firm, of course, and they were entirely devoted to the holiest of causes. Yet such is human frailty that even the bravest fear death. Had not some of the saints themselves, though assured of the rewards that awaited them in eternal life, recoiled from the glory of martyrdom?

The three men, braced by their visit to the Café d'Apollon, gathered again around the cart. Limoëlan spoke in a low voice to his companions and left in the direction of the Seine River. Carbon seized the bridle of the horse and looked around. He whistled at a young woman, who hurried away.

Limoëlan walked along the embankment that followed the Louvre galleries. He paused, took off his gold-rimmed spectacles and wiped them with a checkered handkerchief. He groaned with impatience. How was he to find what he wanted in this fog? He pushed to the Pont-Royal, the "Liberty Bridge," as the scoundrels now had the impudence to call it. He crossed the river. On the Left Bank, he recognized the massive outline of the former Hackneys' Office, which had recently been turned into barracks. Among the flow of the passersby, he finally distinguished two slight figures standing under a streetlight by the entrance. Children, apparently. He approached. Now he could see their skirts. Two girls, little street vendors, stomping their feet in the cold. Each carried a wicker tray, attached by a leather strap to her shoulder.

Limoëlan paused. Either girl would do, but he only needed one. It bothered him to make that choice. Then, when he drew very close, he saw that the tray of one of the street vendors still contained a few cakes and biscuits. The other girl had already sold all of her wares and was apparently waiting for her companion to be done. No doubt it was a sign. *She* was the chosen one.

Limoëlan addressed her gently. A smile lit her pockmarked face when he put a silver coin in her hand. She giggled, slipped the strap above her head and handed the other girl her empty tray.

"Take it home to Mama, will you?" she said in a cheerful tone.

As the girl followed Limoëlan across the river to Rue Nicaise, he turned around to glance at her bony frame, dressed in a tattered striped skirt. She was gathering around her neck the collar of a woolen coat. The sleeves were too short and left her wrists, red with cold, bare. How old was she? Twelve, thirteen? He had not asked her name. It did not matter. He shivered and resolved not to look at her again.

"Hurry, will you?" he said, looking straight ahead. "We haven't all night."

She pressed on and almost caught up with him. They joined the cart and the other men. Limoëlan gave the girl the bridle to hold.

"Remember, no matter what, the horse must not move *at all*," he said as he handed her the whip. "It is very important, do you understand?"

She nodded. "Oh, don't worry, Sir, I'll be very, very careful."

The horse was covered with sweat and kept its head down. It was content to sniff noisily at discarded cabbage leaves on the cobble-stones and seemed in no mood to canter away. The girl waited, shifted her weight from one foot to the other, patted the horse's neck, toyed with the whip. Limoëlan pulled his watch. The time was near. He exchanged a glance with Saint-Régent and nodded.

Limoëlan left to post himself at the intersection of Rue Nicaise and Place du Carrousel. Soon he saw a cortege of carriages leaving the Palace and heading his way. He shuddered. At last. He had waited so long for this moment. A few more seconds, and it would be all over. He knew he had to signal to Saint-Régent, but somehow his heart stopped and he was unable to raise his hand. He was still frozen, overcome by an emotion he could not define, when the first carriage passed him by and turned onto Rue Nicaise.

The girl looked up when she heard the rattling of wheels and the noise of hooves. She gaped at the squadron of dragoons in splendid uniforms surrounding the procession of elegant carriages. One of the guards of the escort, saber drawn, galloped ahead to the cart and shouted to move it out of the way. His horse shoved Saint-Régent against the wall of a house. The girl, her mouth still open, held on to the nag's bridle. She was staring at the gold braid on the dragoon's green jacket, at the horsetail that flowed down his back from his shiny helmet, at the claws of the spotted pelt that served as his saddle blanket. In her entire life she had never seen anything so strange and beautiful. She paid no attention to Saint-Régent, who had swiftly recovered his balance and reached under the tarpaulin.

But the coachman of the first carriage had noticed it all. He swore at the top of his voice, whipped his horses and drove away at a gallop. A blinding burst of light tore at the night. Thunder shook the air. The horses of the guards reared up, neighed wildly, slipped and fell. Cobblestones, roof tiles, parts of walls, entire chimneys, shards of glass, shreds of flesh were raining down on the street.

All that was left of the nag was the head, intact like a trophy, one front leg and one side of the chest and rump. Straw poked out from the remaining half of its leather collar.

2

Chief Inspector Roch Miquel would never forget what he was doing on the evening of the attack. He had left the Police Prefecture earlier than usual to reach the tavern of the Mighty Barrel, located on Rue Croix-des-Petits-Champs, in time for dinner. That establishment belonged to his father. Old Miquel now acknowledged the old holidays again, in his own way. He liked to share a roast goose with his only son and a few friends on Christmas Eve.

When Roch pushed the door open, he was greeted by the mixed smells of lentil soup, roasting meat and tobacco. The voices of the patrons, calling to the waiters, mingled with the dull noises of the mugs hitting the wood of the tables, polished by years of spills. Through billows of smoke Roch saw his father, leaning against the counter, surveying the room. Old Miquel, in the manner of a peasant, wore a wide-brimmed hat and leather leggings that buttoned from his knees down to his hobnailed shoes. A shaggy mongrel, his black hair streaked with much white, was crouching at his feet. The dog rose stiffly and, wagging his tail, went to nuzzle Roch's leg. Old Miquel's eyes gleamed with pride at the sight of his son. Roch seized his father's hand and kissed it. The older man slapped him on the shoulder.

Miquel *père*, a former rag-and-bone man, had seen his son rise to the rank of Chief Inspector, with a salary of 6,000 francs, and Roch was barely twenty-five. Such a feat would have been unconceivable before the Revolution, and it gave Old Miquel a singular satisfaction to have seen Roch achieve such early success. The years of struggling to afford a decent education for his son had been amply rewarded.

The two men addressed each other in the Roman language, the tongue of their native Auvergne. They spoke it for the pleasure of remembering the mountains of the old country, where they had not visited in many years. Also, it was not understood by most of the tavern patrons, and allowed for more candid talks.

Roch tried to keep the conversation away from politics, a topic that was sure to infuriate his father these days. Unfortunately Old Miquel's eyes fell on a copy of *The Free Men's Journal* lying on one of the tables. He seized the newspaper and brandished it in Roch's face.

"*The Free Men's Journal!*" he snorted. "As if we had any free men left in France! I just buy this filthy rag because I need something to put in the latrine. All I read about is our glorious Bonaparte. It's his victories in Italy here, the pacification of the West there. Well, let's talk about their *pacification*. Those Royalist bandits, those *Chouans*, ask them if they are *pacified*. They're still attacking stagecoaches out there."

Roch opened his mouth to protest, but Old Miquel was not to be stopped so easily. "No, son, don't tell me it isn't so. You think I'm a fool? Even in the so-called *Free Men's Journal*, they say that from now on all the stagecoaches going west'll be escorted by five soldiers. Pray what's that for, if it's so quiet, so *pacified* there? But in the same article, they tell you that all the Chouans have laid down their arms. They're all agape with admiration at Bonaparte, they say. That's just the kind of drivel you should expect from the papers that're still open nowadays. Those that told the truth, they had their presses seized, their journalists arrested."

Roch shook his head. "You are right, Father, those newspapers had been useful to spread the ideals of the Revolution. But now they had to be closed because they excited the populace against the Royalists. Everyone is ready to forget the old hatreds. I agree that the Revolution brought us great things, the equality of all before the law, the abolition of the old privileges, all that. But now people are tired of the chaos, of the bloodshed, of the corruption. They want order, they want to unite behind a strong leader. That's why they like the First Consul."

Old Miquel's palm hit the table. "A strong leader all right! Did you know they're going to demolish the statue of Liberty on the Place de la Révolution? To replace it with one of your strong leader, of course! They say in the paper they can't decide if they're going to have him on horseback, in his uniform, or standing in a toga, like a Roman Consul. I wish they'd ask me. Have Bonaparte up there stark naked, I'd tell them. It'd make it easier to kiss his ass."

Roch frowned as he looked around uneasily. Old Miquel's rants, even in the Roman language, might be understood by some of the patrons. That would create trouble for both of them. And the name *Bonaparte* was certainly easy to recognize in any idiom. He had to admit that his father had a point: it was imprudent to criticize the First Consul in public.

"When you think that Bonaparte owes the Revolution everything!" continued Old Miquel. "Without it, he'd still be a piddling lieutenant in some small-town garrison, and his greatest title to glory'd be to belong to a family of penniless Corsican nobles that no one—"

To Roch's great relief, shouts drowned his father's voice and the din of the room. All conversations stopped as two fellows in workmen's caps rose from their benches, facing each other across the table.

"Don't you ever say again that Eugénie's a whore!" one of them cried, rising his fist. "Else I'll kill you."

"Oh, for sure, she's a whore. She bedded you, and me, and Leriche too, and half of the people in here."

The first man roared and caught the other by the lapel of his jacket. "Then I'll kill you. And I'll go kill her too after that."

Old Miquel swore as he walked to the combatants. He grabbed both by their collars, pulled them from the table and threw them out onto the street.

"Enough!" he shouted in French. "Go kill each other outside, you drunkards. A big loss that'll be."

Old Miquel had large muscular arms and a broad chest. A heavy oak wood staff, fitted with an iron tip, hung by a leather thong from one of the buttons his jacket. Like Auvergne peasants, he also carried in his pocket a folding knife, ready to open with one flick of his thumb. Though past the age of fifty, he was more than a match for disorderly patrons.

"Scoundrels," he said as he walked back to Roch. "Where do they think they are? I'll have no foul language here, specially tonight. I invited Vidalenc, and Alexandrine of course, for the *réveillon*." He wagged his forefinger at Roch. "Now here's a girl who'd make a good wife, dutiful and hardworking. Though not as good as your dear mother, may her soul rest in peace."

Roch was not surprised to hear of the choice of guests. Vidalenc was a wine merchant and his father's oldest friend in Paris. As for Alexandrine, Roch did not dislike her at all. He had, when they were both children, treated her with the condescension owed a girl, a younger one at that. She had received some education and had pleasant, unaffected manners. He would not have minded spending the evening in her company but for his father's repeated hints.

"But then," continued Old Miquel, "you wouldn't find a wife like your poor mother nowadays, specially in Paris. Still, Alexandrine's a good girl. Pretty too, which can't be too much of a hindrance. And she's Vidalenc's daughter, not any stranger whose parents you wouldn't even know. As it is, she has a dowry of 50,000 francs, and she's an only child. She'll get all of Vidalenc's money when—"

Old Miquel paused when Vidalenc, a stocky man with white hair and piercing blue eyes, entered the common room. Alexandrine was on her father's arm. Roch had to admit that she looked pretty, even elegant, in a white taffeta dress, embroidered in blue around the hem and sleeves. A cashmere shawl, also blue, was modestly draped around her shoulders, but the swell of round breasts could be guessed underneath. She had expressive gray eyes and her honey-colored hair, with just a hint of red in it, fell in large curls on firm, broad shoulders.

Predictably, she blushed when she saw Roch, which made him all the more uncomfortable.

Old Miquel showed his guests into the private dining parlor behind the tavern's common room. The mongrel followed and settled stiffly in front of the hearth. Within moments he was whining in his sleep, his hind legs twitching. Perhaps he was dreaming of the far-away days when he would run away from the Mighty Barrel to pursue amorous adventures through the neighboring streets.

Alexandrine pulled from a basket on her arm a crown-shaped object wrapped in an immaculate towel, and presented it to Old Miquel. It was a *fougace*, a traditional Christmas cake from Auvergne. Roch breathed in its delicate aromas of orange blossom and dried fruit before they were overwhelmed by the smell of the goose, already golden brown, roasting on a spit in the fireplace. Old Miquel, beaming, removed his hat and kissed Alexandrine on both cheeks.

"Thank you, dear," he said. "Still warm from the oven, I see. There's no finer gift for the season. For any season, in fact."

"I know you are so fond of it, Citizen Miquel," said Alexandrine, smiling. "I baked it myself for you."

"Then it'll taste still sweeter. We'll have it for dessert, with some fine Sauternes wine."

Old Miquel placed the *fougace* at the center of the table, between two uncorked bottles of wine, one red, one white. They were coated with dust, not the gray dust of neglect, but the brown, sticky dust acquired during years of careful aging in a cellar. Roch surmised that, unlike the dubious beverage served to the tavern's patrons, these bottles did not come from Vidalenc's warehouse. On the walls of the dining parlor, copper basins reflected the light of the fire, next to a framed copy of the *Declaration of Rights of Man and of the Citizen* in gold letters against a black background. The table was set with plates painted with bright images of the storming of the Bastille, ten years earlier, and other patriotic motifs of the young Republic.

Old Miquel pulled a chair for Alexandrine to sit by his side, facing his son. Still standing, he poured red wine and raised his glass. "Some say that all things get worse with time. Not true. Like they say in Auvergne:

> *Good friends and good wine,*
> *The older, the better."*

He raised his glass, looking at Vidalenc. "To old friendships!" Then he winked at Alexandrine and Roch. "And to new love!"

Roch glanced at Alexandrine. Her cheeks were flushed and she kept her eyes fixed on the tricolor flags that decorated her plate. Maybe she fancied him. He was generally reckoned handsome. Well, not quite so. His nose was too long and aquiline for that, but it did not seem to bother women. They seemed to like the direct gaze of his brown eyes. He was unusually tall, just under six feet, and well built without being heavyset, with a mass of dark curly hair, cropped short. He very much looked like his father twenty years earlier, except for the fact that Roch was now dressed as a gentleman, in an immaculate linen shirt, black velvet coat and waistcoat, bronze-colored breeches and fine leather boots.

But, for all the attention he paid to his own appearance, he was not conceited. On second thought, he was not sure at all that Alexandrine liked him. Perhaps she was simply embarrassed by the naïve scheming of their respective fathers. If so, that was all to her credit. For all Roch knew or cared, she might be madly in love with some other man.

Vidalenc, grinning, had now risen in turn. He cleared his throat, his glass in hand. Roch cringed at the idea of more talk of young love, but he never heard Vidalenc's words, cut short by a tremendous blast. The entire room seemed to be lifted off its foundations and brutally dropped back down. A wine bottle toppled on the table. The framed *Declaration of Rights* crashed to the floor with a cling of broken glass.

Old Miquel, swearing, straightened the red wine bottle before much of its contents could spill. Alexandrine, silent, was very pale. Vidalenc was still standing, holding his glass aloft, words frozen on his lips. The dog rose and began barking furiously.

"Quiet, Crow!" shouted Old Miquel. "What the hell's this? They

disturb the peace of honest citizens, just to sound the cannon to celebrate some victory or other. All for your Bonaparte's greater glory!"

Roch shook his head. "I doubt it, Father. This doesn't sound like a
cannon. And if this were a celebration of anything, there would have
been a salvo of twenty-one blasts." He put his napkin down on the
table and rose. "You must excuse me."

Roch took his leave, too preoccupied to respond to his father's
protests. All that was on his mind was Blanche's safety.

3

*R*och, on the doorstep of Mighty Barrel, wondered about the location of the blast. It had sounded so close. He could not keep his thoughts off Blanche Coudert, his mistress of several months, in whose company he had spent a few most enjoyable hours that afternoon. He knew that the première of *The Creation of the World* would begin shortly at the Opera, only a few hundred yards away. All of fine society would attend. Blanche and her husband had their own box, and she loved music. She would be there, of course. He imagined her injured, bleeding, dying, far from any help.

He ran towards the Opera. Everywhere he had to force his way through anxious crowds, which became more and restless as he drew closer. But then, when he reached the entrance to the Palais-Egalité, he realized that the center of the uproar must be further to the south, towards Rue Nicaise. He felt relieved. Blanche was safe then. Her carriage, even if it had arrived fashionably late, would not have taken that route to go to the Opera.

Roch prepared to turn into Rue Nicaise, but paused for a minute. There was no street there anymore, only a sort of tunnel, a gaping hole, its edges softened by drifting smoke. All the lamps had been extinguished, and the scene was only lit by wobbly points of light in the distance. Roch entered the darkness. A gust of wind, carrying the stench of gunpowder and fire, hit him in the face. He tripped on an unseen obstacle and cursed under his breath. After a few dozen yards, he distinguished a dozen characters, male and female, in strange costumes, their faces caked with white powder and rouge, huddled together. A man shivering in a Roman toga, his bare feet in antique sandals, held a lantern. Roch remembered that the Théâtre du Vaudeville was nearby. A popular entertainment for those Parisians who could not afford the Opera. Roch approached the little group.

"Police!" he said. "If you don't mind, Citizen, I will borrow your lantern."

The actors gathered around him and proceeded to ask questions all at the same time.

Roch raised his hand. "No," he said, "I have no idea of what happened. Go home now and report to the nearest police station in the morning to give your statements."

He headed further down the street. Shards of glass briefly reflected the light of the lantern and crushed under the heel of his boot. Sometimes his foot sank with a wet noise into soft, spongy, indefinable things, which he preferred not to imagine.

There were more lanterns ahead. Those were not moving. They were fitted at the top of poles planted into the rubble that covered the ground. He saw a large gathering of men, but these were no actors. He recognized his colleague Sobry, the Police Commissioner for the district of the Tuileries. Sobry was a former attorney, a tall man with a handsome, thoughtful face. He was giving orders to blue-uniformed National Guards. Other men, in civilian clothes, were bent over prone bodies. All the physicians in the district must have rushed to the scene.

"A bomb, an infernal machine," Sobry said in response to Roch's question. "On a cart, apparently. Several witnesses noticed it, stopped in the middle of the street, not far from the Café d'Apollon. The bomb exploded just as the First Consul's carriage drove by."

Roch frowned. "So Bonaparte . . ."

"No, amazing as it sounds. Not a scratch, though I heard that the windows of his carriage were shattered. His lucky star again, I guess.

Apparently none of his attendants were seriously injured either. His carriage simply drove on to the Opera."

The image of Blanche returned to Roch's mind with renewed urgency.

"What about the Opera? What's going on there? Another bomb?"

"No, all is safe there, apparently. Bonaparte may be there already. They must have searched the place before they let him set foot inside."

Roch pictured Blanche, by her husband's side, seated in her red velvet box at the Opera. Her white skin must have turned paler than usual at the news of the attack. But at least she was unhurt.

He turned his attention to the crater, several yards across, that gouged the street. The fronts of the nearby houses had collapsed. Blackened paneling, shattered furniture, half-collapsed ceilings were exposed to his view. An hour earlier, those had been ordinary rooms, filled with ordinary people, in a well-to-do district. Now there was something oddly immodest about the sight of those private places, suddenly exposed to anyone's view.

"I can't imagine how Bonaparte escaped this," muttered Roch.

He looked around at the bodies littering the street. Some were moaning, and a woman's shrill cries pierced the air. Roch, trying to shut off all noises, squatted next to the remains of a horse, yards away from the crater. He examined the animal's sole remaining hoof. The shoe was bright and shiny in the light of the lanterns.

"From the extent of the mutilation," he said to Sobry, "it looks like the horse that drew the cart. See this? The shoe is new. This poor beast must be taken to the Prefecture. A blacksmith may be able to recognize it." Roch looked around. "What about the cart itself? Did you find the plate number?"

"No, only the two shafts, each on one side of the street. They seem quite ordinary. As for the plate, it may have been shattered or blown onto nearby roofs. We will search there as soon as day breaks."

"Where is the Prefect?" asked Roch.

"On his way, I guess. I sent him word of the situation."

"And what about the Minister?"

Sobry looked straight at Roch. "Like you, I report to the Prefect. *He* will inform the Minister as he deems appropriate."

"How many dead?"

"Too early to tell. So far we discovered eight bodies. I had them taken to the police station on Rue Thomas. But there must be more buried in the rubble, and there are scores of wounded, many gravely so. A butchery." Sobry nodded in the direction of an intact house down the street. "I had the stables in there turned into an infirmary."

Roch was staring at a dark, elongated form a dozen yards away, in the midst of the rubble. "Sobry, have you seen this?"

The object had the color and texture of charcoal. It looked like a large log, blown off from a fireplace. Followed by Sobry, he walked cautiously towards it. He stopped when he saw tufts of reddish hair still sticking to the far end. A human skull. He turned away and took a deep breath, then willed himself to look again. Now he could see that both arms were missing.

Sobry shuddered. "Poor thing. He, or she, must have been very close to the infernal machine to be so badly burned. Some witnesses mentioned a child, poorly dressed, holding the bridle of the horse and playing with a whip. Most say a girl, but some swear that it was a boy."

Roch nodded, still too nauseous to speak.

"You know how it goes," continued Sobry. "You can never get two people to agree on anything. True, it was hard to tell, with this fog."

Sobry ordered two National Guards to deposit the charred body onto a door that was found lying on the street, and Roch followed them to the police station. There was no end to the night's horrors. On the floor lay eight corpses, some almost intact, some barely evoking a human form. Severed limbs had been piled in a corner. The physicians were all busy attending to the wounded, a guard told him, and no one had come to examine the bodies yet. The only information available was the names of the dead, at least those who had been identified thanks to their *Cartes de Sûreté*. Roch wrote them down in the booklet he always carried in his pocket. He was relieved to leave in search of a cart to take the carcass of the horse to the Prefecture.

He walked away in the direction of the Louvre Embankment. Once he left Rue Nicaise, the reassuring glow of streetlights reappeared. He breathed in deeply the cold air. He could smell the river now. He looked around and saw a familiar figure, slim and raggedy, among a band of street urchins. Perhaps they expected to scavenge something out of the wreckage, once the guards and policemen left.

Roch beckoned to one of the boys. He often used him as an informer, a *mouchard*, in Parisian slang, an *interposed person*, in the official language of police reports. Pépin was thirteen, small for his age and fleet of foot.

"Come here," called Roch, "I have something for you."

The boy approached, grinning. "Always at your command, Chief Inspector, Sir. Looks like you've your hands full tonight. So Bonaparte's tripe's blown all over the street? The King'll come back, eh? Are they goin' to guillotine you, Sir? Or maybe hang you, like in the ole days? That'd be a pity."

"Shut that damned trap of yours, little snot. The First Consul is unharmed and no one's going to hang me."

Roch pulled his booklet and scrawled a few sentences on a blank page. He tore it off, folded it and addressed it in pencil to *Citizen Fouché, Minister of Police*. He handed Pépin the note. The guards at the Ministry knew him by sight and would let him pass. As the boy took it, Roch seized him by the fraying collar of his jacket.

"You're going to take this to the Minister. Right away. If for any reason it doesn't reach him within ten minutes, I'm going to send you to jail. About Bicêtre? I'll see to it that you're thrown into the *Pit*, in the middle of fifty common criminals. A *mouchard*, especially a fresh young one like you, will be quite a treat for them."

Pépin looked chastened. "My apologies, I'm sure, Sir."

Roch let go of him. As soon as the boy's feet rested on the ground again, he took his cap off. "Really, Sir. No offense meant."

"None taken. Just remember that the *Pit* awaits you if you play any tricks."

Roch threw him a copper coin. The boy caught it deftly and saluted before disappearing.

4

Roch, followed by a cart and its sullen driver, returned to Rue Nicaise, where he oversaw the removal of the horse's remains. He agreed with Sobry that, after stopping at the Prefecture, he would go to L'Hôtel-Dieu, the hospital where most of the wounded had been taken.

Roch headed for the Isle of the Cité. He left the carcass of the horse in the care of the guards on duty at the Prefecture of Police, and continued in the direction of Notre-Dame. The massive square towers of the Cathedral stood darker than the night sky. Roch walked past the Enfants-Trouvés, the Foundlings Hospital. There were abandoned the orphans, the little bastards and the offspring of paupers who could not afford to feed them.

L'Hôtel-Dieu was next door, to the side of the cathedral. It had officially been called L'Hospice de la République since the Revolution, but Parisians had never stopped using its old name. *Hôtel-Dieu* means "House of God," an odd term, Roch always mused, for a place that had been for over a thousand years the repository of all of the misery of the great city. But perhaps all misery was the work of God. Everything in the world was, apparently, even the atrocities of that night.

Roch had forgotten most of the catechism the parish priest had taught him when he was a child in the small town of Lavigerie. Still he remembered Old Miquel, in the days before the Revolution, stopping by every cross they met during their long yearly journey between

Auvergne and Paris. Both father and child would take off their hats and kneel. Together they recited a prayer in the Roman language before resuming their progress:

> *Holy Cross, planted Cross,*
> *Don't let my soul be lost.*

Little by little, *sol* by *sol*, the old man had saved some money, and borrowed more from his friend Vidalenc. He had purchased the Tavern of the Mighty Barrel and settled permanently in Paris. Then the Revolution had happened in 1789, when Roch was fourteen. Old Miquel had become a proponent of the new ideas of liberty and equality, a fervent admirer of Robespierre, the Jacobin leader. Like him, he would mention a deity called the Supreme Being, but in terms so vague as to mean nothing to Roch. Now all Roch knew for sure was that most of Paris paupers died, four to a bed in cavernous common rooms, in that earthly House of God.

Roch tried to ignore the howls coming from the hall of the women in labor. He breathed in a mix of excrement, putrefaction, unwashed bodies and cabbage soup. It was the odor of poverty, familiar from the time of his childhood. Here the sense of smell outlived all other perceptions, the stench stuck to the skin, to the hair, to the bedclothes. It accompanied the dying to the doors of eternity.

Citizen Naudier, Chief Surgeon, led Roch to the room where the victims from Rue Nicaise had been taken. They had been given separate beds, with clean sheets, and segregated from the other patients.

Roch walked past the bed of a young woman, her stomach bulging under the sheets. She was unconscious, so wan that Roch surmised she might never experience the trials of childbirth. In the next bed lay a man, his eyes wide open. Muffled cries came out of the bandage, stained red, that covered his mouth.

The plump woman down the line of beds resembled a pincushion. Her body was pierced by dozens of thin, sharp wooden arrows, which a young surgeon was extracting with pincers. She was screaming at each of his attempts.

"A musician, according to her *Carte de Sûreté*," explained Naudier. "These must be the shards of her instrument."

Roch nodded. He was beginning to despair of gathering any information when he walked to the last bed of the row. There lay a man, rather handsome, about forty years of age. He did look pale, but his eye was steady when it met Roch's.

"Captain Platel," said the Chief Surgeon. "Thigh and leg broken, multiple cuts on the torso and abdomen."

Roch would have guessed that Platel was a military man. Two side braids hung in front of the ears, while the rest of his dark blond hair was gathered in two more braids that joined on the nape to form a queue. Those *cadenettes* protected the cheeks and neck in close combat and were popular with soldiers.

Roch drew a chair by Platel's bedside. "I am Chief Inspector Miquel," he said. "Can you tell me what you saw?"

"I was walking down Rue Nicaise with my landlady, Widow Lystère, when the carriage of the First Consul drove by. We were returning home after visiting friends who live near the Palais-Egalité. We saw the guards and carriages coming our way and we huddled against the houses on the right side of the street to let them pass. And then all I remember is the explosion."

"Are you on leave from your regiment, Citizen Captain?"

"I was wounded in the leg in Egypt, at the battle of the Pyramids, eighteen months ago, and received a discharge." Platel sighed. "I have yet to see the first *sol* of my pension."

"This must be quite a hardship. Have you a family?"

A deep blush overcame Captain Platel's pallor. "My wife lives fifty leagues away, in Lille, with our four children. I came to Paris, alone, to find employment. With little success."

"So how do you manage?"

Platel's blush deepened. "Not very well. I owe Widow Lystère 850 francs for room and board." The man paused. "Actually she is not widowed. She divorced her husband. On grounds of insanity."

"Very sad indeed. Please tell me about the explosion. What time was it exactly?"

"We left the Palais-Egalité shortly after eight o'clock, so it must have been ten or fifteen past the hour. There was that dreadful noise. Then, when I came to my senses, Citizen Lystère was no longer there. What happened to her?"

"Did you notice anything unusual before the explosion?"

"Yes, we had passed a cart stopped in an awkward manner, midway down Rue Nicaise. You could say it blocked the traffic, and we had to walk around it. It was covered, down to the hubs of the wheels, with a gray tarpaulin. And a girl was holding the bridle of the horse."

"A girl? Are you sure?"

"Quite sure. I remember her skirt, with blue and white stripes. And she wore a blue kerchief on her head. I didn't see her face, for she had turned away."

"Did you notice the plate number of that cart?"

"I didn't pay attention to it. I guess it was covered by the tarpaulin."

"Anything else unusual, Captain?"

"I saw a man standing at the corner of Place du Carrousel, a dozen yards ahead of us, just before the explosion. He wore a loose blue jacket, of the kind worn by stallholders. But he didn't look like a stallholder. I caught a glimpse of the gold frame of his spectacles in the light of a lamppost. He had a distinguished bearing, like a former aristocrat. I paid attention to him because I was surprised to see such a man dressed in this manner."

"How would you describe that man?"

"Rather tall, slender. Long face, long nose."

"What about the color of his hair? His eyes? His complexion?"

"He wore a cap, low on his forehead. That is all I can tell you. It was dark. I wouldn't even have noticed the man at all but for his spectacles."

"So apart from the girl in the striped skirt, did you notice anyone around the cart?"

"No, no one in particular. The street was busy." Captain Platel drew a sharp breath and winced. "I am sorry," he said. "When you think I narrowly escaped having my leg amputated after the battle of the

Pyramids. And now this . . . The surgeons here haven't told me yet what they intend to do, but it's all too easy to guess." He hesitated. "What about Madame Lystère? She is so brave, trying her best to earn a bit of money. She gives English and piano lessons to support her infirm mother and her three little children."

And you too, thought Roch. Then he chided himself. Captain Platel did not look like a vicious man. Maybe he had loved Citizen Lystère. Maybe he had been kind to her, to her mother and children. Maybe he would have paid her the back rent as soon as his pension arrived at last. Who was Roch to pass judgment on that pitiful little happiness, now that it was all over?

"So you don't know anything about Citizen Lystère?" insisted Platel. "She was on my arm at the time of the explosion."

"She must have been sent to another hospital. We will track her down, I am sure. You have been most helpful. You should take some rest now."

Roch was in no mood to tell the truth. In fact, the name of Citizen Lystère was written down in his booklet. He had seen her body at the police station among the other corpses. She seemed asleep, and her pretty dress, brown with white dots, was not even soiled. Roch hoped she had met a quick and painless end.

5

Fouché, Minister of Police, was still at his desk when an usher handed him Roch Miquel's note. He pursed his lips as he read on. He called back the man just before he had reached the door of the office.

"Order my carriage, please. Right away."

Not a word from the Prefect about the attack, of course. The scheming imbecile would no doubt wait until the next day to send him a detailed report. Fouché walked to the mirror above the red marble fireplace and pulled a horn comb from his coat pocket. He deliberately combed his thinning, graying hair towards his temples and forehead. It was easy to guess what was happening now: Bonaparte had gone on to the Opera, as Miquel wrote in his note, to quash any rumors of his death, but he would hardly be in the mood to enjoy *The Creation of the World*. He would promptly return to the Palace of the Tuileries.

Fouché saw no need to visit the crime scene. Miquel and Sobry were both competent policemen, and between themselves they would take all appropriate measures. The Minister's presence, however, was urgently required at the Tuileries. Bonaparte's generals, his other ministers, his courtiers, all the parasites whose lives and fortunes were closely tied to his, would hasten there to offer the great man their heartfelt congratulations on his miraculous escape, laced with much flattery and advice. Maybe Dubois, the Prefect of Police, was already there, drooling at the idea of being appointed Minister. But no, thought Fouché as he put the comb back into his pocket, Dubois was too much of a coward to face the brunt of Bonaparte's wrath tonight.

The carriage was ready. It crossed the Seine River and stopped in front of the Tuileries. Fouché paused a moment to look up at the stately façade and the high central cupola. Once the Royal Palace, then the National Palace, now the official residence of the First Consul. What came next? Many things had happened in such short time. Barely over ten years ago, Fouché had been a monk, a teacher at the School of the Oratorian Friars in the seaport of Nantes. France had a King then, but soon it also elected an Assembly and in short order found itself in the midst of a Revolution. How fast Fouché had embraced the new ideas and discarded the habit!

He had married, very well. A rich, rational, fertile, thrifty, devoted woman. And his fortunes had risen. He had been elected a Representative, he had become a leading Jacobin. He had even voted for the King's execution. There was still far more to Fouché's revolutionary record, things he never mentioned anymore. There had been compelling reasons at the time, and anyway, why dwell on the past? He had atoned for any excesses by several years of retirement from politics, which he had put to good use. He had sold hogs to the Republic's armies, and made millions. For whatever Fouché did, whether it was teaching, marrying, dealing in livestock, being the Minister of Police, he did very well.

When he entered the Throne Room, in what had been the King's apartments, all he saw at first was a crowd of men in uniforms. The room was abuzz with whispers and indignant cries. All conversations stopped abruptly at his sight, and all faces, unfriendly faces, turned to Fouché.

The crowd parted in silence to make way for a sallow man with an angular face. His First Consul uniform, a red velvet coat and white breeches embroidered in gold, stuck to a thin body, all bones and sinews.

"Ah, here you are!" cried Bonaparte. His blue eyes had an icy glare. "Are you still going to tell me now the Royalists did it?"

"Oh, yes, Citizen First Consul, without a doubt the Royalists did it," replied Fouché quietly. "Not only do I say so, but I shall prove it."

The courtiers stared in astonishment, and Bonaparte's lips only tightened more.

"Nonsense!" he exclaimed. "Can you not see the obvious? This atrocity is the work of the Jacobins. If they had only sought to kill me alone, I might have been inclined to show some leniency. But this is an attack on the people of Paris, on the Nation itself. The Jacobins will pay for this. They have been tolerated, even protected, too long. By *you!* That vermin conspires night and day under your nose, and you do nothing!"

It took more than Bonaparte's tirades or the stares of his entourage to intimidate Fouché. "As I said, Citizen First Consul, this is the work of the Royalists, the Chouans. All I need is a week, one single week, to prove it."

"A week! When your so-called police could not even prevent this!"

"I agree, Citizen First Consul: the police could be more efficient. It would certainly work better if it were united under one command, instead of being divided into several forces. We have the *Gendarmerie* here, the Military Police there, and now the latest, the Prefecture for Paris . . ." Fouché paused to look around. "Speaking of which, I do not see our good Citizen Prefect here tonight. Hard at work in his office, no doubt. An outstanding functionary, Dubois . . . In any event, of this grand patchwork of polices, my Ministry is but a modest part. Yet, in spite of the limitations imposed on it, you may remember, Citizen First Consul, that I recently pointed out in some detail the activities of certain Royalist agents. As much as some would like to blame the Jacobins for everything, this is simply not reasonable."

Fouché paused to look around at the crowd of courtiers. "Too many resources have been wasted watching the men of the Revolution. Dangerous though they may have been in the past, they are now disarmed, powerless. In the meantime the émigrés, the Chouans, the agents of England have been allowed to roam Paris freely despite my warnings. If one had listened to me, this horror would never have happened."

Bonaparte, still frowning, bit the nail of his little finger. He now seemed more preoccupied than furious.

General Lannes cleared his throat and said, "Well, Citizen First Consul, perhaps the Minister has a point. If there is even a remote possibility that the Royalists may be responsible for this atrocity, they cannot be allowed to escape."

The only woman in the room, an elegant brunette in a white satin dress embroidered in silver thread, rose from a sofa. Madame Bonaparte moved with the quiet grace, the poise of a queen. In fact, she was already queen in all but in name, and she seemed to find herself quite at home in the late Marie Antoinette's apartments at the Tuileries. The only thing poor Joséphine lacked to quite fit the part, reflected Fouché, was the ability to bear her husband an heir.

She gently put her hand on Bonaparte's arm and whispered into his ear. He shook his head, frowning. Fouché waited without betraying any emotion or meeting her eye. Joséphine and he were better friends than most, including Bonaparte himself, imagined. The 1,000 francs a day Fouché paid her to keep him apprised of what went on within the Tuileries, within the First Consul's bedroom itself, was not wasted, and at this very moment her help was more precious than ever. She was a spendthrift, always desperate for her next *sol*, and she gladly accepted the flow of the Minister's gold without putting any malice in it.

The glare of Bonaparte's eyes was once more fixed on Fouché. "All right, Citizen Minister, you have a week to bring me proof of the Royalists' guilt."

6

Joseph de Limoëlan was walking briskly towards Saint-Régent's lodgings. He still wore his gold spectacles, but he had traded his stall-holder jacket for an elegant blue coat. Blond curls fell loose on his shoulders.

It seemed that everyone in Paris was on the streets now, and Limoëlan had to elbow his way through the crowd. He was not a happy man. All the preparations, all the care and trouble, all the expense, all had been for naught. He had seen Bonaparte's carriage drive away, intact. He had talked to people on the street. Everyone said the First Consul had gone on to the Opera as though nothing had happened. Now George would be waiting for an explanation.

And George was not famous for his patience. He was the only man in France known to his followers and enemies alike by his given name alone. He was Georges Cadoudal, the supreme commander of the insurgents in the West, the Catholic and Royal Army, the Chouans, as they called themselves, after the name of one of their early leaders. George was a peasant's son, fair-skinned, fair-haired, hefty, very tall, almost a giant, amazingly strong. Legend had it that he could bend a silver coin of six francs between two of his fingers.

Limoëlan, who had served under George's direct command in the Catholic and Royal Army, knew that it was not true. George was simply the kind of character about whom people liked to tell such tales. He was more than a man, he was a legend. But much of the legend was true. For instance, George believed in only one penalty against his enemies, and those of his friends whom he suspected of incompetence, or of betraying the cause.

Months earlier, during the spring of 1800, at the time of the so-called *pacification* of the West, George had been granted safe passage and a private audience by Bonaparte. He had believed, like many Royalists at the time, that the First Consul was intent on bringing the King back from exile and transferring the reins of government to the legitimate monarch. But no, all Bonaparte had to offer George was the rank of general in the regular army, along with a bribe of 50,000 gold *louis*, if he abandoned the Royalist cause and rallied to the new regime. Actually, Bonaparte had not made an offer, he had *ordered* George to accept those things. And George took his orders from the King, not from some uniformed Corsican upstart. He had declined with contempt, of course. His sole regret was that he had failed to seize the moment. "I could have easily choked him to death with my bare hands, that shrimp of a man, and I did not," he had told Limoëlan.

Right now George was waiting, from his hiding place near Cancale, in Brittany, to hear of the outcome of the attack. And what would Limoëlan, who was in charge of the operations in Paris, tell him?

George would not be pleased with the number of dead and wounded, which Limoëlan supposed to be great. That would have been fine, of course, if Bonaparte had perished, but now that the usurper had escaped unscathed, the populace would talk of nothing but the *victims*. That might hurt the cause in the eyes of many. Limoëlan thought briefly of the little biscuit vendor, but soon dismissed any regrets on her account. With her looks, no man must have meddled with her. For sure she had kept her innocence. God would welcome her sacrifice and receive her in heaven among the blessed. Indeed it was probably a far better fate for her than going through the daily drudgery of her miserable existence. Yet those who knew nothing of politics, weak-hearted imbeciles, would weep for her.

So Limoëlan had good reason to be unhappy that night. And now his unhappiness focused on Saint-Régent. The two men were from the same country, on the Brittany coast, and they had known each other since childhood, without ever becoming friends. Limoëlan's father had been the foremost lord and landowner there, while Saint-Régent's family, though also noble, struggled on the fringes of poverty. Limoëlan had received a careful education at the College of the Oratorian Friars in Rennes before purchasing a commission in the prestigious Regiment of the Prince of Savoie-Carignan. Saint-Régent had enlisted in the Navy as an ensign at the age of twelve, to make his way up the ranks as he could.

Then the Revolution had burst out in faraway Paris. War had been declared and a draft instituted. The peasants in the West had rebelled. Limoëlan and Saint-Régent, like many other officers, had first emigrated, then returned to Brittany to join the insurgency. The chances of war had at times united them, at times separated them for months. They had been caught on occasion, but they had always escaped and survived in the midst of the carnage. Then, last June, George had instructed Limoëlan to head for Paris, with another Chouan, François Carbon, posing as his valet, to prepare an attack on Bonaparte. Saint-Régent, also on the orders of George, had joined them in Paris a few months later. They had discussed the most efficient means of ridding France of the usurper, and finally agreed on an infernal machine.

Had not Saint-Régent volunteered to light the barrel of powder himself? Had not Limoëlan, time and again, insisted that his second-in-command use an ember held with pincers? That way there was no need to worry about the length of the wick, the dryness of the tinder, and all the things that could go wrong, no matter how methodical one was in one's calculations. With an ember, the conflagration was sure to be immediate. But no, the bomb had exploded a few seconds late.

Now Limoëlan was certain that Saint-Régent had lost his nerve. The coward must have hidden a fuse under the tarpaulin and lit it with his tinderbox. Of course, an immediate explosion would have meant certain death for Saint-Régent, but was he not, were they not all prepared to die for the cause? Had not Limoëlan's own father done so, seven years earlier, when he had climbed the stairs to the guillotine? Well, Saint-Régent apparently was not ready to sacrifice his own life. He had to put his personal safety ahead of the most sacred of ends. He would pay for this.

Limoëlan turned onto Rue des Prouvaires. There he went to the sixth alley to the right and pushed an iron gate. Fortunately it was still unlocked in spite of the late hour. Limoëlan walked up to the third floor and knocked at a door. A woman, her graying hair pulled tight under a white stiffly starched cap, opened the door. In the parlor, an old man, a younger one and a girl of fifteen or so were playing cards by the light of a smoky oil lamp. They rose to bow or curtsey upon Limoëlan's entrance.

"Good evening," he said curtly. "Has Monsieur Pierrot returned yet?" Of course, the Guillous had no need to know Saint-Régent's real name, nor his own, nor many other details.

"Yes, Sir, thank God," said the older woman. "Oh, I'm so relieved it's you. I was worried it'd be the police, after that big noise we heard. What was that? We looked out the window. We saw a crowd, and horses, all in an uproar. I asked my son to go see what it was, but you know Guillaume . . ." She nodded in the direction of the young man, who looked away.

Limoëlan knew Guillaume indeed, and made no comment.

"Monsieur Pierrot came home about twenty minutes ago," continued the Guillous woman. "He didn't look well, Sir, not well at all. All pale and odd-looking, he was. I offered him a bowl of hot soup, 'cause, you know, he's fond of his soup when he comes home at night, but he wouldn't even answer me. He went straight to his room. I reckon he's in bed now. I didn't want to disturb him."

Limoëlan crossed the parlor and opened the door to one of the bedrooms without knocking. Saint-Régent was lying on the bed, still dressed in his blue jacket, over the covers. His breathing was raspy and shallow. He did not move as Limoëlan approached cautiously.

Limoëlan noticed that Saint-Régent's freckles, usually hidden under this tan, now stood out against his pale skin. Blood traced red lines from the corners of his mouth to the *cadenettes* that framed his face. It also trickled from his ears, a sign Limoëlan knew all too well from his years as a Chouan. Saint-Régent's nose was narrower and pointier than ever, as though pinched by an invisible hand. Yet the man was conscious. His half-closed eyes had traveled in the direction of the door as soon as Limoëlan approached. He stuttered. "George . . ."

Limoëlan's anger waned. Saint-Régent's death would make it easier to explain things to George, and there would be no need to carry out an execution in the midst of Paris, which was always awkward. He put his hand on Saint-Régent's shoulder. "Rest easy, friend."

"The . . . Sacraments . . ." whispered Saint-Régent.

Limoëlan nodded. He left the room and beckoned to the Guillou woman. "Monsieur Pierrot needs a priest," he said. He looked sternly into her eyes. "A *real* priest."

"But, Sir, I don't know of any 'round here," said the woman in a plaintive tone.

Limoëlan glared at her. And these people were supposed to be devoted to the cause! He shrugged. "Don't bother. I will fetch one myself."

There was but one priest he trusted in all of Paris, his uncle, Father de Clorivière. Limoëlan hurried down the stairs.

7

*L*imoëlan headed for the Pont-Royal to cross over to the Left Bank. His mood was still somber, but the realization of his comrade's impending death had put things into perspective. As desperate as things looked, all was not lost. The usurper could still be killed if those who remained recouped their forces and continued to fight for the cause.

After a half hour Limoëlan had crossed the river over the Pont-Royal and reached Rue Cassette, a genteel street, quite deserted at this time of the night. The explosion, if it had been heard here, had caused no lasting turmoil. He pulled a key and let himself into a vast house. Mademoiselle de Cicé, in her entresol overlooking the court-yard, must be in prayers on this Christmas Eve. He did not wish to disturb her pious meditation. In a few hours the dear old lady, with Limoëlan, would attend the Midnight Mass his uncle would celebrate in the little makeshift chapel upstairs. Limoëlan had hoped to impart great news. And now . . .

Limoëlan knew his way around the house in the dark, and ran up to the attic. He knocked on one of the walls. Three long knocks, two short ones, repeated four times. A door, disguised in the wood panel-ing, opened. In its frame stood a tall, gaunt elderly man. He embraced Limoëlan and let him inside a room no more than four feet in width. A cot, a chair and a narrow wooden table, covered with a piece of lace and gold liturgical ornaments, occupied all of it.

"One of our friends has been injured, Reverend Father," said Limoëlan. "For the cause. He needs to confess and receive Extreme Unction."

Father de Clorivière frowned. "Was it tonight? What of Bonaparte?"

Limoëlan paused before answering. "Bonaparte escaped. This time. Let's make haste, Father."

The priest reached for a little gold box on the table, genuflected and kissed the altar. He threw a black coat on his shoulders and followed his nephew.

The two men walked briskly in silence in the darkened street. At last Father de Clorivière sighed and broke the silence: "Why tonight, of all nights? The eve of the Nativity of Christ . . ."

"What better time was there, Father? Bonaparte's death would have heralded a new era. The return of the King, atonement for the atrocities of the Revolution, the restoration of the rights of the nobility."

"Yes, my son, only the King can bring a penitent France back within the fold of our Holy Mother the Church. So tell me what happened tonight."

"We detonated an infernal machine on the path of Bonaparte's carriage."

Father de Clorivière blessed himself.

"Is it not rightful to kill a tyrant?" asked Limoëlan. "Indeed it is more than rightful, it is one's duty. Is it not what Saint Thomas Aquinas teaches us?"

"To kill a usurper like Bonaparte is justified, yes, without any doubt. So that was this awful noise we heard . . . Mademoiselle de Cicé was all shaken. She came up to ask if I knew what it was. Where did the machine explode?"

"On Rue Saint-Nicaise."

Father de Clorivière stopped and stared at his nephew. "At that time? What have you done, Joseph? How many innocents have you sacrificed?"

"We must hurry, Father. Innocents perish in any war, you know it. These at least perished for a just cause."

"Who appointed you, Joseph, the judge of life and death? You bring me to your friend's bedside, but what about *you*, about the salvation of your soul? When will I hear *your* confession?"

"I would confess if I could, Father, but it would not do any good. I feel no contrition, no repentance. This was no sin. My only regret is to have let the usurper escape."

Father de Clorivière shook his head in silence. "God help you. I will pray for you. You need it more than your friend."

When they reached the Guillou house, Saint-Régent, now in his shirt, was tucked under a plump red comforter. But what caught Limoëlan's attention was the sight of a moon-faced young fellow standing by his comrade's bedside.

Limoëlan glowered at the Guillou woman. "Who is *this*?" he hissed. "Are you out of your mind?"

"I thought it'd be a good idea to fetch a physician as well, Sir," she hastened to say in a tremulous tone. "This is Dr. Collin, Sir. Oh, you needn't worry. I know him well, he's a friend. He won't say nothin' to the police. I told him it that Monsieur Pierrot is here on account of the cause."

"Indeed, Sir," Collin intervened, "I came as fast as I could. Madame Guillou caught me just as I was coming home from a delivery class at the Charité Hospital."

Limoëlan frowned. "A class? What do you mean, Sir? You are still taking classes? Aren't you a physician?"

The man flushed. "Well, not quite, Sir, but I will have completed my studies next year." Collin spoke very fast. "The patient's condition seemed quite serious when I arrived, and the pulse was very rapid. Monsieur Pierrot complained of great deal of pain in his eyes and ears. I understand that he fell from his horse, and yet I could not find any contusion or open wound. So I bled the patient, which is always the thing to do when one is in doubt of the diagnosis. And since Monsieur Pierrot also complained of discomfort in the lower abdomen, I applied leeches around the anus."

Limoëlan winced. The medical student smiled proudly and pointed at Saint-Régent's face, as white as the pillow on which it rested. "As you can see, Sir, the patient is already much improved."

Limoëlan shoved the medical student outside the room. As he was closing the door behind them, he saw Father de Clorivière pull a wooden statuette of the Blessed Virgin from his pocket and bring it to the dying man's lips.

Limoëlan, once in the dining parlor, walked to the fireplace. The medical student had left already and the Guillous, gathered around the table, were shaking their heads sadly and exchanging brief sentences in hushed tones.

8

It was still dark when Roch Miquel left L'Hôtel-Dieu early in the morning of the 25th of December, and Paris was awakening as usual. Roch surmised that, had Bonaparte died in the attack, the city would have digested the news overnight, ready for a new ruler to settle in the Palace of the Tuileries the next morning. To many it did not matter much whether the master of France was the restored King or another victorious General, and there was no shortage of those.

It was five o'clock now. The sky was still dark and streetlights still burning, but bakers, powdery with flour, were taking down the shutters of their shops. The bread that was to feed to city that day was already turning brown in the ovens. Prostitutes, their rouge smeared on their cheeks, their lips swollen with too many kisses, were scurrying back to their garrets. They kept their eyes cast down after the exertions of the night, too weary to glance at a last customer.

Roch let himself into a genteel building on Rue de Jouy, on the Right Bank of the Seine. Before the Revolution, it had housed clerics attached to the Cathedral of Notre-Dame, but now it was rented to well-to-do families of shopkeepers and various functionaries. Roch climbed the stairs to his third-floor lodgings and went straight to the kitchen. There he found his maid, her stiff gray locks still loose under her nightcap, a woolen shawl thrown over her shoulders, lighting the wood stove. She curtseyed and handed him a note, sealed in wax. It was unsigned, a mere scrawl, but Roch recognized the seal as that of Fouché, the Minister of Police.

> *I want you to find a Pierre de Saint-Régent, alias Pierrot. Age 33 or so, average height, slightly built, long, pointy nose, eyes blue, close-set.*
>
> *Also a François Carbon, alias Short Francis. Age around 43, 5 feet 4 inches, stocky, scar on his left eye.*
>
> *Both Chouans, involved in several campaigns against the Republic. Both believed to be in Paris at this time.*

Roch frowned. He had never heard of these characters. And this was almost too easy. How could Fouché, only a few hours after receiving Roch's note, put him on the trail of the Rue Nicaise assassins? This must mean that the Minister had already received word from his informers.

True, the Catholic and Royal Army in the West was full of them. And Fouché had many *mouchards* in Paris as well. They were prostitutes, tavern keepers, merchants, beggars or former nobles. The Count de Bourmont, for instance, a former General of the Chouans, was now a recipient of Fouché's largesse.

While the maid was grinding coffee, the bacon was already frying on the stove with a delicious smell. The maid broke two eggs, which landed in the pan in the midst of tiny grease splatters. Soon the fragrance of the fresh coffee mingled with that of the meat. She set the breakfast on a tray, which she took to the dining parlor.

Roch sat down at the heavy walnut table. He never felt at home in this room. The lodgings were rented furnished, and he had brought nothing of a personal nature beyond his clothes, a pair of razors and a few toiletries. Indeed the only mementos from his youth had been an assortment of pens, books and booklets from Monsieur Veau's Academy for Boys. Old Miquel might have kept them in the attic of the Mighty Barrel, but Roch had never cast a glance at them since leaving school.

He rose, seized the plate and ate standing by the window. He was staring into the pool of darkness at the bottom of the courtyard below. At last he gulped down a cup of coffee and went to his bedroom.

He stripped to the waist and proceeded to lather his face. He liked the warmth of the water against his skin, the cold bite of the razor blade, even the burning feeling of his freshly shaven cheeks. He glanced at the maroon velvet drapes of his bed, and was tempted for a moment to lie down. Daylight would not come for another two hours. Yet he did not feel any fatigue. He would be more tired if he took a brief nap than if he eschewed sleep altogether. He put on the clean shirt his maid had laid on the bed and buttoned his waistcoat.

On his way to the Prefecture, he kept thinking of Captain Platel's testimony. The man seemed a reliable witness, not suspiciously eager to remember things. Who was the tall bespectacled fellow in the blue jacket? He did not seem to fit the description of either of the two men mentioned in Fouché's note.

Roch returned to the Isle of the Cité and turned right towards the Quai des Orfèvres, the Goldsmiths Embankment. There, on Rue de Jérusalem, behind the main courthouse, the Police Prefecture was housed in a decrepit warren of turrets and unsteady walls, reeking of dry rot, dust, mildew and old paper. The guards on duty at the entrance saluted Roch. He followed several sharply angled corridors. The steps of a corkscrew stairwell shook under his boots as he made his way up to his office. It was located under the eaves, and in places its ceiling was so low that Roch had to bend slightly lest he hurt his head. But he had this room to himself, a favor he had enjoyed since being promoted to the rank of Chief Inspector at the beginning of the year.

Roch pulled from a drawer of his desk the list he kept of all characters suspected of harboring unfriendly feelings towards the First Consul, and there were many. They fell into two main categories: the most vocal in Paris were the Jacobins, who insisted on keeping France a Republic. They distrusted Bonaparte and his ambitions. And then there were the First Consul's other enemies, the Chouans. Old Miquel was right. In spite of the pacification of the West, they continued hoping, and fighting for the restoration of the King.

The current pretender, the so-called *Louis XVIII*, was a younger brother of Louis XVI. He had sought refuge abroad and been forced to wander from city to city to flee the victorious French armies. That man of forty-five, so obese that he could barely walk, did not seem a fearsome foe, but to the Chouans he was the King. Yet to Roch royal blood, whether shed on the guillotine or flowing in the veins of raggedy pretenders to the throne, was of no account. France was a Republic now. Even Bonaparte understood it.

Roch perused his lists, eager to find any character resembling the fellow with the gold spectacles, or the men described in the Minister's note. He frowned. No, no one, whether Jacobin or Chouan, seemed a match. He opened the door and shouted to a clerk to bring him the lists of all persons who had traveled to or from Paris, on stagecoaches or private carriages, during the previous months. These lists, kept daily by the Prefecture, included names, descriptions and places of residence.

There too Roch's search was fruitless. Of course none of the suspects was stupid enough to arrive in Paris on a public conveyance. They would have reached the capital secretly, traveling on horseback, or even on foot, from friendly farm to friendly farm, and would have crossed the city barriers hidden amidst the piles of linen of a washerwoman's wheelbarrow or among the vegetables of a farmer's cart. Roch dropped the lists and swore under his breath.

At last a white dawn was creeping above the rooftops. This was the hour when Dr. Huzard, the Prefecture veterinarian, was to examine the remains of the horse. Roch was fond of horses. As a child, he had for years slept in a corner of the stables of an inn. Those accommodations were less expensive than even the smallest and filthiest of garrets. Old Miquel would spread a blanket on the straw for them to lie down. The horses nickered, shifted in their stalls, kicked the wooden partitions, but Roch was so used to them that their night noises only eased him to sleep.

Now Roch went down the rickety stairs that led from his office to the courtyard. He frowned when Dr. Huzard pulled away the oilcloth that covered the carcass. This was the first opportunity for Roch to have a look at the animal in full daylight. He was thankful for the cold weather, for it had not begun to smell. It was a small draft horse, with a bay coat and a ragged mane.

"It looks like a cannon ball hit it," said the veterinarian, his eyebrows raised. "Most of the internal organs are gone."

"Male or female?" asked Roch.

Huzard bent over the cavity at the rump end of the carcass. "A mare," he said, pointing at a reddish mass. "See? This is a piece of the womb."

The veterinarian then examined the long, yellow teeth. The lips were curled back in a final snarl.

"Not a young horse either," he continued. "It had a rough life. Look at these scars on the head." He squeezed the muscles of the neck. "But it is fat enough. It had been well fed lately."

Huzard asked the guards to turn the carcass over so that he could examine its intact side. The hair had turned white where the shafts of a cart would have rubbed against the flanks, but there were no brands or other marks of ownership. The veterinarian pulled a measuring tape from his pocket and announced a height of one meter, fifty centimeters at the withers. Roch thanked Huzard, who went inside to write his report.

Roch had ordered all of the blacksmiths in Paris pulled from their beds before dawn. They waited in a room of the ground floor of the Prefecture for their turn to look at the horse. One after the other, they stopped in front of the carcass. Dozens had already looked at the remains and shaken their heads. Roch was beginning to despair when at last a large man with huge hands and arms, by the name of Legros, cried:

"Aye, that's her!"

"You recognize this animal, Citizen?" asked Roch.

"Oh, yes, I shod her a week ago. Three men brought her to the smithy. Her old shoes were all worn out, see."

"Can you describe these three men?"

"One of them was a short fellow, not much over five feet, I'd say. Fat, he was, with a round face and flattened nose. Funny-looking, if you get my meaning, Citizen Chief Inspector." Roch was thinking of the man whom Fouché, in his note, had called *Short Francis*.

"In what way was that man funny-looking?" asked Roch.

"He was ugly, for one thing, and he had a funny scar on his eye."

"Which eye?" The blacksmith only knit his brows. "What kind of funny scar was it?" continued Roch. He imagined that, if it had not been so cold in the courtyard, beads of sweat would have formed on the man's forehead at the unwonted effort of putting his thoughts into words.

Roch sighed. "Show me, Citizen," he said.

"Like this." The blacksmith pulled on his eyelid with a fat finger, next to his left temple.

"How old would you say that man was?"

"Oh, I'd say forty."

"And what about the other two men?" asked Roch. "Were they funny-looking too?"

"Guess not, 'cause I can't remember them. They looked younger than the short one, maybe. Taller too, specially one of them. But it was the short one that was doing all the talking."

"Did one of the men wear spectacles?"

"Well, Citizen, now that you mention it, could be. The tall one."

"What kind of spectacles?"

"Well . . . you know, spe'tacles."

"Were the frames made of steel? Of gold? Round? Oval? Square?"

The blacksmith stared at Roch as though he had never before considered the existence of so many kinds of spectacles.

"How were those three men dressed?" Roch asked.

"Oh, like reg'lar bourgeois. Nothing out of the ordinary, really."

"Were you not surprised to see *three* bourgeois bring a draft horse to your smithy, when one groom could have done just as well?"

The man hit one of his palms with his closed fist. "Yeah, of course, I was surprised!" He beamed at Roch and shook his head up and down with undisguised admiration. "See how clever you've got to be to work for the police! At the time, I knew there was something pe-culiar 'bout those three fellows, but I couldn't put my finger on it. Now, seen in that light, that *was* funny, wasn't it, Citizen?"

Roch took the blacksmith inside, where the man signed his state-ment with a cross.

9

Roch could never look at the emaciated, worried face of his superior, Citizen Dubois, Prefect of Police, without deep animosity. This was odd, because the man was quite unremarkable. Dubois had been an attorney under the Old Regime. During all the years of the Revolution, he had never expressed any political opinion, defended any noteworthy case, been a member of any club, participated in any event of any import. He had simply avoided being noticed. Absent some extraordinary mishap, men of such stubborn, deliberate mediocrity survived the stormiest of times.

Bonaparte, it was rumored, had designed the new function of Prefect of Police, though in theory subordinate to that of Minister, with the specific intent of curtailing Fouché's influence. Roch had not been surprised when Fouché had warmly supported Dubois's appointment as Prefect. For weeks Roch had heard the Minister repeat with great conviction that "Dubois was a man who knew Paris well, very well indeed." That might be true, but it was a distinction Dubois shared with the remainder of the 700,000 inhabitants of the city.

The Minister's purpose in wanting a man of such limited abilities for a rival was obvious. And Roch had no reason to complain, because, when the Prefecture had been created, Fouché had ensured his promotion to the rank of Chief Inspector.

When Roch entered Dubois's office on the 4th of Nivose, he saw all of the Division Chiefs already gathered there. Piis, the Secretary General, Dubois's second-in-command, was standing by his superior's desk. Piis was a former nobleman, an affable man, an excellent character even. His only defect was a profound lack of interest in police work. All Piis cared about was poetry and plays, his own in particular. Sheets of his latest work stuck out of his coat pocket, and he was always ready to read it to his colleagues at the slightest hint of interest, or even without any such prompting. His features, too large for his smallish face, tended to give him a slightly comical aspect. That day Piis, uncharacteristically, kept his large bulging eyes away from Roch and fixed on a flowery detail of the carpet.

As soon as Roch stepped into the office, all conversations halted. The Prefect looked at him coldly.

"Glad you could join us at last, Miquel," he said. "Have a seat." Dubois cleared his throat to underscore the solemnity of his speech. "As you all know, we were able to derive helpful information from the remains of the horse that pulled the cart suspected of harboring the infernal machine. We had the presence of mind to have the carcass brought here forthright. Thanks to ou diligent investigation, we were able to obtain from a blacksmith the description of the authors of this heinous crime."

We, our, thought Roch, a thin smile on his face. Dubois could have given him or Sobry a little credit here, but this was fair enough. The Prefect was after all their superior, and entitled to claim as his own any accomplishments of his subordinates.

"Descriptions of that horse and the suspects," continued the Prefect, "are being printed as I speak. Within hours, they will be posted all over town. The clerks at the barriers have been ordered to search each and every cart and carriage entering or leaving Paris. All coffins headed for the graveyards located outside the city limits shall be opened. Furthermore, the Minister is offering a reward of 2,000 gold *louis* for any information leading to the arrest and conviction of the Jacobins who committed this atrocity."

Roch raised his hand. "Are we sure yet that the Jacobins are to blame, Citizen Prefect? I compared the descriptions of the suspects, as given by the blacksmith, to my lists. They do not match any known Jacobin."

Dubois squinted at Roch. "Well, Miquel, then your lists must not be as accurate as you would like us to believe. And pray, according to you, who would be the culprits?"

Roch had never heard a kind word from the Prefect, but he was nevertheless taken aback. He would have accepted, and not worried a great deal about a one-on-one reprimand, but now Dubois was trying to humiliate him in front of his colleagues. That prompted Roch to fight back.

"The Chouans also could have done it, Citizen Prefect."

Dubois snorted. "The Chouans! You are out of your mind, Miquel. This bears all of the hallmarks of a Jacobin atrocity."

Bertrand, the Chief of the High Police Division, in charge of all political cases, intervened. "Maybe, Citizen Prefect, Miquel's memory is no more reliable than those so-called lists of his. Maybe he forgot all about the Conspiracy of Daggers." A sneer further distorted Bertrand's misshapen face. "Now, if that wasn't a Jacobin plot!"

Roch had always loathed Bertrand, a sort of giant, lame and almost blind in one eye. Indeed Roch had not forgotten about the Conspiracy of Daggers. A few months earlier, a police informer, a Captain Harel, had befriended a few vociferous Jacobins, prodded them, shamed them for being content with words where action was needed. Finally, under the Prefect's supervision, Harel had hatched a plot whereby twelve men were supposed to surround Bonaparte and stab him to death during a representation of the play *The Horatii* at the Opera. The problem was that all of the supposed assassins had stayed home that night. Nevertheless, several Jacobins, including the painter Topino-Lebrun, had later been arrested and were still languishing in jail.

"Exactly, Bertrand," opined the Prefect. "Were not the assassins in the Conspiracy of Daggers planning to stab the First Consul *at the Opera*? And pray, Miquel, where was the First Consul going during last night's cowardly attack? *To-the-O-pe-ra.*" The Prefect detached every syllable, as though Roch had been a particularly slow-witted schoolboy. "Is not the similarity evident to you?"

There was no arguing with such nonsense. Piis himself kept silent.

Bertrand, his only eye alight with malice, intervened. "And I'd like to hear what Miquel has to say about Chevalier's infernal machine. Wasn't he experimenting with a barrel of powder fitted with a lighting mechanism when we arrested him?"

"Yes, precisely!" said the Prefect. "And Chevalier is a notorious Jacobin."

"Certainly, Citizen Prefect," answered Roch, "there is a connection between Chevalier's device and the bomb used in last night's attack. Yet in itself it does not prove the Jacobins' guilt. The Chouans might simply have copied Chevalier's idea. It is too early to exonerate anyone. I am only saying that it might be unwise to neglect clues that would lead to the Chouans. We do not know enough yet."

"I disagree with you, Miquel," said Henry, Chief of the Common Crime Division. "We have more than enough evidence to arrest all notorious Jacobins."

Henry, a thin little man resembling a weasel, had been in the force since the days of the Old Regime, when the chief of Paris police was still called the Criminal Lieutenant. Henry knew every pickpocket, swindler, forger and burglar in town. In Roch's opinion, he even knew them a bit too well, but the man was fond of repeating that "one needed a thief to catch a thief."

Now even Bouchesèche, Chief of the Food Supply and Safety Division, gravely nodded his approval. Bouchesèche had written a *Historical and Geographic Description of Hindustan.* He was a quiet, lumbering fellow with a high, balding forehead, and had the reputation of a fine scholar, though Roch could hardly be a judge of that, for he knew little and cared less about the geography of India. Still, until today, he had found Bouchesèche a pleasant colleague.

The Prefect pursed his lips. "So according to you, Miquel, we should ignore all the glaring clues that point to the Jacobins. We ought to wait for proof positive of their guilt before making any move, is that right? Instead we should chase after shadowy Chouans escaped from the countryside of the West?"

The Prefect's thin, prominent nose jutted more decidedly in Roch's direction. "Well," he added, "I am afraid this is not how police work is done. But I can guess, along with everyone else, why you are so keen on defending the Jacobins. This is to be expected from you, Miquel, considering who and what your father is."

Bertrand bellowed his hilarity and slapped his thigh repeatedly with his huge hand. But Roch's anger was not directed at the brute. He closed his eyes for a moment and imagined the degree of satisfaction he would feel if his closed fist were allowed to hit the Prefect's angular face. Unfortunately, this was not to be. So Roch swallowed the insult, steadied himself and looked straight at his superior.

"What do you mean exactly, Citizen Prefect? Unlike Bertrand, I did not catch the joke."

"It is about time you caught people's meanings, Miquel. And this is no joking matter. You have twenty-four Inspectors under your command, plus an untold number of *mouchards*, and yet you failed to get wind of this conspiracy. You and your men did nothing to prevent this. An unforgivable negligence, Miquel, and one that has not gone unnoticed in high places, I can assure you. How is it that the streets along the path of the carriage were not secured?"

Roch, his face reddening, was no longer hiding his anger. "You, Citizen Prefect, gave me strict orders not to meddle with any matters concerning the personal safety of the First Consul. That was supposed to be the exclusive province of General Duroc and his Military Police."

"Enough, Miquel. Do not compound your incompetence by your insolence. I will not tolerate either much longer."

Roch had no opportunity to respond. The Prefect was now looking at Bertrand and his other subordinates. "I will expect every night on my desk a detailed report from each of you. Even from you, Miquel."

Dubois rose and announced that the meeting was over. Roch's colleagues, casting furtive glances in his direction, left promptly. Only

Bertrand tarried. Still grinning, he bent towards the Prefect, covering one side of his mouth with his giant hand, as though to share confidential information. The Prefect, smiling, nodded in silence. Roch clenched his fists to hide the trembling of his hands and returned to his own office.

10

The reward of 2,000 *louis* offered by the Minister of Police produced immediate results. Crowds flocked to the Prefecture and waited in long lines to be heard by the next available policeman. People reported their friends, foes, neighbors and relatives for speaking ill of the First Consul, for carrying a few hundred francs in their pockets, for going to the tavern and getting drunk. Roch had to listen patiently as a man told him in hushed, breathless tones that his next door neighbor had given a dinner to "several people around a table lit by four candles" on the night of the 3rd of Nivose.

A woman described to Roch the activities of her cousin, who spent his spare time crafting miniature windmills in his attic. Those devices had always attracted the deponent's distrust, but now it was all too clear that those were models for bombs like the one used in the Rue Nicaise attack. Roch was mesmerized by the woman's fingers, mimicking the clockwork movement of the wings of the windmills. He had long stopped listening to her drivel. He was thinking of the meeting in the Prefect's office. Of course his superior had always disliked him, but now the new turn of events had given free rein to the man's animosity. Dubois was no longer afraid of Fouché. And that was very unfortunate news for Roch, who was completely dependent upon the Minister's patronage.

Roch started when an usher interrupted the woman's narrative and his own train of thought to hand him a note.

"From the Prefect *himself*," announced the man with due solemnity.

Roch held his breath. For a moment he believed that he was being dismissed, without even the benefit of a personal interview with his superior. But no, the note only ordered Roch to go question a Citizen Vigier, who had reported hearing someone or something fall into the Seine River next to his bathing establishment.

This was better than anything Roch could have expected. Not only did he keep his position, at least for a while, but he remained part of the investigation. He rose, thanked the windmill woman and pushed her firmly towards the door, assuring her that he would keep her informed if her cousin were arrested thanks to her testimony. He reached for his hat and left the Prefecture.

Vigier's Baths consisted of two separate barges, one for men and the other for women, moored next to the Pont-Royal, the Liberty Bridge, formerly the Royal Bridge. The place would have been bustling during the heat of summer, when Parisians flocked there to enjoy the pleasures of cool water, but in winter it was deserted. Yet a fine day it was, the sky the lightest shade of gray. The thin haze that rose from the river veiled the towers of Notre-Dame in the distance.

Sobry, a scowl on his face, the collar of his coat turned up, already stood on the deck of one of the barges, under a sign that advertised in bold letters: *Private and Public Ladies' Cabins, Showers and Baths*. He watched as his men, armed with nets and long poles fitted with hooks, dredged the bottom of the river from a dozen rowboats.

"Any luck?" asked Roch.

The other man grunted. "Do I look lucky? Oh, we fished out old boots, a female fetus, a few dead dogs and of course enough animal entrails to fill the Tuileries. Those butchers from the slaughterhouses of the Châtelet toss the offal into the river. So no, no luck. Very little to show for a day spent chilling myself here."

Sobry paused to gaze at Roch. "About you? Things going well with the Prefect?"

Roch grinned bitterly. "Who told you? Bertrand?"

"No, not Bertrand. Another sort of animal, of the weasel kind: Henry. You were begging for trouble, Miquel, with your Chouans. Everyone knows the Jacobins did it."

"No one knows any such thing yet. *I* certainly don't."

"Then you should. The First Consul himself said so the other night at the Opera. Piis was there, sitting in the box of some fellow aristocrat, and he told me about it. According to him, Bonaparte promised that the Jacobins would pay, and pay dearly for the attack, and he said it aloud. He meant to be heard by everyone."

"Bonaparte was furious," said Roch. "Quite understandable at the time. By now he will have quieted and realized that there is no evidence pointing one way or the other."

"I am not privy to what he has realized yet, but I would not bet a *sol* on Fouché's future. They say the First Consul has given him no more than a week to prove the Jacobins' innocence. How can that be done in such a short time? Fouché will be fortunate to avoid arrest himself. He is a former Jacobin, after all, and Bonaparte has never trusted him."

"Bonaparte owes Fouché everything. His coup last year would never have succeeded if Fouché had not looked the other way."

"Bonaparte expects more than that from his followers. Fouché was content to do nothing, wait for the outcome, and then side with the victor."

"Doing nothing was already a great deal for a Minister of Police, when he had to know of Bonaparte's projects."

"Maybe, but Fouché didn't rally to Bonaparte's banner until the result was clear. Would he have hesitated a moment to arrest Bonaparte if the coup had failed? No, believe me, Bonaparte has tolerated him so far, but he will seize this opportunity to rid himself of the man."

Sobry looked intently at Roch. "Everyone at the Prefecture knows you to be Fouché's creature. It was fine, of course, as long as Fouché was powerful, but now it puts you in a dangerous position. Switch allegiances, friend, before it is too late. What is stopping you? Loyalty? Fouché himself has betrayed everyone and everything in due time. Go to the Prefect *today*. Tell him that you realized your error, that you are now absolutely convinced of the Jacobins' guilt. He won't be fooled, of course, but he might spare you when Fouché falls, in a few days."

Roch remained silent. He was staring straight ahead at the river. It ran slowly like molten lead in front of his eyes.

Sobry shrugged. "Always stubborn as a mule, I see. Oh well, have it your way, Miquel, but don't be surprised if you find yourself sharing Fouché's fate, whatever it may be."

Roch felt the need to change the subject. "So what has Citizen Vigier to say?" he asked. "I came here to question him."

Sobry waited a minute before answering, then nodded in the direction of one of the houses on the embankment. "I already talked to him. He lives right there. He only heard a splashing noise shortly after eight last night. Since his baths are closed in this season, he didn't come out to see what it was. He didn't think anything of it until he learned of the attack this morning."

"He didn't hear the explosion? He must be deaf as a pot! From here, the racket would have been enough to awaken the dead. Much louder than any splash in the river a few minutes later."

Sobry grinned. "You will question Citizen Vigier yourself, of course, but he didn't strike me as the sort of man who would come out by himself in the dark. Especially if there were any chance of a risk to his personal safety."

"So what do you think that splashing noise was?"

"Could be anything, related or not to the attack. Perhaps one of the assassins jumped into the river, but he must have had a damned good reason to do so. No one could survive more than a few minutes in the river in this season. Perhaps the man was burnt by the explosion and wanted to quell the pain."

"Or perhaps the assassin did not jump into the river at all. He could have thrown something away."

"If he did, we have yet to discover what it was."

Roch went to take the statement of Vigier, who had nothing more to say, and again joined Sobry on the deck of the barge until dusk. The Seine only yielded more garbage as they looked on.

11

*I*t was full dark when Roch reached the Prefecture after his afternoon at Vigier's Baths. The streetlights barely pierced the fog that
rose from the river. He did not follow Sobry's recommendation to go
to the Prefect to express contrition. Instead, he was content to prepare
his daily report to his superior, along with an unofficial copy he would
send discreetly to the Minister. Then, with his colleagues, Roch spent
the rest of the night in his office, receiving more statements from
witnesses, or people who fancied themselves witnesses. Hundreds
of men and women were still patiently waiting for their turn to be
interviewed.

Roch's eyes were burning from fatigue, and he could not help
yawning while taking one statement after another. He had almost
abandoned any hope of garnering useful information when, well
past midnight, a Widow Peusol, a street vendor, was shown into
his office. The woman entered cautiously. She clutched her tattered skirts with both hands, her chest slightly bent forward in a
half bow. At least here was a witness who was not full of her own
importance and did not address him in a conspiratorial tone. He
rose and offered her a chair, scratching his ear while he waited for her
to speak.

"It's my daughter, Citizen Chief Inspector, Sir," she began, "my
little Marianne. She didn't come home two nights ago."

Roch stared at the woman. "Do you mean the night of the attack?

The 3rd of Nivose? You waited *two days* to report your daughter missing?"

The woman opened her mouth like a fish out of water and looked at him with a mix of fear and desperation.

"It's all right, Citizen Peusol," he continued in a softer tone. "I understand." Indeed he knew that the poor preferred, sometimes with good reason, to limit their dealings with the police to a minimum.

"So I won't be in trouble, Sir?"

"No. I guarantee it. Please tell me what happened to Marianne on the 3rd."

"She left with her tray full of biscuits, like every day. I buy'm at the pastry shop, see, an' then she sells'm on the streets for a *sol* more a piece. That's not much, Citizen Chief Inspector, but at least this way she earns a bit of money. We're so poor that more often'n not I worry we won't have twelve *sols* pay next week's rent. Then we'd be thrown out by the lan'lord an' we'd end on the streets, abeggin' for our bread . . ."

"Yes, Citizen Peusol. So where does Marianne usually sell her biscuits?"

"She goes stand by those barracks near the Pont-Royal—" The woman stopped suddenly and cast a worried look at Roch. "Scuse me, Sir, the Liberty Bridge, I should've said. You know, where the Hackneys' Office used to be in the ol' days. It's a good place, with all the soldiers comin' in an' out. So she left with Jeanne, the girl nex' door. An' Jeanne told me that a man came to talk to Marianne."

"A soldier?"

"No, Jeanne didn't say it was a soldier." Citizen Peusol wiped her eyes with a corner of her ragged apron. "He gave Marianne twelve *sols* if she'd come an' take care of some horse. Jeanne saw him put a silver coin in Marianne's hand. An' she was so happy, and she followed him across the bridge, my poor little girl!" Citizen Peusol was now sobbing.

Roch sat up. "I need to talk to that Jeanne right away. What is her full name?"

"I can't tell you. You'd arrest her. Then people'd say that I am nothin' but a *moucharde* an' that I cause trouble to the neighbors. I'd lose my good name."

Roch sighed with exasperation. "Of course I will not to arrest Jeanne, but she must give us a description of that man she saw walking away with Marianne. Do you not want us to find out what happened to your daughter? How old is Marianne, Citizen?"

"She's fifteen, jus' like Jeanne."

Roch shook his head. A fine idea it was to send two girls of fifteen to sell cakes in front of barracks! The man who had lured Marianne away could have been a pimp.

Roch remembered the day when Old Miquel had taken him to Rue Tire-Vit, Pull-Cock Alley. He was fourteen then, and had stared at the women, reeking of strong perfumes, and still stronger animal odors, the bodices of their garish dresses pulled down low enough to reveal their nipples. The whores, mistaking the older man's purpose, had pointed out Roch to one another, giggled and called to them sweetly, enticingly. His father had given him a shove on the shoulder.

"Take a good look at these, son," he had said. "Smell them. Infected with horrible diseases that'll rot your privates. Leeches, all of them, waiting to take whatever money's in your pocket."

Old Miquel's lessons were not lost on Roch. He had kept from that visit a distaste for prostitutes, though, as a policeman, he had learned how helpful they could be as informers. He was always dismayed to see yet another girl join the legions of Paris whores. Now he could picture young Marianne, her face painted white and red, clad in a soiled satin dress, peddling her allurements on Pull-Cock Alley.

"What does your daughter look like, Citizen Peusol?" Roch asked.

"Well, she's red hair, an' a big nose. An' she's very much marked by the smallpox. She was taken awful sick when she was nine."

That settled it. Marianne would have been safe from any pimp.

But the mention of red hair gave Roch a pang. He remembered the skull of the charred body lying in the middle of Rue Nicaise.

"An' she's a bit of a squint too," continued Citizen Peusol. "God knows her brothers tease her enough about it, poor thing. They tell her one of her eyes says shit to the other."

Now Roch felt his anger rising. Was Marianne chosen for the grim task of holding the horse's bridle because of her looks? Would the criminals, those cowards who had run away to save their own skins, have sacrificed a prettier girl?

The Peusol woman joined her hands in a gesture of supplication. "What do you think happened to her, Sir? It can't have been her on Rue Nicaise?"

"What was Marianne wearing that day?"

"Oh, that's easy, 'cause she's but one set of clothes. A skirt with blue an' white stripes, an' her gray woolen jacket. She's grown much this year, so it's quite a bit too small for her. An' of course her blue kerchief on her head. We're not rich, but I wouldn't let my daughter out on the street with her hair uncovered." The woman continued, her voice quavering. "So it can't be her, eh, Citizen Chief Inspector?"

Roch sighed. This was not going to be easy. It never was. He rose and put his hand on the woman's shoulder.

"I am sorry, Citizen Peusol. You will have to be brave. Yes, actually, this seems to match the description of the girl some witnesses saw that night. It may indeed have been your daughter."

The woman burst into a wail. "Oh, I knew it. I knew it, but I didn't want to hear it." She raised her eyes to Roch. "She was a nice, sweet girl. She'd never hurt anyone in her life. Why did they kill her? Can I see her? I want to see her. Jus' one last time."

Roch remembered the blackened, faceless remains of the girl. One of her arms had been discovered the day after the attack on a nearby rooftop. The other one was still missing. It was not a sight for a mother.

"To say good-bye to my little girl," moaned the woman. "Please, Sir."

Roch had to think of something very fast. "No, Citizen Peusol," he said, "I cannot let you, as the next of kin, see her. It would be against the rules. Perhaps you have a relative who could come here to identify the body?"

The woman nodded, tears flowing down her face. "Well," she said, catching her breath between two sobs, "there's my brother . . ."

Roch opened the door and called to a guard to bring some liquor.

12

A clerk brought Roch a note, left by a messenger who had hurried away without waiting for a response. It simply said: *Meet me this afternoon at three o'clock, dearest, dearest love, at the usual place. I know how busy you must be, but please try, just for me. I will be waiting for you.*

Roch had barely caught any sleep since the Rue Nicaise attack, and he had not had much time to think of his next assignation with Blanche. For several months now they had met two or three times a week in a room above Citizen Bercelle's millinery shop. He had last seen her on the afternoon of the 3rd of Nivose, the day of the attack.

Before Blanche, there had been other women, usually the wives of well-to-do merchants. Roch kept clear of maidens. A single moment of carelessness, of lust, of distraction, and he would be expected to wed a girl he did not even like.

Yet Blanche Coudert was not the same as Roch's prior mistresses. For one thing, she was no shopkeeper's wife. Old Miquel would have called her a *ci-devant*, the contemptuous name given to former aristocrats. Blanche had been educated in a convent, and her mother had been a noblewoman before the Revolution, though she never spoke of her father. Also Blanche was lovelier than any of Roch's other mistresses, indeed than any other woman he had ever seen. Even the name *Blanche* seemed to have been designed for her. Her skin was indeed white, all the more so under her crown of wavy dark hair.

Roch had met Blanche in the exercise of his official functions. He had been entrusted by Fouché, who was an astute judge of men, with the task of collecting from the gaming parlors and houses of convenience of the Palais-Egalité the weekly contributions it pleased those establishments to bestow upon the police. Roch did not return the bawds' knowing smiles when they handed him heavy purses, which he delivered promptly to the Minister.

Among the establishments visited by Roch was the gaming salon of Madame de Cléry. It was no brothel, but she would receive him in her bedroom, sometimes lying on a sofa, an embroidered slipper dangling from one toe, sometimes seated at her dressing table, tying her garter around a firm, round thigh. She did not seem a young woman, but he could guess at the curves of a very handsome body. She would yawn, smile at him, rise and walk lazily to a strongbox, disguised by an elegant mahogany veneer. He disliked the woman's familiarities and ignored the squeeze of her hand as she gave him her weekly purse. He always hastened to leave.

It had been during one of those visits that he had met Blanche. She entered the bedroom while Madame de Cléry, who had seemed colder than usual, handed Roch her purse. At the sight of the young woman, he felt no less embarrassment than if he had been surprised in an intimate position with Madame de Cléry. He flushed with displeasure.

But Blanche seemed to ignore his awkwardness. She simply smiled at him. It was the smile of innocence, wandering lightly, without affectation, on a small, round, red mouth. And it did not stop at the mouth, but lit the fine dark eyes and carved dimples in the still childish cheeks. Her gown, a dark green silk with a gray sash, seemed delightfully modest next to Madame de Cléry's sheer negligee. Roch was astonished at finding such a creature here, like a flower growing on a dunghill.

"Why, Mama," she asked the older woman, "do you not introduce this gentleman?"

Roch stared. He had trouble believing that the young woman was Madame de Cléry's daughter.

"Well, Blanche dearest, Chief Inspector Miquel is from the police. You know that the Minister kindly extends his protection to my establishment." Her eyes turned away, she waved in Blanche's direction. "Sir, this is my daughter, Madame Coudert."

Roch frowned. He was unpleasantly surprised to learn that the young woman was married. But then, why not? He had heard of Coudert, the banker, who had already been one of the richest men in Paris before the Revolution. He had to be at least thirty years older than this wife of his.

Blanche, still smiling, held out her hand to Roch.

"I am delighted to make your acquaintance, Sir. Will you do me the honor of calling on me tomorrow night? It will only be a simple musical gathering. I live on Rue de Babylone."

Roch took Blanche's proffered hand and made no response. She seemed to take his silence as an acceptance, and she fled the room as lightly as an apparition. All that remained of her was a fragrance of carnation and lily of the valley. He left promptly, avoiding Madame de Cléry's eye.

Roch wondered about Blanche. The Cléry woman must be rich. The gaming salon, judging by its ample contributions to the coffers of the Ministry, appeared to prosper. Why had Blanche married Coudert? For his money? Madame de Cléry could certainly have spared Blanche a mercenary marriage. Had Coudert used other arguments to pressure the mother into giving him her daughter? Now there was pity, disgust and some curiosity mixed with Roch's admiration of Blanche's loveliness.

Roch hesitated before accepting her invitation. Yet the next day he walked to the Coudert mansion, located at the far end of Rue de Babylone. The weather was dry, fine for a late September evening. He passed the monumental gates, crossed the front courtyard and made his way past the row of carriages bringing Madame Coudert's guests.

He whistled softly as he climbed the flight of steps that led to the front door, flanked by a row of marble columns in the antique style. Madame Coudert lived in a palace. He was wearing his best black coat and white silk stockings, but hesitated before crossing the threshold. He chided himself for his cowardice.

Who were those people anyway? He imagined what his father would say. Upstarts who, since the beginning of the war, eight years earlier, had grown rich providing the armies with *riz-pain-sel*, rice-bread-salt, or speculating on the precipitous decline of the *assignats*, the Republic's paper money. Opposing parties and their leaders had risen and fallen, but the war, with its many opportunities, continued to this day. And now those people, their fortunes made, were trying to ape the *ci-devant* nobles, the former aristocrats.

A servant in a red livery, a sneer on his face, raised his arm to stop Roch. The man must have seen that he had come on foot, but let him pass upon hearing his name. Roch muttered, loud enough to be heard, "Lackey."

He followed other guests up the stairs, lined with bouquets of ferns and the last roses of the season. The movement of the crowd and the noise of violins being tuned guided him to a vast salon, entirely paneled with gold-framed mirrors. They reflected to infinity the lights of crystal chandeliers and giant bronze candlesticks. Naked Roman deities, their pink flesh resting on plump pillowlike clouds, peered down at the company from the painted ceiling.

The men were dressed in black like Roch, or wore brightly colored uniforms trimmed in gold or silver braid. The women were clad in short-sleeved gowns, stiff with embroidery and covered with diamonds, emeralds and rubies set in flower patterns. Many had the thick, ruddy arms of former washerwomen, which did not prevent them from displaying row after row of glittering bracelets. The glare of the lights, the gold, the jewels, multiplied by the mirrors, dazzled Roch for a moment.

Men kept to one side of the salon, women to the other. Roch wondered whether the two groups were going to mingle or even acknowledge each other in the course of the evening. An invisible partition seemed to divide them. He remained standing, surveying the room and its occupants. So *this* was high society. This party seemed a particularly stupid way to spend a night. He could have been sitting on a straw chair at one of the tables of the Mighty Barrel, playing checkers with his friend Mulard over a bottle of excellent Burgundy from Old Miquel's personal reserve. Even dinner with Alexandrine and her father would have been a treat compared to this.

Roch's reflections took a more pleasant turn when he saw Madame Coudert walk towards him. She wore a Greek gown of white muslin, trimmed around the hem with embroidery of the same color. A string of pearls rested on her black hair and pale forehead. More pearls circled her neck and cascaded in drops from her ears. She smiled at Roch in the same manner as in her mother's bedroom. The simplicity of her attire, the soft glow of her pearls against her skin were a delight to the eye next to the gaudiness of the other women's dresses and jewels. Blanche was pretty, very pretty. A delicate figure, tall yet graceful, perfectly proportioned limbs. Maybe that sight alone justified the waste of an evening.

At first, Roch observed her beauty complacently, but coldly, as he would have admired a painting, or a statue in a park. Then his thoughts took a more personal turn. He pictured her with her hair undone, flowing freely down her back, and her pearls, unstrung, hitting the floor one by one, bouncing on the shiny parquet with little tapping noises. Then he imagined the pleasure he would feel in slowly unlacing her gown, which already exposed her shoulders and throat, and pulling it down to her waist. Now her long black curls rested between her bare, white, round breasts. He was ready to follow his reverie further when he realized with dismay that she was leading a stout man towards him.

"Chief Inspector Miquel," she said, "I am delighted to see you here tonight. Allow me to introduce my husband, Monsieur Coudert."

Roch frowned when he heard the word *Monsieur* instead of *Citizen* and eyed Coudert with increased unfriendliness. The man could not be any younger than fifty. His hair, straight and short, was the same gray as his eyes. He looked carefully, earnestly, but without hostility at Roch and bowed.

"Good evening to you, Citizen," said Roch, who bowed slightly in turn. Indeed he did not find the directness of Coudert's gaze unpleasant, and might have liked the man but for the fact that he was Blanche's husband.

No man went over to the women, except Coudert, who paid the ladies a few perfunctory compliments. Then a lackey announced *la Signora Casaretti*, and a very handsome woman, greeted by excited whispers, entered the salon. From then on Coudert dedicated himself to this new beauty, from whose side he did not stray for the whole evening. The rest of the women were left to themselves.

It seemed to Roch that every man in the room was either a general, a banker or a senator. He had nothing to say to anyone and, after the Couderts left him to attend to their other guests, nobody seemed to pay him the least attention. The musicians, a string quartet, finished tuning their instruments and the concert started.

He took a chair in the part of the salon occupied by other men and tried to listen. He was in no way adverse to fine music, but this did not seem a congenial setting to enjoy it. He rose as soon as tepid applause announced that the first piece was over.

As he was ready to leave the salon, he felt a gentle tap on his elbow. He started and turned around, his heart beating a little faster in the hope that it would be Madame Coudert. Indeed she slipped her delicate hand, gloved in white satin, under his arm. An intimate, almost tender gesture. She was smiling at him once more.

"Are you leaving us already, Chief Inspector?" she asked. "You are going to miss Beethoven's *Sonata Pathétique*."

"With great regret. Duty calls me away."

Her lips seemed to pout, but there was a mischievous glimmer in her eyes. "And you were going like this, without taking leave of me? I hope you spent a pleasant evening."

"Quite. I thank you for your invitation."

"You found my party dull, did you not?"

What was he supposed to say under the circumstances? He did not feel like lying. He looked straight at her and made no response.

"Well," she continued, "I find it rather dull myself. Except for the music, of course." Her eyes sparkled. "*That* was beautiful, was it not?"

He nodded. She looked around at her guests and pursed her lips. "Mama says that society was much more polished before the Revolution. Gentlemen devoted themselves to the ladies. Conversations were animated, brilliant. Dinners would turn into balls on a whim, guests would play the pianoforte and sing, suppers were improvised." She giggled. "It sounds like people had so much fun then."

He looked into her eyes. "I really cannot tell. My father is a tavern keeper. He knew little of fine society before the Revolution. Even now he tends to stay away from the most fashionable salons."

She blushed slightly and bowed her head. "I will not detain you any longer. It was a pleasure seeing you again."

A few guests were walking in their direction. Blanche dropped her white lace fan and put her hand to her mouth to muffle a little cry of dismay. Roch bent to his knee to pick the object off the floor. His face brushed against the flimsy fabric of her skirts as he rose.

"See how clumsy I am!" she said.

He ran his forefinger on the mother-of-pearl sticks of the fan and admired for a moment the carved pattern of leaves, flowers, butterflies and ribbons. It was an object of exquisite beauty, fortunately unbroken in its fall. He returned it to her. Their hands touched. He felt something being slipped into his.

"Thank you, Chief Inspector," she said. "I am much obliged."

He almost ran down the stairs and out of the Coudert mansion, fingering the tiny slip of paper in his pocket. This party had not been a waste of his time after all. Lovely Madame Coudert would be his. She was already his. Yet, despite his feeling of triumph, he could not help being somewhat disappointed. Perhaps he had expected her to be less forward. But then he no longer knew what he had expected.

He paused under the yellow glow of the next streetlamp. The note, in an elegant script, read: *Madame Bercelle's millinery shop, at the sign of the Five Diamonds, Rue du Pélican. The day after tomorrow. Three in the afternoon.*

He grinned. *Women,* he thought.

13

Roch had gone to the Five Diamonds at the appointed time, and found Blanche already there. Those two days spent waiting for her had increased his desire to the point where it had become almost unbearable. Thankfully she had not dallied with him. She had let him undress her in haste. He had found her as beautiful as he had expected, maybe even more so. He had done all of the things of which he had thought at the musical evening, then other things of which he had dreamed since, and then more. She had not put up any show of mock shyness, and seemed to share in his passion. They had been lovers since, and his need for her increased with each of their encounters.

He shook himself. All that had happened before the Rue Nicaise attack. His affair with Blanche, more than anything else in his life, now seemed to belong to another, ancient, happy, carefree era.

Roch went to L'Hôtel-Dieu Hospital to have Captain Platel sign his statement. None too early. The man was still conscious, but drenched in sweat, shaking with fever. His leg had been amputated above the knee. Much to Roch's relief, he did not ask again about Widow Lystère. Someone must have told him of her fate. Roch left the hospital promptly.

Just outside, a girl in rags was singing a ditty in a powerful, shrill voice:

Let's 'ear the true tale
Of the most 'orrible attack
Agai'st the gover'ment,
On Rue Nicaise.
Listen, good people,
'Cause the story o' that foul deed
Makes mankin' shudder.

Passersby stopped to listen to the little street singer. Roch threw a copper coin at the red and white kerchief spread at the girl's feet and pressed on, impatient to reach the Five Diamonds millinery on Rue du Pélican.

From the street he glanced inside at several *grisettes*, shopgirls, seated at the counter, who were sewing ribbons, lace, feathers and silk flowers onto bonnets. The young woman closest to the window looked up from her work and smiled at him. He had noticed her during prior visits and would normally have tarried to smile back, for the simple pleasure of gazing for a moment at her pretty face. He was in no way adverse to *grisettes*, though they made so little money at honest work that they tended to be rather demanding in all matters financial. But that day he ignored the shopgirl. He pulled a key from his pocket and opened a door to the side of the shop.

He followed a narrow passage and ran up a flight of stairs. Before he could knock, the door opened and Blanche threw herself into his arms. She pulled him into the room. It was furnished with a large bed, draped in faded blue silk, two matching chairs, a bidet in the corner and a dressing table. In its drawer Blanche kept a hairbrush, a curling iron and a box of hairpins.

Roch recognized the fragrance of carnation and lily of the valley. Blanche would leave a little perfume bottle open, probably to mask the odor of the room, the mercenary smell of a place where too many had passed and no one lived. Yet Roch forgot about the mixed scents, about the roundish stains on the chairs and the flowery coverlet. He wrapped his arms around Blanche and kissed her greedily. He realized how much he had missed her during those three days since the attack.

"I was so worried about you the other night," he whispered. "I thought of you that night at the Opera, of what could have happened to you."

She shuddered. "Oh, you are an angel, but I was in no danger."

Roch had never felt such comfort in her presence. After the charred, torn, bloodied, tortured flesh he had seen during the past two days, it was a delight to behold her white skin. He undressed her slowly, with unspoken apprehension, as if afraid that each item of clothing he was peeling off her would reveal a heartrending gash or burn. No, of course, she was smooth, intact, unblemished, flawless. Naked on her side on the bed, she glowed like mother-of-pearl.

He stripped in a hurry, impatient for their skin to touch. He straddled her on his hands and knees, caressing her with his entire body. That was the time when he would decide how to take her. He usually liked to ponder all options at his leisure, but now he did not hesitate. He pushed on her shoulder to roll her from her side to her back. He needed to feel her mouth, her tongue, her breasts, her hands, to see her face, all the more beautiful when he was inside her, to lose himself in the darkness of her eyes.

He was not rough, not gentle either. He was relentless, insistent. Soon she held her breath and shuddered. He felt her contract around him. Yet he did not pause. He was only becoming more aware of every part of her he could reach. After a few minutes her spasms returned. She was now moaning aloud, almost sobbing.

There was no holding it. It sprung from his loins, up his spine to explode in his skull. Each pulse felt like a bolt of white light, blinding him from within. A yell, deep from his stomach, tore through his throat. For a moment he remained frozen in an arc of pain and pleasure. Then he rolled over on his back, shaking, empty, his eyes closed, not knowing whether the next breath would come.

Thankfully she did not speak or try to touch him afterwards. It would have been unbearable. He struggled to get hold of his own mind. *La petite mort.* The little death indeed. Never before had it felt so like the real one. There was none of the light-headed glow of drunkenness that usually followed his first taste of pleasure.

When he opened his lids at last, Blanche's eyes were on him, wider than ever.

"You frightened me," she said.

He shrugged and smiled faintly. "Perhaps I frightened myself too." He raised himself on one elbow, brushed his lips against hers and sat up on the bed. She rested her head on his thigh. It would normally have been the beginning of more play. She would have toyed with him, teased him tenderly under the guise of cleaning him. She always knew how to bring him back to life, eager for more of her.

Not this time. He stopped her. The memory of the Rue Nicaise attack intruded upon his thoughts. He could not reconcile her beauty with the horror he had witnessed over the past days. He took her head between his hands and pushed it back gently onto the pillow. Then he took his time spreading her hair like a black fan against the whiteness of the linen.

"What is the matter?" she asked.

"Thanks to you, Blanche, I forgot about this Rue Nicaise business for a moment, but it is back." He closed his eyes. "I have seen terrible things, things I can't forget."

She shivered. "Those poor people. I dream of them at night. I see their shadows standing right behind me when I look at myself in the mirror."

He bent to caress her cheek. "Poor Blanche. It must have been terrifying that night at the Opera, not knowing what horror to expect next."

She threw herself against his chest. "This dread has never left me since. Oh, Roch, I see death everywhere now."

He closed her arms around her and rocked her like a child. "The shock will pass, dearest. The assassins will be caught, and they will pay for their crime. Then everyone in Paris will be safe again. You too, my Blanche." He ran his finger over her lips.

"Are you certain of it? How is your investigation progressing?"

His jaw tightened. "I can't discuss it, of course, but yes, we are making good progress. The assassins will be caught, and they will finish their days on the guillotine, as they deserve. Which reminds me that I should go back to the Prefecture, little as I wish to leave you."

He rose, seized the ewer on the dressing table and sat astride the bidet. The cool water flowed down his stomach, washing away the slickness, the smell, the memory of love. He gathered his clothes and dressed in haste.

"When will I see you again, Roch?" she asked.

"As soon as you can make time for me, dearest. I too need you. Send me a messenger, and I will try my best to come here, even if I can only spare a few minutes."

He bent to kiss her cheek lightly and cast a last look at her before closing the door gently.

14

Roch continued questioning hordes of self-styled witnesses, reviewing reams of letters. Most information was worthless. Jeanne, the street vendor who had accompanied poor Marianne Peusol on the night of the attack, confirmed Captain Platel's description of the man with the gold spectacles, without adding anything new. Roch wrote his daily reports to the Prefect, who seemed content with them. Or if he was not, he kept his thoughts to himself, which was the same, or even better to Roch.

His colleagues now risked cautious glances in his direction. If nothing worse happened to him, in the course of a few days, they might be emboldened enough to acknowledge him once again in the corridors.

Sleet had been falling on Paris all day, and the carcass of the little mare, whose description had been posted all over Paris, had been moved from the courtyard to an unheated room on the ground floor.

A guard knocked at the door of Roch's office and poked his head in.

"There's a grain merchant waiting for you, Citizen Chief Inspector. A Citizen Lambel. He says he used to own that horse downstairs."

Roch ran down the stairs to join Lambel, a thin man with shrewd little eyes, set deep in a wrinkled, leathery face. The grain merchant took a step backwards when a guard pulled away the oilcloth that covered the carcass. In spite of the cold, the stench of decomposition was now sickening.

"That's a pity," said Lambel, shaking his head sadly at the remains. "A good little mare. But then she wasn't worth 200 francs, even with the cart."

"So you used to own this animal?" asked Roch.

"Yes, I'd had her for five years. That is, until the 26th or 27th of Frimaire last, I don't remember which. That would've been the 16th or 17th of December, right? I'm always losing my reckoning with the new calendar."

"You are not alone, Citizen Lambel. How did you come to sell this mare?"

"Brunet, my neighbor, brought me a man who was looking to buy a horse and cart. And at the time mine were stopped right in front of my shop, so I showed them to the man. He was a stallholder, he said, he sold cloth at fairs and he needed a cart to take his wares across the country. I hadn't thought of selling the horse before, but then he offered me 200 francs, plus six francs *pour boire*, as a tip."

Lambel pointed at the carcass. "That's a pretty high price for a horse like this one, that wasn't so young as it used to be. And it'd been due for a shoeing for a while. So I went inside the shop to talk to my wife, and she said that if some ninny wanted to buy the horse for 200 francs, I'd better sell it fast, before he changed his mind. So I went back to the man and we shook hands. He gave me a gold *louis* as earnest money. An' the next day he returned with the rest of the price, and we spent the six francs *pour boire* over a few pints of wine at the tavern. I invited my neighbor Brunet along. That was no more'n he deserved, mind you, 'cause he was the one who'd brought the man."

"Did the man tell you his name, Citizen Lambel?"

"I asked him, but he pretended like he didn't hear me, and I didn't press him. I didn't want him to change his mind about buying the horse, specially for 200 francs. Still, I'm curious. *Always poking your nose in other people's business*, like my wife says. So I was itching to know more 'bout that man. After he'd drunk his fill at the tavern, I asked him, innocent like, where he lived, and he said he stayed with his sister."

"Did he tell you his sister's name, or her address?"

"I asked, of course. But he looked like he felt a bit silly for telling me about his sister. Like he'd sobered up all of a sudden. So he wouldn't tell me no more about her after that."

"And what was the man like?"

"Oh, he was no beauty, that's for sure. Short, fat. With a big round face." Citizen Lambel pulled his arms away from his slender body and puffed his usually hollow cheeks to mimic the man's appearance. "And a flat nose, like he'd run into a wall. And a scar that pulled on his eyelid, the left one. Around forty years of age, I'd say. He had curly hair, and he wore it powdered, which I found mighty odd for a stallholder. And he wasn't dressed like one either, at least the firs' time I saw him. He had a dark blue coat, and yellow breeches, tied around the knees with ribbons. And stockings that had stripes that went up and down, and he wore laced shoes and a round hat. Fancy, he looked, but vulgar at the same time, if you catch my meaning. To tell you the truth, Citizen Chief Inspector, I wouldn't have liked him half as much if he hadn't been so fond of parting with his money."

This seemed to fit the description of François Carbon, alias Short Francis, in the Minister's note. "You are very observant, Citizen Lambel," said Roch. "I am sure this is not all you have noticed about that man."

"True, I don't keep my eyes inside my pockets, so to speak. I can tell you the man snuffed tobacco. From a small wooden snuffbox. Round, it was. There was a fine picture of a horseman on it, with a sword at his side. My wife said it looked like the King of England, but I asked her: *How d'you know, woman? You clapped your eyes on the King of England yet?* You see, I don't like telling things when I ain't sure."

Lambel paused to catch his breath. "But when the short man came back the next day, he was dressed like a stallholder that time, in a blue jacket. He even told my wife that he'd paid ten francs for it. A vas' deal of money it is for a jacket like that, if you want my opinion,

Citizen Chief Inspector. But I kept mum 'bout it, 'cause he didn't ask my opinion, did he? And I reckoned it'd be foolish of me to give him ideas like he was paying too much for things. Then he said he wanted to buy a bushel of peas and another one of lentils, and he needed a barrel as well to keep them. I charged him twice the price for the whole thing, but he didn't say nothing 'bout it. If a man likes to spend his money freely, it's his business, eh, Citizen Chief Inspector?"

"Exactly, Citizen Lambel. I don't see that you did anything wrong."

The man shook his head with satisfaction. "Aye, that's the way me and my wife see it too. I asked the man if he had any place to keep the horse and cart, 'cause I could rent him my own shed, where I'd kept them. I liked his custom, see. But when he took a look at my shed, he said it wouldn't do 'cause it didn't lock. He said you don't feel at home in a place that hasn't a good lock. Then he said he needed to get a cover for the cart. I told him Brunet could make one. I owed Brunet a good turn, see, for bringing me such a fine customer."

"And Citizen Brunet made this cover?"

"Oh, yes, but he told me later that the man wasn't happy 'cause it was too short. Brunet'd made it like usual, but the man wanted it to go down to the hubs of the cart, or else his wares'd be spoiled by the rain. Brunet'd never heard of a cover needing to go down so low, and me neither, but he didn't say nothing 'bout it, and he made the cover fit the way the man liked."

"What kind of cover was it?"

"A tarpaulin. A plain gray tarpaulin."

"Was it the last you saw of the short man?"

Lambel sighed. "Yes. A pity, 'cause I wish I'd more customers like that."

"So where did he take the horse and cart?"

"That I don't know. Some place with a good lock, I reckon."

Roch ordered the guard to replace the oilcloth onto the carcass. Lambel cast a last look at the horse. "When you think he'd promised to take good care of her!" Squinting, he turned to Roch. "Say, Citizen

Chief Inspector, about that reward of 2,000 *louis* that's posted all over town?"

"Well, Citizen Lambel, you have provided very helpful information. Once the guilty parties are brought to justice and convicted, I encourage you to apply for the reward. You certainly deserve it."

Roch grinned happily at Lambel. Things were taking a hopeful turn. Fouché, in his note, had pointed Roch in the correct direction: the man nicknamed Short Francis was indeed involved in the Rue Nicaise attack. And he was a Chouan. This meant that Roch, whatever the Prefect said or thought, had been right to suspect the Royalists. Now he was vindicated. But what a pity the grain merchant's shed did not lock!

Now the carcass of the horse had run its course. Roch was not sorry to have it leave the Prefecture for one of the veterinary pits outside the city limits. There stood the shops of the *boyautiers*, the men who skinned the carcasses and sold the bowels to makers of musical instruments. But the belly of the little mare had been blown away by the explosion days before it reached the pit. Her innards had been denied the ultimate grace of finishing as the strings of a fiddle.

15

Roch felt that he deserved the luxury of a lunch with someone who was not a fellow policeman or a witness. He decided to call on his friend Mulard, a painter and for many years a faithful patron of the Mighty Barrel. Old Miquel liked the fellow and regularly forgave his debt to the tavern.

Now Roch crossed over to the Right Bank by way of the Pont-Neuf and turned in the direction of the Louvre. It was now called a *museum*, and the King's collections had been opened to the public after the fall of the Monarchy. The inner courtyard was occupied by temporary constructions where painters' studios were housed. Roch winced at the smell of urine as he walked by the latrines that had been built against the blackened walls of the former palace.

Roch pushed the door to the construction occupied by the studio of the famous painter Jacques-Louis David, under whose direction Mulard practiced his art. Two of the master's best-known works, *The Oath of the Horatii* and *Brutus*, each occupied one of the walls. A male model, clothed in an antique drapery, was seated on a sort of dais, his eyes raised to the heavens. Spare furniture and plaster mannequins were stored in a corner of the room, painted a drab greenish gray. A dozen young men and a woman were gathered there. A male student suddenly burst into song:

The insane fanaticism,
Sworn enemy of our liberties,
Has expired.

It had been written as a war song for the Republic's armies in the fight against the Chouans. Apparently diverse political opinions were represented in David's studio, for some students joined in heartily, while others greeted the song by jeers and whistles.

Roch spotted Mulard in his threadbare coat. The painter cut a conspicuous figure, with his fiery beard that contrasted with his darker, unkempt locks. Not many people in Paris, save a few artistic types, wore facial hair. Apparently oblivious to the uproar, Mulard was applying touches of his brush to two life-size figures, outlined in chalk and already partially painted against a blank background divided into a grid. Next to him sat a young woman in a black bonnet and an elegant pelisse lined with sable. She too seemed unfazed by the song. She was drawing on a sheet of paper resting on a portfolio on her lap.

"Ah, Miquel," cried Mulard. The commotion died down, allowing conversations to resume. He turned to the young woman. "Please, Madame de Nallet, allow me introduce my friend Roch Miquel. I say *friend*, in spite of his rather unfortunate profession. He is Chief Inspector at the Police Prefecture."

Roch bowed slightly. He knew Madame de Nallet by name. A *ci-devant* noblewoman, a society lady. Blanche had on occasion mentioned her in connection with various parties. Though her features were not regular, Madame de Nallet had a small, delicate figure and fine brown eyes. She smiled pleasantly and inclined her head.

"Madame de Nallet has been my pupil for over a month now," continued Mulard. "She wishes to improve her skills at painting flowers, and already shows much talent for it."

Roch pursed his lips. Flowers, of all things! This woman was not there to learn history painting, or to become a portraitist. Of course she was rich, she did not need the money. Her artistic ambitions must be limited to painting fans, screens and knickknacks to decorate her salon and display to rapturous friends. But Roch understood that Mulard was poor, and needed the fee this fair student could afford to pay.

"No disrespect to my friend Mulard," Roch asked Madame de Nallet, "but why did you not seek Citizen David himself as an instructor?"

"Oh, he was the one who referred me to Monsieur Mulard. Monsieur David, much to my regret, does not take any students who wish to specialize in light subjects. I am nevertheless fortunate, for he visits here every day and kindly offers me his guidance." She smiled at Mulard. "It is already a great honor to be allowed to work in the Master's studio, under the direction of one of his pupils."

"The honor is all mine, Madame," said Mulard. "And, if I may be so bold, the pleasure as well. Madame de Nallet's company and conversation are a welcome change here. Before you arrived, Miquel, she was telling me of her brother. His name has just been removed from the list of the émigrés."

Roch inclined his head slightly. "My congratulations, Citizen Nallet."

"Thank you, Sir." The young woman was flushed with evident pleasure. "My brother left France in 1792. He used to fight in the army of the Princes, but now he can return safely to Paris. I expect him any day. Can you imagine that it has been eight years since I saw him? I have missed him so!"

Roch's disdain for the young woman gave way to a warmer feeling. "I do wish you and your brother joy, Citizen."

"Indeed, Sir, it is time for those who lost entire fortunes, and sometimes family members, to the horrors of the Revolution to receive justice at last."

Roch frowned. In his opinion, the laws that made it a crime for an émigré to return without prior permission were still justified. Many of those men and women came back to France with the sole purpose of stoking the unrest in the West, spying for the benefit of England or brewing trouble of some kind or other. His dislike for Madame de Nallet returned in full force.

"What returning émigrés are receiving," he said dryly, "and it is already a great deal, is a pardon. They should expect no more. I, for one, am all in favor of national reconciliation. It behooves France to be generous in victory and open its doors to its misguided citizens, provided that they agree at last to abide by the laws of their country."

Madame de Nallet's smile had frozen on her lips. Roch turned his attention to the figures on Mulard's canvas.

"So, Mulard, what is your subject?" he asked.

"Virginius Showing Appius The Dagger With Which He Just Killed His Daughter."

"Daggers, blood, killings . . . You like the same subjects as David."

"Oh, these days David has no time for history painting. He is busy finishing his portrait of *General Bonaparte Crossing the Alps*, and I spend much of my time upstairs, assisting him. Believe me, it will be a masterpiece. Madame de Nallet can tell you about it: David showed it to her the other day."

Roch felt a great desire to escape the young woman's company. "Is that so? Would you mind showing it to me?"

"Let's go then."

Roch bowed rather stiffly to Madame de Nallet and followed his friend up a flight of stairs to a brighter room, better lit and painted white. In the far corner stood a wooden horse, on which sat a mannequin dressed in a blue uniform coat, its arm extended. A matching hat, trimmed in gold braid, covered the blank head. The next thing Roch noticed, resting on an easel, was a life-size portrait of the First Consul on horseback.

Roch drew closer and gazed at the image of Bonaparte, riding a prancing black-and-white horse and pointing to distant snowy summits. A column of soldiers pulling a cannon climbed a mountain pass in the background. They seemed minuscule under the horse's hooves. That gave Bonaparte's figure a gigantic, heroic dimension. The horse's nostrils flared, the veins of its belly seemed to throb with the contained emotion of the scene. Roch remained motionless, fascinated by the power of the painting.

"Bonaparte looks dashing here," he said, now gazing at the face of the portrait. David had given the First Consul angular, handsome features, and dark hair that was blown into his face by the wind. Roch had seen the First Consul from afar on the occasion of military reviews, and he remembered him as a man of average height, thin to the point of emaciation.

"I am not struck by the likeness," said Roch. "Does Bonaparte come here to sit for David?"

Mulard laughed. "Bonaparte, come here? No, he has neither the time nor the patience to sit for anyone. That's why he invites David to the Tuileries almost every day. In that fashion David has become familiar with his features and can paint them from memory. Frankly, I don't think Bonaparte cares much about the likeness. But, as for the clothes," said Mulard, nodding at the mannequin, "you are looking at the very uniform he wore on the battlefield of Marengo."

Roch grinned. "So the uniform might be truer to the original than the face."

Mulard nudged Roch's elbow. "Don't repeat it, but I tried the hat the other day, when David was gone to lunch at the Tuileries. It is so large that it came down to my eyes. Bonaparte has a huge head!"

"Your secret is safe with me. Speaking of lunch, I am hungry. Let's go to the nearest tavern. My treat."

Mulard's face brightened. "Thank you, Miquel, you are a true friend. Madame de Nallet brings a lunch basket every day, and she insists on sharing with me her cold meats, fine pastries and hothouse fruit. It embarrasses me not to be able to return the favor."

After the two men sat down to a dish of salt cod and potatoes, Mulard asked, "So how is your father?"

"Very well, as usual, thank you. Still managing the Mighty Barrel with an iron fist. But tell me more about this new student of yours."

"Madame de Nallet? She is charming, isn't she?"

"Yes, she seems pleasant enough. Did you hear her talk about her brother receiving *justice*? Does it not strike you as an odd coincidence, this Nallet woman trying to become David's student, coming to his studio daily, and doing everything to ingratiate herself with him, just at the time when she is seeking permission for her brother to return to France?"

"You always see suspicious motives behind everything, Miquel. That's a bad habit you've acquired in your line of work. All I can tell you is that she is a very assiduous student. She arrives at the studio without fault every day at eight, quite a feat for a fine lady like her. If she tries by the same token to help her brother by currying favor with David, so what?"

"Bonaparte, from what you say, seems quite enamored of David."

"The feeling is mutual. David admires Bonaparte, sincerely so. He can't help it: he has always been in thrall to power. Before Bonaparte, at the height of the Revolution, it was Robespierre. But David, in spite of his faults, is generous and does not forget less prosperous friends, like Topino or me. He pays us handsomely whenever we assist him, and he sends us students of our own. But then he hardly needs the money these days."

Roch easily believed it. A few months earlier, Mulard, who had received free tickets, had taken him to the exhibition of David's giant painting, *The Sabine Women*, at the Louvre. It was the first time an artist dared charge a fee to display his work to the public, and yet all of Paris was still flocking there to admire the masterpiece.

"Say, Miquel," asked Mulard in a lowered voice, "speaking of Topino, what is happening to him? You know as well as I do that he had nothing to do with that Conspiracy of Daggers nonsense. When is he going to get out of jail?"

Roch had met Topino on occasion, when Mulard had brought his fellow painter to the Mighty Barrel.

"Frankly, Mulard, I can't tell. After that Rue Nicaise business, the government is in no hurry to release men linked, however tenuously, to any plan to assassinate the First Consul."

"Well, I will tell you why Topino was arrested. He was arrested for his political opinions. He is a Jacobin, and he used to be a juror of the Revolutionary Tribunal. Mark my words, those are the only true charges against him. I worry for him, Miquel."

"I understand, Mulard, but things are moving in the right direction. We are making progress on the Rue Nicaise investigation. When the bastards responsible for this atrocity are arrested, and they will be soon, the situation will return to normal. Men like Topino will be cleared of any suspicions and released. All in due time."

Roch paid for the meals and rose. He slapped Mulard on the back and returned to the Prefecture. Whatever he did, he could not escape the investigation.

16

*R*och had ordered a thorough search of every courtyard and shed within five hundred yards of the shop of the grain merchant Lambel. The little mare, according to Dr. Huzard, was old and tired, and Roch could not picture Short Francis taking her very far.

That afternoon, he repressed a cry of triumph upon hearing Inspector Alain's report. Alain had just spoken to a woman, Citizen Roger, who had rented a shed to a short, squat man on Rue de Paradis, three hundred yards from Lambel's shop.

Roch decided to go question the witness and inspect the premises himself. Rue de Paradis, Paradise Street, unpaved and flanked by dingy houses, did not quite live up to its name. Number 778 was a six-story building of no better appearance than its neighbors. The bony woman sweeping its doorstep grunted in response to Roch's greeting. Her broom still in hand, she paused to squint at his Prefecture card, which bore his name, title and an eye, symbol of the police.

"I hear, Citizen Roger," said Roch, "that you may have information of great importance for us."

The woman, scowling, resumed her sweeping. "All I know's that I'm bein' bothered to no end by people that come askin' questions that're none o' their business."

"But you might be handsomely repaid for your pains. If what Inspector Alain told me is correct, you may have information on the

Rue Nicaise assassins. Perhaps he forgot to mention the 2,000 *louis* reward for information leading to their arrest."

Citizen Roger's eyes narrowed and her expression lightened to a mere frown. "Well, yer man's a ninny, 'cause he didn't say nothin' 'bout no reward." She snorted. "So yes, a stallholder, a short man rented a shed here. Fat, ugly fellow. Citizen Leblanc, he called hisself."

"How did you know he was a stallholder?"

"He told me, course! He said he sold sugar an' dry goods at fairs. He asked 'bout rentin' that shed, back in the courtyard, to put his horse an' cart. An' he kept pesterin' me till I showed it to him."

Citizen Roger's narrative was interrupted by the furious barking of several dogs. She shook her fist in the direction of the racket. "Listen to that! The Vincent woman went out, an' she left her dogs locked in her room again. D'you want to know what the whore does with her damn dogs?"

"Not at this time, Citizen Roger. I can imagine how busy you are."

She shrugged. "Ah, you said it! The work I have keepin' the place halfway clean, with all that filth we have here as tenants!"

"Can I see that shed?"

The woman sighed. She put down her broom and led him across the courtyard. There she reached the depths of her pocket for a key and unlocked the double door to a shed. Roch took a peek inside without entering. The place was large, about ten yards square, and empty. A layer of straw covered the floor. He would ask Inspector Alain to come back with a couple of National Guards to sift through it.

"That short man, Leblanc," continued Citizen Roger, "he tried the lock several times to see if it worked. Like he couldn't take my word fer it! An' then he said he liked the shed, because it's so large, an' he'd have room to sleep in it. To tell you the truth, Citizen, I'm none too fond o' rascals that sleep in sheds. Then he said that he'd take it fer ten days. *Ten days?* I said. *What d'you think this is, an inn? Ness thin', I'll have to come an' tuck you in bed, maybe. Don't waste my time no more*, I said, *go talk to Citizen Ménager.*"

"Citizen Ménager is the landlord? So he rented the shed to that man Leblanc?"

"Yes. But not fer ten days, course, jus' like I'd said. Fer three months. So the short fellow came back that night, with a horse, an' a cart that was covered with a big gray tarpaulin. But that time he wore a stallholder's jacket, you know, one o' those blue ones. An' an hour later, I saw two other fellows I didn't know pass by my lodge an' cross the courtyard. I was wary, course, 'cause the short one hadn't said nothin' 'bout no other fellows. I'd thought it was jus' him an' his horse, an' that was plenty, given that one wasn't prettier'n the other. So I come out o' my lodge to see what's happenin', an' what d'you think those two rascals do, but come an' join the short man in here! An' they closed the door. Like there's not enough goin' on 'round here, with the Vincent woman an' her dogs!"

Citizen Roger shook her head, indignant. "*So*, I thought to mesself, *that's why the bastard was so keen on the lock!* So I ran here, an' I banged on the door with my fists an' shoes, an' I gave'm a piece o' my mind. They opened the right away, let me tell you. They told me not to shout, that I'd have the whole district in an uproar, that it wasn't what it looked like. But they didn't fool me a bit. They still had their breeches on, but they looked mighty worried all the same."

"It is indeed fortunate that you showed such presence of mind," said Roch, nodding gravely. He could have remarked that the Revolution had abolished the crime of sodomy, but he thought it wiser not to annoy this witness with niceties. "I am certain, Citizen Roger, that you took a good look at those other two fellows."

"Fer sure I did! One o' them was tall, with gold spe'tacles an' a long face. Fair-skinned an' pretty-lookin', with long yellow hair. *He* was the pussy, I bet." She shuddered. "Gives me the woollies jus' to think of it. An' the third bugger, he had a pointy nose like a rat, an' his hair braided in *cadenettes*."

"So what happened that night?"

"Nothin' happened, not so long's I'm the porter here. I told'm that I wouldn't let more'n one sleep in here. So they all left. Went someplace else to play their damn games, I reckon. The ness day, the short bugger came back by hisself, an' he asked if I knew someone that'd put iron circles around a barrel. So I asked, *What's that fer?* I was wary, min' you, after the happenin's o' the night. He said he jus' wanted to put sugar in that barrel an' he'd pay to have the iron circles made. So I told him my husban'd do it fer fifteen francs. An' later he asked my husban' to drill two holes into the side o' the cart. An' then he asked me fer a funnel. *No, I don't have no funnel,* I said. Course I've a funnel, but I wouldn't give it to him. He said 'twas to fill the barrel with sugar, but you never know what a bugger'd do with a funnel, do you? But since he'd given my husban' a bit o' money, I gave him some ol' cup to fill his stupid barrel. *An' be sure to clean it 'fore you return it,* I said. But I needn't tell you how filthy men are. No better'n swine, like I tell my husban'. Damn buggers still worse'n the rest, I guess. So when the short fellow returned the cup, it stank o' gunpowder, like those fire-works after Bonaparte's big *victories,* like they call'm. A fine waste o' money, that, if you ask me. Keeps honest people up all night with their racket. So I washed the cup mesself, like I haven't nothin' better to do. That's what comes o' bein' too obligin' . . ."

She paused, her jaw suddenly slack. "So that could've been the powder they used to blow up Bonaparte? So that's why you were talkin' o' the reward?"

"Indeed, Citizen Roger. And you will receive your share of it once the culprits are caught and punished." From the corner of his eye Roch saw a lanky man in a brown jacket, with the air of a whipped dog, cross the courtyard and enter the porter's lodge. Citizen Roger's husband, by the looks of it. "And then what happened?" asked Roch.

Citizen Roger's tone was softer now. "The short bugger came back every day. Sometimes the other two also, but I'd told'm to leave the door open whenever there was more'n one in there. There was always one posted like an idiot outside the shed. An' then, on the 3rd o' Ni-vose, aroun' five in the afternoon, the short fellow came to the lodge to return the key. Rat Face an' Pussy were with him. Dressed in their blue jackets, all three o' them. He said they didn't need the shed no more after all. Imagine that, after payin' fer three months! An' they left together with their horse an' cart. I wasn't sorry to see that sort o' gentry go. But when I came back here to make sure they'd locked the door 'fore leavin', what d'you think I saw?"

Citizen Roger, shaking all over with indignation, pointed at a spot in the straw. Roch waited with bated breath.

"They hadn't cleaned up after their damn horse, the stinkin' buggers!"

Roch repressed a groan of disappointment. "And you never saw those men again, Citizen Roger?"

"Never."

Roch thanked Citizen Roger warmly. He then spoke to her husband, who had nothing of interest to add.

Before leaving the place Roch looked around at the gray walls of the courtyard, pierced by a multitude of narrow windows. Pots of half-frozen cabbages were crowded on the sills. The final preparations for the Rue Nicaise attack had taken place right here, under the porter's nose, without her suspecting anything other than buggery.

The alleged Leblanc and the man Citizen Roger called Rat Face fit the description Fouché had sent him of the Chouans Carbon and Saint-Régent. There was no longer any doubt that the Rue Nicaise attack was a Royalist plot. And the man with the gold spectacles kept appearing with those two characters. All that remained was the small matter of discovering his identity, and arresting all three assassins. Roch would have the usual Chouan haunts in Paris closely watched.

17

The short afternoon was drawing to a close. It was getting colder now. Roch put on his gloves and turned up the collar of his coat. When he crossed the Pont-au-Change, the Bridge of the Money Changers, a thin layer of fog covered the river. At his feet, a puddle of what seemed like urine had frozen into yellow ice. Frost gave a silvery sheen to the bare trees on the embankment. The air was very still, and wisps of smoke, barely visible against the white sky, rose straight from the chimneys on the Isle of the Cité.

At the Prefecture, a guard stopped Roch. "A youn' lady's been waiting for you for over an hour, Citizen Chief Inspector. She asked for you by name, and she said it was very important. So I took her to the little room downstairs."

Roch's first thought was of Blanche. But no, it could not be. Blanche would never compromise herself by coming to the Prefecture, even in an emergency. Instead she would have discreetly sent a messenger.

Roch frowned. "A lady? What sort of lady?"

"She wouldn't say her name, Citizen Chief Inspector." The guard smiled and winked. "But she talked like she knew you personally, if you catch my meaning. So I didn't press the point."

"What is she like?"

"Oh, real pretty, with gray eyes and blond hair, sort of red almost."

Roch felt a rush of anger. How dared Alexandrine disturb him now, when she must know how busy he was? He thought he guessed the purpose of her visit.

In the course of the previous spring, Vidalenc had run into trouble for trading in adulterated wine. Indeed the beverage the old man supplied to the Armies of the Republic and to the taverns of Paris, including the Mighty Barrel, had little to do with wine, apart from its color and a distant similarity in tartness. His warehouse on Bernard Embankment, the wine port of Paris, had been searched by the police, and the composition of the liquid had been uncovered. It consisted of a decoction of various woods, in which carrots and turnips had been left to macerate. Purplish food coloring was added for good measure. The remains of a cat, wonderfully preserved, fur, whiskers and all, had even been found at the bottom of one barrel.

Vidalenc, when confronted with the evidence, had stared blankly and retreated into an idiotic silence. Not a shadow of a ledger was found within his warehouse. One of his clerks explained that the old man barely spoke any French, and could neither read nor write. It was all true, though Vidalenc understood French perfectly well when it suited him. Roch also suspected him of keeping very accurate accounts in his head.

Old Miquel had beseeched Roch to help his longtime friend. Roch had refused at first, but the old man had reminded him that Vidalenc had lent him the money to send Roch to school, and also to purchase the Mighty Barrel, without any security but Old Miquel's word.

So Roch had yielded to his father's entreaties. He had gone to his colleague Bouchesèche, Chief of the Food Supply and Safety Division, and, his face the same color as Vidalenc's fraudulent beverage, asked that the case be allowed to slip into oblivion. Bouchesèche had agreed. True, Roch was deemed Fouché's protégé, and Fouché had been all powerful then. Vidalenc had escaped with a stern warning that, should he ever be caught again, his name would be erased from the list of Army suppliers.

Now, thought Roch, the old rascal was up to the same tricks. He was again in trouble, and he had sent his daughter to the Prefecture in hopes of having the charges dismissed a second time. Well, he would be disappointed. Under no circumstances would Roch go again through the humiliation of applying to Bouchesèche on Vidalenc's behalf. It might be useless anyway, perhaps dangerous, now that Roch's position at the Prefecture had become so unsteady. He would send Alexandrine on her way with a firm admonition never to approach him again with such a plea.

Roch walked to the waiting room. The door, painted a grayish green, bore marks of grimy fingerprints around the handle. It was ajar. The young woman was indeed Alexandrine. Her back was turned, but he recognized the tall, upright figure, the reddish blonde curls on her nape, beneath the black silk bonnet. She was wearing a gown made of remnants of blue and white fabric stitched together at odd angles. She had been dressed like a fine lady on the 3rd of Nivose, on account of Christmas, but now she wore her ordinary clothes. Yet this dress showed her figure to advantage. Roch was almost certain that she had sewn it herself, and that, for a reason he could not understand, made him all the more unhappy to see her.

"Good afternoon, Alexandrine," he said in the Roman language as he pushed the door open. "What is it? I have not much time now."

Alexandrine turned around at the sound of his voice. Her eyes were red and swollen. That was unlike her. He had never seen her cry before, except on the day her mother had died, and she had been a child then.

"What is the matter, Alexandrine?" he asked more gently.

"I am sorry to disturb you, Roch, but I had to tell you right away. It is about your father."

Roch grasped both of her elbows. "What about Father? Speak!"

"He was arrested this morning."

Roch swore. "Arrested?" Now he hated Alexandrine with a passion. "It's about your father's wine again, I bet. Damn the old scoundrel!"

"No, Roch, please listen to me. It can't have anything to do with that wine business. Your father was taken to the Temple."

Roch let go of Alexandrine. He felt as though he had been hit in the stomach. Only political opponents were imprisoned there. Old Miquel must have been arrested because of his past Jacobin sympathies.

Roch bit his lip. "Thank you for coming here, Alexandrine. I am sorry to have been so rude to you. I do apologize, but I need to be alone now."

She opened her mouth, seemed to hesitate, then walked to the door and closed it gently behind her. Once she was gone, he collapsed in a chair, his face in his hands.

18

*R*och cursed himself. All he had worried about had been his own troubles, and he had not given a thought to Old Miquel's danger. How could he have been caught off guard, after the stormy meeting in the Prefect's office? That coward, now that he believed Fouché powerless, felt free to attack the Minister through Roch, and Roch through his father. And this was only a preparatory, tentative move. Sobry was right: if the Minister fell, Roch would be dismissed, maybe even arrested.

Both his father and he would rot indefinitely in jail, like the unfortunate painter Topino-Lebrun and his supposed accomplices in the Conspiracy of Daggers. Roch had easily dismissed Mulard's concern over Topino, and offered bland comfort and vague assurances. Now he understood how it felt to be uncertain of the fate that awaited a loved one.

Roch was pacing the little waiting room. He paused and rested his forehead on the cold window pane. He stared at the spot, down in the courtyard, where the carcass of the little mare had rested under its oilcloth cover. It was easy to guess whence the decision to arrest his father came. Bertrand, the Chief of the High Police Division, must have a hand in it. He had acted out of personal malice, or on the orders of Dubois, or both. In any event, Bertrand must have consulted the Prefect before taking such a measure against the father of a colleague of equal rank. Or perhaps the idea came from the Prefect himself.

That meant that only one man could order the release of Old Miquel. It was Fouché, Dubois's superior. And Fouché, whatever Dubois believed or hoped, was still the Minister of Police. He could overrule the Prefect's decisions and order Old Miquel's release.

Roch ran down the stairs. He left the Prefecture and crossed the river in the direction of the Left Bank, where the Ministry was located. Roch's father hated Fouché, whom he called *The Traitor*. Of course, in Old Miquel's eyes, many deserved that epithet, but none more than the Minister. At the height of the Revolution, Fouché, the defrocked monk, had organized shameful masquerades where jackasses, covered with priestly vestments, with prayer books tied to their tails, were made to drink from chalices.

But there was much worse. He had been sent by Robespierre, the Jacobin leader, to Lyon to quell the Royalist insurrection there. Under Fouché's direction, thousands of opponents had been gathered by the side of vast open graves and shot by firing squads, or, when more expeditious means were required, by cannons that simply aimed at the helpless human mass. All without trial. Robespierre, once informed, had been horrified and immediately recalled Fouché.

And Fouché understood the precariousness of his own situation. He had joined those conspiring to overthrow Robespierre. While the memory of the atrocities in Lyon was still fresh, Fouché disappeared from the public eye, until at last the shades of his past faded away. Then he had been appointed Minister of Police. As such, he had not hindered Bonaparte's coup, nor had he been dismissed afterwards.

Roch, hurrying along the Malaquais Embankment, was looking straight ahead. Certainly, to Old Miquel, Fouché was the worst of men: cruel to those who fell into his power, servile to his superiors and ready to betray everyone, high or low, in the pursuit of self-interest. Yet to Roch, he was a providential patron. Fouché had noticed Roch, who had languished as a lowly clerk at Ministry for a few years, and had entrusted him with a few missions that required discretion, loyalty and wits. Roch, who made no mystery of his ambitions, had given full satisfaction. Within months, he had been appointed a Police Inspector, then, when Bonaparte created the Prefecture, Chief Inspector.

Roch could never have hoped for such swift promotion but for Fouché's patronage.

Of course, he harbored no illusions as to the Minister's motives. Fouché had not acted out of benevolence, but simply needed a dependable man, a man who owed him everything, within the Prefecture to spy on Dubois. Roch understood those things, and Fouché's reputation did not bother him. The horrors of Lyon had taken place seven years earlier, after all, and the Nation had been in great peril then. Was not a man like Fouché just as respectable as the imbecilic Dubois, who had done nothing, and had nothing but his outstanding mediocrity to recommend him?

Roch finally reached the splendid Juigné mansion, where the Ministry of Police was located. It was probably no coincidence that the Prefecture had been assigned its shabby premises on the Isle of the Cité. Fouché wanted to make his superiority of rank over the Prefect perfectly clear to the most casual of observers. Roch was shown without delay into the office of Marain, the Minister's private secretary.

"Well, if this is not Chief Inspector Miquel!" The man raised his eyebrow. "An unexpected pleasure, I must say. It is two days early for your appointment with the Minister. Did the collections from the bawdy houses come ahead of schedule?"

"No, but I need to see the Minister. It is urgent."

Usually Marain greeted Roch with friendliness and showed him promptly into Fouché's office. Now he seemed in no hurry. "I will see whether the Minister can receive you."

Marain disappeared for a few minutes. He returned with a grave look on his face. "You have five minutes," he said.

Roch could not find himself in Fouché's presence without marveling at the resemblance of the man's face to a skull. The sallow skin seemed glued to fleshless bones. The gray hair, brushed forward onto his forehead and temples, gave the impression that he had been hit from behind by a powerful gust of wind. His eyelids were no more than half open, though Roch never suspected the Minister of being sleepy.

Fouché was writing at his desk and did not look up. "What good wind brings you here, Miquel?" he asked.

"I apologize for disturbing you in such a manner, Citizen Minister, but it is about my father. He was arrested."

Fouché looked up at last and put down his quill. "Arrested, was he?" he said in a flat tone. The Minister never expressed much emotion, but this was obviously no news to him. Roch felt a knot in this stomach.

"Yes, Citizen Minister, arrested. And he was taken to the Temple, so his must be deemed a political case. Is this related to the Rue Nicaise attack?"

"I would not be surprised if it were." Fouché nodded in the direction of a seat. "Make yourself comfortable, my dear Miquel. You seem ready to pounce on me, hovering like this over my desk."

Roch sat on the edge of the chair. Fouché joined his hands as though in a gesture of prayer. "Your father, need I remind you, is a former Jacobin. He should have remembered that many of his friends only narrowly avoided the guillotine after Robespierre's execution, and some were not so fortunate. But no, instead of letting the past be forgotten, as it should be, he has expressed his opinions rather freely. About the First Consul, for instance. About me too, I might say, though *that* does not matter. I am accustomed to these kind of remarks."

Of course Old Miquel had never made any mystery of his opinion of Fouché. The conversation was not taking the turn Roch had hoped. "This is all harmless banter on my father's part, Citizen Minister."

"My dear Miquel, what passed for harmless banter a few days ago is now a threat against the safety of the First Consul. Which is to say, a threat against the survival of the Nation." Fouché paused. "And we are talking about more than banter in this case. Topino-Lebrun, that painter arrested for the Conspiracy of Daggers, was seen drinking in your father's establishment with some of his friends."

"Surely, Citizen Minister, all the owners of all the taverns Topino ever patronized can't be arrested. My father never had anything to do with that plot, and you know it."

"What matters is not what I know, but what the First Consul

believes, and still more importantly, what he wants people to believe. And people have been shocked, outraged. Women cry over the fate of that little street vendor, that ... What is her name again? That Peusol, or Pensol girl. They demand justice. And do you know what people mean when they clamor for justice? It is revenge they want, and they care not a jot whether those punished be innocent or guilty, as long as the punishment be exemplary. No one is inclined to question the judgment or truthfulness of our great leader at this time of national grief. Later people may come to see things differently, but now they absolutely trust the First Consul. And the First Consul ordered me to have a great many Jacobins arrested. I obeyed."

Roch glared at Fouché. "So *you* ordered my father's arrest."

A thin smile appeared on Fouché's face. "I did not. Our esteemed Prefect did. Oh, he came here to ask for my permission beforehand, of course. No doubt with the notion that I would oppose that measure and that he would then hurry to the Tuileries to denounce my own Jacobin sympathies to the First Consul, who would then overrule me. It is very easy to thwart poor Dubois's schemes, because they are always so pitifully obvious. In this case I complimented him on his zeal. He left my office looking very much puzzled. But, as you know, it is not unusual for him."

"But my father is innocent. You could explain it to the First Consul."

"Not with any chance of success under the present circumstances." Fouché's sleepy eyes, which had been fixed on the fireplace, traveled deliberately to Roch's face. "I should tell you, Miquel, that things will not stop at mere arrests. The news will be made public tomorrow. The First Consul has asked me to prepare a list of 150 Jacobins, who will be deported to Guiana."

Roch clenched his jaw. When he had been an Inspector, he had attended the departure of the deportees from Bicêtre. Their heads had been partially shaven, their clothes and hats hacked off in a ridiculous manner to make them easily recognizable in case of any escape attempt. That seemed unlikely in any event, for long chains linked the iron collars that encased the necks of the convicts.

Once overseas, those who had lived through the rigors of the voyage were starved and beaten. Most convicts did not survive this regimen for more than a few months. Deportation was called the *guillotine sèche*, the "dry guillotine."

It was unbearable to imagine Old Miquel, chained like a criminal in the middle of the vast courtyard of Bicêtre, ready to leave France and his son forever. Roch struggled to steady his voice. "No court of law will sentence my father to deportation for speaking ill of you and serving a few mugs of wine to Topino."

"But you do not understand, Miquel. Who is talking of *courts of law* here? The First Consul believes that trials are unpredictable, fussy, disorderly proceedings. No, those Jacobins are to be deported by way of executive orders. The First Consul will request from the Senate, and no doubt receive the authority to issue such orders in case of an emergency."

"And I suppose the emergency will be left to the First Consul's appreciation."

"Exactly."

"So, Citizen Minister, you will establish that list of deportees?"

"What choice have I? Believe me, I would much rather not. Some of those men are, or used to be, my friends. Yet if I were so unwise as to decline, someone else would be happy to undertake the task, and even zealously add a few hundred names to the list."

Roch glared at Fouché. "What about my father? Will you keep his name off that list?"

"Ah, that is the question! The good news for your father, my dear Miquel, is that his fate depends on *you*. You will forgive me for doubting you, but I worried that you might defect to the Prefect's side. So many of my friends have already abandoned me in the course of a few days."

"Then you must not know me very well, Citizen Minister. What have I ever done to make you doubt my loyalty to you?"

"Nothing, I grant you. I apologize for my suspicions. I do, most sincerely. Indeed I trust you, Miquel, as much as I trust anyone. Unfortunately, this is not saying much. Recent history teaches us that one cannot be too mindful of one's safety when circumstances become dire."

Fouché rose from behind his desk and put his hand on Roch's shoulder. Roch repressed an instinctive movement of disgust. Maybe there was hope.

"Now, Miquel, listen to me," continued Fouché. "The British fleet now controls much of the Atlantic, and the First Consul does not want to put a large ship at risk for the sole purpose of ridding France of *that vermin*, as he calls the Jacobins. He wants the deportees embarked in small groups of no more than forty, on light schooners."

Roch struggled to contain his impatience. "Pray what is this to my father? What difference does it make whether he is deported on a frigate or a schooner?"

"A very great difference. Since schooners are going to be used, and the First Consul does not want an armada to attract the attention of the British fleet, the deportations will be staggered over several weeks." Fouché withdrew his hand from Roch's shoulder and began to count on his fingers. "Let us see . . . Today is the 7th of Nivose. The last schooner might leave in a month or so. Around the end of January in the old calendar, the 27th to be exact. What I can do, out of friendship for you, is keep your father's name off the list of deportees until that last schooner sets sail forth. This gives you a month. More than enough."

Roch gaped at Fouché. "Enough for what?"

The Minister returned to his position behind his desk. His eyes were wide open now, and he was looking intently at Roch. "You received, I trust, my note about those two Chouans, Saint-Régent and Carbon. I want them both arrested. Then your father will be safe."

Fouché seized his quill and the interrupted letter. "Time presses, Miquel, for me and for you. You have one month to arrest those two men. Your father, in the meantime, will remain in the Temple. I hear that Citizen Fauconnier, the turnkey, is a friendly, congenial character."

Fouché had resumed writing. "It is always a pleasure to chat with you, Miquel. Thank you so much for calling."

Roch rose, shaking with anger. He strove to contain himself. This was not the time for rash action. "If my father is to remain in the Temple, I must visit him."

Fouché raised his eyes from his letter. "I believe you will make a wiser use of your limited time by concentrating on the task I just assigned you."

Roch bowed and left without another word. He paused along the Malaquais Embankment for a minute to catch his breath. He quickly wiped a tear with his gloved hand. It was the sharpness of the wind, and his eyes prickled from a feeling of sorrow, of rage, of humiliation. He had come to the Ministry in the hopes of securing Old Miquel's release. Not only had he failed, but now his father was threatened with a slow, painful, disgraceful death.

He had been very naïve to hope for Fouché's help. What had he expected? Gratitude for his past services? He was nothing but a pawn. Sobry had been right. Fouché was a traitor, and a man who could not be trusted could not bring himself to trust anyone.

Roch shook himself out of these reflections and headed for the Prefecture. All of this bitterness served no purpose. Certainly it did not help Old Miquel. Roch had no choice but to do the Minister's bidding, and do it fast, before the allotted month had elapsed. Right now he would send the turnkey of the Temple 200 francs. That would at least ensure that Old Miquel received a bed and decent food.

Back in his office, he found a letter waiting on his desk.

Dear Roch,

Things were so hurried when I last saw you that we had no time to discuss some practical matters. I had meant to tell you that, unless you instruct me otherwise, I will keep the Mighty Barrel open in your father's absence. I believe that is what he would wish.

I cannot tell you how very sorry I am for what happened. Please do not lose heart: all of your father's friends, and yours too, stand ready to help. My own father sends word that, should you need any money, he will be more than happy to lend you whatever is necessary.

As for me, I went to the Temple to see your father, but was told that absolutely no one is allowed to visit him. This can only add to your sorrows, but he is a brave man, Roch. I am sure that he will bear this ordeal with his usual courage. Please do not hesitate to ask for anything you may need.

> *Your devoted friend,*
> *Alexandrine*

Roch let out a groan. Why did Alexandrine, like everyone else, feel the need to bring up Vidalenc's money at every opportunity? Roch would die before touching a *sol* of it. And that talk of *friends*! As if he and his father could still count on any at this point.

He reread the letter and realized that he was unfair to Alexandrine. She meant well, and she was right on one point. Old Miquel would want the Mighty Barrel to remain open in his absence. She would know how to manage the waiters, keep the patrons quiet and happy, and do the accounts. She understood business. She was Vidalenc's daughter, after all.

19

Outside the sleet was giving way to snow. Joseph de Limoëlan, seated at a little table by the window of his room, was nursing a mug of mulled wine between his hands, relishing the warmth of the beverage. He breathed in the sweet aromas from the bakery downstairs.

On the table, next to his blond wig, was the note his mother had sent him.

> *My Son,*
> *The Minister wishes to speak to you.*
>
> *Renée-Jeanne de Limoëlan*

Madame de Limoëlan was not given to exuberant displays of maternal fondness, especially when it came to Joseph. She had never forgiven his political positions.

Madame de Limoëlan loved comfort, peace and quiet. She used whatever she had managed to salvage from her late husband's vast fortune to keep an elegant but discreet house in Versailles, three leagues west of Paris, far from Brittany and its troubles. There she lived, with her four grown daughters, all unmarried, and a dozen servants. The girls were a bit past their prime, and suitable matches were few, for she held any prospective sons-in-law to high standards. Dear Marie-Thérèse, Joseph's favorite sister, had found her true love in the person of a distant cousin, but the gentleman's suit had been dismissed by Madame de Limoëlan on account of the uncertain state of his finances.

When Joseph had arrived in Paris last June, he had visited his mother and sisters and discovered with horror that she had been paying an active court to Fouché, that criminal whose hands were stained with the sacred blood of King Louis XVI. But that did not repel Madame de Limoëlan. She had even insisted that Joseph meet the Minister. At first he told his mother that he would not have anything to do with a *régicide*. Limoëlan also suspected a trap. But Fouché had given Madame de Limoëlan sufficient assurances of safe passage for her son, and the two men had met three weeks before the Rue Nicaise attack. Limoëlan had expected the Minister to ask him to betray the cause, and he was of course prepared to refuse. But nothing of the kind had happened. Fouché had in fact been quite conciliatory, almost friendly.

Now he wished to see Limoëlan again. Why? Did he now want Limoëlan to betray Saint-Régent and Francis in exchange for immunity? Limoëlan had no taste for this kind of bargain, and the risk of arrest was far greater now, after the failure of the attack. Ignoring an offer from Fouché was a dangerous move, but less dangerous than agreeing to meet the scoundrel. And Limoëlan had no intention of climbing the steps to the guillotine as his father had done seven years earlier.

Joseph had not witnessed the execution. Then twenty-four, he had been abroad, in Jersey, already an émigré. Yet he could picture with perfect clarity the scene that had taken place in Paris, the double row of gendarmes on horseback accompanying the two carts, the outline of the guillotine sitting on the stately Place de la Révolution. The waters of the Seine River, the bayonets of the gendarmes, the triangular blade of the machine reflecting the glare of the June sun.

It was Father de Clorivière who had told his nephew Joseph of the scene. That afternoon the good priest, disguised in the coarse trousers and jacket of a workman, stood in the midst of the crowd. His eyes shifted from the approaching carts to the guillotine, a few dozen yards away.

Some around Father de Clorivière were jeering, some cheerful. Be-

fore his eyes the business of death proceeded briskly. Several decapitated bodies were already piled in a waiting cart when his sister, her
graying hair cut short on her nape, climbed in turn the steep stairs to
the scaffold. Her step was steady, but Father de Clorivière's courage
failed him. He felt light-headed and had to close his eyes now. His lips
were moving silently in an ardent prayer for the repose of her soul as
he heard the dull thud of the machine.

When Father de Clorivière opened his eyes again, he recognized
his niece Angélique. He had not seen her in years, since the time when
she was barely more than a pretty child. The crowd quieted all of a
sudden. It went very fast. The young headless body too was thrown
into the cart. Her skirts, caught on the uprights, revealed pink stockings and white thighs.

"A pity," said a buxom woman, standing next to Father de Clorivière, to a friend of hers. "Look how fair this one was. An' youn' too.
She couldn't be much more'n twenty!"

But Father de Clorivière no longer heard the conversations around
him. He watched as his elder brother, who had been waiting patiently,
was tied last to the plank. It swung forward and the blade hit. It was
all over. Blood, the blood of the martyrs, Father de Clorivière had told
Joseph, was streaming on the cobblestones.

In Joseph's mind a patient, tenacious hate and the passage of
time had given these images the vivid colors of memories. They now
seemed more real than any of his true recollections of his father, gathered during the few weeks spent at the Château of Limoëlan every
summer, when Joseph came home from the Oratorian Friars' school
in Rennes.

And there was his father's last letter to Marie-Thérèse and her
sisters, written from his jail cell:

> *I have loved you, dearest children, until the last moment of*
> *my life. I am not asking you to pray for me, for soon I will be*
> *happier than you. Comfort your mother, always obey her, and*
> *whenever you think of me, let it only be to rejoice in the grace*
> *God gave me to die for Him.*

Marie-Thérèse had shown this letter to Joseph, urging him to forgive, as their father himself had wanted them to do. But how was that possible? Joseph could not drive out of his mind the image of a man being led, helpless, his hands tied behind his back like those of a criminal, to the scaffold.

The elder Limoëlan had been arrested during a meeting of Royalists at his sister's château in Brittany. They had been betrayed, for the policemen knew the exact spot where to dig in the garden. There were found, buried in a jar, weapon inventories, lists of the King's supporters in the region, leaflets calling for an insurrection against the Republic. More than enough evidence for the Revolutionary Tribunal to sentence the elder Limoëlan, his sister, brother-in-law and niece to death.

Against those who had betrayed his father and kin, against all traitors, against the Revolution and its howling mobs, against the people of Paris, Joseph's anger had simmered for those seven years.

2O

*R*och was pacing the dingy bedroom above the Five Diamonds. Just before the appointed time, he recognized Blanche's step, light, hurried, on the stairs. He went to open the door, and she threw herself into his arms. He moaned as they kissed hungrily.

She tossed her bonnet on a chair, undid the buttons of his waistcoat and shirt, her fingers reaching down his chest toward his belly. For the first time, he felt more pain than pleasure at her touch.

He had hoped Blanche's hold on his mind was enough to dispel the darkness that engulfed him, to take him far away from a world where his father was in jail, awaiting deportation, and assassins were roaming the streets of Paris, ready to kill again. But even with Blanche so close to him, those things would not go away. What business had he to seek his own happiness at this time?

Roch seized both of Blanche's hands in his. He sat on the bed and pulled her next to him.

"I may not be a very lively companion today," he said.

"But I know of a way to make you lively enough, my love." She pouted. "If you will let me, that is."

"No, Blanche, no one, not even you, nothing can cheer me much now. My father was arrested."

Blanche covered her mouth with her hand. "Arrested? But what for?"

"It's that horrible Rue Nicaise business."

Blanche's face had become very grave. "But your father had nothing to do with it."

"No, but that doesn't seem to make any difference."

"You work at the Prefecture, after all. You will be able to clear up things and have him released very soon."

"So I thought, but I was wrong. Guilt and innocence don't matter anymore. Think of all those poor people slaughtered on Rue Nicaise. Of what were they guilty? I saw them, Blanche, the dead, the dying. I saw them with my own eyes. They were innocent, and yet they died. It is the same with Father. How can his innocence protect him? And I can do nothing. Not only am I unable to secure his release, but now he faces deportation."

Blanche shuddered. She rested her head on his shoulder. "Oh, Roch, I had no idea . . ."

He stroked her black hair, closed his eyes and breathed in her lily of the valley and carnation fragrance. She wrapped her arms around him. He could not think of any greater solace than this, having her so close. They remained silent for a long time, locked in a quiet embrace.

Blanche was the first to speak. "Roch?"

"What is it, dearest?"

"If I asked you for something, would you give it to me?"

"Of course, if it were in my power to give it to you."

"I would like a present from you."

He felt a twinge of guilt. True, he brought her tiny bouquets, ribbons, fans, trinkets she could wear without attracting her husband's notice, but he knew that he could afford not anything approaching the beauty of the jewels Coudert had given her. That set of pearls she had worn on the night of the musical party at her home had to be worth more than 100,000 francs, many times his yearly salary. Still, he should have brought her small gifts of jewelry once in a while.

"So, my Blanche, what would you like?"

"A ring."

"What kind of ring? How about an emerald?" He caressed her fingers, long, white, thin. "A green stone would look so lovely on your hand."

She looked straight at him. "No. I want a plain gold ring."

He drew back, startled. "Like a nuptial ring?"

"Yes."

"I don't understand. You already have a nuptial ring."

"But I want one from you."

He turned away and stared out the window. She had just spoiled that brief moment of respite. Why did she need to remind him of her marriage at this moment?

"Is your husband's ring not enough for you?"

She frowned. "Are you jealous, Roch?"

"I don't like the thought of Coudert being your husband, that's all. I know that it sounds ridiculous. So yes, I guess I am jealous."

"You shouldn't be. There is nothing anymore between my husband and me. There hardly ever was, in fact."

Roch bit his upper lip. He realized that she had told him almost nothing of her life with Coudert, beyond cursory mentions of the shows and entertainments they attended together. Roch thought again of the musical party at her house, of his brief meeting with her husband.

"Why did you marry that man, by the way?" he asked. "Were you in love with him?"

"No, never." She too stared straight ahead now. "I had fallen in love with another man, and given myself to him. Then he left me. Once Mama found out, she was very angry, and she said no respectable man would have me anymore. About that time Monsieur Coudert, who was a longtime friend of hers, proposed. So I accepted."

"Because you thought no one else would marry you? It was silly, Blanche. So this is why you agreed to marry Coudert?"

"I was grateful to him. I liked him. I was too young to know any better. Now I regret it, but it is too late."

"Why do you say that? You are so young. It is not too late."

"Oh, yes, Roch, it is for me."

Blanche seemed lost in her thoughts. He wondered about what could have happened if she had not married Coudert. Would she have wed Roch? He chided himself. He was the son of a tavern keeper. He was not rich enough, not refined enough. He could never afford the luxuries to which she had been accustomed.

He thought of her Paris mansion, her army of servants, her jewels, her horses, her country houses, her carriages, her parties. Now he tried to picture her in his lodgings on Rue de Jouy, with their dull yellow upholstery, and his maid for sole company. No fine society friends would ever call on her there. No, loath as he was to admit it, she was meant to be Coudert's wife.

Roch shook his head sadly. "Forgive me," he said. "I have no right to be jealous of your husband. It should be the reverse, in fact. But about that ring, what would you do with it, really? Wear it next to your other nuptial ring, on the same finger?"

"No, I will wear yours, only yours. It will be our secret, and no one but us will ever know the difference." There was a tremor in her voice. "But if it upsets you, let's not talk about it anymore."

"Poor Blanche," he said. "No, of course it doesn't upset me. I will buy you that ring."

He bought her hand to his lips. She meant so much to him, especially at this time.

21

lready two weeks had elapsed since the Rue Nicaise attack and winter was now entrenched in Paris. The current month of the Revolutionary calendar, *Nivose*, was named after the Latin word for snow, and snow it did. Not the dazzling snow of the mountains Roch remembered from his childhood, but dirty city snow that mixed with the filth of the streets, melted into a gray slop and then froze at night.

He continued searching for any trace of Saint-Régent and François Carbon. He had all the usual haunts of the Chouans watched. Descriptions of Short Francis's flattened mug and Saint-Régent's weasel face were now posted all over Paris, and all policemen, all *mouchards* were on high alert. In vain. And only twenty days of the time allotted by Fouché remained to arrest them. How would one find two men who had crawled into a hole in a city of 700,000?

Roch was leaving the Prefecture in the evening of the 18th of Nivose, the 7th of January in the old calendar, when he heard his name called. He turned around and saw a clerk ran after him. The man was out of breath, and from his look, something must be amiss.

"The Prefect's been asking for you, Citizen Chief Inspector." The man, panting, shook his head. "He doesn't look too happy."

Roch sighed. What scheme was Dubois hatching now? He steadied himself before knocking at his superior's door. The clerk had been right about the Prefect's mood. Dubois scowled at Roch. "So, Miquel, you are indeed a disgrace to the force. Harassing good citizens to pursue your ridiculous fancies."

Roch raised his eyebrows. He thought at first of Citizen Roger, the porter on Rue de Paradis. But no, they had parted good friends, her eyes aglow with the prospect of the reward.

"Which good citizens am I accused of harassing, Citizen Prefect?"

"Citizen Gillard, the proprietor of the Mayenne Inn."

Roch's lips formed a silent whistle. That Gillard was certainly an impudent fellow to complain to Dubois.

"Well, Citizen Prefect, I have had all of the Royalist haunts in Paris watched. That includes the Mayenne Inn. I have placed an Inspector nearby to watch it discreetly. What is Gillard's complaint?"

"Do you think law-abiding citizens like to be watched by the police? Your Inspector must be less discreet than you think. I know Citizen Gillard. He is a perfectly respectable man, a Captain in the National Guard. And what if the patrons of the Mayenne Inn were all former Chouans? Pray who told you to watch the Royalists in the first place?"

"But, Citizen Prefect—"

"Enough. You will pull all of your men from there. I do not want to hear another word of complaint from Citizen Gillard. Is it clear?"

Roch simply nodded. He was wondering about the Prefect's motives. He had long surmised that the Chouans had infiltrated the ranks of the police. Even Piis, for all his friendliness, was a *ci-devant* aristocrat. Now was the Prefect himself only displaying his usual imbecility, or deliberately hindering the investigation?

"Be careful, Miquel," added Dubois as Roch was turning around. "I will not tolerate any more insubordination."

Now Roch would have to follow the Prefect's orders and pull his men from the vicinity of the Mayenne Inn. But, with less than three weeks left before Old Miquel faced the horrors of deportation, it was out of the question to leave the place without surveillance. Pépin, the little beggar, might again prove helpful.

22

*R*och had settled on red velvet seats by the large iron stove at the Pinecone Café. He was watching his colleague Sobry, who was engaged in a game of *dames*, or "ladies," with a thin, elderly man. Roch tried to watch a few moves of the black and white pawns on the checkerboard, but his mind kept drifting off the game.

He seized a copy of the *Journal des Débats* lying on a nearby table and began to read. The men held for their participation in the Conspiracy of Daggers were going to stand trial. That indeed was news. It meant that the plot was no longer deemed a buffoonery concocted by the Prefect. Also the paper reported that, as predicted by Fouché, the Senate had given the First Consul the power to order the deportation without judgment of any individual deemed a threat to the safety of the Nation. And the newspaper printed the list of the first seventy Jacobins who were to be shipped to the Colonies.

Roch read the list twice, his heart pounding, expecting the name *Antonin Miquel* to jump at him from the page. Fortunately, no, it was not there. But, as the newspaper pointed out, more deportations were to follow shortly. This was but a respite.

Roch looked up when he heard a triumphant chuckle. Sobry's adversary was rubbing his hands, where prominent blue veins pulsated under loose skin. The old man seized one of his "ladies" and flew over three of Sobry's pieces.

"Now what do you say to this, Citizen Commissioner?" he asked, beaming.

"What can I say? I cannot move. You won, Citizen, as usual."

The elderly man pulled his watch. "Time to head home," he said. He grasped his hat and umbrella and wished the company a good evening. Sobry pushed the board towards Roch.

"Want to take your turn trouncing me, Miquel?" he asked, smiling ruefully. "You are more skillful than I with the 'ladies.'"

"No, thank you, Sobry. I am in no mood to play tonight."

Sobry became grave. "I can imagine."

"You heard about my father, then?"

"The Prefect didn't make a mystery of it. I am sorry, Miquel. What about you? Are you making any progress in the investigation?"

"Not much. Do you know of the Mayenne Inn?"

"Of course. No Chouan comes to town without setting foot there, or being connected to the place in some manner or other." Sobry looked into Roch's eye. "There you go again with your Chouans. This won't help your father."

"On the contrary, the only way to help him is to find the assassins."

"In any case, leave the Mayenne Inn alone. The owner, Gillard, has friends in high places."

"You mean Dubois?"

"Yes. And the Prefect has grown bolder in protecting his friends. He must think that it is only a matter of days before Fouché is dismissed. Dubois hopes to be appointed Minister of Police then."

Roch stared at Sobry. "Dubois? Minister of Police? You can't be serious." This would be the worst news of all. Dubois would then make sure that Old Miquel be deported immediately.

Sobry nodded gravely. "Oh, I am quite serious, and so is Dubois. He never liked you and, mind you, he is not alone."

"I know."

"And you underestimate the Prefect's determination. Once again, Miquel, leave the Mayenne Inn alone, for your own sake and that of your father."

"Yes, of course," muttered Roch.

There was no point in arguing with Sobry. Roch drained his glass of wine and bid his colleague a good night. He was more intrigued than ever by the Mayenne Inn and its proprietor. The place warranted further investigation. Instead of going home directly, Roch decided to drop by the Mighty Barrel to borrow a few things of his father's.

23

At this time the common room of the tavern would be busy, though it was not the same crowd as during the day. Now the patrons would be the habitual drunkards, purple-faced and dull-eyed, who took large gulps from their mugs, and those, wide awake, whose business kept up at night.

Going through the common room would require exchanging a few words with Alexandrine. Roch struggled to think of what he was going to say. It was always awkward to talk to her, and now, after having been so rude to her the other day, he had to thank her. This was not going to be easy. Even with the best of intentions, nothing he ever said to her sounded right.

He decided to go through the back alley. Pulling a key from his pocket, he climbed the outside stairs that led directly to his father's apartment. Once inside, he undressed to his shirt and underwear and threw his clothes on the bed. He opened the squeaky doors to an ancient oak wardrobe and pulled breeches and a jacket made of coarse cloth, along with a pair of hobnailed shoes. Roch buttoned leather gaiters around his legs and donned a round hat. Finally, he squatted by the fireplace, rubbed his hands inside the cold hearth and smeared soot on his face. On the top shelf of the wardrobe he found his father's knife. Old Miquel must have been arrested early in the morning, before he had time to put it in his pocket. Roch looked around the room one last time and also seized his father's staff. Instead of fastening the strap to one of his jacket buttons, he slipped his left wrist through it.

Before leaving the apartment, Roch, from the corner of his eye, caught sight of the image reflected in the mirror above the fireplace mantel. He started. Of course this was not a ghost, and thankfully Old Miquel was still alive, but the image in the mirror was, down to every detail, the memory Roch kept of his father twenty years ago. Old Miquel was a rag-and-bone man then, and one of the lowest description, for society knows gradations of rank, even among those who survive on its refuse. He was a *pelharot*, as they say in the Roman language, a rabbit-skin man.

Father and son would go door-to-door throughout Paris. In the poor districts, they climbed many flights of creaky stairs to ask house-wives whether they had any rabbit skins to sell, and even the most destitute did. Roch and his father also knocked at the service en-trances to the comfortable houses of the bourgeois and the mansions of the nobles. There, the maids would sell the pelts, for that minuscule benefit was traditionally deemed theirs. After each house, the load became heavier until the backs and heads of the man and child alike disappeared under an array of all colors of fur. The rancid smell of animal grease preceded them, and dogs barked at them long before their arrival. Once in a while, a mother would point at Old Miquel, who was not old then, and tell her child: "Be quiet now, or I'll sell you to the rabbit-skin man."

Every night at dusk, Roch and his father would stop by the hatter's shop to sell the skins, which would be turned into felt, except for the white ones. Those, more valuable, were used as cheap imitations of ermine fur. Then man and child repaired to the stables that were their home and stripped to their waists in the courtyard. They would wash their faces and chests in the trough from which the horses drank in an attempt to rid themselves of the tenacious stench before going to sleep.

At last, after long years of that drudgery, Old Miquel had saved, *sol* by *sol*, enough money to purchase the Mighty Barrel with the help of a loan from Vidalenc. Roch was very happy to have left those days behind. Yet tonight he looked again like a *gagne-denier*, a penny-earner, as he had done in the days of his childhood.

He left through the wooden exterior staircase. It led to an unpaved alley by the side of the tavern. There a group of men had now gathered, groping at one another for balance, bellowing lewd songs.

Roch ignored the acrid whiffs of vomit coming from the direction of the drunkards and walked away in the damp chill of the night. Certainly, as a policeman, he had been ordered to leave the Mayenne Inn alone, but nothing prevented him, as a private citizen, from paying the place a visit. Roch turned onto Rue du Four-Honoré and soon saw the Inn's sign, representing a basket of pears. That fruit was a traditional crop of the *département* of Mayenne.

He looked around and saw a tiny figure crouching in the shadows of a carriage door. He approached softly. Pépin yelped in terror and took to his feet.

In a minute Roch caught him by the back his jacket and clapped his hand over the boy's mouth. "Quiet, imbecile," he hissed. "It's me."

Pépin nodded. He was breathing fast when Roch relaxed his grip. "Sorry, Sir, I'd never've thought it'd be you, dressed like this. I must've shit in my eyes."

"I hope not, if you are to keep them on the Mayenne Inn. What's happening there?"

"Nothin', Citizen Chief Inspector. There's nobody goin' in or out today, save an ol' manservant goin' to the bakery jus' before dark. Mighty funny for an inn."

"You didn't see either of the men I told you about?"

"No, Sir."

"Well, stay here and keep watching the place."

Roch proceeded to the inn. When he pushed the door open, he saw half a dozen men playing billiards in a common room, but the game, along with all conversations, ceased abruptly upon his entrance. A large, tall fellow put down his cue and walked deliberately to him. The man looked at Roch from head to toe without returning his greeting.

"You the clerk?" asked Roch, exaggerating his Roman accent, which was usually so slight as to be barely discernable. Now his French was but a string of guttural consonants. The men around the billiards table burst out laughing. Roch had heard those puffs of scorn often enough when he had canvassed the streets of Paris with his father, and he knew how to respond: say nothing, do nothing.

The large man grinned. "Why would a filthy *Auvergnat* want to know that?"

Roch kept his right hand inside his pocket and fingered his father's knife. "If you were the clerk, you'd take me to Short Francis."

Suddenly all laughter ceased.

"And what sort of business would you have with Short Francis?" asked the big man.

"I've a letter for him."

"Give me the letter, and I'll make sure it gets to him."

"No. The man said to give the letter to Short Francis. Not to some big fat oaf who's too stupid to know if he's the clerk."

The large fellow squinted at Roch. "There's no clerk here. *I* own this inn. Now give me the letter, will you?"

So this was Gillard, the Prefect's friend. "No. The man said if Francis ain't around, then give it to Saint-Régent. You know, the one they call Pierrot. So if you'll take me to Pierrot, I'll give it to *him*."

Gillard clearly hesitated, his mouth open, his distrustful little eyes trying to read Roch's purpose. The billiards players had left the table and were now gathered around him. One of them, auburn-haired and handsome, in an embroidered waistcoat and an elegant coat of English cut, seized the owner by the elbow and whispered to his ear.

"Aye, that's right, My Lord," said Gillard, nodding. He looked at Roch. "Short Francis and Pierrot packed their things. They left two weeks ago. That's the last I saw of them."

"Then tell me where I can find them."

"You don't understand, rascal, do you? They left town."

"I don't mind. I'll go find'm. I'll earn a gold *louis* if I give'm the letter."

"Too bad. I don't know where they went."

"I find you very insolent in your persistence, Auvergnat," intervened the elegant fellow, who took a step in Roch's direction. "Maybe my friends and I could teach you proper manners."

Roch snapped his knife open inside his pocket. Gillard started at the small popping noise and held out his arm to stop the nobleman.

"Don't come close to this wretch, My Lord," he said. "The likes of him can be nasty."

Gillard was right. As a child, Roch had learned to fight, even when he was outnumbered. As Old Miquel had explained to his son, it was wrong to kill, but one had to be respected on the streets. Roch could have stabbed the fop without the knife ever leaving his pocket. Even a mere cut, if painful enough, sufficed. Then, when the adversary was doubled over, his breath stopped, Roch's knee would rise to hit the man's groin with full force. That would make anyone crumple like an empty sack. Then it was just a matter of a few kicks of the hobnailed shoes in the face and belly. One had to be careful not to be carried away by one's bellicose mood, for sometimes, like now, there were more foes to attend to after the first one was down.

The elegant fellow was fortunate. Roch was not there to look for a fight with a *ci-devant* aristocrat. The innkeeper, breathing hard, kept his eyes fixed on Roch.

"I don't want any trouble here," he said. "Go away."

Roch cleared his throat and treated himself to the pleasure of spitting on the fop's shiny boots. Then he walked slowly backwards, mindful not to turn around until he was clear of the Mayenne Inn. He threw Pépin a coin as he passed the boy.

Roch was happy. A short but fruitful visit that had been. It was clear that Gillard, that old acquaintance of the Prefect's, knew Saint-Régent and Short Francis, and also of their whereabouts. Perhaps the man would be worried enough to send them word that a sinister character was enquiring after them. And if shaken, the rats might leave their nest.

24

It was eleven, the mandatory closing time, when Roch returned to the Mighty Barrel. Still eschewing the street entrance, he climbed the back stairs and stepped into his father's bedroom. As he undressed, he heard, coming from the common room downstairs, the headwaiter's voice raised as the man pushed the last drunkards out onto the street. Soon the place would be empty. Roch slowly undressed. He felt the folding knife in his father's jacket and, after a moment of reflection, slipped it into his own coat pocket. The skin of his face felt dusty and dry from the soot he had rubbed on it.

Shivering in his shirt and underclothes, he washed his face in the chilly water that remained in the basin on the dressing table. He glanced at the bed and closed his eyes. For a moment he pictured Blanche lying naked there. The image was intensely, painfully real.

It would have been so comforting to go home to his bed at night and find Blanche there, to awaken her gently, to enjoy her and then to fall asleep by her side, his arm around her waist. Or maybe not even awaken her. Just feel the warmth of her body and nuzzle her neck. How could that ever happen with Blanche, who was another man's wife? He remembered the ring she wanted and felt again the bite of regret, of jealousy too.

Downstairs the front door of the tavern closed with a clang. Alexandrine would be alone in the common room now. What if she had heard his footsteps upstairs? It was better to go and talk to her for a little while. It would not have to be long: in a moment one of her father's menservants would come and take her home.

Roch slipped on his clothes and climbed down the stairs that led to the common room. Alexandrine was seated at one of the tables, writing in Old Miquel's ledger. A single candle threw a circle of yellow light on her pensive profile, the pages of the vast book and an inkwell. Alexandrine raised her eyes and put down her quill. She did not seem surprised or frightened, as though she had recognized his step in the dark. A smile lit her face, though she looked sad and tired. The memory of their last conversation came back to him in full force. He was embarrassed, but she acted in a natural, unaffected manner.

"I am so glad to see you, Roch," she said in the Roman language. "See, I just finished today's accounts."

"And I am glad to have this opportunity to thank you." He hesitated. "I came here tonight to fetch some things of Father's upstairs." He looked around. Something familiar was missing.

"Where is Crow?" he asked at last.

Alexandrine shook her head sadly. "I sent you a note at the Prefecture, but you must have left before it arrived. Poor Crow died this afternoon. He had refused to take any food over the past few days. Oh, he was as sweet as ever, but he wouldn't even drink. He just lied here quietly at my feet. It broke my heart when he would raise his head and prick his ears every time the door opened, and then whine when he realized it wasn't your father."

Roch looked down. He remembered Crow as a puppy, a ball of black fur in Old Miquel's pocket, and as a very old dog, when the shaggy, slobbery hair around his muzzle had turned all white, like a wise man's beard.

"I am sorry, Roch," continued Alexandrine. "I know how your father will miss Crow when he returns." She paused. "Speaking of his return, what do you think of my offer to manage the Barrel in the meantime?"

Roch shook his memories away. "What do I think? You are right, of course, this place should be kept open and in good order. I am sure it is what Father wishes. Thank you so much for offering to do this."

He wanted to say more, but words did not come easily. "Alexandrine?"

"Yes?"

"Forgive me for the other day. I was horribly rude when you told me of Father's arrest."

She was staring at the floor. "I understand how you must have felt. I couldn't believe it myself when I heard it. I still have trouble believing it."

"You are a true friend, Alexandrine."

Her face was still lowered, but he would have sworn that she was blushing to the roots of her hair. He looked away and noticed a basket full of blue and white hyacinths on the table. The fragrance of the blossoms, both sweet and earthy, was powerful enough to overcome the tavern's reek of wine and tobacco. He felt transported back to the mossy woods of his childhood in the mountains of Auvergne, far from the Mighty Barrel and Paris.

A knock at the door interrupted his reverie.

"Oh, this must be Fraysse," said Alexandrine. "It is time for me to go home."

Roch frowned. Then a sudden inspiration struck him. "Do you think your father would mind if I walked you home? And, more importantly, would *you* mind?"

Alexandrine smiled. "Of course not."

Roch went to open the door to Fraysse, a hulking fellow with grizzled hair. The man had been in Vidalenc's service as far as Roch could remember. In spite of his age, he retained a fearsome figure.

"Good night to you, Fraysse," said Alexandrine. "Citizen Miquel here has kindly offered to walk me home."

Fraysse cast a look of deep suspicion at Roch. "All right then, I'll jus' walk one hundred yards behind you youn' people."

Outside a chilly wind was blowing shreds of clouds very fast in front of the half-moon. Roch offered Alexandrine his arm. Though Fraysse walked too far behind to hear them, his presence seemed to stifle any attempts at conversation. Alexandrine was content to huddle against Roch in silence as they walked. Yet there was no awkwardness in her silence. She seemed to be simply enjoying the quiet of the night.

"You must be very tired after a day and evening spent in the noise and smoke of the Barrel," said Roch.

"Oh, I am fine. But I am not used to the odor of tobacco. This is why I brought the hyacinths."

"Did you grow them yourself? It is quite a bit of trouble to get them to bloom in this season, isn't it?"

"No, no trouble at all. I love flowers, and it's such a joy to see them bloom in the dead of winter." He could hear some amusement in Alexandrine's voice. "I didn't know you were interested in hyacinths."

Roch tried to imagine her, keeping her father's house. He and Old Miquel had often been invited to dinner there. It had been built over a century earlier, at the eastern point of the Isle of the Fraternity. Then, during the Revolution, its noble owner had emigrated, it had been sold at auction and Vidalenc had purchased it at a bargain price. It remained a very fine, old-fashioned mansion.

"I love to grow roses too," continued Alexandrine, "but all I have is a tiny enclosed garden. There's too little sunlight for them. They grow all mildewy and leggy. So I am content with the hyacinths."

Roch realized that he had never given any thought to Alexandrine's everyday occupations at home, her likes and dislikes. "Doesn't your bedroom have a small balcony?"

He immediately regretted his words. This was hardly a suitable topic with a proper young lady, especially one he was still expected to marry.

But Alexandrine did not sound flustered. "Oh, yes," she said cheerfully, "I have a bit of room for potted flowers there in spring and summer." Her pace slowed down, and her eyes seemed to look away in the distance. "Do you know, Roch, what I would really like? I know it sounds selfish and childish, especially now, in the middle of all this sorrow . . . What I would like is a garden of my own. A country house by the river, maybe a league or so from Paris. A garden full of roses. Pink ones, white ones, all fragrant. It would be so beautiful in the fair season."

"One could easily find a house like this, around Charenton maybe. I am sure your father would move there if you asked him."

"I know, Roch. This is why I would never dream of telling him. He would do it to please me, of course. But he wouldn't like it at all there. He likes to keep an eye on his warehouses on the Saint-Bernard Embankment from home. We used to live right there, do you remember? In those little lodgings next to the place, before Father bought the mansion on the Isle of Saint-Louis. Mama was still alive then."

Alexandrine's words had brought an image to Roch's mind. He imagined her standing in a garden by the river. It was spring, and the air was still a bit chilly, but the sun was shining. She was standing under an arch over which she had trained those roses of hers, and her white muslin dress billowed in the wind that was playing with loose strands of her honey-colored hair.

They were walking under a streetlight now. He turned to her and looked at her hair more closely than ever before. He noticed pale blond streaks around her temples, and in the locks that escaped from under her bonnet, on her nape. Her hair was both flaxen and reddish, almost straight in places and tightly curled in others, a mix of hues and textures.

"I hope I don't sound ungrateful," continued Alexandrine. "I am very fond of Father's house on the Isle. I even heard someone say it is, or used to be, one of the most beautiful mansions in all of Paris. You were asking about the balcony off my bedroom. Well, when I stand there, looking down at the river, I feel like I'm on the deck of a mighty ship."

They had reached the river now. The masses of the islands, dark in the moonlight, obscured the view of the other bank. "When I was younger," continued Alexandrine, "I liked to stand on that balcony and imagine that the house escaped its moorings, that it floated downstream like a ship towards the ocean . . . Oh, Roch, do you know I have never seen the ocean?"

"Neither have I," sighed Roch. "But I remember the day when Father took me to the top of the towers of Notre-Dame. It was my very first Sunday in Paris."

"I too remember that day. You and your father came to dinner that night. That was the first time I saw you, and I was very curious about you."

"This can't be. I was only eight. You were too little then."

"I must have been four, but I do remember it as if it were yesterday." She laughed lightly. "You didn't speak much, especially to me."

"I was overwhelmed by what I had seen that day. The whole city of Paris. I had just arrived from Auvergne with Father a few days earlier, and he took me to the towers of Notre-Dame to introduce me to Paris. We climbed more steps than I had ever climbed at a time. I remember an array of huge bronze bells, or so they seemed to me. I remember the *bourdon* was taller than Father. Then I looked around, and the sight took my breath away."

Alexandrine was silent. Roch let the memory submerge him. Old Miquel and he, the child fresh from his mountains, were at the high point of the Cité, the largest of the islands of Paris. L'Ile Saint-Louis, now called the Isle of the Fraternity, where Alexandrine lived now, trailed behind, followed by the last and smallest of all, L'Ile Merdeuse, the "Shitty Isle," undignified, uninhabited, huddled against the Right Bank.

On the banks, between the bridges, boatmen were busy unloading parcels and barrels. Roch's eye wandered across the mazes of obscure, winding streets, the busy squares, the mansions of the rich, the spires of a hundred churches. And all around, the wide boulevards lined with trees formed an oval belt. Further away still, the wings of windmills and the straight lines of vineyards crossed the heights of Montmartre.

"Can you imagine, Alexandrine, that was seventeen years ago . . ."

Old Miquel had pointed at the gardens of the Tuileries and the Luxembourg, still filled with greenery on that sunny September day, the golden dome of the Invalides, the huge medieval fortress of the Bastille to the East, the square tower of the Temple, with its four turrets crowned with pointy slate roofs. This brought Roch back abruptly to the present.

"Yes," said Alexandrine, "so many things have changed: the names of the streets, bridges and buildings. The statues of the Kings were overthrown, the Bastille was demolished . . ."

"But the Tower of the Temple still stands," said Roch bitterly. "When Father and I looked at it that day, we never thought someday he would be locked there. It was not even a prison then."

"Well, Roch, I am sure you will set your father free. I am not saying this to soothe you, but because I trust in you."

Without thinking of it, they had crossed over to the Isle of the Fraternity and found themselves in front of Vidalenc's stately home.

"Here we are already," Alexandrine said softly. "Thank you."

"No. Thank *you*."

Roch bent slightly to let his lips brush against her cheek. Of course proper manners forbade such familiarities with a young lady, on a street too, but now these things did not seem to matter anymore.

25

Joseph de Limoëlan was hurrying under the sleet. In spite of the weather, he wanted to speak to Saint-Régent. The two men had a few remaining things to discuss, and Saint-Régent, by the looks of it, might not last much longer. The street was unpaved, and the gutter overflowing, turning it into a torrent of mud. A man in clogs and a patched green jacket had installed a wide plank, fitted with wheels at an extremity, atop the flow. This device allowed passersby to cross without soiling their shoes and clothes.

Limoëlan walked across the plank and put a copper coin in the man's palm. But the rascal begged for more in a heavily accented, guttural voice. Limoëlan shrugged and went his way. Another Auvergnat. Those scoundrels were little better than beggars, and the whole city was infested with them. A few feet away a woman, unable or unwilling to pay the man's toll, unceremoniously rolled up her skirts and piggybacked on her companion.

At the Guillou house, Limoëlan was taken aback when he saw his comrade sitting in an easy chair in his bedroom. Saint-Régent was still pale, but his gaze was steady. The man, in spite of his light build, was resilient. He had been wounded on many occasions before, in the King's Navy before the Revolution, and in skirmishes during his years as a Chouan. Limoëlan frowned. This unexpected recovery might complicate matters.

"You look well," said Limoëlan thoughtfully. He paused. "I have bad news."

"You mean *more* bad news?"

"Francis had a note from Gillard this morning. A man, an Auvergnat, came to the Mayenne Inn last night. And he asked about you and Francis by name."

Saint-Régent swore. "Francis is still living with his sister and niece, isn't he? Snug and comfortable, ensconced in that filthy hole."

"Come, Saint-Régent, you never liked Francis, but this is hardly the time—"

"I don't see what's to like in that fellow. And you could think of nothing better than to send him to Bourmont to offer his services as a valet. Bourmont, that traitor who now visits Bonaparte daily at the Tuileries!"

"Precisely. George wanted me to keep an eye on Bourmont. And Bourmont had been Francis's General before the Pacification."

"Then unless he is a complete fool, he must have seen through Francis all along. How could you expect a man like Bourmont, who has a young wife, to keep Francis as a servant under his roof? All the scoundrel got was to work in Bourmont's stables. The result is that Francis learned nothing about Bourmont, but Bourmont may well have learned the address of Francis's sister." Saint-Régent glowered at Limoëlan. "And what if Bourmont tells his new friends about Francis? If arrested, Francis will talk. Don't try to deny it, you know it as well as I do. You may be willing to take that risk, but I am not."

"So what do you propose?"

"Bring Francis under some pretext to the Bois de Boulogne tonight. Any secluded spot will do. I guess you are too fond of him to deal with him yourself, but I am feeling better now. I will be waiting for the two of you and make sure he gets what he deserves. A bullet between the eyes."

Limoëlan flushed with anger. "It is out of the question. I am in charge of this, and I want you to leave Francis alone. At least until I receive George's instructions."

Saint-Régent's breathing became more rapid. There was fear, and anger too, in his eyes. "You really don't understand, Limoëlan, do you? This is an emergency. There's no time to wait for George's orders. Francis is a danger to all of us, to the cause. Why are you always protecting that piece of filth?"

"I simply don't want him killed at this time. Why draw attention to us?"

Saint-Régent shrugged. "If that's your only objection, I can kill him somewhere on the banks. I will push the body into the river, and no one will be the wiser."

"Again, leave Francis alone!" said Limoëlan in a sharper tone. "After all, *he* didn't do anything wrong."

"Are you suggesting that *I* did?"

"You used a fuse to detonate the powder, didn't you? After I told you to use an ember!"

Saint-Régent's knuckles turned white as he grasped the arms of his chair. "Are you calling me a coward? The fuse wasn't the problem. The problem was that English powder you gave me. The best quality, you said! It was garbage, it detonated two or three seconds later than it should have. And since we're talking of cowardice, pray let's speak about *you*. *You* were supposed to signal the arrival of Bonaparte's carriage."

Limoëlan flushed. "And I did!"

"Do you think I am as blind as you? It was all you had to do: signal to me, and from a safe distance too. But no, you couldn't even do that! What was it? Last minute remorse? Or were you soiling your trousers? Whatever the reason, I didn't get the advance notice I needed. I only saw the carriage when it turned onto Rue Nicaise. That left me precious little time. One of the guards shoved me against the wall and almost knocked me out. But I still rushed back to the cart to light the powder. The explosion nearly killed me." Saint-Régent half-rose from his chair. "Now don't dare say this is my fault, or call me a coward. Mind you, I wrote George about the disaster, and your part in it. If it were not for you, your incompetence, your weakness, Bonaparte would have perished."

Limoëlan, his pulse racing, drew away from Saint-Régent. "There is no point in quarrelling at this time. This is exactly what the enemies of the cause would want us to do. Let's wait for George's decision. For everything."

Saint-Régent, breathing fast, sat back wearily in his chair. "What about Francis?" he asked, his brow furrowed. "If you want to keep him alive, you must move him to a place that scoundrel Bourmont doesn't know."

"What of the Convent of Saint-Michel? Blanche Coudert should be able to help. She could convince her friend the Mother Superior to hide Francis."

"I wish you would leave Madame Coudert out of this. She is doing enough for the cause as it is."

Here Limoëlan's assessment differed from Saint-Régent's, but there were a few things Saint-Régent did not know. In any event, this was not the time to discuss Blanche's merits.

"And I don't like the way Francis watches her," continued Saint-Régent. "You would think he is ready to pounce on her."

"It doesn't mean anything. Francis watches all women like that."

"But Madame Coudert is not like any other woman. Keep that swine away from her. And another thing: you will need to move Francis's sister as well. She knows too much. You can't expect the Mother Superior to house both Francis and his sister. Their little habits might be a bit disconcerting to the nuns."

"I know of another place for the sister. In fact, I am going to take care of this right away. Take some rest and don't worry about a thing."

He patted a sullen Saint-Régent on the shoulder.

Limoëlan headed for Rue du Faubourg Saint-Martin, where Francis lived with his sister. On one point Saint-Régent was right. Those two would need to be separated. But it might not be easy to pry them apart. What if, in spite of the risk of arrest, Francis balked? Well, Limoëlan would use Blanche for that as well. Saint-Régent might not like it, but he did not need to know about it.

That ridiculous infatuation of Saint-Régent's seemed to have begun as soon as the man had arrived in Paris last November. He and

Limoëlan would meet Blanche at Mademoiselle de Cicé's modest entresol on Rue Cassette.

"It was a hard life waging war on the Republic," Saint-Régent would tell the ladies. "I, as an officer, was dressed in bits and pieces of uniforms taken from the enemy, when I didn't wear a peasant's clothes. We all survived on a few francs a month, a pittance doled out by the English government." Yet now, thanks to the generous funds received in preparation for the attack, Saint-Régent was dressed in the latest fashions.

"When I think of the sufferings you brave young men have endured for the cause!" exclaimed Mademoiselle de Cicé.

Blanche, her face slightly inclined to the side, said nothing. She was content to smile graciously at Saint-Régent and make little sympathetic noises. Limoëlan was sure that the recitation of Saint-Régent's exploits, though ostensibly addressed to the company, was meant to impress her. Yet Limoëlan very much doubted that Saint-Régent had much of a chance. Blanche accepted his attentions, but Saint-Régent was not rich enough, brilliant enough, handsome enough to tempt her. Actually it was not even a matter of looks.

Certainly, Saint-Régent, with his ferret's face and narrow shoulders, was no beauty, but it was the grinding poverty of his childhood, the harsh years in the Navy, and finally the horrors of the insurgency that had left their mark. There always remained something rustic, uncouth, unpolished, cruel too about him.

"We would ambush the Republic's troops in moors, in woods, in villages," Saint-Régent continued, his gaze fixed on Blanche's face. "Oh, Madame Coudert, you have no idea . . . Those villages! Once bustling, now deserted, reduced to blackened rubble around the ruins of churches. There was no quarter, for neither side took prisoners."

Mademoiselle de Cicé blessed herself.

"And after each skirmish," continued Saint-Régent, "I would retreat to my *green château*."

He paused. Blanche asked with mild curiosity: "Your *green château*? You were hiding in a château, Sir?"

Saint-Régent beamed at Blanche. "Oh, Madame, this is the name

I gave my retreat. A matter of derision. In fact, it was a sort of burrow, made of mud and branches, deep in the forest of Récœur."

Blanche giggled. "You are quite the humorist, Monsieur de Saint-Régent!"

What Saint-Régent was not saying was that, at the time, he kept a concubine, a peasant girl by the name of Lucile, in that *green château* of his. But, guessed Limoëlan, there was no need to bring that detail to the attention of the ladies.

"Then, last spring," intoned Saint-Régent, "when Bonaparte declared the West *pacified*, some cowards among us stopped fighting. Not me. Never! I went from village to village, tearing from the walls of town halls the proclamations that offered us an amnesty."

Blanche, her mouth slightly open, gave a very good impression of interest in Saint-Régent's narrative, and the poor fellow clearly believed that he was making progress with his fair listener. Limoëlan watched it all with faint amusement and shrugged.

"But the insurgency was not quelled," continued Saint-Régent. "We only changed tactics. I took the head of a group of trusted comrades, and we attacked the stagecoaches that carried the government's gold. That money would otherwise have fed the Republic's armies and its godless schools. All I was doing was seizing it in the name of the King, its rightful owner. It was all sent to George's treasurer, except for what I needed for myself and my men."

"I would not doubt it for a moment, Sir," said Mademoiselle de Cicé, nodding gravely.

Limoëlan was becoming irritated. To him those stagecoach attacks, though condoned by George, seemed uncomfortably close to vulgar highway robbery. "I heard, Saint-Régent," he interjected, "that, in the process of confiscating the Republic's gold for the King's benefit, you also relieved travelers of their money and jewelry."

Saint-Régent jumped in his seat and glared at his comrade. His piercing blue eyes, set too close to his pointy nose, flashed with anger. "Only those travelers who were enemies of the cause."

He returned his attention to Blanche. "I am not the one to sing my own praises, Madame Coudert, but I rather distinguished myself by a series of daring feats. One day, you see, my men and I ambushed the stagecoach on which the newly appointed Constitutional *Bishop* of Quimper was traveling to his Episcopal See. A renegade, a defrocked priest who had sworn allegiance to the Republic, to the Revolution!"

"Indeed, Monsieur de Saint-Régent," said Mademoiselle de Cicé, "those so-called constitutional priests make a mockery of the sole true Church."

Blanche was now paying full attention to Saint-Régent. "So what did you do?" she asked in a low voice.

Saint-Régent grinned proudly. "What do you think, Madame Coudert? I pulled the false *Bishop* from the stagecoach and shot him right between the eyes." Saint-Régent, with an expression of childish delight, extended his arm and pointed his index and middle fingers at her. "Like this, point-blank!"

He did not seem to notice that Blanche shuddered and turned pale. That was one of the problems with Madame Coudert: she seemed to believe that one could make an omelet without breaking any eggs.

But she was beautiful enough to turn most men into beasts, which could prove very helpful on occasion. Sometimes one had to use de-filed instruments in the service of the cause. Limoëlan had no scupples asking Blanche to take full advantage of her allurements. She certainly had no virtue to lose. Thanks to Mademoiselle de Cicé, he had known from the time of his arrival in Paris that Blanche was no better than a slut. She was utterly depraved, in fact.

She was the very opposite of Mademoiselle Julie d'Albert, Li-moëlan's fiancée. Certainly Julie lacked Blanche's startling beauty and elegance, but the sweetness of her face matched the purity of her soul. He had seen angels beaming down at him from heaven on the day when his sister Marie-Thérèse had introduced them and Julie had smiled at him for the first time.

26

*I*n Blanche's bedroom the maids had long closed the shutters and drawn the pink silk curtains, but she could hear the patting of heavy rain on the cobblestones of the courtyard below. She walked to a dainty mahogany and gilt bronze table and picked up a copy of *Les Souffrances du Jeune Werther*, a present from Roch. Not to read it, for she no longer found any comfort in reading. The leather volume opened at the page where, an hour earlier, she had slipped Limoëlan's note.

> *I will be waiting for you in front of Saint-Sulpice at eight o'clock. Be on time.*

Already it was past seven. She twisted the scrap of paper between her fingers. The Couderts had received an invitation to a ball at Félicie de Nallet's tonight, and now Blanche would have to excuse herself. Of course a sudden cold was nothing out of the ordinary in this season, and Félicie was enough of a friend to forgive this transparent last-minute illness. But Blanche worried about Coudert. She would try to convince him to leave her at home, and he would probably insist on keeping her company. There would be a discussion, questions, explanations, lies, and Blanche would never reach Saint-Sulpice by eight.

Her first reaction had been to disregard Limoëlan's note, and go to Félicie's as planned, but she had reconsidered. Limoëlan's tone was not friendly. Oh, he had never directly threatened her, but he had made no mystery of his unhappiness with the failure of her latest mission. Yet what else could she have done? Now she had to buy time, and the only way to pacify Limoëlan for a while was to do his bidding tonight.

A single silvery chime of the clock on the mantel startled her. Half past seven already. There was no time to change her gown. It was new, of white satin, embroidered in gold at the hem with a Greek pattern, and it would undoubtedly be ruined if she went out on foot in this downpour. But that was of little account. Blanche tossed away her dainty matching shoes across the room and hurried to her wardrobe. She seized a pair of sturdier riding boots, which she promptly laced up. Then she picked at random a red velvet pelisse, threw it on her shoulders and ran down the service staircase. An astonished footman gave way to her.

Now she was on the street, running away from her house. She had forgotten to take an umbrella or even put on a bonnet, and it was too late to return. The rain drenched her black hair, so carefully curled by her maids, and ran in icy rivulets down her neck and between her breasts. She shivered, paused to slip on her pelisse and prayed to meet a hackney soon.

At last one was coming her way. She waved and hailed it at the top of her voice, but if the driver saw her, he made no sign of pulling on his reins. She huddled against the wall of a house and closed her eyes as the carriage passed her by. Droplets of mud prickled her lips. She wiped them with the tips of her fingers and resolved to walk to Saint-Sulpice.

Water oozed out of her boots with each step, but she pressed on. She was out of breath by the time she came in sight of the round towers of the Church of Saint-Sulpice. Her heart quickened when she distinguished, under the bare chestnut trees, a waiting hackney, black and shiny in the rain. She steadied herself and knocked at the window of the carriage.

Indeed Limoëlan was waiting inside. His face was hidden in the shadows, but his lanky frame was unmistakable.

"You are late," he remarked coldly.

"I couldn't find a hackney."

"So I see, Madame." She detected a hint of amusement in his voice and shivered. It felt still colder inside the hackney. "This is an emergency," continued Limoëlan.

"Is this about Saint-Régent? Is he doing better?"

"Our friend is making a full recovery, it would seem. This is not about him. I need your help with Francis."

Blanche shuddered. "Francis?"

"Yes, Francis. He needs a new hiding place. The Convent of Saint-Michel will do perfectly. You are a great friend of the Mother Superior, and she will give him shelter if you ask her."

"I can't ask Mother Duquesne to do such a thing! It would be too dangerous for her, for all the sisters."

"They are all friends of the cause, are they not? They should be prepared to take some risks."

"I don't want Mother Duquesne to take any risks."

Limoëlan bent forward. "It is about time, Madame Coudert, for you to realize that what you want, or don't want, doesn't matter in the least." His voice was down to a hiss now. "I am asking you to do something for the cause, and I fully expect you to comply. One would think you should be anxious to show your loyalty these days. I, for one, have begun to entertain some doubts in this regard. Those two fellows at the Prefecture should have been easy prey for someone like you."

"What do you mean by *someone like me*?"

"Need you ask? I mean, of course, a person of your incomparable allurements. I am at a loss to explain your failure, to myself and to others."

"But I told you they are wary. They are policemen, after all. I need more time."

"How much more? You have been assigned that mission for months. I have come to rely solely on my own man at the Prefecture, and you know it is not the same." Limoëlan shook his long blond curls and drew closer to Blanche. Now he was only inches away from her face. "I am running out of patience. Out of trust too. So tonight, dear

Madame Coudert, you will convince the Mother Superior to hide Francis at the Convent, and you will convince him to stay quietly there. You should be extremely grateful for this opportunity to make amends. Be sure, however, that there be no dallying, no excuses this time. Let's go. Francis is waiting for us."

Limoëlan reached for the cord to signal to the driver to set forth, but Blanche reached out to stop him. "All right, I will ask Mother Duquesne to hide Francis, but let's not go there in a hackney. It's too dangerous."

Limoëlan shrugged. "If you wish. Soaked as you are, a bit more rain can't hurt you."

He stepped out of the hackney, opened a large green umbrella and offered her his arm. They crossed the square and stopped in front of a carriage door in a neighboring street. Blanche recognized Francis Carbon in the pudgy figure huddled in the shadows.

27

Carbon had seized Blanche's free arm. He was squeezing it through the velvet of her pelisse. She shook him off.

"I am grateful for the offer of your arm, Sir," she said, "but you are hurting me."

Francis let go of her. She pressed on. All that mattered now was ridding herself of this valet, this foul, hideous man, as fast as possible.

In five minutes they had reached the convent. The heavy front door creaked on rusty hinges, and Blanche engaged the elderly porter in a hushed conversation. She left her two companions in his lodge and crossed the courtyard to find the Prioress in her apartment.

Mother Duquesne was still dressed. A white wimple and black veil surrounded her full face, where an aquiline nose and square jaw were the most prominent features. When she opened the door, she let out a cry at the sight of Blanche.

"My dearest, look at you!" she said, pressing the young woman upon her ample breast. "Whatever happened to you? You are going to catch your death."

Blanche let herself be pushed into a chair by the fireplace. She wearily removed her pelisse and her wet, chilly boots and stockings. She extended her feet, red and swollen, towards the hearth. The heat of the blaze hurt as the flow of blood returned to her toes. She felt more tired than ever before, and yet the worst was still to come.

Mother Duquesne fetched a bottle of alcohol from her bedroom. Over Blanche's protests, she knelt before her and proceeded to vigorously rub her feet and legs.

"What possessed you, child, to walk here in such weather?" mumbled the Prioress. "I wouldn't throw a dog out tonight."

Blanche could not utter a word. In Mother Duquesne's presence, she was a little girl again. Within the walls of the convent, under the protection of the Prioress, no evil could befall her. She was still shivering, but a wonderful numbness was overcoming her.

Mother Duquesne pulled a comforter from her bed and wrapped it tightly around Blanche. She pulled another chair next to Blanche's and sat down. "So now, dear, will you tell me why you are here tonight?"

"Mother, I came with Monsieur de Limoëlan and a friend of his, a man who has just returned from London without papers. He needs shelter for a few days, until his family gets his name cleared from the list of émigrés."

"Can Monsieur de Limoëlan vouch for this man?"

"Certainly, he will."

"And you, Blanche, can you vouch for this man?"

Blanche's lips trembled.

"You cannot, can you?" asked the nun.

"No, dear Mother, I cannot."

"And yet he must be very important to you, or you wouldn't have come here tonight."

"Oh, yes. I will be in great danger if he is caught. And yet I hate to ask you to help him."

Mother Duquesne sighed. "I have heard strange stories lately, Blanche. About some Chouans being linked to the attack on the First Consul. You know that our little community here is only tolerated as a girls' boarding school. The morning after the Rue Nicaise attack, I had a *Te Deum* celebrated in our Chapel on account of the First Consul's quasi-miraculous escape. These days one cannot be too tepid in the display of one's patriotic zeal. And this is the time you choose to ask me to give shelter to a man of whom you cannot tell me anything, at least anything I can believe."

Blanche threw herself at the feet of the Prioress and seized both of her hands. "Forgive me, dear Mother. Yes, I lied to you. But I will tell you everything now. This man is not an émigré. He is—"

Mother Duquesne put her index finger on Blanche's lips. "Be silent, child. I cannot hear your confession, nor do I wish to learn who that man is, or what he has done. The less I know of him, the safer for you, I suppose. All I want is an answer to this question: if I agree to give him shelter, will it put the Convent at risk?"

"Yes, I believe it will."

Mother Duquesne stared into the fire. "This is what I feared. Not an hour passes, Blanche, without your being in my thoughts, and my prayers. I worry so about you. And I have much to reproach myself with. If it were not for me, you would not have met Monsieur de Limoëlan, and you would be much safer. Father de Clorivière and Mademoiselle de Cicé had always spoken so highly of him. Now I realize how little I truly knew that man. He seems to have dragged you into some terrible trouble, and that is in part my fault. Alas, what is done cannot be undone, no matter how bitterly I regret it."

"Oh, but you did nothing wrong. How could you know? And if it were not for you, dear Mother, I would not be who I am."

Mother Duquesne caressed Blanche's cheek. "In any event, dearest, I cannot desert you now. I will receive that man here and trust in God's mercy."

Blanche buried her face in the folds of the Prioress's habit. "Oh, Mother, how could I ever ask you to do such a thing?"

"It is done. Now rise, Blanche. Let me find you some dry clothes."

Ten minutes later, Blanche, dressed in a schoolgirl's uniform, followed Mother Duquesne to the porter's lodge, where Limoëlan and Francis were warming themselves in front of the fire. The Prioress frowned at the sight of Carbon, his striped stockings and beribboned breeches. She cast an alarmed look at Blanche and kept her hands folded within the vastness of her habit sleeves.

"Welcome to His house, Sir," she said. "Madame Coudert tells me that you are in need of shelter. Because she requests it, you may stay here for some time. We rent a room to an elderly gentleman boarder in our front building, and will be happy to extend the same hospitality to you. The only thing I request is that you respect the peace of this house, and not interfere with the education of our girls."

Carbon grinned and opened his mouth wide, but Limoëlan promptly interrupted him. "In the name of my unfortunate comrade, Reverend Mother, let me thank you from my heart. But then I expected no less from such a devoted friend of the cause."

Mother Duquesne fixed her dark blue eyes on Limoëlan. "Reserve your thanks for Madame Coudert, Sir. As for your friend, let him keep to his room, and remember that this is a place of prayer. Now Sister Ursule will show him the way."

"With your permission, Reverend Mother," said Limoëlan, "Madame Coudert and I will accompany him. We still have a few things to discuss."

Mother Duquesne turned to Blanche and pressed her in her arms. "God be with you, child."

She bowed again and left. Sister Ursule, candle in hand, led the three visitors up a flight of corkscrew stairs to a small room, simply furnished with a white bed, a chair and table with a wash basin. She knelt in front of the hearth to light a fire.

"This will do very well, thank you, Sister," said Limoëlan. The nun bowed and retired in silence.

Limoëlan smiled at Francis and Blanche. "Well, you two must look forward to becoming better acquainted. I will let you do so at your leisure, and bid you a good night."

Blanche flushed in anger. All of her weariness had vanished. "I am leaving too," she said. "Francis must be tired, and I need to go home. My husband will worry."

"Oh, your *husband*?" Limoëlan squinted at Blanche. "A half hour earlier or later won't make any difference to him, will it? Surely you can spare a few minutes for our friend Francis."

Carbon was gaping at her with a look of expectant imbecility. Blanche felt she might be able to handle him better if they were alone. She turned to Limoëlan. "If it makes Francis happy, yes, of course, I will stay a moment longer."

Limoëlan, after a last pointed look at her, took his leave. As soon as he had closed the door, Francis approached with a broad grin. He wrapped his arms around her waist and pushed his tongue into her ear. She stiffened with disgust, but resisted the impulse to wipe the slobber away. It was out of the question to cry for help, for Limoëlan might be lingering around.

"Oh, my little darling," Carbon whispered hoarsely into her wet ear, "I like you so!"

She giggled while pulling away from him. "How fast you are, Francis! Are you always like this with the ladies?"

"Well, you'll be my first real *lady*, so to speak. But usually girls don't mind my manners a bit, and they beg for more once they've tried me."

"I am not in the least surprised, dear Francis. I hope you did not mistake my little show of reluctance in front of Monsieur de Limoëlan. I couldn't give way to my feelings before him."

"Oh, you needn't worry 'bout Monsieur de Limoëlan. He knows you fancy me. *Madame Coudert pretends like she's givin' you the cold shoulder,* he said, *but that's jus' the ways of a fine lady. Don't let it fool you, Francis, I know she's had her eye on you for a lon' time.* And me too, I've always fancied you. And tonight, in your little schoolgirl dress, I like you still better'n usual. You look like you couldn't be older'n fifteen, Blanche. You like it when I call you Blanche, eh?"

Blanche forced her most winsome smile. "Yes, certainly, Francis."

She drew closer to the door, but he pinned her against the wall. He was several inches shorter than she, but far heavier. She felt the bulk of his belly pushing against her thighs and stomach.

"Tonight," he continued, "I was none too happy at first to leave my sister and my niece. I'm fond of those wenches, see. They're family, and whatever people say, family's family. But when Monsieur de Limoëlan said you'd make it worth my while to come here, then I agreed right away. Jus' for your sake, little darling."

Francis had wrapped one arm around Blanche's shoulders and with the other raised her skirt and petticoat. He was kneading her buttocks forcefully. She whimpered at the touch of his calloused hands. This seemed to embolden him, for he inserted a fleshy tongue deep into her mouth. She fought back nausea and pushed him away firmly.

"Well, dear Francis, Monsieur de Limoëlan was right about my fancying you, but on one point I was not dissembling: I cannot tarry any longer tonight."

His face became tense and his tone peevish. "Now don't make me angry. You can't leave me like this. Feel this?" He seized her hand and rubbed it against his groin. "See, I'm ready for you."

Blanche wiggled to disengage herself and move ever so slightly towards the door.

"Well, Francis, there's a thing you may not know yet about us ladies. When a lady loves a man passionately—"

Carbon was beaming at her. "So you love me, eh, little darling? Me too, and I bet you won't be disappointed when I give it to you."

"Not doubt about it. But, as I was telling you, no matter how impatient a lady is to yield to the ardors of her suitor, she does not want to surrender the first time in a hurried, awkward manner. It has to be perfect. So I want us to have all the time in the world. This can't be tonight, but it will be tomorrow. We will have the whole day together. In this fashion—"

He pinched her buttock so harshly that she could not repress a cry.

"Oh, no, it can't wait till tomorrow. We'll do it in a jiffy right now, and send you on your way. Then you'll come back tomorrow, and you'll show me all of your fine lady tricks, and I'll show you a few of mine too. In the meantime, jus' turn around and hold your skirts up like a good girl."

Blanche's only chance of escaping now was to pretend to faint, and pray that Carbon would be afraid enough not to take advantage of it. She bent her knees and let herself slip against the wall.

Francis caught her roughly by the armpit. "Eh, what's that? Blanche, you're all right? Little darling?"

Suddenly the door opened. The heavy figure of a nun appeared in the frame.

"Madame Coudert," said Mother Duquesne, "your husband is waiting for you downstairs. He is very worried." She turned to Francis. "As for you, Sir, I suggest you take some rest."

Blanche pulled free and dashed for the door. As she ran down the stairs, she wiped at last the spittle off her lips. Limoëlan would pay for this.

28

*B*ack at the Prefecture, Roch resumed his review of the mail that continued to pour in. Inspector Alain came to report on his progress, or lack thereof. The search for Saint-Régent and François Carbon remained fruitless. Roch groaned. His visit to the Mayenne Inn had not brought the results he had expected. He remembered the first days of the investigation, when he had seemed to make headway so fast, so easily. Now, at the time of his father's danger, nothing seemed to be happening anymore. It was already the 11th of January, the 22nd of Nivose, only two weeks away from the time set by Fouché for Old Miquel's deportation.

The Prefect again had Roch called to his office. Maybe word of Roch's visit to the Mayenne Inn had reached the Prefect. Dubois pretended to continue writing without taking any notice of Roch, who looked out the window. It was already dark outside. After a few minutes, the Prefect raised his head.

"Ah, yes, Miquel, here you are!" he said. "Chevalier's case will be reviewed by a Military Commission tonight. You are to fetch the man from the Temple and take him to the Ministry at nine o'clock, and then to the place of execution."

Roch felt a pang at the mention of the Temple. So now the Prefect was sending him to the place where his father was imprisoned. He took a deep breath to compose himself. "Chevalier?" he asked in a detached tone. "That engineer who experimented with an infernal machine?"

"Yes, of course, the same."

Roch could not help asking, "And if Chevalier were acquitted by the Military Commission, should I take him home?"

The Prefect leered. "I told you already to be careful, Miquel. I am tired of your witticisms. Maybe your mood will be less jocular tonight when . . . anyway, be sure to bring Chevalier to the Ministry at nine o'clock."

Roch bit his lip. He could ill afford to provoke his superior these days. He left the Prefecture at seven that night and went to a nearby tavern. Standing at the counter, he hastily swallowed a bowl of hot onion soup before hailing a hackney.

Why was the Prefect sending him on this pointless errand? Military Commissions, which dealt with matters involving the safety of the Nation, were the exclusive province of the Army. The attendance of a man from the Prefecture was not normally required.

The hackney stopped in front of the Temple. It was difficult to imagine that the place, so grim now, had been one of the palaces of the King's brother before the Revolution. These days it housed, in addition to Old Miquel, scores of other opponents to Bonaparte. Beyond the former palace loomed the massive square tower. Tiny windows projected points of light from all of its stories. Roch asked the hackney driver to wait.

The prison clerk, Fauconnier, recognized Roch, whom he had met on occasion. The man's greeting lacked warmth and his eye kept shifting to the far corners of the room. Roch could not take his thoughts off his father, so close and yet out of reach.

"Ah, yes, yes," the clerk said. "The Military Commission, obviously. Yes, it's about Citizen Chevalier. I received my instructions all right. I'll take you to him right away, Citizen Chief Inspector. The soldiers should be here in a moment to escort you to the Ministry."

Roch followed the clerk across the courtyard, lit by lanterns, and down a narrow stairwell to the basement of the tower. They found Chevalier, lanky, sullen, unshaven, standing in his cell. Roch was chilled to the bone, and the dampness oozing from the bare stone walls reminded him of the cold sweats of agony. He turned up his collar and tried not to think of Old Miquel, who was perhaps housed in a similar cell. No one spoke. Chevalier's Adam's apple kept moving up and down. He avoided Roch's eyes and kept staring out a barred window, just under the ceiling, that opened at the level of the courtyard.

Roch looked up when he heard noise outside. The hooves of many horses, orders barked by a hoarse voice, then heavy footsteps beating against the cobblestones. The military escort must have arrived. At least the wait was over. A soldier tied his horse's reins to the bars of the window. Only the man's boots and the animal's legs were visible. Voices resonated within the prison, mingled with the metallic clang of heavy doors opening and shutting. A captain, accompanied by two privates, entered the cell. The soldiers, after saluting Roch, proceeded to shackle Chevalier's hands. It was half past eight.

In the hackney Roch could feel the prisoner, seated next to him, shivering. They drove in silence to the Ministry of Police, where the proceedings of Military Commissions were held on the second floor. The captain pushed Chevalier inside a room while Roch remained in the corridor.

He expected the wait to be short. Military Commissions were composed of a few officers. No attorneys were allowed nor were any witnesses required, and the sole record of the proceedings consisted of a few lines sending the accused to his death. When the door opened again fifteen minutes later, the sentence could be plainly read on Chevalier's face.

The hackney was still waiting for them in front of the Ministry. Soldiers climbed into their saddles. It was quite a way to the place of execution, but traffic would be no hindrance at this time.

In the hackney the prisoner's face was briefly lit at regular intervals by the streetlights, then it fell back into complete darkness. They drove by the great classical front of the Ecole Militaire, the Ecole de Mars, as it had been called during the Revolution, half drowned in the fog. Roch knew the place very well. Old Miquel had enrolled him there, after Veau's Academy for Boys had closed, to receive at the Nation's expense the education of a future warrior of the Republic.

With his comrades, he had performed physical exercises for hours, always outdoors, always in the nude, even in the biting cold of winter that shriveled their genitals to nothing.

At last the Ecole Militaire disappeared in the fog and the hackney stopped in an empty plot just outside the Grenelle Gate. When the captain opened the door, the prisoner started at the sight of the cart waiting for what would soon be his corpse. Roch wondered about this strange twilight, when one was still fully alive, and yet moments away from certain death.

The captain ordered Chevalier to stand with his back to the wall that marked the city limits. A soldier took a lighted lantern and placed its strap around the prisoner's neck.

"Makes an easier target at night," he explained to Roch. "No good for anyone if we miss the chest."

Now the man's face was lit from beneath by the lantern. His features looked still grimmer than before, his clenched jaw jutted, his orbits were empty holes, as though the head had already been reduced to the bones. A dozen soldiers, dark figures shrouded in fog, gathered in a line in front of Chevalier. The points of the bayonets attached to their rifles were only a few yards from the man's chest. The captain commanded, "Present arms." The soldiers brought the butts of their rifles up to their shoulders. Sharp clicks resonated in the cold night air. The soldiers, hunched over, took aim. The captain now shouted, "Fire!" Orange flames shot from of the barrels of the rifles, billows of white smoke mixed with the fog. The thunder of the explosion startled Roch. The horses barely nickered.

The smell of powder hovered over the scene as on Rue Nicaise on the night of the attack. Roch felt his mouth fill with saliva. He turned towards the wall against which Chevalier had stood. His stomach pulsed, the muscles of his belly contracted. He retched. The taste of vomit filled his mouth before its stench filled his nostrils.

One of the soldiers asked, "You all right, Citizen Chief Inspector?"

Roch drew himself up and pulled a handkerchief from his pocket. "Never better, soldier," he said, wiping his mouth.

His step was steady when he walked to the body. It had fallen facedown. The captain, with the point of his boot, turned it over onto its back. The chest was nothing but torn flesh, still shaken by tremors. The bloodstains on the shirt seemed black in the light of a soldier's lantern. The captain pulled a pistol and fired it down into the man's head. Roch braced himself before the shock and avoided looking at what was left of the face.

"Well, now he's all yours," said the captain.

For Chevalier all was over. But Roch was not done. The soldiers grabbed the body and lifted it onto the cart. They mounted their horses and headed for town, talking and laughing quietly between themselves, their task accomplished. Roch climbed once more into the hackney, which followed the cart to the graveyard of Vaugirard. There he pulled the clerk from his bed, wrote and signed the death certificate, and watched the body thrown without ceremony into the open pit of a common grave. The other corpses there had been sown into burlap sacks, but Chevalier's would be denied even that modest rite. The surly graveyard clerk was content to open a barrel and shovel a layer of lime over the body.

Roch stepped back wearily into the hackney. As soon as they reached the city limits, he pulled the cord to make it stop. Walking home in the cold would help him cleanse his mind of the night's memories.

Roch was thinking of Chevalier, the dead man. He had built a bomb, an infernal machine similar to the one used in the Rue Nicaise attack. What could his purpose have been, if not to kill Bonaparte, probably along with many innocents? He must have deserved to die. But then why had he not been tried by a regular court?

And why had Roch been asked to witness this grisly masquerade? Once at home, he removed his boots and dropped heavily onto his bed without bothering to undress. He fell asleep very fast.

29

*E*arly the next morning, before Roch left for the Prefecture, a messenger brought a note. He felt weak in the knees when he recognized the seal of the Ministry and Fouché's handwriting. For a moment he could not bring himself to open it. Maybe it simply contained more clues, more directions for the investigation, perhaps even the name of the third man, the fellow with the gold spectacles. But the note might also seal Old Miquel's fate. Roch shook himself and tore it open. It only said *You may visit your father at five o'clock this afternoon.*

Roch threw his head backwards and took a deep breath. He was relieved, happy, of course, but what if he found Old Miquel weakened, thinner, a shadow of his former self? What if this were the last visit before his father's deportation or execution? He could not banish from his mind the impressions of Chevalier in the face of the firing squad.

Roch went to the Prefecture as usual that morning, but he had trouble concentrating on his work. A report to Dubois, which should have taken no more than ten minutes to compose, had to be started over many times, and Roch, after reading its latest draft, still was not sure that it made any sense. No matter, it was probably good enough for Dubois.

All day Roch kept looking out his office window at the pale winter sun. A fine day, dry and crisp for the season. At last it was four o'clock. He set off on foot and reached the Temple in less than half an hour. The prison clerk, Fauconnier, greeted Roch with a warmth that contrasted with his embarrassment of the night before.

"Ah, Citizen Chief Inspector," he said, "I expected you. Received the instructions today from the Minister *himself*." He shouted an order to the guards and turned his attention back to Roch. "There's not a better man than your father, and I'll be sorry to see him go when his time comes. I mean when he is released, of course. But then, mind you, we have nothing but the cream of the cream here. True, we lost Citizen Chevalier last night, as you know, but we still have three generals, seven judges, and dozens of *ci-devant* noblemen. And also Citizen Topino-Lebrun, the history painter, and his accomplices in the Conspiracy of Daggers. You won't find any common criminals here, no, Citizen."

The clerk, swelled with pride, patted the prison register. "I could show you the names of the *ci-devant* King and Queen in here. They sent me a thief the other day, imagine that! But I saw the mistake right away, and I refused to receive the scoundrel. A common *thief*, here!"

Roch nodded in response. He did not want to show any weakness now, especially before his father, and drew himself up. A door opened, and at first all he could see was a blurry figure, flanked by two guards. He had no time to bring his father's hand to his lips, and felt a pair of arms wrapped tightly around his shoulders. Once the embrace relented, he drew back and looked at Old Miquel. Indeed his father did not seem altered at all.

"Roch," he cried, "I haven't been so happy in weeks!"

"Thank God I find you in good health, Father. And in good spirits too, it seems."

The turnkey was smiling in a sanctimonious manner, his head cocked to the side. Roch, impatient to be rid of him, slipped him a silver coin.

"You'll be comfortable by yourselves in there, Citizens," the man hastened to say. He unlocked the door to a square room, fitted with a barred window, and furnished with a table and two straw chairs.

Old Miquel patted Roch on the shoulder before taking a seat.

"I knew you'd worry. Of course, the first day, they only gave me a piece of bread and a bowl of that greasy slop they call *the soup*. And I spent my first night on a straw mattress they threw on the stone floor of the common room, without even a blanket, so I was mighty cold. But we've slept in worse places in the old days, you and me, and eaten food that wasn't much better, haven't we?"

Roch clenched his jaw. He recalled what Fouché had said about Old Miquel being comfortable in prison. So that was what the scoundrel's assurances meant.

"But things took a turn for the better the very next day, thanks to you," continued Old Miquel. "After the turnkey got your money, I got my own cell, and now I take my meals at the paying table. Also, I can play ball in the afternoons with the others in the courtyard." Old Miquel chuckled. "Turns out I'm one of the best, at my age too! I can still kick that ball, and run faster than most young fellows. And I get to read the papers too. So I know what happened since my arrest, at least what's printed in those rags."

Old Miquel smiled at Roch. "I even read your name a couple o' times. Made me feel all funny, proud and sad at the same time. Then at night after dinner the guards herd us, there's a roll call and I am locked back in my cell."

"Did they put you in a decent place at last?"

"Oh, yes, it's quite all right. A little chamber, up in the tower. It used to be occupied by Madame Elisabeth, the *ci-devant* King's sister, before she was guillotined too, poor thing. Too many people died then, for sure." Old Miquel shook his head pensively. "See, Roch, I sleep in the bedroom of a princess now. Never thought that'd happen to me. And then, because it used to be Madame Elisabeth's cell, all the Chouans in the Temple come and visit. The turnkey charges them a fee to bring them up there. So they kneel, and say prayers for the repose of her soul, and the souls of the royal family. A *pilgrimage*, they call it. So now I'm used to people kissing the filth on the floor at the foot of my cot, and I move out of the way. I don't agree with their ideas, but that's no reason to bother them, is it? Then, when I see they're done with their prayers, I talk to them for a bit."

"Really, Father? And they talk to you?"

Old Miquel shrugged. "Oh, yes, they're even quite nice. Normally I wouldn't make friends with *ci-devant* aristocrats, but in jail you can't be too fussy about the company you keep. So I've discovered we've something in common: we all hate Bonaparte, and here the differences between us don't matter anymore. See, once in a while the guards call someone to take him before one of those Military Commissions, and everyone knows what it means. Sometimes we read his name in the papers the next day, sometimes not even that. That can happen to any of us, any day, so that makes it easy to understand one another."

Roch closed his eyes, then, very fast, reopened them. The scene of Chevalier's execution had come to mind again with fresh intensity.

"I read in the papers about those Jacobins who got deported," continued Old Miquel. "And they say it's only the beginning. So I reckon that, even though I missed the first ship, someone'd make sure I got on the next one, or the one after that."

Old Miquel, from prison, had a perfectly clear understanding of his own situation. Roch, dumbfounded, had not expected this. He was torn between the desire to confide all he knew about Fouché's threat and the fear to confirm his father's all too perceptive assumptions.

"It's not for me to decide, of course," continued Old Miquel, "but if I'd my say, I'd much rather die cleanly with my chest full of lead after a Military Commission than be sent to rot alive across the oceans, in a place that's too hot for people, and full of vermin and mosquitoes."

Roch was still uncertain of what to reveal, but was spared that decision, for Old Miquel hastened to say: "Enough talk about me. Tell me about you and that investigation of yours."

"I am sure the Jacobins are innocent. So far, I have three suspects, all Chouans. And Fouché sent me information leading to the identification of two of them."

"Nothing about the third man?" mused Old Miquel. "Yet I bet Fouché knows about that one just as well. Maybe he's protecting him. Maybe he's made an alliance with some Chouans against Bonaparte."

Roch stared at Old Miquel. "The Chouans wouldn't have anything to do with him. They hate him. Remember, Father, he voted in favor of the King's execution in '93."

"Oh, like I told you, I've talked quite a bit with the Royalists here. Now I understand better what they think of many things and many people, including Fouché. They hate him all right, and they'll never forgive him for voting to kill Louis XVI, but they'd be mighty happy if he'd help them get rid of Bonaparte. Then, with Bonaparte dead, they'd turn on Fouché. Many people here talk of having him drawn and quartered, which, come to think of it, isn't a bad idea for a man like that."

"I must have been very naïve, Father. I hadn't thought of that."

"Neither has Fouché, I bet. He's clever, but less than he thinks. So yes, Roch, he could've turned around and made friends with some of the Chouans, without realizing the risks to his precious person."

"So you think Fouché might be betraying Bonaparte? Indeed I have heard that Bonaparte does not trust him at all."

Old Miquel nodded. "Our glorious General may be right about that. Just make sure you don't trust Fouché either. I've always thought you were too keen on the man. He doesn't care about you, or Bonaparte, or anyone else. He only cares about himself, about his position, his safety, his money. Help him, and he'll be your friend. Until he betrays you, that is."

"I am afraid you are right. I didn't want to believe that of him before."

"Be careful, that's all. Now tell me about the Barrel. Everything's all right there?"

"Alexandrine has offered to keep it open in your absence. I thought you would like that, and I accepted."

"Well, of course I like that. That's kind of Alexandrine, but then she's always kind. And old Crow likes her. He'll feel a bit lonesome, after all these years we spent together."

Roch looked away. "Crow died three days ago, Father. Quietly, at Alexandrine's feet."

Old Miquel opened his mouth without uttering any sound. At last he pulled a red and white handkerchief from his pocket. "Poor Crow," he said, noisily blowing his nose. "Changes aren't easy, for old dogs or for old men. At least Alexandrine was there with him. She must've petted him when he went away. Be sure to thank her."

"I already did, Father."

Old Miquel tucked his handkerchief back into his pocket and looked into Roch's eyes. "I mean thank her *properly*, from the heart. I've noticed that you're not always so very pleasant with her."

Roch flushed. "I regret it now. I am beginning to appreciate her as she deserves."

"Good. And you should thank her on your own account too," added Old Miquel. "It's better for you if the Barrel remains open, because you'll get a better price for it when you sell it."

Roch looked intently at Old Miquel. "It belongs to *you*. Alexandrine is keeping it open for you, until your return."

Roch's words sounded hollow to his own ears. His father simply gazed at the darkening sky outside the barred window.

"Well, Roch, you should know that I put my affairs in order a few months ago. Like I knew what was coming. Actually it wasn't so hard to guess. Mignon, my attorney, will give you all the details, but everything goes to you, of course."

Roch felt a lump in his throat. "Please don't talk like this, Father."

Old Miquel seemed to hesitate. "I don't like it either, Roch, but we need to talk now, because I don't know if we'll get another chance. There's something I have to tell you. Yesterday afternoon the clerk told me that I'd be taken to a Military Commission at nine o'clock that evening and—"

"The bastards!" Roch hit the table with his closed fist. "If—"

"Don't let your anger govern you. That's no good." Old Miquel patted Roch's arm. "Anyway, I reckoned I'd have a close look at the guns of the firing squad in a matter of hours. But then at night they locked me in my cell as usual, and they told me someone'd given other orders to the contrary. Still, in the meantime, I tidied up my mind, so to speak. The good thing's that I'm leaving everything in order. I owe no money, and if I've ever harmed anyone, it was done without malice, and I'd beg their forgiveness if I could. The only thing that bothered me, and it bothered me quite a bit, was about you. I know it'd cause you a great deal of pain."

"They made you go through that agony!" muttered Roch between his teeth. "I failed you. I should have prevented that."

"You didn't fail me, and it was no agony."

Roch bit his closed fist. "I too have something to tell you, Father. I was here, at the Temple, last night. To take Chevalier to a Military Commission. I attended his execution."

"Yes, I'd heard he'd been taken to a Military Commission. Only I didn't know it was by you."

"And on the same day, the clerk here tells you that the same is going to happen to you. And then someone orders otherwise. Then today they allow me to see you. All in less than twenty-four hours."

"Wait a moment, Roch. When you say *they*, who's that?"

"If only I knew, Father. It was the Prefect who told me to attend Chevalier's execution. When I think of it now, I believe he was taunting me. He must have known that you were scheduled to appear before the Military Commission at the same time as Chevalier. The bastard wanted me to witness your execution." Roch paused. He had never understood the true intensity of the Prefect's ill will. "But then Fouché must have given orders to save you. And it was Fouché too who allowed me to visit you today."

Old Miquel frowned. "So I'd owe Fouché my life? It doesn't sound right. Why'd he do that for me, or for you?"

"It's not all, Father. There is no point in hiding it since you have guessed anyway. He told me that he would have you deported if I did not arrest those two Chouans by the end of January."

Old Miquel shook his head pensively. "Aye, that's more like Fouché. Now I think I understand what he was doing. He ordered my execution, knowing that the Prefect'd tell you to attend, and then he gave orders to the contrary at the last minute. Just to rattle you. If I'd been shot last night, he'd have lost all power over you. With this threat of shipping me to the Colonies, he can make you do his bidding. I told you, Roch, beware of that bastard."

Old Miquel seemed lost in his thoughts for a while. Then he shook himself and grasped Roch's arm. "I want you to remember something. For my sake. Whatever happens to me, I don't want you blaming yourself for it. It's my own damn fault if I talked so freely about Bonaparte and Fouché. You warned me to be careful, remember, and I wouldn't listen to you. I don't regret it on my own account, because I had a good life, and I am old enough to go. But I should've thought more of you. You're my only child now, and I couldn't have wished for a better son. D'you hear me, Roch? I want you to promise you'll remember that. Say it."

Roch concentrated on fighting the sobs that were choking him. He swallowed hard before he could utter the words. "I promise, Father. I will always remember it."

"Good. I believe you, and I can rest easy now. I think it's time for us to say good-bye."

Roch knelt on the floor and removed his hat. "Father, please give me your blessing."

Old Miquel rose and extended both of his hands over his son's bowed head. He said the ritual words:

May God bless you,
May He give you health
And keep your soul in happiness.

*In the name of the Father, and Son, and Holy Ghost.
Amen.*

Old Miquel raised his son to embrace him. Then he walked to the
door and knocked to call the guard. He left the little room without
looking back.

30

Roch's hate for Dubois had taken a new turn, personal, vivid. He felt the same kind of dislike, to a lesser degree, for the rest of his colleagues. They seemed to understand it and avoided his eye whenever they met him in the corridors of the Prefecture. He limited his direct contacts to his Inspectors, who kept searching all of Paris for Saint-Régent and Carbon, still without success.

Yet when he crossed the path of Piis, the Secretary General, on the morning of the 15th of January, he was surprised to see a smile parting the man's thick lips.

"Ah, Miquel," exclaimed Piis. "Am I glad to see you! I have a little something here on which I would like to have your opinion."

Piis, without waiting for a response, pulled a folded sheet of paper from his pocket. Roch cringed. The fact that Piis again spoke to him was probably a good omen, but he had no desire to listen once more to the readings of his colleague's poetry.

Of course, Roch had studied the classics, Virgil, Ovid and Horace, as well as French poetry, at Monsieur Veau's Academy for Boys. It was not a fond memory. He could barely read and write when he had arrived at the Academy, and he had been three years older than any other pupil in his class. During the first six months, he had been flogged without fail every Saturday for his ignorance and unruliness until the Latin teacher took pity on him and tutored him, free of charge, at night. Thanks to that kind soul, Roch caught up with the boys of his age, and was on his way to graduate with honors if the Academy had not abruptly closed due to the emigration of its proprietor. Now poetic endeavors of any kind held little interest for him, and he was not in any mood to humor his colleague.

"Thank you, Piis," he said, "but perhaps you should read it to Bertrand. He used to own a bookshop."

"Bertrand? That mindless brute? All you have to do is look at that snout of his to tell that he doesn't understand the first thing about poetry. No, I want *your* opinion. A good-looking young fellow like you must be in love."

Roch was not sorry to disappoint his colleague and remained silent.

"So?" asked Piis with some impatience. "Are you?"

"A good-looking fellow? You flatter me, Piis. I hardly know what to say."

Piis rolled his eyes and let out a groan. "No, Miquel, you know perfectly well what I mean. Are you *in love?*"

"I generally reserve the avowal of my feelings for the lady who inspires them."

"Ah! We have a lady here! And even if you are not in love, it may be close enough." Piis lowered his voice. "You see, Miquel, in my case, there's a rather delicate situation. I have declared my flame to my lady, but she won't have anything to do with me. She says she will never like me because I work at the Prefecture."

"Perhaps she worries that you might take advantage of your functions to read her police file." Roch arched his eyebrow. "Did you?"

Piis puffed with indignation. "Of course not! No man of honor would read his beloved's police file. But this little sonnet should mollify her. Now listen."

Piis put one of his hands upon his chest, holding the sheet at arm's length with the other.

"*Oh, Photis, cruel Photis, thy charming name—*" he began.

"*Photis?*" scoffed Roch. "Like that little minx of a maid in *The Golden Ass?* Where did your paramour get a name like that?"

Piis knit his brows. "*The Golden Ass?* Now that you mention it, yes, there might be a character by that name in it."

"And do you remember what that Photis does in *The Golden Ass?*"

"I must have forgotten," said Piis.

"Well, I remember that novel fairly well because it was the only time I found reading Latin enjoyable. The book had been smuggled into Veau's Academy by one of my schoolmates, who had stolen it from his father's library. So, for your information, Photis is a luscious little hussy who shows the narrator a delightful time in bed, then turns him into a jackass. Hence the title. Beware, Piis. The same could happen to you. Only without the delightful time in bed."

Piis bit his lip. "Well, you see, Miquel, *Photis* is not my beloved's real name. I made it up for this sonnet, and it worked for the rhyme. Also, her real name is too plain for poetry. In fact, it is too plain for her. I wish you could see her, Miquel. Such eyes! Such a complexion! And what a figure! Light and gracious and yet voluptuous . . ." Piis's eyes wandered away for a minute. "And then, I don't want to compromise her. She is married, you know. Imagine if this poem became an instant success. I wouldn't want her *real* name on everyone's lips."

Roch refrained from remarking that perhaps his colleague overestimated that risk. Some of Piis's comedies had made it on occasion to vaudeville stages, where they had garnered but lukewarm reviews, and his *Poésies Fugitives*, published one year ago, had already sunk into obscurity.

Who indeed cared a jot about Piis's poetry? Roch looked into his colleague's eyes and asked, "Say, Piis, how is it that you are again talking to me?"

Piis blushed. "Well, you see, everyone said that Fouché would be dismissed, and the Prefect was to be the next Minister, so—"

"Yes, I understand perfectly well why you *were* not talking me anymore. What puzzles me is why you have changed your mind."

"Oh, that! I guess you have not heard the news then. Fouché had Bourmont arrested last night."

"Bourmont? The *ci-devant* Count de Bourmont, the former Chouan general?"

"The one. But wait, that's not all. The arrest took place at the bottom of the grand staircase of the Tuileries, just as Bourmont was leaving the First Consul's private apartment." Piis leaned towards Roch and shielded his mouth with his hand. "They say the First Consul and Madame Bonaparte have become friends with Bourmont and his wife, and that he was furious to have one of his guests arrested in that manner, practically on his doorstep. So Fouché was summoned to the Tuileries right away. But this morning, he is still Minister, and Bourmont is still in jail, in spite of everything."

Roch stared out the window. This was the best news he had received since the attack. Fouché must have had proof positive of the involvement of the Chouans to provoke the First Consul in this manner. The Minister was now enjoying the sweet taste of revenge. The tide must be turning at last. None too soon, because Roch had begun to despair of finding the Rue Nicaise assassins within the remaining two weeks of the allotted time.

"Now, if you don't mind," continued Piis, "we shall go back to my little piece. Make sure you don't interrupt this time. It breaks the rhythm of the verse, and you won't be able to appreciate the flow of it." Piis's hand returned to his chest. He cleared his voice. "*Oh, Photis, cruel Photis—*"

"Now, Piis, have you considered the fact that maybe your Photis is in no way adverse to the police in general? *I* have never found it to be a hindrance. Perhaps she only says that because she doesn't want to hurt your feelings. What if she simply doesn't like you? Or maybe she can't abide your name?"

Piis sighed. "Really, Miquel, you have no idea how many tasteless jokes circulate about it. Do you think my beloved heard any of them? I can't imagine how anything so base could ever reach her ears, but perhaps you are right. Maybe if I adopted a nom de plume . . ."

Roch slapped his colleague on the back. "And what of the literary fame you have already achieved under your *real* name? I am afraid it's too late. No, Piis, don't look any further: your beloved simply doesn't like the fact that you work at the Prefecture. She says so herself, does she not? Perhaps you should glance at her police file after all. There must be something interesting there."

Roch proceeded to his office without waiting for Piis's answer.

31

*R*och called all of his Inspectors to his office to discuss their progress and devise new ways of locating Saint-Régent and Short Francis. The date set by Fouché for Old Miquel's deportation was but twelve days away now. Roch was more convinced than ever that the Mayenne Inn was at the heart of the Rue Nicaise conspiracy and silently cursed the Prefect for preventing him from posting his men there. Little as he liked it, he had no choice but to rely solely on a little beggar to watch the place.

The Rue Nicaise investigation did not absolve Roch of his usual duties. It was the day of the week when he was to visit the Palais-Egalité in his professional capacity. Blanche's mother was not the only one to have opened a gaming salon there. The Palais-Egalité had been called the Palais-Royal before the Revolution, when it belonged to the Duke d'Orléans, cousin to the King. The Duke had conceived the idea, novel for a prince of the royal blood, to rent part of his palace to shopkeepers to supplement his already enormous income. Then, during the Revolution, the Duke had been guillotined for conspiring to make himself King in place of his cousin.

Yet the shops, unlike him, survived. The rents were twice as high as anywhere else in town, and often drove the tenants into bankruptcy, but much of the business of Paris was still transacted there. A multitude of shops around the pillared galleries sold shiny fabrics, dresses, flowers, jewels, ribbons, toothpicks, jars of rouge, clocks, trinkets, perfumes, embroidered garters and every other imaginable sort of merchandise.

The sound of raised voices burst from the cafés where the Stock Exchange brokers and their customers gathered. Music came from the Frères Provençaux restaurant, while the fragrance of roasting meat rose from the kitchens in the basement. Inside the vast dining parlor, huge mirrors reflected pyramids of pâtés, pastries, jellies, and even peaches and cherries, grown in hothouses during these winter months.

Military men in bright uniforms ambled in the galleries. Austria had been defeated at the battle of Marengo by Bonaparte himself last June, and again at Hohenlinden by General Moreau. The Holy Roman Emperor, Francis II, *the tyrant of Austria*, as Old Miquel called him, had been forced to beg for an armistice. Negotiations for a peace treaty had already commenced. The considerable territorial gains of the French Republic in Germany, Italy and the Netherlands would no doubt be confirmed. England would have to carry alone the burden of prosecuting the war against France.

Roch passed a bookshop that displayed, in the midst of an assortment of libertine prints, *Justine or the Misfortunes of Virtue*, the notorious novel by the *ci-devant* Marquis de Sade, and its counterpart, *The Anti-Justine*, by Restif de la Bretonne. Roch knew Restif, who was a clerk at the Ministry of Police and a prolific author of novels and pamphlets, including *The Pornographer*. The man claimed that his *Anti-Justine* provided the same kind of entertainment as Sade's works, without indulging in their excessive cruelty. He had boasted to Roch, while presenting him with a free copy, that *only one* woman was cut into pieces and devoured in the *Anti-Justine*. Roch had never finished the novel. He had found the sexual exploits of the characters mildly entertaining at first, though a bit repetitive, but even a single dismembered woman was one too many for his taste.

Many houses of convenience were also located in the Palais-Egalité, but this was no Pull-Cock Alley. The presence of prostitutes was hardly noticeable during the day, when they remained in the bawdy houses. Roch made his rounds of those, and finally climbed the stairs that led to Citizen Renard's establishment. Two ladies, yawning, greeted him without rising from the plump sofas where they rested. Both were young and pretty, and their rouge was tastefully applied. They wore no undergarments, and their dresses were so sheer that every detail of their bodies was revealed, from the pink-brownish rosettes of their breasts, down to their nether hair and the embroidered garters that tied their flesh-colored stockings. Roch took a moment to enjoy the sights before turning his attention back to the business at hand. Citizen Renard, a buxom woman of mature years, handed him her weekly purse.

"There, Citizen Chief Inspector," she simpered. "Please be kind enough to send my respects to our dear Minister, as always. And did you know that we have a fresh piece? Arrived last week from the countryside. Would you like to meet her? I will go awaken her if you wish. Our patrons simply rave about her." She pointed to the two reclining ladies, who smiled sleepily at Roch. "Unless you prefer Rose, or Fanny. Or both. Courtesy of the house, of course."

Roch put the purse into his already heavy briefcase and took his leave, politely declining the bawd's offers. Once he went back to the galleries downstairs, he passed the window of a jewelry store and stopped for a moment. He looked at delicate filigree earrings, at gold ornaments shaped like roses, cupids or birds. All lovely things, and he would have been happy to present Blanche with any of them. He was ready to push the door to the shop open, but reconsidered. He did not want to give her anything tainted by an association with the Palais-Egalité. In any event, the shop must specialize in trinkets destined to the whores upstairs. It was the last place in Paris to purchase a nuptial ring, even for a lady one could not marry.

He now had to call on Madame de Cléry, which he found still more disagreeable than all of his other visits to the Palais-Egalité put together. Blanche must have told her mother of her liaison with Roch, because ever since the older woman had introduced them, her flirtatious attempts had given way to the coldest of manners. Roch, without meeting her eye, was content to seize the purse she handed him.

He was done at last and looked up at the white, opaque sky, laden with a promise of snow. So he hailed a hackney as soon as he left the Palais-Egalité and drove to the Ministry. He had no wish to see Fouché, but Marain, the private secretary, as though expecting a request for an interview, pointedly informed him that the Minister was not there. Roch walked back to the Isle of the Cité. Now the first snowflakes, plump and light, were dancing in front of his eyes. Roch hated snow and pressed ahead.

Shortly before reaching the Prefecture, on the Goldsmiths Embankment, he stopped in front of a shop window displaying a variety of silver platters, tea sets and ice buckets. *This* place might sell wedding rings. A bell rang cheerily when he pushed the door open. The shopkeeper, a comely young woman in a black silk dress, smiled graciously at him from behind the counter. He told her of his errand.

"Allow me to offer my congratulations, Citizen," she said, her eyes lowered, as she pulled a tray full of nuptial rings.

Roch tried to examine the rings, but they all seemed the same. He pointed to one at random.

"A wise choice," said the young woman. "Any other jewelry for the fortunate young lady? We have these bracelets, in three tones of gold. Quite the fashion these days, and very appropriate as a wedding gift." She pointed at a case behind the counter. "And a silver porringer for the little ones to come, perhaps? You know that it is considered good luck to purchase it *before* the marriage."

Roch felt his cheeks burning. Now this wedding ring business seemed sillier than ever. The shopkeeper was looking at him in an inquisitive manner, with a half smile on her lips.

"No, thank you, Citizen," said Roch. "Just the ring, please."

"Certainly."

He noticed a large diamond on her finger as she weighed the ring on a goldsmith's scale. She announced a price of thirty francs and put the jewel in a case.

"My congratulations again, Citizen," she said, smiling. "You may find that you need something else before long. Do not hesitate to come and ask. Anytime."

She pressed his hand slightly as she gave him the tiny parcel. He hastened to leave.

Roch was too preoccupied to give the elegant jeweler's offers any consideration. He kept thinking of Blanche and her mother while walking the few dozen yards that separated him from the Prefecture. He remembered Piis's words: *No man of honor would read his beloved's police file*. Perhaps Piis was right. Roch, until now, had never thought of doing such a thing, or even sought to discover whether there were any files at all at the Prefecture on Blanche, her husband or mother.

Yet now he felt that something was amiss. Instead of going straight to his office, he walked to the archives, where, as usual, he winced at the odor of musty paper. Indeed many files here dated from before the Revolution, for the archives of the old Police Lieutenant had simply been moved to the Prefecture. "Governments change, the police remains," his colleague Henry liked to say.

Roch followed with his finger the shelves marked with the letter *C*. He saw a folio marked with the name *Cléry* and proceeded to pull it. He started when a tiny ball of gray fur, followed by a long pink tail, scurried away with a squeak. Roch had a peasant's aversion for mice. He had already complained to Dozier, the archivist, about the damage the little pests wrought and had suggested the introduction of several cats.

But fortunately the *Cléry* file was intact. It contained several sheets. The earliest dated from decades before the Revolution. Renée-Amélie de Cléry was born in Paris in 1750, into a family of ancient but impoverished nobility. So she was fifty, older than Roch would have guessed. She had married a Louis-Célestin de Cléry, an obscure gamester who styled himself Captain de Cléry without having ever belonged to any known army. The man had wisely fled to America in

1775, to avoid his many creditors and charges of forgery of promissory notes.

Abandoned penniless in Paris at the age of twenty-five, Madame de Cléry had resorted to the profession favored from times immemorial by females in financial distress. She had become a kept woman. The birth of her only child, Blanche, was recorded in 1780, and so was, at the same time, the opening of her gaming salon in the galleries of what was still called the Palais-Royal. Madame de Cléry had sought, and been granted, a divorce as soon as the Revolution had made it possible, in 1790. Her former husband might still be alive somewhere in America. Or, for all anyone seemed to care, he might have died years ago. Roch bit his fingernail. What was sure, he reflected, was that the fellow had disappeared years before Blanche's birth.

Another sheet in the file related that Madame de Cléry had been jailed during the spring and summer of 1794. She had been suspected of spying for England and being a Royalist conspirator. Roch frowned. That was the time of the Great Terror. It did not take much then for anyone to be accused of counterrevolutionary activities, jailed or sentenced to the guillotine. The woman might have been compromised by an unwitting association with patrons of her gaming salon. Or she might have really been an English spy. But then he would have expected a steady stream of entries in that regard. There were none. All recent notes concerned routine matters dealing with the gaming salon and the renewals of its license.

On a separate sheet was a list of the men reputed to have been Madame de Cléry's lovers. It seemed to contain the name of everyone rich or fashionable in Paris before the Revolution. Yet Roch's eye was caught by one name in particular: that of Albert-Firmin Coudert, banker, who was reported to have kept the Cléry woman from 1778 to 1780. 1780! Roch clenched his fists. 1780 was the year of Blanche's birth. All was clear now. Not only was Coudert old enough to be Blanche's father, he *was* her father.

There might have existed a separate file on Coudert, maybe yet another one on Blanche herself, but Roch felt no desire to peruse either. He had read enough.

Roch's first impulse was to find Coudert and beat him to a pulp. Then, when his heartbeat slowed a bit, he realized that he needed to speak to Blanche first. Not to confirm his guess, because he did not doubt its correctness for a moment, but to hear the truth, painful as it was, from her lips.

32

Roch set forth for Blanche's mansion on Rue de Babylone. He had not returned there since the day of the musical party, when Blanche had slipped him the note summoning him to their first assignation. What a fool he had been then, and since. He remembered the ease with which Blanche had seduced him. After a chance meeting at her mother's gaming salon, after an exchange of only a few words, she had invited him to share her bed, as though it were the most natural thing in the world.

At the Coudert mansion a footman in a powdered wig and red and gold livery answered the bell. Before the man had time to open his mouth, Roch said, "I need to see your mistress."

"I am afraid Madame is not home, Sir."

Roch pushed his Prefecture card in the man's face. "Police. She'll be at home for me."

The footman stammered before recovering his disdainful composure. He let Roch in and opened the door to a salon on the ground floor. "Very well, Sir. Please wait here while I go announce you."

"I won't wait, and let's dispense with all of this buffoonery. Take me to Madame Coudert directly."

The footman seemed frozen, his eyes and mouth wide open.

"Faster, if you please," said Roch, "or I'll have to arrest you."

The lackey, without a word, led Roch up the grand staircase and down a corridor before stopping in front of a door. Roch shoved him aside before he had time to knock. He stepped into a vast bedroom, hung in pale pink silks. In the far corner, facing a window, Blanche was seated at a mahogany dressing table supported by life-size swans of gilded bronze. Her maid was adjusting white egret feathers in her hair. She turned around and stared as Roch approached.

"So, Blanche, my love," he said, "is there anything at all you have forgotten to tell me?"

She turned crimson, from the roots of her black hair to the embroidery that decorated the bodice of her white dress. Her eyes darted wildly from the maid to the footman. She motioned to both to leave. Roch slammed the door shut behind them, pushed the lock and returned to post himself in front of Blanche.

Her eyes, flashing with anger, or maybe fear, were fixed on his. "How dare you come here uninvited? Speak to me in this manner in front of the servants? What if they tell my husband?"

He hit his forehead with the palm of his hand. "Ah yes, your husband! Silly me, I was forgetting about that fellow."

"I don't understand what you want."

"I want the truth, Blanche."

"What truth? Of what are you talking?"

"*What truth?*" he repeated between his clenched teeth. "Is Coudert your father?"

She swallowed large gulps of air.

"Is he?"

"Yes," she whispered, her eyes closed.

"Little whore. Liar."

Now her eyes were wide open, defiant. "I didn't lie. You never asked."

"*Never asked?* Is that a question one is supposed to ask? But I did ask why you married Coudert, didn't I? Wasn't that enough of an invitation to tell me the truth? Instead all I got was that ridiculous tale about no one else wanting to marry you."

Her face was firm, but the silky egret feathers in her hair were quivering, as if agitated by an emotion of their own.

"Come, Blanche, tell me the truth at last," he continued in a calmer tone. "You knew that Coudert was your father when you married him, didn't you? Have you no decency? No shame?"

"I am not one of your suspects, Roch, someone you can bully at your pleasure. If you want the truth, I will tell you, but you must listen to me." She took a deep breath, staring straight ahead. "Yes, Monsieur Coudert is my father. And I have always known it, since I was a little girl. But he is not my husband."

Roch swore. "Do you take me for an imbecile?"

"We only wed in a civil ceremony. This doesn't make us husband and wife before God. And he never touched me."

"So why would he have married you?"

"He married me out of kindness."

"Out of kindness? Are you mocking me?"

"Please listen to me. He never touched me. He only married me to help me. You don't know, Roch, how things are at Mama's gaming salon. Many of the patrons court her, and some began courting me as well. This is how I met the Count de Rivoyre, Armand. I was fifteen. He was young, handsome, dashing. I fell in love with him. He convinced me to wed him secretly, without telling Mama—"

Roch glowered at Blanche. "What? You were married before?"

"You wanted the truth, Roch. I pretended to go stay in the country with a friend, a former schoolmate, while in fact I joined Armand at his Paris lodgings. We were married secretly by a Franciscan Friar, and we spent a week together, the happiest of my life. Then he had to leave for England. He promised to claim me as his bride as soon as he returned to Paris."

Blanche caught her breath. "In the meantime Mama had called at my friend's country house, and discovered my absence. She was furious, of course. When I came home at the end of my week with Armand, I had to tell her the truth. She said no one would ever be able to find the monk who had celebrated my marriage, that Armand would probably deny it, that he had disgraced me."

Roch sneered. "Let me risk a guess: the scoundrel had bedded her as well. So you stole your mother's lover?"

"I was truly, passionately in love with Armand. I believed him when he said he would come back to me and acknowledge our marriage. I still believe that he would have done so. But he was captured a few months later, during the Bay of Quiberon invasion. He was part of the army of French émigrés the British fleet brought to the shores of Brittany to join the Chouans. He was captured, court-martialed and shot for treason, along with hundreds of others."

"You and your mother must have been heartbroken."

"I was. Then I discovered that Armand had left behind in Paris all of the letters I had written him. One of his former mistresses, who still had a key to his lodgings, found them when she went through his papers after his death. Out of spite, she showed them to other people. Soon they began to circulate in society. Mama had been right on one point: there was no way of proving my marriage. The Franciscan Friar, an unsworn priest, had disappeared, and both of our witnesses had been shot at Quiberon with Armand. My reputation was ruined. It was terrible to mourn my husband, to miss him as I did, and to know at the same time that people were laughing at my sorrow. Mama was always trying to convince some man or other to marry me, but no one would have me, no matter how much money she offered for my dowry. I didn't care anyway, because I didn't want to marry any of them either. Mama and I had terrible arguments about that all the time."

Tears were gathering in Blanche's eyes. "Then one day, when I was eighteen, Monsieur Coudert took me, without Mama, for a ride to the Champs-Elysées in his carriage. It was a beautiful October day, the trees were all golden in the sun. He asked whether I was happy like that, living with Mama. I told him that no, I wasn't happy at all. Then he proposed. He said that he would never touch me, of course, that he would try his best to make me happy. I agreed right away. But Mama was very angry when she heard of it."

"I wonder why! She finally displayed some common sense." Roch frowned. "You told me the general outline of this story last time. You only omitted a few minor details, such as your supposed marriage to that Rivoyre fellow, and Coudert being your father. He was only a *longtime friend* of your mother's then. But I am sorry, I interrupted your narrative. Please proceed."

Blanche opened a reticule lying on the dressing table. She pulled a tiny lace handkerchief and blew her nose.

"At first Mama was adamant in her refusal," she continued, "but Monsieur Coudert insisted. He promised to leave me everything upon his death, and he is very rich. He said that it would be far easier for me to inherit his fortune if I we were married. He couldn't acknowledge me as his daughter because Mama was married to Monsieur de Cléry when I was born. So she finally relented. She said I was making a grave mistake, that I was still a child, that I would regret it later. But I guess she was tired of fighting with me all the time. So Monsieur Coudert took me away from her. He gave me everything I wished for, most of all my freedom. I reconciled with Mama very soon afterwards."

"You never saw anything wrong with marrying that man?"

"I didn't care at the time. After Armand's death, I thought I would never love again. I only wanted to leave Mama, have my own house, my own life, to see the friends I liked, to be at liberty of doing the things I thought right. And in the two years we have been married, Monsieur Coudert has never breached his promises. He has mistresses, and he never tried to touch me."

Tears were welling up in her eyes. "It is only when I met you that I realized Mama had been right. I began to regret what I had done. I didn't want to see you only in a place like the Five Diamonds, only for a few stolen hours. I wanted you to take me to the countryside, I wanted to walk on your arm in public places. I wanted some happiness at last. I even thought sometimes of asking Monsieur Coudert for a divorce, but I never had the courage."

Roch sneered. "Hence the ring."

"Yes. It would have made me feel as though you wanted to marry me." She raised her eyes to him. "So you understand now? You believe me?"

"Yes, I think I understand. And I may be enough of a fool to believe you. But you deceived me about so many things, Blanche. At this time I can't bear it. Yours is a sad story, and I feel sorry for you. But you lied to me when I was begging for the truth. Can you imagine what *trust* means to me at this moment? How can I ever trust you again? I don't even know who you are now. Every time I would look into your eyes I would wonder what else you could be hiding."

"So you don't want me anymore?"

"It breaks my heart to give you up, but no, I don't want you anymore."

Silent tears were rolling down her cheeks. This was too painful. He turned around and softly closed the door behind him.

He crossed the river over the Pont-au-Change, the Bridge of the Money Changers, to reach the Prefecture. As a gust of wind lifted the tails of his coat, he felt in his pocket the jewelry case containing the ring. He stopped in his tracks and pulled the circle of gold out of its box. It was perfect, round, free of any scratch or blemish. Roch gazed at it intently as he held it between his thumb and forefinger. He leaned over the parapet and dropped ring and case into the river. They were swallowed by the waves in an instant and disappeared without a ripple.

33

*F*or the rest of the day Roch immersed himself in his work in an attempt to chase away the thought of Blanche. There were ever more witnesses to interview, none with anything of interest to say, ever more clues to follow, all leading to nothing. At least he was busy, and that was his sole comfort now. It was past ten when he reluctantly closed the door to his office that night. As he was leaving the Prefecture, a slim figure appeared from the wisps of fog that rose from the river.

"Ah, here you are, Citizen Chief Inspector," chirped a familiar voice. "I thought I'd freeze to death waitin' for you. It's mighty cold 'round here."

"Pépin! Why didn't you ask the guards to take you to my office?"

"No offense, Citizen Chief Inspector, but I'm not sure it's safe to be seen too much with you, if you catch my meanin'..."

"So you must have a good reason to wait for me out here."

"I'll say. You owe me some silver this time."

"Silver? What for?"

"It's about the Mayenne Inn, Sir. You'll want to hear my story."

Roch sighed. He doubted that there was much to learn, but any news was better than no news. He pulled a coin from his waistcoat pocket and held it in front of Pépin's face. The boy grinned.

"Well, Citizen Chief Inspector, I was abeggin' in front of the Mayenne Inn. Nothin' wrong with earnin' a *sol* or two more'n what you'll give me, eh? An' it made me look like I was doing somethin' beside watchin' the place. Like I told you, usually there's almos' nobody comin' in and out. But then some big sack o' lard opens the door. An' what d'you think he does?"

"He grabs you by the scruff of the neck and skins your scabby ass for begging in front of his door?"

"No, Sir. I'd be too fast for him. He looks right an' left, then he beckons to me: *D'you want to earn three* sols, *boy?* he says. *Yes, Sir,* I say, *I'd do 'most anythin' for three* sols. So he says, *You take this to Catherine Vallon, Rue du Faubourg Saint-Martin, above the Biré grocery, in front of Saint-Martin Church.*"

Roch held his breath. "And did you go to that Catherine Vallon?"

"Oh, yes. An' is she ugly! A reg'lar witch, with her bones poking out of her skin, an' a big red nose, an' a screechy voice too, like a cat in season."

"And what did you take to her?"

"Oh, jus' a letter, an' not a thick one. I'd tell you more, but I can't read."

The boy reached for the coin, but Roch closed his hand. "When did you say that happened?"

Pépin scratched his hair under his cap. "I'm not too sure, really."

Roch dropped the coin. Pépin crouched to pick it up. Before the boy had time to reach it, Roch seized him by the ear and slowly raised him to his feet. "Now think well, Pépin. When did that happen?"

The boy winced. "Could've been a week ago, maybe."

Roch threw Pépin against the wall of the Prefecture and pinned him there by the shoulder. "A week ago? Little bastard! Do you know what a week's delay means to me?"

The boy let out a yelp. "Please, Sir, it's not my fault. They said your father'd been arrested, an' I couldn't keep on dealin' with you."

Roch pushed harder on Pépin's shoulder. "*They?* Who said that?"

"Chief Bertrand, Sir, the big ugly one. I came here to tell you right away, jus' after I took the letter to that witch Vallon, but you weren't in your office. So Chief Bertrand saw me. He said they'd get rid of you at the Prefecture, and he'd arrest me if he ever saw me tryin' to talk to you again. But I saw you're still workin' here, so I reckoned it was safe enough to wait for you, after dark."

Roch's anger was now taking another direction. He relaxed his grip somewhat. "Have I your attention, Pépin?"

The boy took a deep breath. "Oh, yes, Sir."

"So listen to me. By waiting a week, you allowed several murderers to escape. Now see this?" Roch, still holding Pépin with one hand, pulled his father's knife from his pocket and flicked it open. "I may be less heavy than Chief Bertrand, but I can be far more dangerous. Don't ever fail me again."

Roch pressed the flat of the knife against Pépin's cheek. "Do you understand?"

Pépin whimpered. "Yes, Sir. Please don't kill me. I'll be sure to tell you right away ness' time I hear anythin'. I promise."

Roch let go of Pépin, who, rubbing his ear, hurried to pick up the coin and blend again into the shadows. Roch reentered the Prefecture and ran to Dubois's office. His visit to the Mayenne Inn had in fact caused as much of a stir as he had hoped. Gillard, the owner, had been shaken enough to warn Francis of the danger, and he had sent a message to that Vallon woman. She must be the sister the short man had mentioned to Lambel, the grain merchant.

If only the Prefect had let Roch keep his Inspectors there, they would have followed Pépin to the Vallon woman's lodgings, and Short Francis might be in custody already. But what else could one expect from that scoundrel Dubois? And what about Bertrand? Had he prevented Pépin from speaking to Roch out of personal malice, or was he too deliberately protecting the assassins?

Roch had not met the Prefect since his visit to his father at the Temple, and glowered as he entered his superior's office. He had no choice but to share Pépin's news, though he simply explained that one of his habitual *mouchards* had reported bringing a message from the Mayenne Inn to the Vallon woman. Roch omitted any mention of Bertrand's part in delaying Pépin's information. He would settle this account himself later, without any interference from the Prefect.

If the Prefect found it an odd coincidence that one of Roch's informers happened to pass by the Mayenne Inn just in time to be entrusted with a note from Gillard, he did not remark on it. He no longer showed any overt hostility. Perhaps he was resigned to tolerate Roch for a while, now that it seemed that Fouché was to remain the Minister of Police.

The Prefect listened to Roch with great interest and marked no hesitation before issuing a warrant to search Catherine Vallon's lodgings, along with the whole building. However, he did not breathe a word of a search of the Mayenne Inn, nor did Roch press the point. The Prefect, whatever his other shortcomings, was a steadfast friend to Gillard.

34

At this time of the night, Roch would have called on his father. Old Miquel would fetch a good bottle from his personal reserve, and the two men would spend some time talking over a few glasses of wine. Instead, Roch had work to do at the Prefecture to prepare the search of Catherine Vallon's lodgings, while his father spent yet another lonely evening locked in his cell in the Temple. And Roch could only hope that nothing worse happened to Old Miquel.

For several years of his childhood, Roch had spent much time with his father, in fact had barely left his side. That was when they walked the streets of Paris in search of rabbit skins, before the days of the Mighty Barrel and Monsieur Veau's Academy.

Yet before the age of eight, Roch only saw his father in summer. Old Miquel would walk to Paris at the end of every September, leaving his wife and children in Auvergne. He did not return until the following June, with four or five gold *louis* sewn in the belt of his breeches. Then one fine summer day, Roch heard Old Miquel announce that his eldest boy was now old enough to follow him to Paris. Roch's mother burst into sobs. His sister, little Anna, stared in shock.

"Enough, woman," said Old Miquel, slapping the table. "You're going to soften the boy. You've spoiled him enough already. Now he'll be useful at last."

Roch's mother dried her tears. Roch also felt much sorrow at the prospect of leaving her, and his sister too, but his pain was mingled with the excitement of seeing the great city and his pride at the idea of helping his father.

At the end of that summer, the two of them adjusted their bundles on their backs and walked northwards for days in the direction of Paris, sleeping outdoors, by the side of hedgerows when the weather was fine, or in the stables of inns when it rained. Sometimes a driver, kinder-hearted than most, would let them climb onto the back of his cart for a league or two.

During this first journey, Roch saw other children, and also grown men, beg on their way. Old Miquel would spit at the sight. On one occasion, Roch turned around upon hearing the hooves of a galloping horse. He was captivated by the beauty of the animal, its glossy bay coat and the rider's fine leather boots. Without thinking, Roch took off his hat and extended his other hand, palm up. The horseman slowed down, took a quick look at the boy and tossed a copper coin at him before disappearing in a cloud of dust.

Roch was still staring at the coin, new and shiny against the dirt of the road, when he felt his father's large hand seizing him by his collar. Old Miquel led him, his feet barely touching the ground, into a little wood by the side of the road. Roch was covered with sweat, but he felt very cold all of a sudden. When Old Miquel let go of him a few dozen yards later, he dropped to his knees.

"I don't know why I did it, Father," he said. "Please forgive me. I'll never do it again."

"Have you ever seen me begging?"

"No, Father."

"Down with your breeches. And roll up your shirt under your armpits," ordered Old Miquel.

Roch, holding his breath, obeyed. His father's oak wood staff had many uses. It served as a walking stick during the long stretches of the journey, and as a weapon. Sometimes people would let loose their dogs after them, but the animals, after one look at the staff and the man wielding it, stopped barking and fled, their tails tucked between their legs. Old Miquel also used it on occasion to discipline his children.

Now Roch heard the staff whistle in the air and braced himself for the first stroke, but gasped when the force of the blow rippled through his body. He shut his eyes tight to hold back tears of pain and shame. This was not the first beating he had received from Old Miquel, but it was by far the longest and harshest. Roch clenched his teeth. He did not cry out, he did not even whimper. He would at least show his father that he could accept his punishment without sniveling like a coward.

"All right. Now look at me," said Old Miquel at last. He grabbed Roch by his hair and raised him to his feet. The boy opened his eyes, releasing tears that rolled down his cheeks. "If I ever see you begging again, I'll double the correction. And I'll triple it if I catch you stealing. We may be poor, but you'll work for every *sol* in your pocket, just like me and all decent people. Is this understood?"

"Yes, Father."

"Good. Now get dressed."

During the following week, Roch could not sleep on his back or sit down. With every step he took, the coarse linen of his shirt rubbed against his burning buttocks. Yet they proceeded briskly in the direction of Paris. Whenever Roch's pace slowed down on the road, Old Miquel, without stopping, applied a sharp stroke of the staff across the boy's bottom.

"Faster, you lazy beggar," he said.

The worst part of the punishment was Old Miquel's contempt. Only during their first night in Paris did he relent. He ruffled his son's hair. Roch seized Old Miquel's hand and kissed it.

"I'll never do it again, Father," he said.

He kept his word. He never begged again, nor was he ever tempted to steal.

For the following years, Roch roamed the streets of Paris by his father's side, carrying his share of the rabbit skins. Every summer, he walked back to Auvergne with Old Miquel. Then that terrible year Roch's mother died, along with his sister and brother. There was no one left of the family in the old country, and the man and the child together remained for good in Paris.

That was what Pépin was missing: the affection and guidance of a father. All the little rascal had learned on the streets was to steal, beg, snitch and, on occasion, drop his breeches for a few *sols*. His chances of turning out well were slim. Roch felt something approaching pity for the boy.

35

*H*opefully Pépin's news, tardy as it was, could still be useful. Roch ordered all of his Inspectors to report immediately to the Prefecture. He spent that evening planning the arrest of Short Francis and his sister. He could not afford to take any chances, with barely eleven days remaining before Old Miquel's deportation.

Once on Rue du Faubourg Saint-Martin, he posted two Inspectors at the back entrance of the Biré grocery, and another two at the front door, while he and half a dozen others, with twice as many National Guards, would search the entire house. It would be watched all night. Any visitors would be allowed to come in and be trapped inside.

In fact, only one man, looking around in a suspicious manner, was seen entering the building around nine in the evening. Finally, at six o'clock the next morning, long before dawn, Roch pounded on the front door to the grocery.

"Police!" he shouted.

He heard the shuffling of feet and muffled voices. Light appeared behind the closed shutters of the grocery, and an elderly woman, a candle in her hand, opened cautiously. Roch stuck his foot in the door.

"Chief Inspector Miquel. We have a warrant from the Prefect to search this entire house. Please step aside, Citizen."

The woman obeyed. She was in her chemise, wearing a nightcap. A blue knitted kerchief covered her sloping shoulders. Another woman, younger, also in her chemise, huddled behind.

"Which one of you is Citizen Biré?"

"It's me, Citizen," said the older woman. "I didn't do anything wrong."

"Are you the owner of this house?" asked Roch.

"Yes, Sir, since my husband died last year, poor man."

"We are looking for a François Carbon and a Catherine Vallon. We know they live here."

"No, Sir, they don't anymore," said the woman. "Catherine Vallon left one fine morning last week, before the sun was up."

Roch cursed under his breath. "And what about François Carbon?"

"Oh, that one! He must've left with his sister, because I haven't seen hide nor hair of him either since she disappeared."

Roch bit his lip. Once again Short Francis was ahead of the police. He must have fled upon receiving the note brought by Pépin. That week's delay had ruined everything.

The woman leaned towards Roch and lowered her voice. "In fact, he wasn't only Catherine Vallon's brother. He slept with her too."

Roch suppressed a start of disgust. "Really, Citizen?"

"And not only that, but he slept with little Madeleine as well."

"Who is little Madeleine?"

"Madeleine Vallon. That's Catherine's daughter. His niece."

"Where did Carbon and his womenfolk go?" asked Roch.

"I wish I knew, because Catherine Vallon owes me forty francs for rent. She's a nasty woman, Sir, always looking for a quarrel. But she was like ass and shirt with that other wench upstairs, Marguerite Davignon. They'd take coffee together, with that Carbon fellow, almost every day. I guess that's where my rent money went. I'm sure the Davignon woman knows where her friend Vallon went, but she won't tell me."

"Where is this Marguerite Davignon?"

"Oh, she's here all right. Third floor, left door."

Roch rushed out up the stairs, followed by two Inspectors. He knocked at the left shaky door on the third floor with his closed fist and yelled, "Police!"

The only response was a woman's shrill cries. Roch kicked the door with the sole of his boot. It flew open with a crashing noise as rusty nails were pulled out of the frame. A woman, holding a petticoat with both hands in front of her ample, naked body, was standing at the far end of the room. Skirts, breeches, a man's coat, various undergarments were strewn on the chairs, the table, the floor, as though a storm had hit the place. One could distinguish a tremulous shape in the bed. Roch pulled on the sheets and uncovered the terrified face of a man. Long, thin, red-cheeked, it did not answer to the description of any known suspect.

"Who are you?" asked Roch.

The man opened his mouth without uttering a sound.

"You are under arrest," said Roch. "Get out of bed!"

"I can't!" cried the man. "I'm naked."

Roch pulled further on the bedsheets and completely uncovered the fellow, who was lying curled in a ball on his side, his knees under his chin. Roch turned to the woman.

"Who is this?"

"I . . . I don't know," she said.

"Oh, you don't? And who are you?"

"Marguerite Léger, married name Davignon."

"So you are married?"

"Yes, Sir."

"And where is your husband?"

"He's not in Paris. He drives the stagecoach to Rennes."

Roch felt sorry for the man. It was not easy work, being out in all weathers. It was dangerous too, especially driving to Rennes, in the West. Any wood along lonely country roads could hide a band of Chouans armed to the teeth. Roch, given his personal situation, was not inclined to cast the first stone at an adulteress, but he could not help disliking the Davignon woman.

"So while your husband earns a living freezing his ass on the seat of his stagecoach," he said, "you keep his bed warm with your lover?"

"But Deniau doesn't usually stay the night!" replied the woman in an indignant tone. "He always leaves around eleven, but last night he'd forgotten his papers. I told him that he'd be arrested by a patrol, that he'd better stay till dawn. If I'd known . . ." She frowned, as if struck by a sudden idea. "My husband won't learn of this, will he?"

"So you say this man is called Deniau, but he has no papers? About you? You have your papers?"

The woman, still holding her petticoat in front of her with one arm, opened the drawer of the nightstand with her free hand. She handed Roch her *Carte de Sûreté*. He perused it.

"At least you haven't lied about your name," he said. "And where is Catherine Vallon?"

"I don't know her."

"She is your best friend. Where did she move?"

"She . . . she didn't say."

"And what of that brother of hers, François Carbon? Where is he?"

Citizen Davignon shook her head vehemently. "I don't know, Sir."

Deniau was howling as two Inspectors pulled him from the bed. Roch squatted to pick up a pair of breeches from the floor and threw them at him.

"You, be quiet," he ordered. He turned back to Citizen Davignon. "You are under arrest too."

She stared at Roch. "But I didn't do anything wrong. And I have my papers!"

"You are giving shelter to a man who hasn't any. And you are lying to a police officer. Now will you please dress and follow us?"

The woman did not budge.

"Fine," said Roch. "We will take you to the Prefecture naked then. But we will need to wrap you in a blanket for the sake of decency."

"No!" she wailed. "Wait, I'll dress."

"Then make haste."

Inspector Bachelot was gaping at the woman's half-exposed thighs and breasts. Roch shoved him to make him turn around. Behind them, Citizen Davignon made little unhappy noises, half hiccups, half sniffles, as she dressed.

At the Prefecture, Roch led Citizen Davignon to the coop, the vast cage holding the prostitutes arrested during the night. It was quite full at this time of the morning, for the whores had yet to be taken for arraignment to the Police Court. Marguerite Davignon, like any new arrival, was greeted by much cheering as a guard unlocked the gate and pushed her inside.

"Look, girls, this beauty's dressed like an honest woman!" cried one of the harlots. "What's she here for, my love?" she shouted to Roch as he was leaving for his office upstairs.

"Whoring," he shouted back without turning around. The cheers turned into hoots. The harlots did not like unfair competition.

Roch questioned first the fellow arrested with Citizen Davignon. He was so shaken that he had some trouble stuttering his name and occupation, René Deniau, poultry merchant. No, he did not live in the Biré house. He only went there to keep his good friend Marguerite Davignon company whenever her husband happened to be away. No, he had never seen or heard of anyone named Catherine Vallon or François Carbon. His business was only with Marguerite. He always tried his best to avoid her neighbors and their prying eyes.

The man seemed to be telling the truth, but he would stay in custody until his story was verified. Roch could not think of a more dismal conclusion to a night of passion than an early-morning arrest. That might be the end of that romance.

Roch pulled his watch. Eight o'clock already. Hopefully the Davignon woman had simmered long enough in the coop. In any case, time was of the essence.

When she appeared, escorted by two National Guards, he noticed that she limped. She seemed to have lost one of her shoes. The cap and kerchief she had worn upon her arrival were missing, and her cheeks were covered with brown smears. Roch, after a glance at her disheveled state, seized a quill and a sheet of paper. He pointed to a chair, in which she sat gingerly. He began writing the usual opening phrases of her statement.

"Well, Citizen Chief Inspector," she simpered, "you're a young man, I must say a very handsome young man, and . . ."

He raised his eyes. Citizen Davignon had gathered herself and mustered what was probably meant as a seductive smile. He put down his quill and looked straight at her.

"And what?" he asked coldly.

She bit her lip and remained silent.

"I am afraid, Citizen Davignon, you fail to appreciate the gravity of your situation," he continued. "Let me explain. You made a mistake by refusing to answer my questions truthfully earlier. You forced me to arrest you. This man you are protecting, this Carbon, is wanted for the Rue Nicaise attack, and his sister is also wanted as an accomplice. You are obstructing the course of justice in a case of the utmost gravity. You will find yourself among the accused, with your friends. If you are lucky, you might escape the guillotine, but you will be sentenced to many years in jail. You will only come out as an old woman, and one does not age well in prison."

Citizen Davignon burst into loud sobs that made the flesh of her breasts quiver like jelly. Roch now hated her. That brainless, spineless, soulless slut knew of Carbon's whereabouts, she held the key to Old Miquel's freedom, and yet she refused to speak, out of sheer stupidity, or, heaven forbid, because she fancied Short Francis. Roch felt the urge to slap her, but he clenched his fists under his desk and waited for the outburst to subside. When he thought she was quieting, he asked, "Are you done now?"

She nodded.

"Good," he said. "Let us start then. Do you know François Carbon?" continued Roch.

"Yes, Sir."

"And of course you knew that he is wanted in connection with the Rue Nicaise attack?"

"No, Sir, I didn't."

"You did not see his description posted on the streets, with the reward of 2,000 *louis*? Can you read?"

"Yes, Sir, I can, I saw that, but I didn't think it was him. Francis wasn't the kind of man who'd do a thing like that."

"How long have you known him?"

"Since last summer."

"Where is he now?"

"I don't know, Sir."

"About his sister, Catherine Vallon? How long have you known her?"

"About five years."

"So you must know the address of such an old friend."

Marguerite Davignon took a deep breath. "She lives on Rue Martin, in front of Saint-Nicolas Church. Number 310, between the wigmaker and the café. On the sixth floor, in front. A house with an iron gate."

Roch pushed away the Davignon woman's statement and hastily wrote a note. He rose and shouted to a guard to bring it immediately to the Prefect. He returned to his seat and looked into Citizen Davignon's eyes.

"What about Short Francis? Does he live there with his sister?"

"No, Sir, I don't think so. I don't know where he went. I swear, Sir."

"When was the last time you saw him?"

"On the 28th of December, in the morning. That would have been the 7th of Nivose. I saw him at his sister's, Sir. Just before she moved. She made coffee, and we had a little chat. Francis was nice and friendly, as always."

"You said you met Carbon last summer, Citizen, is that right?" asked Roch in a softer tone.

"Yes. He was a bit raggedy then, but he's been far better dressed of late. He wears his hair powdered now, and nice starched shirts. And silk stockings, with stripes lengthwise. And he snuffs tobacco, from a pretty snuff box, with the picture of a horseman on it. He has a silver watch too. He looks quite the gentleman."

So the woman liked Carbon. Indeed, all tastes were found in nature.

"It apparently was common knowledge," said Roch, "that Carbon slept with his sister, and with his niece Madeleine."

Citizen Davignon hesitated. "Well, I'm not one for meddling with what's none of my business. Francis is fond of a joke, and you never know what nasty people'll make out of that. Sometimes he'd have Catherine and her girl Madeleine sit in his lap and pinch them.

Or he'd raise their skirts to slap their bottoms. Playfully, mind you. That's all there was to it."

"He did that in front of you?"

"Oh, yes, he'd wink at me, and I'd wink back. It was all done in good cheer. Catherine liked it too, I could tell. It's only that Madeleine girl that kept a sour look on her face. She doesn't promise much, that one."

"I see. When did you last see Catherine?"

"Three days ago, at her new lodgings. Francis wasn't there. She said he wasn't living with her anymore."

"Where did she say he lives now?"

"She wouldn't tell. She said she didn't like my questions about Francis. She looked like she'd had a bit too much to drink, and it wasn't coffee, if you get my meaning. She got angrier and angrier, and finally she accused me of sleeping with him. She said she'd tell my husband when he came back from Rennes, and he'd give me a good whipping. She even said I was nothing but a dirty trollop."

"Imagine that! So you slept with Francis?"

Citizen Davignon put her hand to her heaving breast. "Me, Sir? No, never!"

Roch found her show of indignation a bit excessive, but he smiled amicably.

"I understand how it all happened, Citizen Davignon. Your husband is away most of the time, and you are fond of company. You felt lonesome. You met Carbon, a dashing, well-spoken man. Who could blame you if you took a liking to him?"

The Davignon woman shook her head vigorously in denial. Roch gazed at her for a moment. He was sure that she was hiding something, maybe something of such crucial importance as Short Francis's whereabouts, but there was nothing more to be had from her now. Not until she had spent some more time in the coop. He finished writing her statement and pushed it towards her.

The woman signed the sheet of paper and raised her eyes to Roch with a hopeful look. "So I am free to go now, Citizen Chief Inspector?"

"Are you joking? You are still not telling the truth."

"But I gave you Catherine's address, Sir!"

"There's much more you haven't told me."

Her lower lip quivered. She began to whimper again. "There, there, Citizen," he said, "do not make yourself unhappy. You are going to stay with us, right here at the Prefecture, until you decide to tell me all you know. The coop should be empty soon, and you will have the place to yourself. Until tonight, that is. In the meantime, do not hesitate to call the guard should you remember anything."

Citizen Davignon, in tears, was led out of Roch's office.

36

The Prefect must have reached the conclusion that it behooved him at this point to display some zeal. He acted promptly on the note Roch had sent him during Marguerite Davignon's questioning. While the woman was signing her statement on Roch's desk, Catherine Vallon and her daughter Madeleine were arrested at their new lodgings.

Roch, once he was done with Citizen Davignon's questioning, stopped to talk to Piis in the corridor. A search of Catherine Vallon's lodgings had yielded men's clothes, including three blue jackets, in addition to a barrel of gunpowder, ingots of lead and bullet molds.

Roch whistled. "Quite a catch!"

"The experts are analyzing the powder to determine its provenance. I would be much surprised it were not of English manufacture."

"And Carbon?" asked Roch.

"No trace of him there, apart from the clothes."

Roch hit the palm of his hand with his closed fist. The scoundrel was again ahead of the police, and time was running out for Old Miquel.

"The Prefect himself will question Catherine Vallon," continued Piis. Roch stared at his colleague in disbelief.

"Dubois?" asked Roch. "*He*, question anyone? His mother would not tell him the time of day if he asked."

"Maybe not," said Piis. "But in a case like this one, he wants to take credit for the arrest of the culprits. The questioning should begin anytime now."

Soon Roch and Piis were standing against the peepholes looking into the room where important witnesses were questioned. The holes were hidden in the flowery pattern of the dingy wallpaper on the other side. Grates let them hear whatever was said in the other room. Such a system allowed several policemen to follow the proceedings without the knowledge of the suspect.

"By the way," whispered Piis, "I must really thank you. I reread *The Golden Ass* after our conversation. You were quite right about the name *Photis*, so I replaced it with *Iris*. Listen—"

Piis's hand was already reaching for his pocket. Roch put his forefinger to his lips. Through the peephole, he had just seen a woman enter the room, flanked by two National Guards. Indeed, Pépin's description of Catherine Vallon had been accurate, and she resembled the traditional image of a witch. The Prefect entered in turn. He pulled a handkerchief, dusted a chair and sat at a table in the middle of the room. Catherine Vallon reluctantly followed suit and cast a malevolent look at him.

Dubois cleared his throat. "Please state your name," he ordered.

"Again? I've already told those other fellows."

An auspicious beginning, thought Roch.

"Then state it again."

"I guess you've nothin' better to do'n harass a poor 'armless woman." She hissed, "Catherine Carbon, married name Vallon."

"What of all those clothes found in your lodgings?"

"You want me and my daughter to go naked?"

"I mean the men's clothes, those blue jackets in particular."

The woman shrugged. "Then you should've said the men's clothes. How'm I supposed to guess what you're talking about?"

"So what about those blue jackets?"

"They're my husband's."

"Where is your husband?"

"Dunno. He's a good-for-nothin' rascal that runs away chasing after whores all the time."

"And that barrel of gunpowder found at your lodgings?"

"I reckoned those were lentils in that barrel. Never looked inside."

"Who brought it to you?"

"Dunno. S'been a long time."

"Did your brother, Francis Carbon, bring the barrel to your place?"

"I don't remember, like I told you already."

"François Carbon is your bother, isn't he?"

"Course." The woman pursed her lips and looked at the Prefect as though she had never faced such stupidity before. "I was Catherine Carbon 'fore I married that piece of filth Vallon. So François Carbon'd be my brother, wouldn't he? That's not too hard to understand, maybe?"

"When was the last time you saw your brother, François Carbon?"

The woman seemed absorbed in the contemplation of her hands. "S'been a long time. Can't remember, really. Two months, maybe." She picked some dirt from under her fingernails. "Dunno where he's either, in case you'd be thinking of asking."

Roch was furious. Any imbecile would have known that this was not how a recalcitrant suspect should be questioned. Two policemen, taking turns, were needed. That was when Bertrand's grotesque appearance could be useful. His clubfoot, his dead eye, his gigantic frame instilled terror in the steadiest of minds. He ranted, raved, threatened, drew himself to his full height, frightened the suspect out of his or her wits. If no information was forthcoming after an hour or so, he left the room. Then another policeman, soft-spoken, friendly, someone like Piis or Roch, for instance, entered the room, offered comfort, even apologies for his colleague's manners. By then the suspect was usually ready to reveal anything.

The Vallon woman must know of her brother's whereabouts. Yet now, thanks to Dubois's skill as an interrogator, she would never speak. But then all was not lost. There remained young Madeleine.

Roch waited for the end of the Vallon woman's questioning, which failed to yield any information, and asked the Prefect's permission to interview Madeleine Vallon. Dubois, mopping his forehead with his handkerchief, granted it with a relieved look.

Roch took Madeleine to his office. She might be more at ease there than in the cavernous peephole room. She was a tall, slender girl with a sad face, though not devoid of charm. There was none of her mother's venomous air about her.

"Good afternoon, Madeleine. I am Chief Inspector Miquel."

The girl muttered in response.

"I know that you would rather not be here, Madeleine, but we are investigating a horrible crime. Many people died. We need to discover who did it." Roch looked into the girl's eyes. "I will ask many questions, and you may not know the answers to all. That is perfectly all right. You simply need to tell me that you don't know. Also, if I say something that is mistaken, you should tell me too."

"And then what'll happen?"

"I will prepare a paper that will state what you told me, and I will read it to you, and then ask you to sign it. I am sure an intelligent girl like you can sign her name."

"Yes, Sir, I can. I can even read a bit too," said Madeleine with the first hint of a smile he had yet seen on her face.

"That is what I would have thought. Now what can you tell me about your uncle, François Carbon?"

The smile left Madeleine's face. She stared at Roch with frightened eyes. "Nothing," she said. "I don't know where he is."

"He's not always kind to you, is he?" asked Roch.

The girl's lips began to tremble.

"I believe," Roch continued, "that he did to you things that shouldn't be done between an uncle and his niece."

The girl twisted her hands. Her nails were bitten to the bone. Her voice caught on her words. "If I tell you, it'll be all written down, and everyone'll know of it."

"Yes, it will be written down, but no one outside the police needs to know about it. There is no reason for any of it to be mentioned at trial. The judges are reasonable men. They will understand that it's a private matter, between you and your uncle, and that it does not concern the crime."

"And I won't go to jail?"

"We have to keep you for some time, because you are an important witness, not because you did anything wrong. Also, we want to make sure that no one hurts you or bothers you."

"And you won't make fun of me?"

"No. I don't see anything funny about this."

Madeleine swallowed hard. "Well, my uncle came to stay with us when he arrived in Paris last summer, and in the beginning he always slept with Mama. Then one night, he slipped into my bed while I was asleep. I cried out. But Mama scolded me. She said she'd throw me out if I didn't let him do what he liked. After that, sometimes he just slept with Mama, and he left me alone. But sometimes he slept with me, or I had to sleep with them in Mama's bed. Oh, I hated it. I could never tell in advance what he'd want to do." She was interrupted by a sob. "I'm ruined now."

"You are not ruined. What he did was wrong, completely wrong, but it was not your fault. You look to me like a fine girl."

"But I'm not! Who's going to marry me now?"

"Some men don't care about this kind of thing, Madeleine. I, for one, don't."

"You don't?"

"No, I don't. I have no intention to marry at this time, but if I did, all I would worry about would be to find a girl who would make a good wife. A pleasant, honest girl, a girl I could trust." He suddenly thought of Blanche and paused until the pang subsided. "What else can you tell me about your uncle? When was the last time you saw him?"

"Two days ago, at the Convent of Saint-Michel, on Rue Notre-Dame-des-Champs. He has a room upstairs. Mama sent me there to bring him clean shirts. Oh, I didn't want to go. I knew what he'd do, but I had no choice."

Roch leaned back in his chair. He could have kissed Madeleine on both cheeks. Short Francis was still at the convent two days ago. The track was fresh.

37

So François Carbon had found a refuge in a nunnery, of all places. Hours before dawn on the 17th of January, the police discreetly surrounded the Convent of the Sisters of Saint-Michel. The Prefect had authorized the use of a full detachment of the National Guard, along with all twenty-four Police Inspectors. Roch had studied at length the plans of the house, which had been filed with the city of Paris at the time of the construction, ten years before the Revolution. The Convent consisted of four buildings forming a square and enclosing a courtyard, at the far end of which was a chapel. The front door opened onto Rue Notre-Dame-des-Champs, Our Lady in the Fields, a genteel, peaceful street, and there were no other entrances.

Dawn was casting a pale shadow in the eastern sky when Roch and the Police Commissioner for the district had ladders laid against the outside walls of the convent. Dozens of men climbed onto the roofs, moved the ladders up and then down to the other side.

Roch himself had already stepped down into the courtyard, whence he was surveying the operations. In a few moments he would be in control of the place. The only laggard among his men was Inspector Bachelot, a tall awkward fellow, heavy in the face and around the waist. Bachelot, puffing, caught his foot in the last rung as he stepped down the ladder. It fell to the ground with a resounding crash, while the man tripped with a cry.

Roch swore. He heard the sound of hands clapping four times, then a pause, and another four claps. This had to be a signal. The nuns had already detected their presence, and were alerting Francis to the arrival of the police. No need to worry about secrecy now. Roch shouted to his men to search all of the buildings and ran towards what he assumed to be the porter's lodge, just inside the carriage door. A man in a coarse reddish jacket appeared.

"Police!" said Roch. "Why did you clap your hands?"

The man stared stupidly without answering.

"What is the meaning of this?" asked a stern female voice behind him.

Roch turned around and saw a middle-aged woman in a white wimple and black habit. She was breathing fast, her hand on her breast. Only then did Roch realize his mistake. Of course he should have remembered that nuns went to bed early and awoke before dawn for the first morning Mass. The entire Convent, including Francis, must be up already. The place should have been secured hours earlier.

"Everyone in this house is under arrest, Citizen," said Roch. "What is your name?"

Her chin held high, the nun folded her hands inside the sleeves of her habit. "I am Reverend Mother Marie of the Infant Jesus, Prioress of this community."

Roch, still furious at his own mistake, had no intention of letting this woman put on airs. He looked straight at her. "I asked for your *name*, Citizen."

A certain trembling behind the firmness of her voice betrayed her nervousness. "Marie-Anne Duquesne. You interrupted the divine service on the Lord's Day. With good reason, Sir, I hope."

"I can't think of a better one. You are giving shelter to one of the Rue Nicaise assassins."

Mother Duquesne's lips turned pale. "I have nothing to do with that terrible misfortune."

"A misfortune! In police jargon, Citizen Duquesne, we call it murder. Take me to your apartment."

Mother Duquesne led Roch through the courtyard, where National Guards were herding a dozen nuns and twice as many schoolgirls in black uniforms. Their excited chatter ceased abruptly at the sight Mother Duquesne, escorted by Roch.

Her apartment was on the second story of the back building. Policemen were already busy there, emptying drawers, moving furniture away from the walls, gathering letters and papers into bundles, pulling the sheets off the bed. Mother Duquesne gasped when two National Guards ripped open her pillows with the points of their bayonets, filling the air with a shower of feathers.

Inspector Bertier burst into the apartment. "We found his room, Citizen Chief Inspector!" he cried. "Empty, but the bed's still warm."

Roch abandoned Mother Duquesne to his subordinates. He ran with Bertier across the courtyard and climbed one flight of stairs to a little room overlooking the street. Roch touched with the tips of his fingers the unmade bed. It was indeed warm. Obviously Francis had not been attending the service in the chapel. He looked out the window. It was too high for Carbon to have jumped out without breaking a limb, and the street below was teeming with National Guards. The short man was still hiding somewhere in the Convent.

"Have you searched the rest of the floor?" Roch asked Bertier.

"No, but a man named Buchet next door, a boarder, told me of an attic above. He thinks Carbon may be hiding there."

An elderly man, slightly stooped, a cunning smile on his lips, was standing in the doorway, watching the policemen.

"Are you Citizen Buchet?" asked Roch.

"Yes," said the old man. "And I have the key to the attic in my pocket. This way you won't have to force the door open. I'm always one for sparing the gentlemen of the police any trouble. If you'll follow me . . ."

Roch pursed his lips. The man's zeal was suspicious in light of the sympathies of the house. He told Inspector Bertier to accompany the man to the attic. Roch remained behind and gestured to a National Guard to follow him into the apartment of the obliging boarder.

He pushed the door open carefully. Inside sat a man, his feet to the fire, quietly warming himself. He was as Roch had pictured him: squat, flat-faced, with deep-set blue eyes and a large scar that pulled on the lid of his left eye. The only unexpected trait was the beard, unshaven for a few weeks. Its hair was tan, with darker spots, like a wild beast's fur. Roch and the National Guard rushed to wrestle him to the ground. He did not try to run, nor did he offer any resistance.

Roch, as he bound the prisoner's hands tightly behind his back, felt such satisfaction as he had never known in his entire career. It was more than pride, more than the hunter's triumph. There was hope too. Now that Carbon was under arrest, the scoundrel would lead the police to Saint-Régent, and Old Miquel would be free at last.

38

Carbon, his hands bounds, was escorted out of the Convent between two Inspectors. Roch followed at a few paces' distance. Just as he was passing the front door and stepping onto the street, Roch saw from the corner of his eye something black running away very fast in the gray light of dawn.

He cursed and, abandoning the prisoner to the care of the Inspectors, set out in pursuit of the fugitive. All he could see ahead was billows of black skirts and white petticoats. A nun, perhaps, or a man disguised as one? The fugitive had a head start of several dozen yards and was fleet-footed, but Roch was determined to catch her, or him.

The distance that separated Roch from his prey was shrinking. Now, from her long flowing hair, it was clear that the escapee was a woman, a brunette more precisely. She turned her head around to look at him, a fatal mistake, for she tripped and fell flat on her stomach. Roch landed on her back in a moment, seized her wrists with one hand and pulled another rope from his pocket.

The woman, spitting out dirt and loose strands of hair, turned her head sideways to look at him while he was tying her wrists. She was very young, probably no more than fifteen, with a round face and turned-up nose.

"Stop this, you brute!" she exclaimed. "You're hurting me."

"Your fault, I guess, for running away."

Roch pulled the girl to her feet. "And pray why were you running away?"

"Why? But this was the perfect opportunity to escape. I had asked Mama many times to put me in another school, but she wouldn't hear of it. So this morning when I heard all that ruckus and saw those men storming the Convent, I hid in a corner of the Chapel, behind the altar of Saint-Joseph, and waited until no one was looking to slip away. And I would have managed to run away, but for you!"

Roch raised his eyebrows. "Really? There's nothing more to it? Did you see that short man we arrested? Do you know him?"

The girl stamped her foot. "How many questions am I supposed to answer at the same time? And who are you anyway?"

Roch seized her firmly by the elbow and walked back in the direction of the Convent. "Chief Inspector Miquel, Prefecture of Police. If you don't mind, I will ask the questions from now on. One at a time. What is your name?"

The girl stared at Roch and smiled proudly. "Well, when Mama hears of this . . . Arrested by a Chief Inspector!"

"Who are you?"

"Pulchérie Fontaine, Chief Inspector. This is what I should call you, isn't it?"

"Citizen Chief Inspector. So what about that man we arrested?"

"He is very ugly, don't you think, Citizen Chief Inspector? Disgusting even." She cast an appraising look at him. "Not like you."

Roch let go of the girl's arm and pushed her in the back. "Let's press on, if you please. Had you seen that man before, Citizen Fontaine?"

"Yes. Three weeks ago exactly. It's easy to remember because it was a Sunday, like today. The Sunday just after Christmas." She stepped on tiptoes to reach Roch's ear and lowered her voice. "I am punished every Sunday."

Roch could not help smiling. "You, punished? Hard to believe." He remembered his own years at school. Saturday, not Sunday, had been his flogging day. But then Veau's Academy had not been a religious establishment. "So what do the nuns do to you when you are punished?"

"Nothing very pleasant, I can tell you. It's always the same. I hear Mass on my knees at the back of the Chapel. That's what I was doing today when your men burst into the Convent. Then the porter locks me in the little basement by the front door. He only gives me bread and water, and he leaves me there all day. Then, at half past eight at night, one of the sisters fetches me and takes me to the dormitory."

"That basement must not be a very nice place."

"Oh, it's horrible! Full of rats. I can hear them scurry around me and squeak in the dark, and I have nothing to do all day but look out the tiny little window."

"And that little window looks out onto the street?"

Pulchérie shook her head. "Yes, Citizen Chief Inspector, and it's fortunate, because else I would go mad. Although the street is so quiet, hardly anyone goes by. So I pay attention to anyone who does."

"And you paid attention to that ugly man?"

"Oh, yes. There's a streetlight there, so I can see well at night. He was uglier than anyone I have seen before, uglier even than that filthy old porter. There were other people with him, a lady and a gentleman."

Roch stopped in his tracks and looked into the girl's eyes. "What were they like?"

"I can't tell, because they walked to the far side of the ugly man. I only saw the gentleman's boots and the lady's skirt. And they were all walking fast. No wonder, it was raining hard."

"Why do you say a *gentleman* and a *lady*?"

"Oh, the man's boots looked like fine leather, in two colors, like fancy riding boots. And the lady . . . well, she was dressed like a lady. Her gown was ruined by the rain, but I could see the hem was embroidered, a really pretty Greek pattern." She looked down and winced at her black dress. "I wish I wore something like that, instead of this hideous uniform."

Roch resumed his walk at a slower pace. "And then what happened to those three people?"

"I couldn't see them anymore, but I heard the front door open, and then close with a clang. That's all."

"And what time was it?"

"Oh, just before Sister Caroline fetched me to take me to the dormitory. So it must have been close to half past eight." She cocked her head to the side. "Say, Citizen Chief Inspector, since I've been so helpful, do you think you could untie me?"

"For you to slip away again? Certainly not. You are too valuable a witness."

They had now reached the Convent's door. "Ah, no!" cried Pulchérie. "Don't take me back there!"

"Have no fear. You are coming with me to the Prefecture. I will have you sign your statement, and I will send word to your mama to fetch you. You can tell her all about your adventures."

39

An hour later, Citizen Fontaine *mère*, outraged at the idea of finding her daughter at the Prefecture of Police, took Pulchérie off Roch's hands. He walked to the office of Division Chief Bertrand, to whom Carbon had been delivered.

When Roch pushed the door open, he paused a moment at the sight of Short Francis, stark naked, bent over the desk. The man's stubby, hairy legs were spread wide while Bertrand, grinning from ear to ear, performed a thorough search of his person. Four of Roch's Inspectors were also there "to prevent any escape attempt," explained Bertrand. Roch, as he was watching the scene, would have been hard-pressed to tell which of the two men, his colleague or Carbon, he found more loathsome.

Roch wondered whether Bertrand had received the Prefect's authorization to proceed in this manner. It was not done unless a man was considered likely to be hiding keys, springs or similar devices on his person, or already sentenced to a term of imprisonment. But Bertrand, as Chief of the Second Division, was in charge of political crimes. So now Carbon belonged to Bertrand.

Bertrand was taking his time pawing every part of Short Francis's body. His grin became still broader whenever his victim yelped or twitched. He ordered the man to stand, to open his mouth, to lie down on the table, to kneel while his hair was inspected, and finally

to squat and cough. Each part of the search was conducted at a leisurely pace, and in a deliberate manner. Yet nothing was found.

At last Bertrand ordered Short Francis to sit on the desk, and
bound his hands behind his back. Carbon's feet could not reach the
floor and his legs dangled like those of a child. His clothes had been
piled on a chair. Inspector Bachelot examined them, one at a time,
feeling linings, emptying pockets.

The Inspector deposited on the desk a snuffbox, lined with tortoise
shell and adorned with the picture of a horseman. Roch picked up the
object and examined it. The Lambel woman, the grain merchant's
wife, had been right: it bore the legend *H.M. King George III*. This
was the snuffbox Marguerite Davignon had so admired.

Next Inspector Bachelot found, pinned inside of Carbon's shirt, a
white silk medallion. It was embroidered in gold thread with a heart
crowned by flames and a cross, and the motto *In hoc signo vincemus*.
Roch remembered enough Latin from his years at Veau's Academy to
know that it meant "By this sign we shall win." It was the image of
the Sacred-Heart-of-Jesus, which the Chouans used as a battle sign.

Chief Bertrand seized the medallion between two fingers, thick as
sausages, and shook it in front of Carbon's face. "And pray what is
this?" he asked.

"A girl gave it to me, back in Brittany."

Bertrand guffawed. "A girl!" He looked down at Carbon's genitals.
"Some wenches aren't disgusted by anything, I guess."

Inspector Bachelot hastened to proceed with his search of Carbon's
clothes. He pulled from the waistcoat pocket a gold watch, enameled
in blue and decorated with pearls. Roch frowned. Marguerite Davignon had said that Short Francis owned a silver watch. She had not
mentioned any gold, pearls or enamel, though she had been attentive
enough when it came to Carbon's finery. Had Carbon acquired this
expensive trinket after he had left his sister's place? And under what
circumstances?

Bertrand squinted at the watch. "Look at this! Is it another present
from a sweetheart of yours? This one must be mighty rich."

"Oh, no, not at all!" exclaimed Short Francis. "I bought it with my own money."

Inspector Bachelot finally opened a red leather portfolio found in a coat pocket, and pulled a folded sheet of paper. Bertrand perused it, then handed it to Roch. It was written, all in capital letters, in an awkward, obviously disguised hand.

> PLEASE KEEP VERY QUIET, DEAR FRANCIS. DO NOT GO OUT FOR ANY REASON WHATSOEVER, AND TRUST ME, AND ONLY ME. DO NOT PLACE YOUR CONFIDENCE IN ANYONE ELSE, EVEN THOSE YOU BELIEVE TO BE YOUR FRIENDS, OR MINE, BECAUSE THEY WOULD BETRAY YOU.
>
> UNFORTUNATELY, I CANNOT CALL TODAY, BUT I WILL VERY SOON, AND WILL KEEP YOUR SISTER INFORMED, SO BE SURE TO REMAIN WHERE YOU ARE. I WILL NEVER FORSAKE YOU. I LOOK FORWARD TO THE PLEASURE OF SEEING YOU AGAIN.

The search was now complete. Roch expected Bertrand to allow Short Francis to dress, and then take his statement forthwith. Instead, Bertrand shoved the man off the table and called for two National Guards to take him to a cell.

Bertrand fixed his sole good eye on Roch. "I know what you're thinking, Miquel. Oh, yes, I'd be delighted to question this scoundrel myself, and with me he'd sing in no time." Bertrand shrugged. "But, what do you know? The Prefect wants to do it. And it won't be until late this afternoon, because he says he has *other things* to do right now."

Roch did not comment. He was astonished at the delay, and dismayed to hear that the Prefect insisted on questioning yet another important suspect. Yet this was excellent news for Short Francis. Bertrand's interrogation methods were appalling. Indeed they were no better than the *question*, the torture that had been an official part of criminal investigations before the Revolution.

After the arrest of the suspects in the Conspiracy of Daggers last November, Roch had heard on several occasions howls of pain and terror coming from Bertrand's office. When confronted by Roch, Bertrand had scoffed and boasted of his favorite technique, very simple, yet efficient. He cocked the hammer of a gun and then released it on the suspect's fingers, crushing them, one bone, one joint at a time.

Roch had reported this to the Prefect, who had dismissed his concerns on the grounds that the search for information of vital importance to the safety of the Nation justified such means. Roch disagreed. Most of what could be obtained in this manner was false confessions or information that reflected what the suspect thought Bertrand wanted to hear. Roch had argued in vain that a skillful interrogator could obtain better information without disgracing himself and the entire police.

"In the meantime," continued Bertrand, "we have all those *ci-devant* nuns and that gaggle of schoolgirls from the Convent on our hands. I'll take the nuns, they can be tough." He sneered. "Do you think you can handle the schoolgirls?"

Roch shrugged at the jibe. For the first time felt some sympathy for Mother Duquesne. He was headed for his office when a guard handed him a note from the Prefect asking him to report, along with all Division Chiefs, to Piis's office. Attached were a list of more than ninety names and addresses of suspected Chouan leaders, and a copy of an order from the Minister of Police himself to arrest them all.

40

*L*imoëlan was almost running in the direction of Rue d'Aguesseau, looking up at the house numbers. For Saint-Régent had moved. One fine morning he had packed all of his things and left the Guillous' lodgings. All without warning.

But Limoëlan knew that Saint-Régent, even before the attack, had discreetly secured lodgings elsewhere. That reflected poorly on the trust the man placed in his chief, his old comrade Limoëlan. Of course Saint-Régent, since the failure of the attack, had good reason to be wary. Any day his fate could be sealed by an order from George. Yet this morning Limoëlan's purpose was purely benevolent.

Hiding Francis in the Convent of Saint-Michel, Limoëlan realized now, had been a mistake. In Mother Duquesne herself his trust was not shaken. She was no fool and must have suspected the truth, but betraying Francis would have been betraying Blanche, and she would never do that. But many other people might have talked: another nun, a pupil, a boarder. The thought of Blanche herself crossed his mind as well. The little hussy was becoming more unreliable by the day.

At last Limoëlan stopped before the soot-colored building that bore number 1336. He pushed the door open. His boot hit crumpled papers and vegetable peels as he ran up the creaky wooden steps, worn hollow in the middle, to the fourth floor. The furious yapping of a small dog answered his knock at the door. "Who's this?" asked a tremulous female voice.

"A friend of Monsieur Pierrot," said Limoëlan. "Open, please. I know he is here."

There was a pause, the noise of hurried steps, hushed voices, more barking. Limoëlan knocked again, harder. Saint-Régent, pale and sullen, opened the door himself. Limoëlan, as soon as he entered the front room, was taken aback by the rancid smell of manure. A makeshift cage of wood and wire was propped against one of the walls. There half a dozen adult rabbits, oblivious to his arrival, jumped leisurely over one another. Many more young ones lay half-hidden in the litter of straw and cabbage leaves that covered the bottom.

Standing in the room were two women, an elderly one and a pretty, freckled, red-haired girl, maybe fifteen or sixteen. Limoëlan looked with curiosity at her dress, obviously new, white with pink flowers. It seemed at odds with the brownish colors of her surroundings. The girl was holding a growling pug dog, its tiny fangs bared.

"Can we talk, Pierrot?" asked Limoëlan impatiently.

Saint-Régent, still silent, led him to a second room and closed the door behind them. A sheet hung from a clothesline in the middle, as a makeshift partition.

"You don't ask how I found you here?" said Limoëlan. "I must admit I was rather surprised when the Guillou woman told me you had left for good." He paused. "Seriously, we need to talk. I heard from Bachelot at the Prefecture. Francis was arrested this morning."

Saint-Régent cursed and stamped his foot. "I was right!" he said between his teeth. "This is your fault! I told you Francis needed to be killed. But no, you had to put us all at risk to protect him."

"Well, I waited for George's orders in your case as well, did I not? Imagine how easy it would have been to kill you right after the attack, when you were wounded. Instead I brought my uncle to hear your confession."

Saint-Régent sneered. "You thought I was dying. Why go through the trouble of killing me?"

Limoëlan shook his head in exasperation. "Enough, Saint-Régent. We need to leave right away."

Saint-Régent looked around.

"No time to pack anything," said Limoëlan. "Let's go."

The two men went back into the front room. On his way out, Saint-Régent stopped to take the pug from the girl's arms. She tried to hold on to it.

"Come, Toinette," he said. "We had an agreement, remember."

Saint-Régent seized the animal in spite of the girl's resistance and its frantic barks. Limoëlan pulled roughly on his comrade's sleeve. "What are you doing? We have to go."

At last the two men hurried down the stairs, the pug tucked tightly under Saint-Régent's elbow. Once on the street, Limoëlan cast an unfriendly glance at the growling animal, which was struggling to escape.

"This thing is meant as a gift for *her*, I suppose?" asked Limoëlan. "How can you worry about such nonsense at this time? *You* are putting us all at risk."

Saint-Régent made no response.

"Where will you be going?" asked Limoëlan.

"Do I ask where you live now? I suppose you decamped from your room above the pastry shop already. You know where to leave word if you need me."

"Fine. Perhaps it's better this way now."

Saint-Régent turned on his heels and disappeared around the corner of Rue des Saussaies. Limoëlan could now return to the new hiding place Father de Clorivière had secured for him.

This business with the pug worried him. He was sure that it was a gift for Blanche. She must have recently met Saint-Régent without Limoëlan's knowledge, and given the man encouragement enough for him to present her with the stupid dog.

41

For Roch, the 18th of January had been a busy and fruitful day. Following Fouché's instructions to arrest dozens of Royalist leaders, all of the Police Commissioners in Paris, with all of their men, and all twenty-four Inspectors had been ordered to report for duty. Detachments from the regular army, more than 300 cavalrymen and foot soldiers, had even lent their assistance for the arrests. Old Miquel would have much company at the Temple.

Roch returned to the Prefecture shortly before nine that evening. He had not slept the night before, and was beginning to feel light-headed, but he went to Piis's office to hear the results of Carbon's questioning.

"Oh, he did not display any of his sister's spirit," said Piis. "He answered the Prefect's questions meekly."

"Did he confess?"

"No, he maintained that on the 3rd of Nivose, at the time of the attack, he was walking on the boulevards. By himself."

"No alibi, then?"

"None. He denied everything at first. Then he reconsidered and admitted to purchasing the horse and cart, and renting the shed, all upon the request of a man he didn't know."

"A likely story! And what does he say he did with the horse and cart?" asked Roch.

"He brought them to that same stranger in the afternoon of the 3rd of Nivose. Then the fellow in question gave him six francs and left."

"And then, what else?"

"Nothing else. The Prefect announced all of a sudden that the questioning was recessed."

Roch stared at his colleague, his eyebrows raised.

"I was surprised myself," added Piis. "The questioning had only begun at four in the afternoon, which I thought was late enough, and it stopped twenty minutes later."

"Why give Carbon time to recover whatever wits he has? *That* was the moment to press for information."

"Well, I am sure that the Prefect has a plan."

"What plan? We need to arrest Saint-Régent and the man with the gold spectacles right away, before they learn of Carbon's arrest. How is it that the Prefect fails to see that?"

A guard knocked at the door and announced that the questioning of the suspect was going to resume. Roch followed Piis to the peepholes.

The Prefect took his seat behind the table. Short Francis was fully clothed, and his face bore the mildest of expressions.

The Prefect cleared his voice. "Witnesses have seen two men with you in that shed you rented on Rue de Paradis. Who are they?"

"One's Monsieur de Saint-Régent, but we call him Monsieur Pierrot between ourselves. Back west, he's a Commander in the Catholic and Royal Army. The other man's My Lord the Chevalier de Limoëlan. He's George's First Major General."

This was fast. Roch had heard of that man Limoëlan, a notorious Chouan leader. He must be George's chief representative in Paris, the head of the conspiracy. During the first session of the questioning, a few hours earlier, Short Francis had seen only one man, and had no clue as to his identity. Now there were two of them, and he perfectly remembered their names. Roch wondered whether Carbon had been granted a private interview with Bertrand during the recess. Yet it did not appear to be the case. His hands seemed normal, not horribly swollen as those of some suspects Roch had seen during the investigation of the Conspiracy of Daggers.

Short Francis proceeded to describe both of his accomplices. It was clear that Limoëlan, tall, thin, long-faced, handsome, "weak in the eyes," was the man with the gold spectacles described by Captain Platel and other witnesses. Roch now expected the Prefect to ask Short Francis for the addresses of his accomplices before it was too late. But no, instead the questioning rambled on the details of Carbon's past service in the Catholic and Royal Army. Roch, his eye still stuck to the peephole, began to kick the wall impatiently. He wanted to walk into the interrogation room, shove the Prefect out of his chair, seize Carbon by the lapels of his coat and wrench from him the addresses of the other assassins.

"Yes, Sir, I'd served in the Catholic and Royal Army for seven years," said Short Francis proudly. "I left with the rank of Captain aroun' the time of the Pacification. After that I came to Paris."

"Under which chief did you serve in the Catholic and Royal Army?"

"Under My Lord the Count de Bourmont."

"Have you seen Bourmont in Paris?"

"Yes, Sir. He gave me thirty-six francs, and let me work as a groom in his stables. That's the way he is, Monsieur de Bourmont. A good master, always kind-hearted."

"Did Bourmont discuss with you the plan of the attack on the First Consul?"

"Oh, no! Monsieur de Bourmont'd never do that. He used to be a Chouan, but now he's full of admiration for the First Consul."

Roch nearly snorted in derision. At least that rascal Bourmont was now behind bars, thanks to Fouché's initiative, but Saint-Régent and Limoëlan were still free. Where were they? Why was not the Prefect asking about that *immediately*? No, instead he dwelled at his leisure upon the happenings at the shed during the days that preceded the Rue Nicaise attack. Short Francis was happy to oblige and rambled on cheerfully.

"And then," he said at last, "we left the shed, me, Monsieur de

Limoëlan and Monsieur Pierrot, all three of us. No, Sir, I didn't know what was on the cart, 'cause the cloth covered everything. Monsieur de Limoëlan was the one leading the horse by the bridle. Then we arrived at Place des Victoires, and Monsieur Pierrot asked Monsieur de Limoëlan, *We don't need Francis no more, do we?* And Monsieur de Limoëlan said: *No, for sure we don't. Go your way, Francis. I'll meet you tomorrow at the shed.* So I left them right there, and I went home to my sister's."

"And did you meet Limoëlan at the shed the next day?" asked the Prefect.

"Yes, Sir, I did."

Another obvious lie, thought Roch. Short Francis had surrendered the key to the shed to Citizen Roger, the porter, *before* the attack. But who cared? The only thing that mattered right now was to capture Saint-Régent and Limoëlan.

"So you are completely ignorant of any plot to kill the First Consul?" continued the Prefect.

"Oh, yes, Sir. That is, I *was* ignorant of it till I read 'bout it in the papers." Carbon sighed and shook his head sadly. "A terrible, terrible thing that was. Then, a few days later, Monsieur de Limoëlan met me at the shed again, and he said, *My poor Francis, you can't stay with your sister no more. It's not safe. I've heard some evil-minded people blaming the Chouans for the attack.* Imagine how upset I was when I heard that! So Monsieur de Limoëlan said, *Go get your things, Francis, and meet me in front of Saint-Sulpice at eight o'clock tonight. I'll take you to a safe place, a place where they'll treat you well.*"

"So did you meet him there?"

"I waited over twenty minutes for him, Sir. In the rain, and it was freezing, almost. But at last he came, and he took me to the Convent of the Sisters of Saint-Michel. He told me to be sure to stay quietly there till the police found the real culprits."

Short Francis entered, with obvious relish, into the details of his life at the convent. His room was small but well heated. His bed was comfortable, the food the Sisters brought him tasty, the wine plentiful. All free of charge. What else could a man wish for?

"Was Limoëlan alone when he took you to the Convent?" asked the Prefect.

"Yes, Sir. It was jus' the two of us."

"Yet a woman was seen with you that night. Who is she?"

Francis gaped for a few moments before answering. "A woman, you say? Ah, yes, I was going to tell you all 'bout that. Just when Monsieur de Limoëlan met me, three ladies came out of a house nearby and joined us. And me, the three ladies, and Monsieur de Limoëlan, we went to the Convent together."

"And who are those three ladies?"

"I don't know them, Sir. And it was dark, so I couldn't tell you what they were like."

The Prefect pulled the note that began with *PLEASE KEEP VERY QUIET, DEAR FRANCIS.*

"Who wrote this?" he asked.

"Oh, that?" Short Francis blinked and seemed to hesitate again. "It's from Monsieur de Limoëlan. The Mother Superior brought it to me, jus' the day after I'd arrived."

"Where are Limoëlan and Saint-Régent?"

At last! Roch held his breath. He had almost abandoned hope of the Prefect ever reaching this point.

"Monsieur de Limoëlan has lodgings on Rue Neuve-Saint-Roch. Above the pastry shop, at the corner of Rue des Moineaux. And his mother has a house in Versailles. I don't know where exactly."

"And Saint-Régent?"

"He has a room on Rue des Prouvaires, with a Guillou family. It's the fifth alley to the right, when you come from Rue Honoré, third floor. It's easy to find, because the alley door has an iron gate. And he also has lodgings on Rue d'Aguesseau, Number 1336, on the third floor, with a Widow Jourdan."

Roch exhaled deeply. It was now four in the morning. Almost twenty-one hours had already elapsed since the arrest of Short Francis. Where had his accomplices gone now?

42

The Prefect lost no more time. He launched his men immediately in pursuit of the suspects. It fell to Roch's lot to go to Rue d'Aguesseau, where, according to Short Francis, one might find Saint-Régent. "Remember that the man is extremely determined and dangerous," added the Prefect. Roch needed no such warning and ordered three of his Inspectors, Bachelot, Alain and Bertier, to accompany him. Saint-Régent's arrest was now the only remaining obstacle to Old Miquel's safety, and Roch did not want to give the man any chance to escape.

A woman opened the door on the third floor as soon as he knocked at the door. There was no way of arriving by surprise up those creaky stairs. The first thing Roch saw, and smelled, was the rabbit cage against the far wall.

"Police!" he said. "Are you Citizen Jourdan?"

"Yes, Sir."

Roch nodded at the pretty girl standing behind the older woman. "And who is this?"

"This is my daughter Marie-Antoinette. Toinette, we call her."

Toinette smiled and curtseyed to the policemen as if this were a social occasion. She must have been born only a few years before the Revolution, and at some point, during the Terror, it must not have been easy to be called *Marie-Antoinette*, like the *ci-devant* Queen.

"Do you know a man named Pierre de Saint-Régent, or Pierrot?"

he asked the mother. "Over thirty, blue eyes, long pointy nose, hair braided in *cadenettes*, slight build?"

The older woman shook her head. "No, Sir, I don't know anyone by that name."

Roch looked carefully at her. In fact, she was not as old as she seemed at first glance. It was that wrinkled, emaciated face, and most of all those hollow eyes, devoid of any expression but fear.

In the rabbit cage, the male, unfazed by the arrival of the policemen, hopped behind one of the females and proceeded to mount her with short, hurried strokes. "Pray what is *this*?" asked Roch, pointing at the animals. "Do you know, Citizen, that it is against the law to raise livestock within city limits? I am going to issue you a citation. These rabbits will cost you a fine of 300 francs."

The look of fear in the woman's eyes became frantic. "Please, Sir, I've never seen so much money. If I can't pay the fine, I'll go to jail, and then what'll become of my poor Toinette?"

"Then perhaps you could answer my questions."

"Oh, I will."

"What about that man Pierrot? We know for a fact that he lives here with you. He is wanted on account of the Rue Nicaise attack."

Citizen Jourdan did not seem surprised. "Well, Sir," she said, "a Monsieur Pierrot did rent a room from me at times."

"Where is he?"

"I don't know, Sir. I haven't seen him in a while."

"How long?"

"I can't remember, Sir."

"How did you meet him?"

"Another man brought him here in the middle of December."

"What other man?"

"I don't remember, Sir."

"And you housed this Pierrot here, without reporting him as a boarder to the police? You broke the law, Citizen."

"But he wasn't really a boarder, Sir. He didn't stay here much. He'd agreed to pay me twenty *sols* a day, and God knows we need the money. He said it'd only be for a few weeks."

"When was the last time you saw him?"

"I don't remember, Sir."

"Please step outside with your daughter while we search your lodgings."

Roch walked to the other room and saw a pile of men's clothes on one of the beds. He looked as Inspector Alain inventoried shirts, clean and soiled, cravats, handkerchiefs, stockings, a pair of slippers and a coat, the pockets of which contained twenty-five silver coins of six francs, some small change and a letter.

Roch read it.

This 19th of December

My dear Pierrot,

I received news of you through our friends. As for you, apparently you still have not yet learned to write. Alas, two weeks have passed, and events proceed at a frightening pace. If our misfortunes continue, I do not know what will become of us all. In you alone rest my trust and our hope. The fate of the cause is in your hands. Farewell.

Your friend,
Gideon

PS: I await news from you by the next mail.

Gideon. George's war name. The Prefecture's experts would compare this letter to the known samples of his handwriting. The date of the letter, the 19th of December, was only five days before the Rue Nicaise attack. There was no postmark. George would never be so imprudent as to correspond with his accomplices through the Post Office. It was common knowledge that the police opened many letters, which were copied, and so cleverly resealed that their recipients often did not suspect the tampering that had taken place.

The lodgings contained nothing else of interest. Roch invited the Jourdan women to reenter.

"We are taking this to the Prefecture," he said, pointing at the sealed bundle of Saint-Régent's belongings. "By the way, we found more than 150 francs in your boarder's pockets. Did you know he had all that money?"

The older woman remained silent, but Toinette opened her eyes wide. "You don't say! When you think that he owes Mama over fifty francs for room and board . . ."

"Here is what I am going to do, Citizen," Roch told the widow. "I will leave with you twenty-four francs of his money as partial payment for his rent. We are taking the rest of his things. And your daughter is coming with us."

The woman wailed. "Oh, you can't do that, Sir. She's too young."

Roch looked sternly at her. "Then stop protecting a scoundrel who took advantage of you. He lived in your home and ate your food without giving you a *sol*, while his pockets were full of money. Answer me. Where is he?"

The woman moistened her lips, opened her mouth, and seemed to hesitate. Roch waited, but no sound came. The two women had to be separated, or the mother would never talk.

"All right then," he said. "I am arresting Toinette."

Tears were rolling down the older woman's face. "Then please arrest me with her. Please, Sir. We've never been apart."

"No. You need not worry about Toinette. I will make sure she is treated well."

The Widow Jourdan was now sobbing.

"Have you a neighbor or friend," asked Roch, "someone who could keep you company tonight?"

"I've an elder sister, Marie-Luce," intervened Toinette, patting her mother's shoulder. "She's married and lives on Rue Lazare. But she doesn't get along with Mama too well, you see. *You let that rotten child govern you*, she always says, speaking of me."

Roch thought that Marie-Luce was probably right. "I will have her fetched to keep you company," he told the widow. "And I will leave three Inspectors with you as well."

Toinette seemed chatty enough. He felt sure that, once separated from her mother, she would talk. He stepped back to let the girl go first out of the lodgings. They were already halfway down the first flight of stairs when he heard Widow Jourdan's plaintive voice. "An' about those rabbits?"

"I don't care," he shouted from the stairwell. "Eat them."

On his way to the Prefecture, Roch was hoping that Saint-Régent had been caught at the other address provided by Short Francis. But no, Piis told him, there as well the police had been too late. Likewise, Limoëlan was no longer in the room above the pastry shop, though a long blond wig had been seized on the premises. In both places the lodgers had been arrested.

Roch had Toinette brought to his office. He imagined what Bertrand would say of the situation. After Madeleine Vallon, after the schoolgirls from the Convent of Saint-Michel, he was making a specialty of questioning ingénues.

Roch, in an effort to hide his somber mood, smiled at the girl. "This is a pretty dress you have, Toinette."

She blushed under her freckles, more from pleasure, he imagined, than from shyness. "It is, isn't it? Monsieur Pierrot gave it to me."

"He did? That was kind of him."

"Oh, but it's an agreement we had. You see, Mama found on the street a pug dog. It looked like it was lost. A little bitch, so pretty. I called her Mirza, 'cause once, on the street, I'd heard a lady call her pug Mirza. Mama complained that we hadn't any money to feed her, but I said that she was so small, she wouldn't eat much. And I'd always wanted to have a pug dog. So Mama saw that I was right, and she agreed to keep her. But when Monsieur Pierrot saw Mirza, he went wild about her, and he said he wanted to buy her to give as a present to a lady of his acquaintance. So Mama asked me if it was all right if we sold Mirza to Monsieur Pierrot, because we needed the money so much. So I said that he could have Mirza, but only if he bought me a new dress. And he did!"

Toinette, pursing her lips, complacently straightened the folds of the skirt.

"Certainly Monsieur Pierrot has good taste," said Roch. "So what is the name of this lady of his?"

"Oh, but he wouldn't say, no matter how often I asked about her. He jus' said she'd be mighty pleased with Mirza." Toinette leaned towards Roch, her eyes shining with excitement. "And not only that, but he'd a collar specially made for Mirza *by a jeweler*. Monsieur Pierrot showed it to me. It was all real sterling silver, lined with green leather, with three little bells, and a medal with an inscription that said *To My Lady*. And the bells and the medal were all sterling silver too."

Roch nodded. "Fancy that! Monsieur Pierrot must be very much in love with his lady. And he stayed at your lodgings all the time?"

"He didn't come very often at first. But we saw him on Christmas Eve, in the morning. That day he gave me twelve *sols* to go buy ten feet of wick. *Get the thickest you can find, Toinette*, he said, *I'll show you something funny*. So when I came back with the wick, he made a little heap of gunpowder on the mantel of the fireplace, with a length of wick next to it. I was scared at first. *Don't light it, Monsieur Pierrot!* I cried, *you'll wreck the mirror. It's already cracked, and then Mama'll be in trouble with the lan'lord*. But he said, *Don't worry, Toinette, I know what I'm doing*. He pulled his watch—it was a fancy watch, all gold, with several little dials—and he said that the powder must explode in two seconds, no more. Then he lit the wick with his tinderbox. The powder made a funny little pop that made me jump. But he was right: the mirror wasn't ruined, at least not more'n before. But he wasn't happy, 'cause he could tell by his watch it wasn't as fast as he'd have liked. So he cut the wick shorter and shorter until the powder popped in just two seconds." Toinette giggled at the recollection. "He's a pleasant man, Monsieur Pierrot. He made Mama laugh, and she doesn't laugh often."

Roch smiled. "So your Mama liked him too?"

"Oh, yes. She said that she couldn't tell me his real name, jus' that he was a nobleman, from the West, and that he'd come to Paris to do something very important for the King, and that we should help him as best we could."

Toinette seemed sincere in her naïveté. She was really no more clever than she looked. "Very interesting," said Roch. "What else happened on Christmas Eve?"

"Monsieur Pierrot left before the morning was over. And he didn't come back until several days later. He arrived after dinner. But he was so altered! He looked all pale. He had trouble walking. But he wouldn't go to bed. He asked Mama for a candle and ink and paper. Mama told me she couldn't go to sleep, with him being in the same room behind the curtain, because he stayed up all night writing. He went out the next morning for about an hour, and he returned, very sick-looking, and after that he didn't go out for several days. Then he began to feel better, and he went out once in a while. He was never dressed the same way, sometimes like a gentleman, and sometimes like a beggar, almost. And sometimes he took his dinner with us, and sometimes elsewhere. But he came back to sleep at our place every night."

So Widow Jourdan had lied. She had given Saint-Régent shelter for weeks on end after the Rue Nicaise attack.

"And when was the last time you saw Monsieur Pierrot?"

"Jus' last night."

"Last night!" Roch stared at Toinette. If Short Francis had been questioned in a timely manner, Saint-Régent would have been caught already. No, instead, precious time had been wasted on the search of Francis's most intimate recesses, on the Prefect's aimless questioning and on such dallying. Roch had to bite his lip to repress a rush of fury against Dubois.

"So what happened last night?" continued Roch, trying to bring his voice under control.

"A man came asking for Monsieur Pierrot."

"A man?"

"A tall, thin man, with gold spectacles, and dark hair, cut very short, still shorter'n yours. He wore a fine blue coat too. He didn't say his name. He jus' said he was a friend of Monsieur Pierrot, and he needed to see him right away. Monsieur Pierrot looked mighty surprised to see him, and none too happy either. They locked themselves in the other room. I heard Monsieur Pierrot's voice raised. That was the first time because, like I told you, he's so pleasant usually. Then he left with the tall man." She sighed. "And he took Mirza with him. Now can I go home to Mama, please?"

"Tomorrow perhaps. You have been very helpful, but we may need you yet. In the meantime, I will make sure you sleep in a decent place tonight."

Roch had Toinette sign her statement and dismissed her. He was confident that the girl had told him all she knew, but her mother had much more to say. Toinette's absence might prompt her to reconsider the advisability of protecting Saint-Régent.

He rubbed his hands over his face. The stubble on his cheeks felt rough under his palms. The dull pain of a headache had settled behind his eyes. The past two nights, the one spent preparing the arrest of Short Francis at the Convent, and the other listening to the man's questioning, had been exhausting, more so than the mere lack of sleep could explain. It was certainly infuriating to have missed Saint-Régent by a matter of hours. And time was not stopping for Old Miquel. Barely nine days remained now.

Hopefully Carbon's arrest would pacify Fouché while the hunt for Saint-Régent continued. Roch decided to go home. He could not go on any longer without rest, and he needed to reflect on the evidence that had been gathered so far.

43

Roch awoke around midafternoon, more tired than when he had gone to bed in the morning, his mind still clouded by lingering shreds of dreams. His father, still in jail, but oddly cheerful, had made an appearance, and so had Short Francis, with his spotted blond and brown beard, in all his loathsome nakedness. Blanche too, smiling her innocent smile, as though nothing had happened. That was more painful than even the thought of Old Miquel.

It was only after Roch had drunk a bowl of vegetable bouillon that he felt refreshed. He removed his shirt and put on a nightgown. He asked his maid to warm water for his bath and in the meantime went to the parlor. Its furniture had been handsome, in the manner fashionable twenty years before the Revolution. Now the velvet of the drapes and upholstery, once perhaps a vibrant buttercup hue, had turned a dull, dusty shade of yellow. His maid, in spite of his instructions, persisted in lining the chairs along the walls, like soldiers at a revue. Paintings of cows grazing in muddy meadows, framed in gold, completed the decor.

Roch dragged the most comfortable chair next to the window. He sat, his chin resting on his hand, staring at a few passersby in the street below. It was a fine afternoon, with a pale blue sky lit by a white winter sun.

First he realized that things were not as hopeless as he had felt before. He must have been worn out then by fatigue and the disappointment of Saint-Régent's close escape. In fact, much progress had been made over the past few days. Short Francis, one of the two men the Minister wanted, had been caught. An ugly man, whose ugliness was more than skin deep, deceitful, devious, cunning in his own stupid way.

Roch thought of the note found in Short Francis's coat, with its odd capitalized handwriting. *PLEASE KEEP VERY QUIET, DEAR FRANCIS.* He could not rid himself that there was more to this missive than met the eye. The letter from George found at Widow Jourdan's lodgings was useful too. For one thing, the Prefecture's handwriting experts had confirmed its authenticity. It showed that George was not in Paris. He directed the conspiracy from afar, hidden in some farm or château in the West.

And then the questioning of François Carbon, in spite of the Prefect's unforgivable ineptitude, had revealed much. The short man had lied aplenty. Yet he had revealed the true names and addresses of Saint-Régent and Limoëlan, and had not hesitated to incriminate Bourmont, his former General and employer. But Carbon had steadfastly protected another person, the woman who, with Limoëlan, had taken him to the Convent. At first he had not mentioned her at all, then, when he had realized that the police knew of her, he had said that *three ladies* had accompanied them. He had tried at all costs to draw attention away from that one woman.

As for the note found on Short Francis, why was its author so worried that Francis would leave the Convent, a place where the man seemed to feel safe and comfortable? And it repeated with desperate insistence the warning not to trust anyone but the author. Trust was obviously a commodity in short supply among the conspirators. No more so, Roch thought with bitterness, than between himself and his colleagues. Did he, for one, trust the Prefect? Or Fouché? Or Bertrand? Or anyone else within the police?

And who was the author of the capitalized note? Limoëlan, as

Short Francis had stated? But Short Francis had lied on other points, in particular to protect the unknown woman, the *lady*, as Pulchérie had called her, who had taken him to the convent. She too might have written it.

And now something else pointed to a woman: the pug dog. To Saint-Régent, presenting it to *his lady* had been worth the risk of having the silver collar specially made by a jeweler, at a time when his life was at stake. He must be in love to take such a chance.

Were Saint-Régent's lady and Carbon's lady one and the same? Perhaps, but the gold embroidered hem of the skirt described by Pulchérie could belong to hundreds of women in Paris.

Roch was startled out of these thoughts when the maid knocked at the door and announced that his bath was ready. He thanked her and went to the little water closet. There he disrobed and stepped into the copper tub. He closed his eyes as he felt the warmth of the water envelop his skin and slowly dissolve his weariness. The comfort of the bath conjured a vivid image of Blanche. Why was it always coming to mind when he wanted a woman?

He shrugged. What a fool he had been! Not so much fooled by her than by himself. He must have loved her, for that was love indeed: the pursuit of the wisp of an illusion. Roch was still angry with Blanche, he was impatient to clear his mind of her, and there was no better way to achieve this end than to replace her, fast, before too many regrets could take hold and fester.

His first thought was of the jewelry store on the Quai des Orfèvres where he had bought the ill-fated ring. The young woman there had seemed eager to become acquainted with him. Yet, given the nature of his purchase, she might ask questions that Roch felt no inclination to answer, truthfully or otherwise.

Then Roch remembered the shopgirl who had smiled at him from the window of the Five Diamonds millinery shop. Of course, she too would be painfully linked to the memory of Blanche. He would normally have preferred a bourgeoise like the pretty jeweler, a better educated, probably less demanding woman, but he had no time to waste on the quest for true love. The shopgirl would do for the moment.

He resolved to go to the millinery. He would ask the shopgirl to show him dozens of spools of ribbon and solicit her advice, as though it were a gift meant for another woman. Then he would make a purchase and present it to her. She would blush and feign surprise. The rest was no less easy and predictable. He had earned these few hours of blissful oblivion.

He stepped out of the tub and put on his nightgown. Still warm from the bath, he shaved carefully and put on the clean clothes the maid had laid for him on the bed. He left in the direction of the Five Diamonds millinery. He was turning onto Rue du Pélican when his attention was attracted by a man, clad in a well-cut blue coat, walking straight at him. He was almost as tall as Roch, with an elongated face that matched his slim figure. He wore gold-framed spectacles. Limoëlan.

It did not take the man a moment longer to read Roch's expression. He turned on his heels and fled. He was fast. Roch shouted *Catch thief!* the cry most likely to grab the attention of passersby. Several men moved towards Limoëlan to stop him, but quickly withdrew when they saw him pull a pistol from under his coat. Roch ran after him and did not bother to draw his own firearm. There was no time to load it, and in any case the street was busy in the late afternoon. It would have been impossible to shoot without risking injuring an innocent.

Apparently Limoëlan felt no such qualms. He stopped and quietly turned around to aim at Roch. *His* pistol must have been already loaded. Roch sought refuge in the corner of a carriage door. He heard the detonation, then the whistling of the bullet. People around ran away shrieking. *Murderer*, thought Roch.

When he cautiously looked out from the carriage door, Limoëlan was nowhere to be seen. He must have turned onto the smaller, quieter Rue Coquillère already. Roch did the same and now pulled his pistol. There was still no trace of the man. Roch walked to the end of the street, which opened on to the much larger Rue du Louvre. Li-moëlan could have mixed with the passersby there, or he might be lying in wait anywhere, behind a door, in a staircase, at a window, his pistol reloaded, ready to aim and fire again. The chase was useless. Roch cursed and turned around. His encounter with the assassin had extinguished any flicker of desire for the shopgirl.

44

*R*och, after a good night's sleep, was at his office at dawn the next morning. He was surprised to see Inspector Bachelot already waiting for him, hat in hand, pacing at the foot of the rickety corkscrew stairwell. Roch had often suspected that his promotion to the rank of Chief Inspector had caused some resentment among the Inspectors, formerly his equals. Most had more seniority than he in the police, and some were far older. That was the case with Bachelot, who was over forty and did not look a day younger.

"What are you doing here, Bachelot?" asked Roch, frowning. "Aren't you supposed to be watching Widow Jourdan?"

Bachelot's flabby jowls trembled. "Well, Citizen Chief Inspector, she doesn't need watching anymore." He stammered. "She . . . she's dead."

Roch glared at the man. "Follow me," he said curtly.

Roch led the way to his office. He slammed the door shut and sat behind his desk without inviting Bachelot to have a seat.

"I am all ears," he said.

"Well, Citizen Chief Inspector, Citizen Jourdan looked very worried last night. She kept talking about her daughter Toinette, about what would happen to her at the Prefecture. Her elder daughter, Marie-Luce, tried to comfort her and finally she convinced her to go to bed. After that, Marie-Luce stayed in the other room, along with

Bertier and Alain and me. We played cards for a while, all four of us, then we went to sleep, Marie-Luce in Toinette's bed in the corner of the parlor and the colleagues in chairs there. I slept in the second bed in the bedroom, the one that's on the other side of that sheet. Saint-Régent's bed, I guess."

"Do you mean that you all went to sleep?"

Bachelot was fingering the hem of his hat. "Well . . . yes, Citizen Chief Inspector."

"Did it ever enter your mind, Bachelot, that I did not leave you there to loll around, or play cards, let alone go to sleep? So anyway, what did happen?"

"I was awakened around four in the morning when I heard Citizen Jourdan stirring on the other side of the sheet. It was pitch dark, but she was all dressed already. She told me she was going downstairs to get water in the courtyard, because she wanted to do her laundry."

Roch cursed. "Her laundry? At four in the morning? I know that you are not married, Bachelot. But perhaps you have a concubine? A maid, at least? How many females of your acquaintance do their laundry by candlelight at four in the morning, in the middle of winter too?"

Bachelot flushed. "I guess you are right, Citizen Chief Inspector. I didn't think of it at the time. After Citizen Jourdan was done with her laundry, she went down to the courtyard again to empty her bucket. Then she told me she was going back to bed, and she disappeared behind that bedsheet."

"Wait a minute, Bachelot. She slept on the window side of the sheet?"

"That's right. I couldn't see what she was doing. I thought she was undressing and going back to bed. But a minute later, I heard a big noise. I rose right away, Citizen Chief Inspector, but I couldn't see her. The window, a sash window, if you recall Sir, was open. Her bucket was lying there on its side, like she'd upset it when she'd stepped on it to jump out of the window. There's no light in the courtyard, so I couldn't see a thing down there. So I called to Bertier and Alain, and we ran downstairs. We found Citizen Jourdan, sprawled on her stomach, just outside the latrine door."

"She was fully dressed?"

"Yes, Citizen Chief Inspector. She was still breathing, but she couldn't speak. I had a physician fetched, and she was taken to the Charité Hospital. I came directly from there, Sir. She died before they had time to take her to a bed."

"Well, Bachelot, I must congratulate you," said Roch. He raised three fingers of his right hand. "I leave no less than three Inspectors there, and between all of you jackasses, you cannot even watch one old woman?"

Roch rose from his chair and walked to Bachelot, who was still standing. "Now do you understand what this means? We have lost a crucial witness, one who could have led us to Saint-Régent. And pray who is going to tell Toinette that she no longer has a mother? I should send you break the news to her yourself."

"Maybe she won't be so surprised, Citizen Chief Inspector. Her sister Marie-Luce told us last night that their mother had already tried to jump off the window two months ago, and that Toinette had caught her by her skirts and pulled her back just in time."

"Then that child has more wits about her than you and your distinguished colleagues put together." Roch paused and looked into Bachelot's eyes. "You realize what public opinion will make of this? That the police killed Citizen Jourdan to silence her?"

Bachelot flinched. "I expected better from you," continued Roch. "When I told you to watch that woman, I meant keep an eye on her at all times, not play cards or go to sleep. Your negligence is unforgivable." Roch pointed to a chair and handed Bachelot a quill. "Sit down. I want a full report immediately."

Bachelot went to work with alacrity, pausing once in a while to reflect, the quill against his lips. Roch, absorbed in his thoughts, barely heard the pen scratching against the paper. Citizen Jourdan had died at a very convenient moment for the Chouans, when she could have revealed much about Saint-Régent, and maybe his accomplices. Roch wondered about Bachelot. Was the man guilty of only gross negligence, or had he, in cold blood, pushed the Jourdan woman to her death?

Bachelot had belonged to the police for ten years, and his record was unblemished. Yet he had dropped that ladder at the Convent on the day of Carbon's arrest, as though to raise the alarm. And the fact that the short man's accomplices had learned so fast of his capture confirmed Roch's suspicions. Also, come to think of it, how had Gillard, the owner of the Mayenne Inn, understood so quickly that the place had been put under police surveillance? The assassins must have at least one informer within the Prefecture. Roch had suspected the Prefect or Bertrand, men he hated, and who returned the favor, rather than an unremarkable subordinate such as Bachelot. That was what happened when he let personal feelings cloud his judgment.

Roch told Toinette of her mother's death. She took the news better than he had feared. She wept, of course, but, as Bachelot had guessed, she did not seem very surprised. She confirmed that her mother had tried to jump off the window two months ago. This, of course, did not mean that the widow had committed suicide the night before.

Roch went to Piis's office to have the girl released as soon as arrangements could be made for her to go live with her sister Marie-Luce.

"So did you learn anything from that Toinette?" asked Piis.

Roch looked intently at the little man. Certainly Piis, in spite of his aristocratic origins, had been mostly friendly and pleasant. Roch had always considered him harmless, if a bit ridiculous, but Bachelot's case showed that such implicit trust might not be justified. And Bachelot's likely guilt did not in the least exonerate Piis. There could be more than one Royalist spy at the Prefecture.

"Toinette saw Pierrot experiment with gunpowder and wicks," said Roch. "And her mother knew much more yet."

"Knew?" asked Piis.

"She conveniently died last night. Jumped out of her bedroom window, according to Bachelot, whom I had left there to watch her."

Piis seemed genuinely shocked. "Do you think Bachelot . . . I would never have suspected him. What are you going to do?"

"I am tempted to suspend him immediately to prevent any further damage. He is at the very least guilty of dereliction of duty. And on the morning of Carbon's arrest, he upset a ladder when we arrived at the Convent, as though to raise the alarm. Yet I am afraid the Prefect will overrule whatever sanctions I take against Bachelot, if only to deprive me of any semblance of authority over my Inspectors."

Piis nodded gravely. "Oh, I would go to him and leave the decision to him. He might be more inclined than you think to follow your recommendation. Now that all those Chouans have been arrested, Fouché's star is shining brighter."

"Well, Piis, you may be right. What about you? Any news from Saint-Régent's other lodgers? What's their name again? The Guillous?"

"Yes, the Guillous. Monsieur Pierrot, as they call him, had been their tenant since the beginning of December. They describe him as quiet, sullen, going in and out at all hours. He had very few visitors, all male, including two who seem to have been Short Francis and Limoëlan. According the Guillou woman, on the day of the attack, Saint-Régent left early in the morning and came back very sick after nine at night. Then the man answering to the description of Limoëlan appeared, and went out again in search of a priest. The Guillou woman also had a physician fetched."

"What about the rest of the family? Do they all tell the same story?"

"Yes, at least the ones who were arrested. There is a grown son, a musician, age thirty-five, and a daughter of seventeen. The father was not home. He is a stagecoach driver for the line that goes to Rennes. He will be questioned as soon as he returns to Paris."

Roch frowned. A stagecoach driver, like the Davignon woman's husband. And both men drove for the same line, the one that went to Rennes, in the middle of Chouan territory. Yet another coincidence, coming upon the heels of the untimely, or too timely, demise of Widow Jourdan. He remembered someone saying that there was no such thing as a coincidence in police work, and now he stumbled upon two of them on the same day.

Roch felt a great desire to meet the coachmen Guillou and Davignon immediately upon their respective arrivals, without giving them time to reach their homes and discover the absence of their families. Davignon's flighty wife was still a guest of the coop at the Prefecture. Maybe she was not the only one in the Davignon household who liked Short Francis and his political ideas.

There was one problem: the stagecoaches from Rennes arrived in the town of Saint-Denis, north of Paris, outside the jurisdiction of the Prefecture. Actually, since the Revolution, Saint-Denis had been renamed Franciade, but everyone had now returned to the old appellation. In any case, regardless of the place's name, pursuing the investigation there would be breaking the law, and there was no need to call the attention of Piis, or anyone else, to such trifles.

"So the Guillou woman had a physician fetched to treat Saint-Régent on the night of the attack?" asked Roch in a detached tone.

"A medical student, in fact. A Basile Collin. Doesn't seem to know much, but he was arrested anyway. He provided his services, without reporting it, to a patient wounded in a suspicious manner."

"And Limoëlan?"

"Still unaccounted for, I am afraid. His landlord, the pastry shop owner, doesn't know where he went."

"How did he meet Limoëlan?"

"Through a family of second or third cousins of Limoëlan, by the name of Lavieuville."

"Were they questioned?"

"Oh, yes. And two wooden crates full of rifles, pistols, knives, sabers and the like were found in Madame de Lavieuville's dressing closet. She would only say that Limoëlan's valet, a man by the name of Francis, had brought them. She never opened them, of course. And she has no idea of Limoëlan's whereabouts either. A pity, she says, *because the children loved to play with him.*"

Piis suddenly hit his forehead with the palm of his hand. "Ah, yes, I was forgetting all about it! We also found Limoëlan's mother. She lives quietly in Versailles with her four unmarried daughters. She says she has not had any contacts with her son Joseph since August, because she disapproves of what she calls *his fanatical pursuits*. She even says the government should have him, and all the Chouan leaders, jailed for a good two years after the Pacification, to teach them to rebel against the proper authorities and make sure they don't cause any more trouble."

"She says that? Of her own son? Do you believe her?"

"When she was arrested, she had just returned from Paris, where she and her daughters had attended one of the First Consul's military reviews. She makes a point of doing so several times a month. Certainly no woman widowed by the guillotine ever expressed more patriotic feelings."

"What? Her husband, Limoëlan's father, was guillotined?"

"Oh, yes. In 1793. Sentenced to death by the Revolutionary Tribunal for Royalist conspiracy. But Madame de Limoëlan did not fail to mention that she personally knows the Minister of Police. She says he thinks highly of her and her loyalty to the government."

"Fouché?" This was becoming more and more incredible. "Limoëlan's mother is acquainted with Fouché?" He immediately thought of Old Miquel's guess. Fouché had indeed been aware of Limoëlan's identity from the beginning, and yet he had chosen not to share this crucial piece of information with Roch.

"Apparently," added Piis, "Madame de Limoëlan asked a common acquaintance, General Hédouville, to intervene with the Minister to have her son's name removed from the list of the émigrés. Fouché agreed to receive her on several occasions over the past few months. But she says she discontinued her efforts on behalf of Limoëlan once she understood that he continued to associate with unrepentant Chouans. Her house is being searched by the Police Commissioner for Versailles as we speak, and she has been brought to Paris for further questioning."

Roch arched his eyebrow. "By the Prefect, I suppose?"

"Yes, by the Prefect. I know what you think, but frankly I would be surprised if she had much more to tell us."

On the contrary, Madame de Limoëlan probably had fascinating things to reveal, in particular about this friendship of hers with Fouché, but Roch chose not to share this thought with his colleague.

"The pastry shop owner, however," continued Piis, "had much to say. He did remember those cousins, the Lavieuvilles, mentioning an aunt of Limoëlan, one Mademoiselle de Cicé."

"The name sounds familiar." Roch frowned. "*Ci-devant* aristocrats like you, are they not? A Cicé used to be one of Louis XVI's Ministers before the Revolution. And I think I remember that when I was a child the Bishop of Rodez, in my country, used to be a Monseigneur de Cicé."

"Oh, yes, these are Mademoiselle de Cicé's brothers. An ancient and powerful family. The brothers emigrated years ago. They live in England now."

"At least we now have a lead for Limoëlan. But we seem to have lost all track of Saint-Régent."

"Indeed," sighed Piis.

This was the time Roch usually dreaded, when inconvenient police matters were fully discussed and out of the way. Piis's hand would travel to his pocket and produce a sheet of paper. Yet it did not move. Roch, to his own surprise, was mildly disappointed.

"What's the matter, Piis? The well of your inspiration has run dry? This must mean that congratulations are in order. You bedded your beloved at last?"

The corners of the little man's mouth fell. "Alas. To tell you the truth, she is never at home anymore when I call. At first, I imagined that these were only the coquettish ways of an elegant lady, that she wanted to pique my passion by avoiding me for a while. But now, Miquel, I am beginning to worry. It has been almost a month since we met. She invited me to her box at the Opera on the night of the Rue Nicaise attack, and I went in hopes of seeing her, but she did not even attend. And since . . ."

"Yes, Sobry told me that you witnessed Bonaparte's outburst against the Jacobins at the Opera. But I didn't know that you were waiting for that Photis of yours."

"Well, I didn't tell Sobry about that. I only open my heart to you."

"And to whoever reads your sonnets. What can I say, my poor Piis? These things do happen to the best of us. If this can be of any comfort, my own romance is over. Beyond any hope of reconciliation. Perhaps I should take to writing poetry myself."

45

*R*och gave no more thought to literary endeavors that day. He sent Bachelot's report to the Prefect, along with his own recommendation that the Inspector be immediately suspended. He received no direct response, but instead instructions to perform a search of the lodgings of Mademoiselle de Cicé, Limoëlan's aunt.

Roch did not know whether to be grateful for this assignment. If Fouché had wanted Limoëlan arrested, he would have been more forthcoming with Roch. Why was the Minister protecting the assassin? On the other hand, that aunt of Limoëlan's might lead him to Saint-Régent, and that was undoubtedly the key to Old Miquel's fate.

Mademoiselle de Cicé lived at Numbers 11 and 874 Rue Cassette. This strange address was that of a single building, though a vast one, but logic had little to do with Paris street numbers. The house might have been the mansion of a great lord before the Revolution, but now it was divided into many lodgings. The peeling paint of the shutters and the tattered curtains behind the windows told of the indignities of genteel poverty. *Vanitas vanitatum, et omnia vanitas*, thought Roch. He wondered why he was remembering more and more of his Latin these days. Perhaps those years spent wearing out the seat of his breeches on the benches of Veau's Academy had not been a complete waste of his time and Old Miquel's money.

Roch asked the porter about the lodgings of Mademoiselle de

Cicé, as Piis had called her. She lived in an entresol overlooking the courtyard. Roch posted one Inspector at the carriage door that served as a street entrance to the house. Then, followed by two other men, he went to the courtyard and climbed down the half-flight of stone stairs with a rusty banister that led to the entrance to Citizen Cicé's lodgings.

A gaunt woman, clad in a black dress reminiscent of a nun's habit, her brown hair pulled back in a tight bun, opened the door herself. Before the Revolution, she must have been a rich lady, with a small army of servants in attendance. Now she was an old maid living alone in a couple of dark, dingy rooms.

"Citizen Cicé?" asked Roch.

The woman inclined her head. He pulled his Prefecture card.

"Police. We have a warrant to search your lodgings."

She stepped aside to let the men pass. "Pray enter, Sir."

"I would like to avoid forcing your locks and damaging your furniture." Indeed, against the mildewed wallpaper, most of the pieces he saw were quite fine, in the ornate style that had been fashionable before the Revolution. "Please unlock everything for us, Citizen Cicé."

The woman pulled a ring full of keys from her pocket and obeyed in silence.

Everywhere were discovered hoards of religious medals made of tin or brass, and reams of letters. Copper, silver and gold coins were scattered in boxes, drawers, purses of all materials and sizes, in envelopes, some with names scribbled on them.

Roch pointed to a secretary desk, decorated with a lattice marqueterie pattern and gilded cherubs. "Is there a hidden compartment in this thing?" There always was at least one.

"You did not ask about any secret compartments, Sir."

Her tone was icily polite. Roch knew what she felt. He even understood her, to a point. To her he was a barbarian, the product of a Revolution that she hated, that had decapitated her King, ruined her family and sent her brothers to exile.

"I said that I did not wish to destroy your furniture, Citizen Cicé.

But if you force me to do so, I will not hesitate for a moment. Your choice entirely."

"I will show you the secret drawer. I treasure this desk, Sir. It belonged to my late mother." She shrugged. "But it is not a thing someone like you would understand, I suppose."

He looked into the woman's eyes. "Unfortunately not, Citizen Cicé," he said in an even tone. "*My* late mother did not own any secretary desk. Indeed she had no use for one, for she could neither read nor write. But it is a thing someone like you would have guessed, I suppose."

Citizen Cicé had squandered any goodwill Roch might have felt towards her. He did not mind *ci-devant* aristocrats as such, and he was even on friendly terms with a few of them, like Piis. But this woman's contempt made him angry. He had been poor, worse than poor, he had been nothing before the Revolution. Because she some- how felt it, she implied that he could not comprehend the bond be- tween mother and child. He had been wrong to think that he was, in her eyes, a barbarian. In fact, to her, he was not even human.

He nodded in the direction of the desk. Citizen Cicé seemed to understand the look in his face and hastened to open a drawer and slip her hand inside. A secret compartment sprung open. It contained a few more letters, several hundred francs in gold coins, and a list of all sums of money scattered throughout her lodgings, with their exact locations.

Behind them an Inspector let out a cry of triumph. He pulled from under her bed a cloth bag, with the mention *Paupers' Purse* written in a spidery handwriting on a paper label. It held five coins of six francs. Another bag, marked *Gentlemen's Purse*, contained 102 francs in silver coins and, in a smaller silk bag inside, five gold *louis* of twenty-four francs. Quite appropriate, reflected Roch. A pauper's purse is always leaner than that of a gentleman.

"Who are the *gentlemen* in question?" Roch asked Citizen Cicé.

"I keep in this purse the proceeds of a collection for the priests and the paupers of La Salpêtrière."

"You did not answer my question. Who are these *gentlemen?*"

"I cannot answer. It would offend my delicacy."

"Would it? Your delicacy is not so easily offended when it comes to aiding assassins like your nephew Limoëlan and his friends."

"Monsieur de Limoëlan is not my nephew, Sir, nor any relation of mine. I only know him."

"How so?"

"Again I cannot answer."

"What about Saint-Régent?"

"I cannot tell you more."

"Then you are under arrest, Citizen. You will be questioned at the Prefecture. Would it also offend your delicacy to empty your pockets, or must we search you?"

Citizen Cicé pursued her lips and pulled a prayer book out of her pocket. Roch held it by a corner of the cover and shook it. A bookmark fell to the floor. He squatted to pick it up. It bore the image of the Sacred-Heart-of-Jesus in bright red against a white background and the motto *La victoire ou la mort.* Victory or death, the emblem and motto of the Chouans.

There was a timid knock at the door. One of the Inspectors went to open. A middle-aged woman, her hand to her mouth, stood on the threshold. The Inspector posted at the front door of the house had instructions to let anyone come in and no one go out. He had been discreet enough not to be noticed by this woman.

"Police," said Roch. "Please state your name and place of employment."

"Marie Danjou, Sir. I am a lady's companion, but have no place now."

"What business have you here, Citizen Danjou?"

"Mademoiselle de Cicé is a friend, a very good friend, I must say. I was calling on her."

Roch did not feel kindly disposed towards any friends of the old maid. "Perfect. You will keep her company then. I am placing you under arrest too."

The woman stared at Citizen Cicé in mute horror.

It would take a while to collect, inventory and seal all of the evidence to be seized. Inspector Bertier was left to watch both females. Roch, with his remaining man, proceeded to search the rest of the house. Those tenants whose names had been written on Citizen Cicé's envelopes were arrested. Also, a man from the western town of Poitiers was found in possession of a valid passport, but he had failed to have it stamped at the Prefecture upon his arrival in Paris. He protested that it was an innocent omission, that he was only visiting an aunt in the capital for a few days. He nevertheless was arrested.

From a narrow window in the attic, barely a slit in the roof, a gray eye was watching the scene. Mademoiselle de Cicé, in the midst of a small group, was waiting on the street below. Father de Clorivière blessed himself. The policemen had failed to notice the entrance to his hiding place. Thank God it was cleverly disguised in the paneling of the attic. His lips formed a silent prayer for dear Mademoiselle de Cicé. This was not her first arrest. She was brave. She would not speak.

46

Roch hailed two hackneys to take the suspects to the Prefecture. He invited Mademoiselle de Cicé, the man from Poitiers and the lady's companion to step into the first one before he settled across from them with an Inspector. The fellow with the unstamped passport sat in a corner with a look of perfect imbecility on his face. The two women were holding hands. Citizen Cicé kept her eyes turned upwards, in the direction of the heavens and, more directly, the shabby roof of the hackney. Now she must fancy herself some sort of martyr for *the cause*.

Roch was watching her. In spite of her charities, did she like the poor, the *paupers*, as she called them, very much? Of course, they were necessary to her as grateful recipients of her kindnesses. But she probably saw them as devoid of true feelings, indeed barely above animals. Her comment about Roch's inability to understand her love for her mother rankled.

For Roch did remember his own mother's love, and he remembered loving her as well. He remembered suckling at her breast, and later watching his sister and brother do the same. She had fed all of her children until they reached the age of four. They were by then old enough to stand on a stool by her side. She would smile and, without bothering to sit down, unlace the top of her bodice for them to latch onto her nipple.

While his father was away in Paris for nine long months, Roch, his sister and brother would all sleep in their mother's bed in the only room of the cottage, and she always kept the place next to her for him, her firstborn. Roch remembered the warmth of her body through her chemise as he nestled against her under the fat down coverlet, with its red silk envelope, that had been all her dowry. During the day he, as the eldest, would graze their tiny flock of sheep along lonely mountain lanes, and, once in a while, try to catch a few hurried hours of study on the benches of the parish school.

Then, in June, Old Miquel walked home from Paris, in time for the hay harvest. He had not much hay to harvest himself, but he earned a few *sols* helping more fortunate neighbors. Upon Old Miquel's return, the mood at the cottage changed. The children would cast cautious glances at their father, and Roch's mother smiled less. During meals, she never sat in her husband's presence. She stood behind his chair, ready to serve him and obey his commands. Such was the custom among peasants in Auvergne.

In fact, Old Miquel was less harsh to his wife than most men of his class. Whenever he was displeased with her, he simply glowered at her and reached for his staff, which was enough to make her cower. He never actually beat her, in spite of the many proverbs that advised a man to correct his wife, hard and often, if he wanted to remain the master of his own house.

Old Miquel called her *fenno*, which means both "woman" and "wife" in the Roman language. Again, that was the usual way in Auvergne. But on occasion, when he was in a cheerful mood, after dancing a *bourrée* at the sound of the bagpipes, or drinking a few glasses of wine, he used her Christian name, Augalio, which translated as "Eulalie" in French. That always seemed to startle her. She blushed and looked up at him. Then, when she saw him grin at her, she would smile back with shy pride, as though he could pay her no greater compliment than to speak her name.

When Old Miquel returned home every summer, Roch would have to surrender his place in his mother's bed, and instead share with his sister and brother a straw mattress on the dirt floor of the cottage. For many nights afterwards, though the other children dozed off quickly, he could not sleep. He lay awake, his eyes wide open in the dark, attentive to the sounds behind the closed curtains of the bed.

It all began with barely audible words, whispered in a hoarse man's voice. Soon followed the rhythmic creaking of the old frame, slow at first, then more and more urgent, and his mother's moans, his father's grunts, and finally inarticulate, muffled cries. The bed fell into silence at last, until the process was repeated. Roch would learn later that Old Miquel did not touch women during his nine months in Paris, and he returned to Auvergne with a ravenous appetite for his wife's body.

To Mademoiselle de Cicé, all of this would have been disgusting, a reflection of the beastly immodesty of the poor, of the coarseness of their feelings. Yet this was how Roch had first learned about lust and love, a mother's love, a wife's love.

But then what kind of love had Blanche in mind when she had asked for a ring? Lovers' love. Blanche herself, like the women he had bedded before her, had been a poor teacher in this regard. He realized that he had wanted from her things, such as loyalty and truthfulness, she could never give him or any other man. Yet her loss left him empty.

47

At the Prefecture Roch sat down with Piis to review the letters seized at Citizen Cicé's lodgings. There were a great many, written by different hands, but in some ways they were all alike: unsigned and full of cryptic references to the *Little Painter*, the *Hermit*, the *shop's main agent*, the *flow of commerce, our dearest Julie*, and the like.

"Now look," said Roch, pointing at a sheet he was reading, "in this one, there is a mention of *S___t Francis*."

Piis jumped in his chair. "And about this one! Listen: *The Little Painter has a few good companions. We hope that it will all happen very soon now. I look forward to giving you in person more ample details that you will find satisfactory.* This could be a reference to Limoëlan, Carbon and Saint-Régent. It seems that Mademoiselle de Cicé was aware of the preparations for the Rue Nicaise attack."

Roch frowned. "I suspect she provided, and may still provide, active support to the assassins."

"And, Miquel, what if she were the *lady* that schoolgirl saw accompanying Carbon to the Convent of Saint-Michel?"

Roch shook his head. "I don't think so. That girl Pulchérie mentioned that the lady in question wore a gown with elegant gold embroidery at the hem. This hardly matches the Cicé woman's clothing. You have not seen her yet, but her attire is very austere, almost like that of a nun."

"Maybe that Pulchérie girl was mistaken, or perhaps Mademoiselle de Cicé dressed differently for that occasion."

"Both highly unlikely," said Roch, seizing another letter from the
pile on the desk.

All of a sudden he sat up. The new letter was written in a bold
hand he had not seen before.

> *Dear Gideon,*
>
> *I learned that Pierrot is trying to blame me for the failure
> of our business venture. He apparently says that I provided
> him with defective wares. This is not true. I simply handed
> him the merchandise our friends had given us. He also says
> that I failed to warn him in time of the arrival of the shipment
> at the Stock Exchange. This is not true either, and he had more
> than enough time to set up the business as instructed. As I
> wrote you before, his cowardice is what doomed our plan.*
>
> *But that you already know. Now you ask why I doubt
> For the King's loyalty. Actually I no longer have any doubts.
> Remember what happened when our competitors seized our
> associate: he betrayed the names and addresses of the venture's
> managing partners, including Pierrot's and mine. Why then
> did not our competitors attempt to seize For the King as
> well?*
>
> *Also, remember how For the King failed us at the competi-
> tion's headquarters. The only explanation for this failure is
> treason.*
>
> *What I propose is that from now on we exclude For the
> King from any involvement in the venture. This means that
> different means must be found for us to correspond. I am send-
> ing this through a trusted friend, and should have some other
> scheme in place shortly. In my opinion, For the King is fit to
> be drowned, but I will be awaiting your instructions.*
>
> *Your devoted friend.*

Roch handed the letter across the desk to Piis. "Gideon is one of George's war names, and this can only be from Limoëlan. Who else could be so closely involved in the Rue Nicaise attack, and so keen on blaming Saint-Régent?"

"I agree," said Piis after reading the letter. "But who is this *For the King* character?"

"Well, Piis, it can't be Limoëlan, who wrote this letter, nor Saint-Régent, who is mentioned here as *Pierrot*. Short Francis has to be the *associate* seized by the competition, which must mean the police. *For the King* is a fourth conspirator, entrusted with a mission to spy on us. So that could be Bachelot, or some other traitor within our ranks. There could be more than one at the Prefecture."

"Not necessarily," said Piis. "Nothing in the letter implies that *For the King* works here. He could be spying on us from the outside."

Roch looked at his colleague in a more pointed manner. The man seemed very anxious to exonerate their colleagues. "True, Piis. Then *For the King* might be a woman. The woman Pulchérie saw taking Francis to the Convent, for instance. Or the *lady* for whom Saint-Régent purchased the pug."

"Also," said Piis, some of the letters mention a *Little Painter*. Who is that?"

Roch, lost in his thoughts, stared out the window. He was reminded of a little painter he had met recently.

"Say, Piis, do you know a Madame de Nallet?" asked Roch abruptly. "She studies, or pretends to study flower painting in David's studio."

"Madame de Nallet? I have known her for years. A lovely lady." Piis scoffed. "You are not implying she could have anything to do with this Rue Nicaise business, are you?"

"This lovely lady could be *For the King*. She has ties to the Royalists through her émigré brother."

"But the same is true of hundreds of other society ladies in Paris. And the letter implies that *For the King* has something to do with forwarding the correspondence between Limoëlan and George. I can't imagine Madame de Nallet doing such a thing. But that could fit Mademoiselle de Cicé. Look at those reams of letters you seized at her lodgings. She could be *For the King*."

"Come, Piis, let's be serious. Would Limoëlan want to drown a woman he considers his aunt?"

"Well, I guess we'll have to wait until she is questioned by the Prefect."

Roch shrugged. "Oh, yes, for all the good that will do."

As he feared, the questioning of Mademoiselle de Cicé threw little light on the investigation. She persisted in saying nothing about Carbon, Saint-Régent or Limoëlan, beyond the fact that the latter was not a relative of hers.

Mother Duquesne and the Sisters of the Convent of Saint-Michel had been questioned by Bertrand. The nuns still denied any knowledge of Carbon's involvement in the Rue Nicaise attack. One of them, Sister Ursule, did remember Mother Duquesne confiding that the short man's presence "was a great inconvenience, and worried her to no end." As for Mother Duquesne herself, she insisted that it was her good friend Mademoiselle de Cicé who had brought Francis to the Convent. The Prefect decided to question both women together.

Roch felt some amusement when he saw through the peepholes the two suspects facing each other. They were both past fifty and dressed in similar black gowns, but Mother Duquesne's full face, with its square jaw, contrasted with the wan, emaciated cheeks of Mademoiselle de Cicé. Mother Duquesne, her eyes downcast, maintained that her friend was the one who had asked her to give Francis shelter at the Convent. The old maid put her hand to her breast in indignation and lost her usual pallor as she vehemently denied the accusation.

Roch tended to believe Mademoiselle de Cicé. He had noticed since their first meeting that she never seemed to lie outright. She only refused to answer questions when she did not want to tell the truth. That meant that Mother Duquesne was, at the risk of compromising an old friend, still protecting the *lady* who had actually brought Carbon to the convent. That unknown woman must be either very dear to the Prioress, or a very important cog in the Rue Nicaise plot. Or both.

48

This was the 30th of Nivose, the last day of a month that had seemed longer than any other in the course of Roch's life. Now Nivose, the month of the snows, was ending to give way to Pluviose, the month of the rains.

Roch left his office and climbed down the rickety stairs. He was ready to go home when he caught sight from afar of the giant frame of Division Chief Bertrand in the corridor. This was enough to make the short hairs on the back of Roch's nape stand on end. Bertrand had noticed Roch as well, for he stopped walking. Roch pressed on. But Bertrand was blocking the passage.

"In a hurry, Miquel? Not in the mood for a friendly chat tonight?"

Roch had never been so physically close to Bertrand, and he could now smell the odor of stale sweat that emanated from the man's armpits. He grunted.

Bertrand was grinning. "No wonder, you must be worn out by all your worries. I heard that some of the Jacobin deportees have left Bicêtre already. Headed for an undisclosed port in the West, where they will board their ship to the Colonies. Well, the first batch of deportees, that is, because more are to follow. In a week or two all those scoundrels will be gone. Who knows, the Prefect, in his goodness, might even let you say good-bye to your father. That way you will be able to see the old man walk away, chained to his friends."

Roch had to close his eyes for a moment. He remembered his father's advice. *Don't let your anger govern you.* Bertrand was only trying to provoke him; he was looking for a pretext to file a complaint with the Prefect.

"Also," continued Bertrand, "Metge, you know, the Jacobin pamphleteer, is going to be tried by a Military Commission tonight. I bet you didn't know that, did you? With three other rascals of the same ilk. All had conspired to assassinate the First Consul."

Indeed Roch had not heard of it yet. He had read some of Metge's writings, though. They were inflammatory. His last pamphlet, *The Turk and the Military Man,* was nothing but a thinly veiled invitation to assassinate Bonaparte. These days expressing such opinions had become a capital crime.

"Those Military Commissions are just the thing," added Bertrand. "Fast, efficient, clean, no appeals, no needless fuss. That's what I was telling the Prefect this afternoon. The government needs to empty the prisons, starting with the Temple, of all that vermin crawling in there. Don't you agree, Miquel?"

Roch struggled to control his breathing. The occasion did not call for rash action. He looked carefully at Bertrand. The beast must be fifty pounds heavier than himself, maybe more, and a good six inches taller. His hands were the size and color of the slabs of beef one saw hanging from hooks in butcher shops. But the left foot was stiffly turned outwards, and the left shoulder was shorter than the other. This was the weak side.

Roch took a step back for momentum, and also to trick the other man. Bertrand grinned more broadly. The fool, as expected, had interpreted the move as a retreat. All of a sudden, Roch plunged headlong into the left side of Bertrand's chest, just below the breast. Bertrand, caught unaware, gave a retching cry, staggered and fell heavily onto his rump.

Roch watched with some pleasure his colleague struggle to get back to his feet. "My poor Bertrand," he said after a minute, "these corridors, though not waxed very often, can be slippery. You should be more careful, especially with your deformity. There, let me help you."

He offered a hand, but Bertrand, still on the floor, bellowed and pushed him away. Roch shrugged. "What's this? Who's not in the mood for a friendly chat now? Oh, fine with me. Have a good night." He stepped over Bertrand's splayed legs and left the Prefecture.

Outside, the crisp, cold night was soothing. Roch was pleased, very pleased with his encounter with Bertrand. It had been long overdue. The fine thing about it was that the man liked to boast of his strength, and would be too vain to bring the incident to the Prefect's attention. Besides, Roch felt sure that the blow, though it must have broken a couple of ribs, had left no trace. It would still hurt for a few weeks.

Yet in one regard, Bertrand had succeeded. He had brought to the fore Roch's anxiety about his father. What was the old man doing at this very moment, in the tower of the Temple? He must be done with dinner. Was he reading the papers, talking politics with the Royalists before being locked in his cell for the night? More importantly, had Fouché made a decision as to his fate?

49

Roch would have given anything for the comfort of a talk in the Roman language with his father. Of course, Alexandrine too could give him the pleasure of speaking their native tongue. She was probably at the Mighty Barrel now. And, in spite of his father's admonition, he had never called on her to thank her *properly*.

Truth be told, he had never paid Alexandrine much attention. Yet his attitude was inexcusable now that she minded the Mighty Barrel. He realized that he had always been angry with her because of things for which, in all fairness, she could not be blamed. He remembered resenting her intensely after the death of his sister. The two girls were about the same age, and little Anna Miquel, whom Roch loved, had died, while Alexandrine had lived. And more recently he had disliked Alexandrine because of the trouble her father's so-called wine had caused. That was not her fault either. Most of all, he had resented the fact that Old Miquel wanted them to marry, while he was enthralled by Blanche. So he had scowled at Alexandrine at almost every opportunity. If only as a friend of many years, she deserved better.

Before Roch realized it, his steps had taken him to the Mighty Barrel. Alexandrine smiled when she saw him push open the front door, but he detected a certain sadness in her greeting. The tavern was busy at this time of the night, but she told the headwaiter to mind the common room and led Roch to Old Miquel's private dining parlor in the back. Steam and the smell of vegetable soup filled the room. In the hearth, flames licked the bottom of a copper kettle resting on a tripod.

"Have you any news of your father?" asked Alexandrine as soon as she closed the door behind them.

Roch sat wearily in a chair by the table and rubbed his eyes. "I was allowed to visit him once in the Temple. He is doing well, much better than I had thought. He has lost none of his spirit."

Alexandrine put a bottle of wine and two glasses on the table. She sat in a chair next to Roch. "I am not surprised. It would take more than jail to break him down."

"There is something else," he continued, "something that makes me very angry. The night before I had permission to visit him, he was told that he would be tried before a Military Commission. You know what that would have meant."

Alexandrine gasped. "But your father cannot be tried for anything, Roch. He didn't do anything wrong. He must have been very upset."

Roch looked at the copy of the *Declaration of the Rights of Man and of the Citizen* that his father had proudly hung on the wall. What did those words mean now? He turned his eye to the low fire in the hearth. He remembered the goose roasting on a spit on the 3rd of Nivose, when he, Alexandrine and their respective fathers had been gathered in this room for the Christmas Eve *réveillon*, moments before the attack. Now Old Miquel might never return to the Mighty Barrel.

Roch sighed. "No, Alexandrine, Father was not even upset. He seemed resigned to the worst, without being despondent. The prospect of the firing squad only worried him because of the pain it would cause me. You are right, he is strong." Roch shook his head. "I was hoping that the discovery of the true culprits would help Father and his friends. I was wrong, I was naïve. And some of the assassins are still at large. I have failed to arrest them all. Father is still threatened with deportation, or worse. Everything I have done, or tried to do so far, has been useless, worthless."

Alexandrine put her hand on Roch's arm. "But nothing, at least nothing that can't be mended, has happened to him yet. There is hope.

I think you are too harsh on yourself. You feel disheartened now because you are tired. You have been working so hard. Of course some good will come of your efforts, very soon. I am sure that your father will be released. Your superiors owe it to you. They have to appreciate your merits, and the results of your work too."

Roch shrugged at the thought of the Prefect's appreciation of his merits. What was still worse than the Prefect's animosity, open or disguised, was Fouché's duplicity.

"No, Alexandrine, things don't work in this manner. My superiors don't like me at all. Neither do many of my colleagues. Some have been jealous of my promotion, some dislike me because of Father and his opinions, and some . . . well, some simply don't find me very likable."

The sad smile returned to Alexandrine's lips. "Perhaps you pay more attention to those who dislike you than to those who like you."

He could not help smiling back. "How true." He reached for her hand. "So what on earth do you find to like in me, Alexandrine?"

Now Alexandrine's smile had turned mischievous. "A pointed question, isn't it? But I will try my best to answer, since you seem to count me among those who like you."

He bit his lip. "I am sorry. I must sound abominably conceited."

"No, please don't apologize. I take your candor as a token of friendship. And you are right, I do like you. For one thing, I have known you since I was four years old, which is almost as far back as I can remember. I have never had any brother, and when I was a little girl I admired you because you were out in the streets all day long, in all weathers, helping your father. Like him, you never let your work or anyone's scorn wear you down. And you are still the same. As proud, as brave as ever, in a different way, and I still admire you for it. Indeed I cannot think of a time in my life when I have not liked you."

Her tone was that of lighthearted banter, but he knew that she meant all of it.

"Now, Alexandrine, I am truly humbled. I have been so often rude to you, and I don't know how to make amends."

"There is no need for amends."

She kept her eyes down. He could not think of what to say, and maybe it was better this way. In spite of her embarrassment, and of his own too, he wanted this moment to linger. In a few words she had dispelled much of the gloom that had been weighing upon him for days. For the first time he was enjoying her company. He was still holding her hand, feeling its warmth. He laid it flat on the table and caressed it with the tip of his fingers. Then, moved by a sudden impulse, he seized it and brought it to his lips. She took a sharp breath and withdrew her hand.

"Forgive me," he said. "I startled you."

"I guess I am not used to seeing you so affectionate." She hesitated. "Roch . . ."

He cringed. He feared that something terribly serious was coming, and did not want to hear it, least of all at this time, when he felt so weak.

"This is not easy to say," she continued, "so please listen and don't interrupt me." He opened his mouth. She put a finger on his lips. "No, please listen to me, Roch. I need to tell you of this. I know that your father and mine would like us to marry, and that most men in your position would be happy to have me, if only for the sake of my dowry. And I know that *you* won't do it because . . . because it wouldn't be right for you, or for me. I understand, and I respect you for it."

She kept her eyes fixed on a few stray embers glowing red in the hearth. "So please do not feel uneasy for not wanting to marry me. Again, I think you are doing the right thing. It shouldn't prevent you from calling here to spend some time with me if it can bring you any comfort. Even if it is to talk of another woman."

She looked straight at him now. Her eyes were shinier than usual, and her nose a little pink. She smiled, and her smile no longer had any sadness in it. "There. I am happy to have said it, and it was not so difficult after all."

Roch felt ashamed of the manner in which he had thought of her before, dismissively, as though she were nothing but a pretty face attached to a sack of gold.

"Your guess is right, Alexandrine. There is, or rather there was, another woman, a woman . . . well, a woman I would like to forget. I cannot tell you of what happened, but in a way I feel that she has deceived me. It doesn't make any sense for me to feel this way, because she was only my mistress. She didn't owe me anything, not even the truth. I shouldn't have expected anything from her, but I did. I left her once I discovered what she had hidden from me. And I have no regrets over leaving her. But I have not forgotten her yet, and it still pains me to think of her. A part of me still yearns for her."

He seized Alexandrine's hand again and kept it in his. "I will be as candid as you," he continued, "and tell you what I want tonight. I want to hold you tight, and I want to rest my head against your breast, like a child in need of comfort. But if I let myself do that, if you pressed me in your arms, before long I would be seeking your lips to kiss you, not as a child, but as a lover, and then I would want more. In fact, just speaking of it makes me want more already. I want all of you."

Alexandrine half rose from her chair and leaned towards him. He held her firmly by the wrist to make her sit back. "I am very unhappy and confused now, dearest Alexandrine, and worried over Father's troubles. But I feel better for coming here tonight, for seeing you, for talking to you. Thank you for saying what you said, and thank you for your friendship. I need it even more than you can imagine."

He rose from his chair. "I should go now."

He brushed his lips against her flushed cheek and fled before she could respond.

50

This was the day when Roch had to visit the businesses of the Palais-Egalité. Before he had broken with Blanche, meeting her mother was simply unpleasant, but now that prospect was excruciatingly painful. His face burned with shame when he remembered looking at a jewelry store window at the Palais-Egalité in quest of a wedding ring. Only a week had elapsed since that day. He resolved to do his rounds at a later time than usual, during the evening. Then Madame de Cléry would be too busy to pay him much attention, and that would limit any exchanges between the two of them to a minimum.

In the meantime, he wished to have another chat with Madame de Nallet. He could ill afford to neglect any clues that might lead to the conspirators, to Saint-Régent in particular, and he realized that he had not paid the little flower painter the attention she deserved.

When he entered David's studio, he saw, standing on the dais, a young man of athletic stature, nude, his clothes neatly folded at his feet, his arm pointing at the ceiling. The position looked painful to hold. Roch could see neither Mulard nor Madame de Nallet. He asked one of a group of students at their easels.

"Mulard? No, I haven't seen him in a few days," answered the man without looking away from his canvas. "Not since the trial of the Conspiracy of Daggers opened. He's a great friend of Topino, you know."

"And where did Madame de Nallet go? She is not here today?" asked Roch.

"Oh, David doesn't allow any female students when we do male nudes. And anyway, she doesn't come to the studio anymore. When I last saw Mulard, he told me that she had decided to abandon her flower studies."

Roch nodded. This was as he had suspected. The woman had remained close to David long enough to have her brother's name removed from the list of the émigrés. So much for her much-vaunted dedication to her art. Whatever Piis's assurances, this warranted further investigation, but for now Roch had no longer any reason to tarry in David's studio.

That night he headed for the Palais-Egalité. The galleries were far busier than during the day. Now they were full of prostitutes, strolling around in pairs, arm in arm, in search of patrons. There did not seem to be any shortage of those either. He saw Rose and Fanny, his acquaintances from Citizen Renard's establishment, shivering in their sheer gowns in spite of fur stoles thrown around their shoulders. They winked at Roch. They had found their quarry, a crimson-faced, paunchy fellow, whom they were steering in the direction of the brothel. Each of the young women had seized one of his elbows and both giggled in his ears. They huddled against him, to prevent any thoughts of escape and maybe also for warmth.

All of the brothels and gaming salons he visited had lost their daytime sleepiness. Roch called on Madame de Cléry last. He heard raised voices and shrill laughter before he pushed her door open. Groups of men and women were gathered around card tables. Some women were dressed like society ladies and kept their eyes fixed on the cards, while others, wearing the same sheer gowns as Rose and Fanny, were seated in the men's laps or standing behind them, their arms draped around their clients' necks. Piles of *louis*, like a gold tide, rolled towards the center of the tables.

In the middle of the crowd, Madame de Cléry cut a conspicuous figure. Roch had never seen her fully clothed. Now the gold fabric of her gown caught the light of the candles, and a scarlet shawl, embroidered in a darker shade of red, was artfully draped around her arms. Her breasts, full and round, were generously exposed. Very similar to Blanche's, thought Roch with a pang, only larger. A gracious smile on her lips, Madame de Cléry was walking from table to table, stopping to address her guests. She looked very elegant, and behaved like a society hostess at a fashionable party.

She drew herself up, frowning, when she recognized Roch, and walked quickly to him. "Here you are, Chief Inspector," she said under her breath. Her whisper was almost a hiss. "I had almost given up any hope of a visit from you. As you can see, I am rather busy at this time. Perhaps it would be more convenient if we kept to our usual hours."

"On the contrary, Citizen Cléry, this time suits me perfectly. It also allows me to watch the operation of your salon. A thriving business, if appearances are to be trusted."

"You happened upon us on a particularly good night. Now if you would please follow me to my apartment . . ."

Roch paid more attention than ever before to Citizen Cléry's bedroom, dimly lit by the fire in the hearth. At the far end, slender mahogany columns, trimmed with gold, formed an alcove around the bed. It was draped in blue silks, studded with little gold stars. The same fabric covered the walls and hung from the windows. Roch's eye traveled upwards to the painted swans that decorated the ceiling. He then returned his attention to Madame de Cléry. She was kneeling in front of a strongbox. Its gold-trimmed mahogany, matching that of the bed, disguised its function. She deftly turned three keys in their locks, revealing a thick steel lining under the wooden veneer, and seized a large purse.

"Are you looking for anything in particular, Sir?" she asked as she rose.

Roch was struck by a sudden inspiration. This was the bedroom of a lady. Indeed Madame de Cléry was a *lady*, though he had never thought of her in that light. What if she were Saint-Régent's lady? She was fifteen years older than the man, but she remained strikingly handsome. And was she also the lady who had taken Short Francis to the Convent?

He looked into her eyes. "No, Citizen, I was just thinking. Of a convent. The Convent of Saint-Michel. Do you know it?"

Madame de Cléry blanched, though her features remained unmoved.

"No, Sir, I have never heard of such a place," she said after a minute.

She handed him the purse. "You may obtain a warrant to search these premises if you wish, but you will find nothing. As you probably know, I had spent half a year in prison during the Terror. I have not forgotten those months. I awoke every morning wondering whether it would be for the last time. That experience has taught me to stay clear of anything that could send me back to jail."

Citizen Cléry's gaze wandered towards the mirror above the fireplace. She seemed very thoughtful now, almost sad. She looked her age. "I made many mistakes in my time, Chief Inspector, some grievous to the point of being irreparable. Some I repent to this day. I learned the value of prudence."

Roch took the purse. For the first time he felt no dislike for her. To a certain point she might be telling the truth, though he was sure she was lying about the Convent of Saint-Michel. He would have her gaming salon watched closely.

51

*R*och hailed a hackney and drove to the Ministry to drop the money he had collected. Though Marain, Fouché's secretary, had an apartment there, he did not seem too happy to be disturbed at this late hour.

As the hackney was driving Roch home, it crossed the Isle of the Cité and passed the main Courthouse. A row of windows at the northeastern corner of the building was still brightly lit. Surprised, Roch looked at his watch. Eleven o'clock. This must be the trial of the Conspiracy of Daggers. Judges and jurors would only remain in session so late for a case of major importance.

Roch pulled on the cord to signal to the driver to stop. He climbed the monumental stairs to the main entrance and walked to the Criminal Court section of the building. His footsteps echoed in the cavernous, empty halls. When he pushed open the only lit courtroom, it was empty, except for the yawning gendarmes and a few men and women scattered on the wooden benches. An iron stove provided adequate heat, but the gaslights hanging from the high ceiling and resting on the judges' desk left the far corners of the room in darkness. Nevertheless, Roch had no trouble recognizing Mulard's large figure and long reddish hair.

The painter started when Roch sat next to him. Mulard's cravat pointed in the direction of his left ear, and dark bluish shadows circled his eyes.

"How are things going?" Roch asked in a lowered voice.

"The jury is deliberating right now. As for the evidence against Topino, there's none. None of any value, that is." Mulard frowned. "Ceracchi, the only witness against him, recanted at trial and kept repeating that his confession had been wrenched from him under torture by your fine colleagues at the Prefecture. Then Harel, the *mouchard*, testified that Topino had not supplied any daggers to anyone. The prosecutor did produce a knife, but two witnesses could not agree on its origin, or whether it had anything to do with any plot to stab Bonaparte. Topino himself has steadily denied any involvement in the conspiracy."

"I have always thought that he would be acquitted if the case went to trial."

"He should be, but then the prosecutor argued that *sketches* of daggers had been seized in Topino's studio, and that, according to him, would be enough to prove his guilt! Of course a history painter is bound to sketch swords and daggers in the course of his work. I do it all the time. As things stand, those sketches are the sole evidence against Topino."

"What about David? Did he testify?"

"Oh, yes, as a character witness. He praised Topino's talent. How is this going to help? As if the jurors gave a damn about painting! They want to punish someone, anyone, for the Rue Nicaise attack."

A door at the back of the room opened and the bailiff announced: "The Court!" The gendarmes jumped to their feet and saluted. Mulard and Roch rose. The five judges appeared, in their black uniforms and plumed hats, the gilded insignia of their functions hanging from tricolor ribbons around their necks. The jurors also reentered the courtroom. The foreman stood up. The sheet of paper he held was shaking in his hand. Roch felt Mulard shaking too. His fists clenched and unclenched convulsively, his jaw was tense.

"Upon our honor and conscience," the foreman read, "we the jury find that there existed, during the month of Vendémiaire past, a conspiracy to assassinate the First Consul at the Opera." The foreman droned on, dwelling on the minutest details of the plot. Roch frowned.

He could not follow the rambling, confusing narrative, nor understand which particular role each of the accused was supposed to have played in the conspiracy. Finally the foreman paused to clear his voice. "Accordingly, the jury finds Dominique Demerville, Joseph Ceracchi, Joseph Aréna and François-Jean-Baptiste Topino-Lebrun guilty of participating in said conspiracy."

Roch barely heard the foreman announce that the remaining accused, three men and one woman, were acquitted. When Mulard heard the name of his friend among those found guilty, he rose all of a sudden and pounced forward. Roch caught him by the tails of his coat to make him sit again. The President, after casting a stern look in the direction of the two men, ordered the gendarmes to bring the accused. They slowly filed into the dock. Roch recognized Topino, young, tall, well built, with dark eyes and curly black hair.

Then everything passed very fast. The actors were weary, most of the audience had gone home, and the outcome of the play left no one in suspense. The accused resumed their seats, the prosecutor began his closing statement. The guillotine was the only punishment befitting the horror of the crime, he argued. The President conferred with the other judges, then read the death sentences and advised the defendants of their rights to appeal. Mulard, very pale, did not seem to listen to any of it. He was staring straight ahead at nothing. Finally, the gendarmes took Topino and the other accused away.

Roch grabbed Mulard by the arm and led him out of the courthouse. Both men walked along the banks of the river. Mulard broke the silence at last.

"Do you realize what has just happened, Miquel? They are going to be guillotined, all four of them, and they are innocent."

"Go to David. Ask him to intervene. Bonaparte might pardon at least Topino."

"I doubt it. Bonaparte likes the idea of befriending a great artist, but he would never listen to David on anything related to politics."

It was a clear night. Mulard's eyes remained fixed on the dark, slow waters of the Seine. The reflections of the lights along the embankments floated like specks of gold on the river.

Mulard looked into Roch's eyes. "No offense, Miquel, but you work for evil men. Your Prefect and his torturers will have innocent blood on their hands. Beware. You are a decent fellow, but before long you will become one of them."

"I will remain what I am."

"What choice will you have? I heard of your father's arrest. I am very sorry. I do hope things turn out better for him than for Topino."

Mulard put his hand on Roch's shoulder. "Listen, Miquel, don't take it amiss if I ask you to stay away from me. I don't hold you responsible for what happened to Topino. I know that this conspiracy business wasn't your idea, that you had nothing to do with it, but I don't trust you anymore. Good-bye then."

He left in the direction of the Right Bank. Roch remained still, listening as Mulard's footsteps resonated in the chilly night air. This friendship was one of the many things he had lost in the course of a few weeks. He shut his eyes tight, took off his hat and wearily ran his hand through his hair.

52

Roch slept poorly that night. In all fairness, after the conclusion to the Conspiracy of Daggers, he could not blame Mulard for wanting nothing to do with anyone linked to the police. But still more ominous was what the verdicts implied for Old Miquel. Anyone could be sentenced to the guillotine on the flimsiest of evidence.

In the morning, the only topic of discussion at the Prefecture was the outcome of the trial. Roch was attending to some routine correspondence when the guard announced a visit from Pépin. The boy removed his cap and remained by the door, at a safe distance. Yet he was grinning proudly.

"Got what you wanted, Citizen Chief Inspector, Sir," he said. "There's a coach arrivin' from Rennes 'round noon, with that man Davignon drivin'. And the day after tomorrow, that other man, that Guillou fellow, he'll be comin' back too."

"This sounds good, Pépin. Anything of crucial importance you forgot to tell me lately?"

Pépin put his hand on his breast. "Me, Chief Inspector? I'll never do that again. Remember, Sir, you've my word of honor."

"As though you had any such thing to give." Roch paused. Instead of tossing Pépin a copper coin, as was his wont, he set it down in the middle of his desk. The boy approached cautiously and began to extend his hand, ready to retreat at the first sign of danger.

"Say, Pépin," asked Roch, "aren't you tired of begging?"

The boy's jaw dropped and his hand stopped midway to the desk.

"I can't stand the sight of your rags," continued Roch. "And you smell like a dead skunk. I bet you haven't washed since your last dip in the river in the summer. Listen, I could find you an apprenticeship with a good master, one who would feed you well, give you a set of decent clothes and teach you a trade."

Pépin retreated backwards towards the door, an uneasy smile on his lips. "Like I tell th' other fellows on the street: *Chief Inspector Miquel, he's my favorite gen'leman in the whole police. Always a joke at the ready for me.*"

"I am not joking, imbecile." Roch looked into Pépin's eyes. "So what kind of trade would you like to learn?"

Pépin stared back. "Dunno, Sir. Never thought of that." His voice had a quivering, high-pitched tone now. It must be beginning to break. "Really, Sir, you'd do that?"

"Are you interested?"

"Of course I'm. Thank you, Sir. It's the first time anyone wants to do anythin' for me. Really for me, I mean. So yes, Sir, I accept. Right away, 'fore you change your mind."

"Not so fast. There is something you should know, little rascal. If I learned that your master wasn't entirely happy with you, I would come after you, personally, and I would give you such a thrashing as you would never forget. So don't take my offer unless you mean to better yourself. Think about it for a week."

"Oh, I've already thought 'bout it. Thank you, Sir. Well, if I ever thought that you'd . . ."

Roch picked up the coin from the desk and threw it to Pépin. For the first time, the boy missed and squatted to pick it up.

"Now run," said Roch.

He would talk to Alexandrine about Pépin. She would think of something suitable for the boy, perhaps at the Barrel or at her father's warehouse. In the meantime, the coachman Davignon would soon arrive in Saint-Denis, and Roch intended to greet him there. He had grabbed his hat and was on his way out of his office when he bumped into Piis.

"Excuse me," said Roch, "I am in a hurry."

"Wait, Miquel, it will only take a minute." The little man seemed distraught. "It . . . it's about your father."

Roch seized Piis by the arm. "My father? What do you mean? What happened?"

"Well, I just left the Prefect's office . . . He was signing various orders and warrants, and—"

Roch shook Piis. "And what? The Prefect ordered my father's deportation? The scoundrel can't do that!"

"Let me talk, Miquel. No, the Prefect cannot order anyone's deportation. But I saw him sign a memorandum ordering your father's transfer from the Temple to Bicêtre. For tomorrow morning."

Roch closed his eyes for a moment. All deportees left Paris from Bicêtre. Old Miquel's transfer there meant that his deportation was now imminent. It might happen as early as the next morning. Roch shoved his colleague out of the way. "Thank you, Piis. I need to go to Fouché this minute."

"For Heaven's sake, Miquel, can't you listen to me for a moment? The Prefect was not acting on his own accord. He had received his orders from Fouché himself this morning."

Roch frowned. This was indeed the 27th of January, the very date set by Fouché for the arrests of Saint-Régent and Carbon. That of Carbon alone was obviously not sufficient to save Old Miquel. There was no point in going to Fouché before Saint-Régent was captured as well, and this needed to happen within the next twenty-four hours. Roch's errand to Saint-Denis was more urgent than ever.

He ran out of the Prefecture and stepped into the middle of the street to stop a hackney. The driver, yelling a volley of oaths, pulled on the reins. Roch opened the door of the hackney, seized the astonished occupant by the lapels of his coat and threw him out.

"Police!" shouted Roch over the driver's curses. "To Saint-Denis, and whip your horse."

53

The guards at the city gates waved the hackney through when Roch showed his Prefecture Card. He jumped off before the vehicle had stopped in front of the Inn of the Golden Lion, the point of arrival and departure in Saint-Denis for all the stagecoaches to and from Rennes. Yet at this time there was no carriage in sight.

Roch rushed into the Golden Lion and grabbed one the waiters by the elbow. The man swore, recovered his balance and steadied the tray he was carrying. "Eh, you, can't you be careful?"

Roch slipped a coin into the man's palm. "Sorry. Did the coach from Rennes arrive yet?"

"Oh, that's why you almos' knocked me off my feet? Your sweetheart's on it? Well, the coach's a bit late today. You never know, with all those brigands on the roads. So what can I serve you to keep you nice an' warm while you wait for your youn' lady? A mug o' wine, maybe?"

Roch thanked the man and went to wait outside. The inn's wine, for all he knew, might come from Vidalenc's warehouse, and he doubted that he could he muster the patience to sit still for long.

A rooster, all brilliant russet and green feathers, and a few hens pecked at the dirt with satisfied clucks. A mongrel, seated on his rump, was scratching his ear with vigorous strokes of his hind leg.

After a while other people joined Roch in front of the inn. Among the small group Roch noticed a man, large, tall and fairly young. A low forehead, long matted hair and thick eyebrows gave him a brutish expression. He was dressed in trousers of coarse canvas and a goatskin jacket. Of course, this was a small suburban town, not Paris itself, but the man's apparel seemed oddly rustic here.

Soon Roch heard the rumbling of wheels and the rhythmic sound of hooves. The coach was approaching at a walk, its horses covered with white patches of sweat. The driver pulled on the reins, set the brake and climbed down stiffly from his seat. Rubbing his lower back, he opened the door for the travelers to alight. Deep lines cut into his face, between his cheeks and his chin, and locks of white hair stuck straight, as though half frozen, from under his hat. This must be Davignon, whose wife, unbeknownst to him, was housed in the prostitutes' coop at the Prefecture at that very moment.

The coachman, once all the passengers had alighted, looked on as two Auvergnats joking in the Roman language proceeded to unload the luggage from the roof and back of the carriage. The travelers claimed their belongings and went inside to stretch their legs and partake of some refreshments before taking hackneys to Paris. Davignon cleared the reins from the leaders while grooms freed the horses from their harnesses. Roch had retreated into a corner next to the stables entrance to watch the scene.

Once there was no one else left around the stagecoach, the goatskin man approached Davignon. They did not greet each other, nor did they appear to exchange a single look or word. Yet Roch saw the driver reach under the leather cover of his seat and hand the other man a sort of portfolio, which promptly disappeared inside the vastness of the hairy jacket.

So this was how George corresponded with his associates in the capital! There must be yet another trick to get the letters past the guards at the barriers, for they had strict orders to search every cart and carriage coming in and out of Paris.

The goatskin man walked away at a brisk pace. Fortunately no horse, hackney or carriage was waiting for him. He passed the massive walls of the Basilica, where the Kings and Queens of France had been buried before their tombs had been destroyed during the Revolution. Roch, thankful for the dark, narrow, winding streets, followed the suspect closely. But soon the man left the boundaries of Saint-Denis, headed towards the countryside, away from Paris. The cry of a rooster could be heard in the distance. Without the cover of the streets and their many recesses, Roch had to give him more headway and worried about losing sight of him.

A fourth of a league from the city limits, on a hillside, was an isolated white stone house, in the style of the aristocratic châteaux built before the Revolution. The goatskin man walked through the gilded gates of its park.

54

*R*och avoided the front entrance and followed the wall that enclosed the grounds. It was in good repair, smooth and too high to allow for easy climbing. After walking a few hundred yards to the west, he found a gate, three feet in width. This would do. He put on his leather gloves, settled his foot on the iron bar at the middle and seized the sharp spikes at the top with both hands. Careful to keep his groin clear of them, he pulled himself up and jumped to the other side.

To avoid detection Roch had to rely on the scant protection offered by the park's clusters of shrubs and trees in the English style. Half crouched, he hurried across the lawns that led towards a terrace at the back of the château. He hoped that no hounds were loose in the park at this hour and regretted the absence of his father's staff. All he had was Old Miquel's folding knife in his pocket.

At last he reached the flight of stairs that led to the terrace. It offered a beautiful perspective of Paris. Roch, without pausing to admire the view, stepped onto the terrace. Sheltering his eyes from the pale glare of the winter sun, he peered into a vast oval room, the windows of which opened to the floor. It took him but a moment to break one of the panes with his gloved fist. He pushed on the handle inside and let himself into a room paved in a checker pattern of black-

and-white marble. The furniture comprised a large mahogany table, twelve cane chairs and sideboards displaying heavy silver ewers and platters. Two sets of double doors were decorated with painted allegories of the seasons.

Behind the panels representing Spring, crowned with flowers, and Summer, holding sheaves of wheat, he heard the ringing of tiny bells, mingled with the yelps of a small dog. With bated breath he flipped his knife open inside his pocket. So this was the home of Saint-Régent's *lady*. He would discover her identity, and the man himself would be within his grasp. Old Miquel would be free at last.

Roch, still holding the knife in his right hand, opened the door with the left one. He found himself in an elegant salon, draped in silks patterned with roses and daisies. A pug ran at him as fast as its bow legs allowed and bit his boot. But Roch was not paying the animal any heed.

What arrested his attention was the sight of Blanche, standing in the middle of the room. She was very still, as pale as her white dress. Her black hair was tied by wide scarlet ribbons in the Greek fashion. She stared at Roch in silence, and he could not keep his eyes off her.

The dog's renewed attacks on Roch's boot brought him to his senses. If Blanche rang for her servants, he would be easily overpowered. He placed himself between her and the bell pull.

"It's over," he said in a quiet tone. "We are surrounded by a squadron of gendarmes, ready to storm the house. It is too late to escape now." He pointed at a chair. "Have a seat. You will forgive me if, under the circumstances, I take the liberty of giving you orders under your own roof."

Blanche slowly sat down, her eyes still fixed on his face. He slipped his foot under the belly of the pug and seized it by the scruff of the neck. He turned the silver medal hanging from its collar between his fingers. The dog, shaking with rage, snapped at the air in an attempt to bite his hand.

"*To My Lady*," Roch read aloud. "So this friendly animal must be Mirza. In truth, whose lady are you?"

She was still staring at him in silence. He let go of the dog, which, growling, jumped onto her lap.

"Listen, Citizen Coudert," he said between his clenched teeth, "if you wish to avoid the guillotine, talk, and fast. First you are going to tell me about Saint-Régent. Where's the bastard? In this house?"

She took a deep breath and spoke at last. "No. I don't even know where he is, Roch. I swear."

"Oh, yes, as you swore to tell me the truth during our last meeting. So you don't know where your lover is hiding?"

"He never was my lover. We met at the end of November, and he fell in love with me. I believe so, at least."

"Ah, yes, another one of those fools." Roch glared at Blanche. "But this won't be quite enough to keep this lovely head of yours on your shoulders. Come, Citizen, let's do better than this. Tell me about this business with the stagecoach from Rennes. All of the letters from George to Paris come this way, don't they? And that servant of yours, that fellow in the goatskin jacket, brings them here. See, I already know."

Blanche hesitated. "I take the letters to Paris in my carriage. They are hidden in a secret compartment in the door panel. And I do the same thing with the letters addressed to George from Paris. It is as fast as the post office, in fact. The guards at the barriers know me well, and they never search my carriage."

The pug burst out into a new frenzy of yelping. Blanche stroked its head. It kept quiet after one last resentful bark.

"And then," asked Roch, casting a malevolent look at the dog, "once the letters are in Paris, you arrange to have them delivered to your accomplices."

"They retrieve them at the Five Diamonds. They also drop their letters to George there."

Roch scoffed. "Well, of course, the Five Diamonds. So beautifully simple. You have everything at your fingertips there: your own little post office, and also a discreet love nest. No wonder I ran into Limoëlan nearby. He was retrieving or dropping his mail at the shop. How did you come to be called *For the King?*"

"That is the name Mother Duquesne gave me at the Convent when I was a child, because I would say that I would lay down my life for the King."

Roch was pacing the room. "Ah, yes, the Sisters of Saint-Michel! And I have known all along that you had been educated in a convent. What an idiot I was not to think of it!"

"Mama sent me there when I was five, and I stayed until the age of fifteen. So actually Mother Duquesne is the one who raised me. I was her favorite pupil."

"It was that fanatic who poisoned your mind with that Royalist nonsense!"

"She is no fanatic, and it is not nonsense! She told me of the late King and Queen, of their lives and martyrdoms, and of the cause. And I still believe in the restoration of the King."

"Oh, do you?"

"Yes, more than ever, though I loathe what Limoëlan did in its name. Those crimes can only hurt the cause. Mother Duquesne doesn't condone them either."

"Yet she gave Short Francis shelter at the Convent."

"Only because I begged her to hide him. Limoëlan told me that Francis was on the verge of being arrested, that I had to convince Mother Duquesne to give him shelter."

"So she agreed."

"Because she thought it was the only way to help me." Blanche hung her head. "And now she is in jail because of me . . . Oh, Roch, what will happen to her?"

"She still maintains that she didn't know anything of Carbon's involvement in the assassination plot. It remains to be seen whether the judges and jury believe her when she stands trial. There's another interesting point, though: she also maintains that the Cicé woman, not you, brought Francis to the Convent. She never stopped protecting you, whatever the consequences to herself."

"My God . . . my God . . ." Blanche whispered. "What have I done?"

"Pertinent question." A vision intruded upon Roch's mind. Carbon. Naked, pudgy, hairy, seated on his narrow bed at the Convent, and Blanche, also naked, kneeling on the floor between his legs. There were more unbearable images: Francis pulling her up onto his lap, kneading her beautiful breasts, spreading her long white thighs apart. Now was the time to press her for the truth.

"Unfortunately for you," continued Roch, "someone else was less discreet. Not only does Francis say you were the one who took him to the Convent, but he boasts that, once there, you bedded him with much enthusiasm. He speaks very highly of your skills and allurements. You made quite an impression on him."

"He is lying, the filthy beast!" cried Blanche. "He is even worse than I thought."

"Think of it. This will make for a few picturesque, memorable scenes at trial: Francis Carbon and Blanche Coudert, lovers and accomplices, seated next to each other in the dock. Posterity will remember you not as a martyr to the Royalist cause, but as the whore of the ugliest, most disgusting man in Paris."

Blanche shuddered. "He is lying. I simply told him I would return the next day. But of course I never went back. I never saw him again."

"Rather odd, I must say. I can't imagine Francis being content with mere promises and letting you go. Come, dear, tell me the truth."

"Mother Duquesne arrived in his room when he was ready to force himself on me. I ran away, and wrote him the next day."

"So *you* sent him that note in capitals!"

"And with it I sent Francis a gold watch, enameled in blue, the most garish I could find. He is very vain, very fond of finery. He fancies himself a great favorite with the ladies, and he even believes I like him. I knew he would be pleased to receive something like that from me."

Roch stared at Blanche's face. "So that watch was a token of your affection. And in that note, you wrote Francis that you would let his sister know where he was."

"I knew that Francis would become restless at the Convent without female company, that he would complain to Limoëlan that I wasn't visiting him. I knew through Saint-Régent that Francis slept with his sister. So I thought he wouldn't miss me too much if she went to the Convent."

"Now that was clever of you! The woman probably thought it was a bit risky, so instead she sent her daughter, who in turn led us to the Convent. What did your saintly friend Mother Duquesne think of those visits?"

"Oh, she left Francis alone in his room."

"Rather wise of her. And what about Limoëlan? How has he such a grip on your mind? You do everything he wants, no matter how revolting."

"I had no choice. He threatened to report me to George as a traitor. He has lost all trust in me."

"Why?"

Blanche hung her head.

"Might it have anything to do with me?" continued Roch. "Please enlighten me. You did not meet me by chance, or become my mistress for love, did you?"

"Limoëlan asked me to seduce you. He knew from his spy at the Prefecture that you came to Mama's salon every week."

"Which spy?"

"One of your Inspectors, a man called Bachelot."

"Bachelot wasn't enough?"

"No. Limoëlan wanted some documents to which Bachelot had no access, like the list of all of the traitors in our midst who worked for the police. So I convinced Mama to arrange a meeting between us at the gaming salon."

"And then what? You thought I would just open my office to you, and let you help yourself to whatever was of interest to your friends? I am afraid you had not a very high opinion of me."

"I realized that you were not that kind of man, that I would never get any information from you. I should have broken our liaison, but I didn't want to lose you." She held her hands to him. "*I* was the one to fall in love."

"And how you proved it!" There was poison in his voice now. "Are you Limoëlan's mistress too?"

"No, he never liked me in that manner, in any manner in fact. He despises me. Mademoiselle de Cicé must have told him of my true relationship to Monsieur Coudert. Anyway, Limoëlan is in love with a young lady, a friend of his sisters."

"And your mother, what part has she played in this business, in addition to introducing us?"

"None. I had to insist a great deal before she agreed to do even that. She wants nothing to do with politics nowadays. She was very angry when she discovered that I had become a fervent Royalist at the Convent. She had a terrible dispute with Mother Duquesne. Mama accused her of betraying her trust, of turning the head of a child with all of those ideas. She forbade me to see Mother Duquesne ever again."

"But you did not obey?"

"I had no choice as long as I lived with Mama. I did not see Mother Duquesne at all for three full years. But as soon as I was married, I went to the Convent again. Mother Duquesne introduced me to her friend Mademoiselle de Cicé, and told her of my old name of *For the King*. One day, as I was leaving, Mademoiselle de Cicé took me aside and asked me whether I still deserved that name. I said that I did, more than ever. Then some weeks later she mentioned that George needed a trusted go-between to forward his correspondence between Paris and Brittany. Right away I thought of this house, which is so close to the stagecoaches, and of the Five Diamonds. I have patronized the shop for years. I was happy to help the cause by forwarding George's correspondence. It seemed innocent enough, even thrilling. But last summer Mademoiselle de Cicé introduced me to the Little Painter, and everything changed."

"The *Little Painter*? Is that Madame de Nallet?"

"Félicie? Oh, no! I have known her forever. We were raised together at the Convent, though she is five years older than I. She doesn't even know Limoëlan. She has nothing to do with any of this."

"Is she the friend who provided an alibi for your little escapade with that man Rivoyre you supposedly married?"

"Yes."

"So then who is the *Little Painter*?"

"Limoëlan. That is what Mademoiselle de Cicé called him before the Revolution, and he still uses it as a code name. She showed me the miniature portraits of his sisters he had painted then."

"Charming. A pity he did not keep to that sort of talent."

"I don't know what he used to be when he was younger, but he is an evil man now. By the time I met him last summer, I had been forwarding George's correspondence for months. I was already compromised, but I still could have refused. When he asked me to seduce you, I thought that I would simply make you fall in love with me, and that would be all. I was still very naïve. Of course things did not go as I had planned. And after my failure with you, I couldn't refuse Limoëlan anything, and he kept pressing me to do more and more things."

"Here is what comes from having fine friends like yours." Roch's eyes narrowed. "So thanks to your accomplices, dozens of innocents were killed, maimed for life, at random, all for nothing. That does not bother you?"

Blanche's fingers were twisting the fringe of the crimson belt that tied her gown under her breasts. "Oh, yes, it does. But then the initial plan was still worse. Limoëlan wanted to blow up the entire Opera House, with Bonaparte in it, in the middle of the show. I was horrified. I realized that the Opera would be full that night, that there would be hundreds of victims, just to kill one man. It would tarnish the cause forever. So I talked to Saint-Régent and begged him not to let that happen. He promised he would convince Limoëlan to change the plan. Then, a few days later, Saint-Régent said that they had thought of a better idea. Both of them, with a few other Chouans, were to ambush Bonaparte on the road to his country house of Malmaison. They would overcome his escort. In that manner only a few dragoons would be killed, and of course Bonaparte."

"This is preposterous! Limoëlan and Saint-Régent, with the help of a few other men, hoped to overcome all the riders of Bonaparte's escort? And you believed that tale?"

"Certainly. Saint-Régent told me that Limoëlan had purchased half a dozen air guns."

Roch whistled silently. He had never handled or even seen air guns, but he knew of them. They were powerful, noiseless, smokeless, for the bullets were propelled not by the explosion of gunpowder, but by a removable compressed-air reservoir.

"How could Limoëlan afford all those air guns? Each would have cost a small fortune."

"George had sent him a great deal of gold he had received from the English government."

Indeed air guns were so expensive that they were not used by the Army, not even by the elite units in charge of Bonaparte's safety. They were remarkably efficient. An automatic magazine, loaded from the breech, could shoot twenty bullets a minute. A small group of seasoned, determined Chouans, armed with those weapons, could hope to overcome all of Bonaparte's guards.

"Who are those other men?" asked Roch.

"I don't know anything about them, only that they were to join Limoëlan and Saint-Régent somewhere on the road to Malmaison."

"Do Limoëlan and Saint-Régent still intend to proceed with that plan?" asked Roch.

"I don't know. Limoëlan doesn't tell me anything, and I haven't seen Saint-Régent in a week."

Roch rested his hands on the arms of Blanche's chair, bending over her. He looked into her eyes. "I want those guns, Blanche."

"Limoëlan has them, and I don't know where he keeps them. I am not even sure anymore that the air gun plan was real."

Roch was struck by a sudden idea. "So you didn't go to the Opera that night. You worried that your friends might blow up the place after all!"

"I no longer knew what to think."

Roch stood in front of Blanche, his hands on his hips. "You stayed home that night. And, like an imbecile, I worried about your safety! What did you tell Coudert? That you had a headache? That you didn't find your gown elegant enough for the occasion? Or is he part of this monstrous business?"

Blanche's eyes were wild with terror. "No, please, he is innocent. He is, Roch. He has never suspected what I was doing. He lets me do whatever I want, come and go as I like. If he knew . . ."

"Maybe he should have kept a closer eye on you. But let us go back to the 3rd of Nivose. You didn't go to the Opera that night. And I happen to know someone, another policeman, who waited in vain for his lady in her box. How rude of you to disappoint an admirer! You are Piis's Photis, are you not?"

Blanche's eyes were averted.

"Are you?" insisted Roch.

"Yes," she answered in a shaky voice, "sometimes he calls me Photis in those sonnets he keeps sending me."

"Your fondness for us policemen is remarkable."

Blanche was fidgeting with the bells of the dog collar. "Limoëlan said that, since I had failed with you, I had to get that list of traitors from Piis. I often met him in society and he seemed to like me. I told Limoëlan that I was trying my best to seduce Piis, while in fact I never had any intention of ever becoming his mistress."

"Always truthful, I see." Roch looked into Blanche's eyes. "Did you think all of this was some sort of game?"

Blanche shook her head slowly. "I have always known that I was risking my life. What comforted me was that the late King and Queen perished on the guillotine too. If they bent to that horrible machine, why should I shrink from such a death myself? At least that is what I used to feel. But now, Roch, I keep thinking of all those people who died on Christmas Eve. I told you of this already. I dream of them at night. Especially that poor little street vendor. I see her, with her biscuit tray, from the corner of my eye, when I least expect it. She startles me. And when I turn my head in her direction, she is not there anymore. And I realize that I am a coward. Oh, Roch, I am terrified."

Roch gazed at Blanche, at the crimson ribbons that tied her black hair, at the white skin of her throat. He pictured the raw flesh of her severed neck, still pulsating for a few moments after the fall of the guillotine blade. He shuddered. His anger gave way to a feeling of sadness, of hopelessness.

"What will happen now?" she asked. "Are you arresting me?"

"I want Saint-Régent and Limoëlan. Both."

"I don't know where they are."

"So you already said, but you are lying. You are protecting Limoëlan, not out of loyalty, but out of fear. This is a mistake. The man considers you a traitor. While he is free, he can either kill you himself or have one of your friends the Chouans do it."

"I know it all too well. I am not protecting him, but I truly have no idea of where he is hiding."

"And Saint-Régent?"

"I told you I don't know where he is either."

"Even if I were to offer you a chance to escape the guillotine? It will be your last one, so think well."

"But you said Francis mentioned my name. How could you save me?"

"Well, you are not the only one who can take liberties with the truth. In fact, Francis hasn't breathed a word about you. So you see, Blanche, all is not lost for you yet. It is down to your life, or Saint-Régent's. Your choice."

She was staring out the window at the beautiful view of Paris.

"I don't quite follow you," said Roch. "You tell me you are horrified by what Limoëlan did, by the carnage on Rue Nicaise. But is Saint-Régent any better? He is the one who set off the infernal machine, is he not? Did he not hurt your sacred cause too? I will tell you what it is, Blanche: you are protecting Saint-Régent because it flatters your vanity to be his *lady*. All this seems a bit childish in light of what is at stake here, doesn't it?"

Blanche remained silent for a minute, then turned slowly towards Roch. "I can leave a note for Saint-Régent to meet me at the Mayenne Inn. I think he will come."

"Then write it. Now."

Blanche rose. She sat in front of a lemonwood desk and dipped her quill into a crystal and silver inkwell.

"Write," growled Roch. "Give him an appointment."

Her quill scratched the paper. *This is For the King, dearest Pierrot. I need to see you at the Inn.* She hesitated.

"Tomorrow," dictated Roch. "At five in the morning. And make it urgent. If he doesn't come, I will have no choice but to arrest you."

He looked over her shoulder as she resumed writing. *Tomorrow, at five in the morning. My life depends on it. Oh, please come, dearest friend. You are my last hope. Do not mention to anyone and destroy this note as soon as you receive it. I miss you so.*

Roch reviewed the note. "Excellent. And it is true enough, for a change: your life depends on it. Have it delivered yourself. Remember, if you play any games, if Saint-Régent is not arrested tomorrow morning, you will be. Now I want you to order your carriage and return to Paris immediately. Once there, do not stir from your house until I tell you so. Do you hear me? Not under any pretext."

She looked up at him. "Roch, I want you to know that—"

"Enough, Blanche. No need to see me out."

He let himself out of the house through the back terrace and returned in haste to Saint-Denis. He never wanted to see Blanche or speak to her again. Thankfully their affair had been over long before this last conversation. The only thing that mattered now was Saint-Régent's arrest, and ultimately the fate of Old Miquel.

55

Pierre de Saint-Régent, alias Pierrot, was arrested before dawn on the 28th of January 1801, old style, as he was ready to enter the Mayenne Inn. Roch, before leaving for the Ministry, delivered the assassin to the astonished Bertrand. As Roch had guessed, his colleague had never breathed a word of their encounter to anyone, and he did not seem any more hostile than in the past.

Until the last moment, Roch had feared that Blanche had once again deceived him. But no, she had indeed betrayed Saint-Régent, and the man had walked into the trap for her sake. He too must have loved her. Roch had kept his own part of the bargain. He had not disclosed Blanche's part in the plot, and had ascribed his knowledge of Saint-Régent's presence at the Mayenne Inn to an anonymous letter.

Roch's father could not have left Bicêtre yet, and Carbon and Saint-Régent, both of the men Fouché wanted, had been arrested. Now he would order Old Miquel's release.

At the Ministry, Marain received Roch rather coldly. "No, Citizen Chief Inspector," said the man, "Citizen Fouché can't receive you. He went to the Tuileries to give the First Consul a report on the new developments in the Rue Nicaise attack."

"So he knows of Saint-Régent's arrest?"

"Of course. We received a note from the Prefect earlier this morning. I understand that you played some small part in it. Congratulations, Citizen Chief Inspector."

"And about my father?"

"Oh, yes. I was forgetting to give you the good news. The Minister ordered Citizen Miquel *père* transferred back to the Temple."

Roch closed his eyes and threw his head backwards. At least deportation was no longer an immediate threat.

"And what about releasing him?"

"The Minister didn't say anything to that effect."

"I don't quite understand. Is the Minister not happy with the results?"

"He seemed in an excellent mood, I would say. I am sure he will send the Prefect his instructions shortly." Marain rose. "Congratulations again, Citizen Chief Inspector."

Roch bit his lower lip. There was nothing for him to do but to return to the Prefecture. He paused on his way on the Pont-Neuf, the New Bridge. He leaned on the parapet and gazed at the slow river beneath. So Fouché still would not order Old Miquel's release. Why should he, besides keeping his word to Roch? The threat of deportation had receded, at least for a time, but Old Miquel was not out of danger. He could still be tried before a Military Commission and summarily executed any day. Fouché wanted it this way. Roch shrugged. He had concentrated all of his thoughts, his energy, on arresting Carbon and Saint-Régent, but that was clearly not enough. He had not guessed Fouché's ultimate purpose.

Once back in his office, Roch wrote General Duroc, the head of the Military Police, an anonymous letter warning of an attack on the First Consul, on the road to Malmaison, by a group of determined men armed with air guns. Hopefully Duroc would double the escort and increase the usual precautions. Without informing his superiors, Roch also sent Pépin to watch Blanche's Paris mansion, with instructions to follow her whenever she left home.

At the Prefecture, Division Chief Bertrand was now in charge of Saint-Régent's case. In Roch's presence, he made the Chouan sit on the same table where his comrade François Carbon had been searched. Naked, Saint-Régent looked almost frail, and the tan of his face and hands contrasted with the whiteness of his body. Yet he was muscular in spite of his slender frame. The witnesses' descriptions had been accurate: a pointy nose, blue close-set eyes, a high forehead, light brown hair, braided in *cadenettes*.

On the chair lay his clothes: a blue coat with shiny buttons that bore the inscription *guilt warranted* in English, a black waistcoat, striped stockings, a round hat and a light gray overcoat. Oddly enough, he was wearing slippers at the time of his arrest. He must have been in a hurry to respond to Blanche's call for help.

Unlike Short Francis, Saint-Régent was immediately interrogated by Bertrand. Roch could hear telltale howls of pain, as during the questioning of the suspects in the Conspiracy of Daggers, coming from his colleague's office.

"Damned fanatic," grumbled Bertrand to himself in the corridors of the Prefecture.

Saint-Régent must have understood that Blanche had betrayed him, and yet he had not named her. Maybe he loved her to the point where his love survived the awareness of her treason.

But Bertrand was not easily discouraged. The yelling resumed after lunch, before the official questioning by the Prefect. Roch, standing with Piis by the peephole, noted that the prisoner's fingers were reduced to masses of purplish flesh, and that he walked with great difficulty. Bertrand must have burnt the soles of his feet. Yet Saint-Régent's face, though tense, was perfectly steady.

"My name is Pierre Martin," he answered the Prefect, "born in Brest, Brittany, formerly sailor. I arrived in Paris two days ago."

"How did you come to Paris?" asked Dubois.

"On foot."

"On foot? You walked over a hundred leagues in these slippers? In the middle of winter?"

"So it is, Citizen."

"And why did you come to Paris?"

"To find work."

"Have you a passport?"

"No, Citizen, I have no papers whatsoever."

Obviously Saint-Régent would not speak, at least not until he was granted a few more sessions with Bertrand.

On the next day, he was presented to his former landlady, the Guillou woman, to her children and husband, for he too had been arrested upon the arrival of his stagecoach in Saint-Denis, and to young Toinette Jourdan. All identified him as the man they had known and housed under the name of Monsieur Pierrot.

The witnesses' statements seemed to achieve more than Bertrand's ministrations.

"My name is Pierre de Saint-Régent," he stated to the Prefect in a weary tone during the second day of his questioning, "born in 1768, in Saint-Régent, Brittany. I used to be an officer in the King's Navy from 1781 to 1791. I was wounded three times in action during that time. My usual residence is my birthplace of Saint-Régent. I arrived in Paris almost three months ago, for the purpose of having my name removed from the list of the émigrés, where it doesn't belong. In fact, I never left France, though I took arms against the Republic from 1793 to 1795. I received a pardon for my activities as a Chouan."

At least the Prefect had obtained from the suspect a truthful statement of his identity. Not bad for Dubois, thought Roch.

"Do you know a man by the name of Limoëlan?"

"I can't remember."

"Was he the one who brought a confessor when you were injured on the night of the Rue Nicaise attack?"

"I wasn't injured. I was sick in bed."

"Who was that confessor?"

"I don't know," answered Saint-Régent.

"Where is Limoëlan now?"

"I don't know."

I don't know remained Saint-Régent's stubborn answer to all of the Prefect's questions, except for the occasional *I can't remember*. In fact, the man did not appear to know anything, or anyone, apart from a few individuals about whom he had no information to provide. Dubois now looked more tired than the suspect.

"Where did you stay on the night that preceded your arrest?" finally asked the Prefect.

"Outdoors. I have not had any abode since the 17th of January, when I left the lodgings of Widow Jourdan. At night I slept on coal barges on the river."

"And during the day?"

"I would go for strolls on the embankments."

"What was your business at the Mayenne Inn when you were arrested?"

"I went there to enquire about a room."

Not a word about Blanche or her note. Saint-Régent was still shielding her, as had François Carbon and Mother Duquesne. The young woman had been fortunate so far. Would Limoëlan be equally kind to her once he too was arrested? Roch doubted it.

The questioning soon reached the issue of Saint-Régent's alibi on the night of the Rue Nicaise attack. Yes, he had seen the carriage of the First Consul drive by, escorted by dragoons. No, he had never accompanied any cart on the 3rd of Nivose. He did not know anything of any girl being told to hold the horse's bridle. No, he had not lit any fuse. Indeed he had not even seen Limoëlan or Carbon that night. The tinder he had asked Toinette Jourdan to buy was to light his pipe, in the manner of the Indians, in America. He had nothing to say about the letter signed *Gideon* that had been seized in his room at Widow Jourdan's lodgings. It must have been placed there by some unscrupulous policeman intent on compromising him.

The interrogation continued on the next day, and the next, though Roch ceased his attendance. There was nothing to be learned of Saint-Régent. Not only did he persist in his denials, but he became angry, he ranted, he growled at the Prefect. And that, reflected Roch, after the man had been tortured for days. The pain in his hands and feet must now be unbearable, it must linger, relentless, between the sessions in Bertrand's office. Roch could not help feeling some grudging admiration for Saint-Régent.

56

A so-called Letter from Topino-Lebrun to the Jury was circulating in Paris. It was in fact an anonymous pamphlet about the inanity of the evidence and the unfairness of the death sentences in the trial of the Conspiracy of Daggers. The Prefect instructed Roch to discover and arrest promptly its author, or authors, and printer. Roch, though convinced that Mulard had a hand in it, chose not to share his suspicions with his superior and indeed displayed little zeal in that investigation.

In any event, the pamphlet served no purpose. Topino-Lebrun and his supposed accomplices were duly guillotined once their appeals were rejected, on the 30th of January. Their fate elicited no sympathy, for public opinion still blamed them for the Rue Nicaise attack in spite of the arrests of Carbon and Saint-Régent.

Yet all the usual Chouan haunts, including now the Mayenne Inn, were under close surveillance. Roch had also posted some of his informants to watch Madame de Cléry's gaming salon and the mansion of Madame de Nallet, the halfhearted flower painter. He put little stock in Blanche's assurances about the innocence of her mother and friend.

Saint-Régent remained steadfast in his refusal to speak. Of Limoëlan there was still no trace. Roch was beginning to worry that the man had managed to slip out of Paris. He looked up from his work when a messenger brought him a note, and frowned when he recognized Blanche's handwriting. What could she possibly want from him now? He tore the seal open and began to read.

> *I understand, Roch, how angry you are with me, justly so, but please read this, not for my sake, but for your investigation.*
>
> *I have long thought of Limoëlan. Contrary to what you think, I do want to help you arrest him. I don't know where he is, but I do know of a way to reach him through an uncle of his.*
>
> *So through that uncle I sent Limoëlan a note asking him to meet me at midnight tonight at the lower end of the Champs-Elysées, on the pier whence the ferry leaves. He will come, if only to kill me.*
>
> *I pray that someday you may find it in your heart to forgive me.*

Roch flushed with anger and crumpled the piece of paper. Blanche was trying to draw him into a trap, as she had done with Saint-Régent. Only this time she was acting at Limoëlan's behest, in an attempt to regain the trust of her accomplice. And by the same token the little minx would rid herself of the only policeman aware of her part in the plot. She would kill two birds with the same stone. And who was that uncle of Limoëlan? Did he even exist? If so, this was yet another thing Blanche had been hiding.

Roch frowned. There was another possibility. He straightened out Blanche's note and reread it, pondering each word. Unlikely as it seemed, what if she told the truth this time? After all, Limoëlan was her most determined foe. Maybe the trap was indeed destined for him, not for Roch. With Limoëlan dead, she could hope to recover her former standing with the Chouans. She was clever enough to dispel George's suspicions as to Saint-Régent's arrest. Roch shook his head in exasperation. Who could ever hope to disentangle Blanche's skein of lies?

The only prudent, reasonable thing was for him to inform his superiors of the fact that Limoëlan might be at the Champs-Elysées tonight. He could even avoid naming Blanche by claiming that he had received the tip from some anonymous informer. The Champs-Elysées would be surrounded by dozens of policemen, waiting to arrest Limoëlan.

But then if Blanche came to the Champs-Elysées, she too would be arrested, then tried, maybe executed. Roch realized that he could not reconcile himself to that prospect. He would go, alone, and take his chances.

57

Aboveground, in the Church of Saint-Laurent, monuments and long-winded inscriptions recalled the titles and virtues of the priests, deacons and aristocratic donors buried below, but down in the crypt only plain stone slabs covered the tombs. Joseph de Limoëlan shuddered. Not that the closeness of the dead disturbed him in the least. These days the dead bothered him far less than the living. But it was dreadfully cold.

Certainly there could be no safer hiding place than the crypt of this deserted church, and he was grateful to his uncle Father de Clorivière for thinking of it, but he was used to the outdoors. He liked the swift, daring attacks on the Republic's troops in the Brittany countryside, the wind whipping his face, the fragrance of the sea, the crash of the waves on the pink granite shores. Now he felt trapped like a rat in that dark, dank, musty, silent hole.

Limoëlan, by the light of a tallow candle affixed to a tombstone, was reading a letter from his uncle, Father de Clorivière.

> *Dearest Joseph,*
>
> *I received the enclosed note, destined for you. I supposed it to be very urgent, and forwarded it immediately.*
>
> *You must be desperate for news of your dear mother. Rest easy, my son. She has already been released. She was questioned, her house was searched, but the police found nothing*

there. She is now restored to the affections of your beloved sisters.

Our dearest Mademoiselle de Cicé, however, is still in jail, and so is Mother Duquesne. I have little hope of a prompt release for either of them. Let us remember them in our prayers, as we remember all of those who suffer for their faith and King.

May God keep you, dearest son, under His worthy and holy protection,

†

Limoëlan had not been overly worried for his mother. He had been sure that, thanks to Fouché's protection, she would be released after some perfunctory questioning. What was far more disturbing was Blanche's note, folded within Father de Clorivière's letter and written in a hurried scrawl.

Dear friend,

I have something of the utmost importance to tell you. You are in imminent danger. Please meet me at midnight tonight at the lower end of the Champs-Elysées, on the pier where the ferry leaves.

For the King

He sneered. Blanche must take him for a complete imbecile. He had already suspected her at the time of Francis's arrest, but he had given her the benefit of the doubt then. Now there was but one person who could have lured Saint-Régent out of hiding. For Saint-Régent was cautious, cunning, wary. Except when it came to Blanche. The fool was in love, and she had used his love to deliver him to his enemies, as Delilah had done to Samson. Blanche had clearly fallen under the influence of that scoundrel Miquel. That was why she had told

Limoëlan for months that she could not succeed. *He* had succeeded with her.

And now the treacherous little whore tried to deliver Limoëlan as well to her lover. She would find some difficulty there. Limoëlan meant to live, and to live free, and he meant for Blanche to die. Without rising, he reached for a thin object, four feet in length, resting against the wall behind him. Steal gleamed in the light of the candle. He grinned as he braced the club-shaped butt of the gun against his shoulder.

58

Blanche fervently prayed that Limoëlan and Roch would both come to the Champs-Elysées tonight. Before sending the messages she had long thought of her situation. It was hopeless.

How could have things come to this? Seducing, deceiving and then getting tangled in her own snares. Betraying the lovelorn Saint-Régent. Worse, helping kill innocents. It could all be traced to Limoëlan. Until she had met him, everything was going so well. She was helping the cause without harming anyone. Then Limoëlan had come to Paris and her life had changed. First he had asked her to seduce Roch. She could have refused that mission. Why had she accepted? She must have been yearning for the romance she had so carefully eluded since Armand's death.

She thought she could play with Roch's feelings without getting caught herself. When she had realized the enormity of her presumption, it had been too late to escape. She had lied to Limoëlan to continue lying to Roch. Limoëlan had sensed her betrayal and kept asking her to do more outrageous things, to seduce Piis, to give herself to Francis. Again the result had been yet more lies, less trust, and more contempt from Limoëlan. All this to keep a man whose love she was bound to lose. Now it had happened, and it was only part of the darkness enshrouding her.

Roch had been right: either Limoëlan would kill her, or he would convince George to order her execution, and some other Chouan would take care of it.

And then there was the police. Even if Carbon and Saint-Régent, against all odds, persisted in shielding her, how much longer could Roch protect her without compromising himself? She imagined herself awaiting death in a jail cell, then stepping onto the cart under the jeers of the people, laying onto the deadly machine, waiting in terror for the fall of the blade. Limoëlan's bullet would bring a speedier, more merciful death.

She walked to her dressing closest. She chose her finest pelisse, a white satin lined with ermine fur. It was a gift from Monsieur Coudert on her last birthday, in November. It seemed so long ago. She brought the soft, shimmering fabric to her cheek and fought back tears. It was sure to catch any glimmer of light, even in the dead of the night. Oh, she would never commit suicide, the only sin for which there was no forgiveness. But maybe tonight on the Champs-Elysées it would please God to deliver her from her earthly burden.

She slipped on the pelisse and was ready to head for the service staircase when she saw a large figure blocking the door.

"Where are you going, Blanche?" asked Coudert in a quiet tone.

"Well, Sir, Félicie sent word that she has a bad sore throat. She asked me to spend the evening with her."

"Félicie? Again? And why did you put on your best evening pelisse to attend to a sick friend?" Coudert shook his head sadly. "I know that we agreed long ago that I wouldn't interfere with your life, but I am becoming very worried, Blanche. You disappear at all hours without warning, you go to Saint-Denis every other day, your friend Félicie is sick every week, and now that young policeman comes here and behaves in an outrageous manner in front of the servants."

Coudert walked to Blanche and took her in his arms. "And you look so sad, so forlorn these days. All happiness seems to have drained out of you. I hardly recognize you. What is it with you, my dearest?"

Blanche huddled against Coudert. She closed her eyes, relishing the comfort of his embrace. For a moment she was tempted to confess everything. But what good would come out of it? She pulled away gently and forced a smile. "Thank you, Sir, but I am all right. I will be fine, really."

Coudert sighed. "I wish you would tell me the truth, Blanche. You should know you can trust me. If you have run into some kind of trouble, I will do anything in my power to help you. Is it a matter of money, dearest?"

Blanche shook her head wistfully. If only it could have been about money! "Oh, no, not at all."

"That's what I suspected. It is far more worrisome, isn't it?" Coudert looked into Blanche's eyes. "Listen, Blanche. I have rendered Fouché some very important services. I will go to him, explain that you made a mistake. You are very young, you were thoughtless. He will help if I ask him."

"It is very kind of you, Sir, but no, not even Fouché could help me."

Coudert looked away. "All right, then, it must be what I have been dreading for some time. Your friends have turned on you, haven't they? What have you done, my poor Blanche?"

"Oh, please don't ask me. If I told you, you too would be in danger."

"So let's both leave Paris tonight. We will go to Moriaz. Surely those so-called friends of yours can't track us down there, in the middle of the Alps."

"Yes, they can. Even if we were to leave France, they could still pursue me. You don't know them, Sir. I would never again have a minute of peace. I would spend the rest of my life in terror."

"So at least tell me where you are going."

"I can't. You must let me go now tonight. This is truly my only chance of escape. Please do not follow me. It would only put me in greater danger."

She threw her arms around his neck. "If I escape tonight, Sir, I promise I will never again give you a moment of uneasiness. I will never again keep any secrets from you. You will see, we will be so quiet and happy."

She realized that she was not only trying to slip away. She meant it. Whatever happened at the Champs-Elysées tonight, she would be free.

59

Limoëlan was making his way towards the pier whence, in daytime, the ferry crossed the river in the direction of the Invalides. It was almost midnight now. All was silent and seemingly deserted at this end of the Avenue of the Champs-Elysées. These were the place and time appointed by Blanche in her note. Whether she would be there herself, he could not tell, but he was certain that her lover, along with many other policemen, was laying in wait nearby.

The soil was sandy in this area, and the dead leaves of autumn had long been swept away by the sharp winds of winter. One could move stealthily, an advantage obviously shared by the scoundrels of the police. The night was fairly clear, and a silvery half-moon glowed behind a film of fog. Rows of trees, planted half a century ago, under the reign of King Louis XV, provided little protection against the illumination of the streetlights, for they were barren in this season. Limoëlan sighed at the remembrance of the hedgerows and thickets of Brittany, so convenient to ambush the Republic's troops.

As intently as he peered through the darkness and listened to any noise, he could not detect the presence of any policemen around the place. He approached the little pier and saw a figure draped in white, glimmering softly in the night. His first thought was of the ghosts whose woeful stories his nurse would tell him when he was a child. He promptly shook away those ridiculous fancies. This was no Brittany moor, shrouded in mist and legend; this was plain, prosaic Paris, and the creature was of flesh and bone. One tree at a time, he drew closer. Now he recognized Blanche. He could not discern her face or hair, because she wore some kind of white hood that covered her head. Yet, even at this distance, there was no mistaking the tall, slim figure, the grace of her movements. For she was moving, pacing the length of the pier, sometimes stopping as though to look at the far-off lights of the Invalides across the river. Sometimes she was facing the Champs-Elysées and, in the shadows, Limoëlan and his gun.

He settled behind a tree, about one hundred paces away from her, well within the range of his gun. With his spectacles, he could easily hit a target at this distance. He was no expert marksman, but his hand was steady and his nerves never failed him.

This was uncannily easy. Limoëlan, to avoid making any noise, had taken the precaution of fitting the compressed-air reservoir and loading the bullet magazine before leaving the crypt of Church of Saint-Laurent. He dropped to his knee on the humid, soft soil. He aimed at his leisure and was ready to shoot when he heard a man's voice to his left. Now he could guess at a figure, half hidden by a tree. Not an easy enough target.

"Blanche, what are you doing here?" shouted the man. "Run! Run away!"

She turned in the direction of the voice, and seemed to hesitate whether to leave the pier. She walked a yard or two, then stopped.

"Blanche, come to me," pleaded the voice. "Don't let him kill you. Please."

Blanche began to run towards the bank. Soon she would reach her lover and the protection of the trees. The man himself had left his position and was headed in Blanche's direction. With a little luck Limoëlan could kill them both, one after the other. A slight breeze pushed a wisp of fog between him and his targets. No matter, he could still guess at their positions. He pulled the trigger. There was no explosion, no fire, no smoke, only a whizzing sound, repeated half a dozen times.

But Limoëlan did not see whether he had hit his targets. All of a sudden he went blind. The pain in the socket of his right eye was so sharp that he dropped his gun.

"Right 'ere, Citizen Chief Inspector!" cried an unknown voice, high-pitched and croaky. "I nailed the bastard!"

Limoëlan put his hand up to his eye. A warm gush of blood was running down his cheek. He staggered and fell to his side. Running footsteps were getting closer and closer.

60

Roch had heard the whistling of the bullets, but the bank of the river remained hidden in mist. From the spot where he had last seen Blanche no noise was coming, not a cry, not a moan, not a whimper, not a splash in the water. She must have moved in time. As for Limoëlan, there was no telling what had happened to him. Certainly he was not shooting anymore, and the odd voice resembled that of Pépin. Roch headed cautiously in its direction. He could not go to Blanche until he was assured that Limoëlan no longer posed a threat.

Roch breathed a sigh of relief when he saw Pépin, holding a slingshot and kicking a prostrate Limoëlan in the belly. The man was doubled over in pain, his spectacles were missing and blood was smeared over the right side of his face.

"Enough, Pépin," said Roch. "Now grab the gentleman's gun and watch him for a moment."

Roch ran back towards the pier. Another gust of wind tore at the wall of fog. He dreaded seeing at any moment something white lying there. Blanche wounded, in pain, dying. But no, all he could see was the planks of the pier and the sandy soil of the banks. She had disappeared as fast, as silently as an apparition, and he wondered whether his eyes had not deceived him.

Roch walked back to Pépin, who was standing, air gun in hand, next to Limoëlan. The man, curled up on his side, his eyes closed, was clutching his belly. That sight infuriated Roch.

"I will take this, Pépin, if you don't mind," he said, seizing the gun.

Limoëlan started at the sound of Roch's voice and rolled over onto his back. He blinked. Roch pointed the gun at Limoëlan's face. The man probably could not see anything without his spectacles, but he recoiled from the heat of the barrel on his cheek.

"Yes, bastard," said Roch, "this is your gun. Now, tell me, how many bullets have we left in this thing? I'd say at least a dozen. And we aren't in any hurry, are we? Nice and slow, one at a time. Where do you think I should begin? The stomach? Or the bowels? Or maybe the groin?"

"Have mercy," whispered Limoëlan.

"Mercy? What mercy? Mercy on Blanche when you tried to kill her a moment ago? On those poor people on Rue Nicaise? Now let's be serious. Give me one reason not to kill you, piece of filth."

Limoëlan opened his mouth, but could utter only a rattling sound.

"None comes to mind, apparently," said Roch.

Roch pushed the barrel of the gun into Limoëlan's belly and was ready to shoot. The man let out a croaking cry. "Wait! I can help you save your father."

Roch had not expected this. His heart was pounding.

"Your father . . ." continued Limoëlan. "Fouché sent him to jail, did he not?"

"How do you know that? Through Bachelot, that traitor?"

"Yes. My father too was in jail, before he was guillotined. I couldn't save him." Limoëlan paused to swallow. "Fouché has no intention of letting your father go. You know that, don't you?"

"You are lying to save your skin, bastard," cried Roch. He was breathing hard. The worst was that Limoëlan might be right. What incentive could Fouché have to release Old Miquel now? Gratitude? Keeping his word?

"Listen to me," said Limoëlan, "and then tell me if I sound like a liar. Fouché asked my mother to arrange a meeting with me. That was three weeks before the attack."

"'I already knew that. He asked you to betray your friends?"

"No. He seemed to know all about them already. He . . . he asked me to put him in touch with George, and with the King's government in London. He wants to remain Minister of Police once the King is restored."

Roch held his breath. Was it out of character for Fouché to plot such a thing? Certainly not.

"I see," said Roch. "Fouché looks the other way while you kill Bonaparte and, as a reward, he gets to keep his position. And what did you do?"

"I wrote George, of course."

"And what had George to say about it?"

"He forwarded Fouché's offers to London."

"Did George put this in writing?"

"Yes."

"Where is that letter?"

"Do you think I carry George's letters in my pockets? I burned them all at the time of Francis's arrest."

Roch looked down at Limoëlan. The barrel of the gun had left a reddish burn on the man's cheek.

"Then this is worthless. There's no proof of what you are telling me. Better think of another story. Fast."

Limoëlan blinked a few times. "Wait. Miquel! If you kill me, you will lose any proof of Fouché's dealings with George. You will be the only man left in Paris to know about that, and it won't put you in a very enviable position, will it? Do you think Fouché would hesitate for a moment to rid himself of you if you were the last witness against him? And where would that leave your father?"

Roch pushed the gun deeper into Limoëlan's stomach. "You are right," said Roch. "Better arrest you. Get to your feet, I am taking you to the Prefecture."

"That won't work either for you. If you arrest me, I will reveal everything I know about Fouché to the Prefect in exchange for immunity. I need not tell you what that means. Dubois hates Fouché and will have him arrested for treason. Now I understand the Prefect is no friend of yours, is he? You will be dismissed, and your father will be tried before some Military Commission. So, Miquel, as much as you hate the idea, you need me alive, and free."

Roch was torn apart. He was Chief Inspector Miquel, one of the upper functionaries of the Prefecture of Police, a man whose paramount duty it was to arrest the assassins and prevent them from killing again. But there was a different Roch, the son of Old Miquel. And Old Miquel, unlike the Rue Nicaise victims, could still be saved. Roch the policeman had lost many of his illusions over the past few weeks. Had his superiors, Fouché and Dubois, displayed any integrity? Of course if Roch let Limoëlan go now, he would be guilty of the same dereliction of duty.

"Listen, Miquel," continued Limoëlan, "if you let me go, I give you my word of honor that I will flee to Brittany, and from there to England. You will never hear of me again."

"Or you might come back to Paris someday and kill again."

"I gave you my word of honor."

"Assassins like you have no word, and no honor."

Roch's heart was racing. Rage almost choked him, but now was the time to think clearly for Old Miquel's sake.

"Pépin, go look for the gentleman's spectacles," he said.

Pépin walked around and soon brandished them with a cry of triumph.

"He won't see too good with'm, though," the boy said as he showed Roch the spectacles. One of the glasses had been shattered and sparkled like diamonds in the glow of the streetlights.

"Oh, better these than nothing. Give them to him. We wouldn't want him to hurt himself, would we?" Roch spat in Limoëlan's face. "Now run," he hissed.

Limoëlan rose slowly, watching Roch through his only intact eyeglass.

"Run, carrion, before I change my mind."

Limoëlan turned around very fast and disappeared into the night.

61

"So you let the vermin go, Sir, after he tried to kill you and Madame Coudert," said Pépin, a twinge of disappointment in his voice.

"I had no choice."

Roch was twisting in his pocket Blanche's last letter. Again she had slipped away when she had seemed so close. Yet to her too Limoëlan's escape was good news. If Francis and Saint-Régent persisted in protecting her, she might not even be suspected. Roch himself did not intend to reveal her part in the conspiracy.

It was Blanche who had in fact led him, unwittingly or deliberately, to all three men in stallholder jackets. She had informed Francis's sister of the short man's presence at the Convent, which had indirectly caused his niece Madeleine to reveal his hiding place. Then Blanche had betrayed Saint-Régent. Now she had risked her life to allow Roch to capture Limoëlan. Had she hoped to find an escape from her troubles and sorrows in death? Roch clenched his fists at the thought that he had let Limoëlan escape, but that very escape, hopefully, would secure Old Miquel's freedom. Yes, what mattered now was the fate of Old Miquel.

Roch shook himself out of his thoughts. "Let's talk about you, Pépin. I haven't thanked you yet. Let me do so." Roch put his hand on the boy's shoulder. "I wish to express my deepest gratitude for your help."

Pépin smiled proudly. "I aimed good, eh, Citizen Chief Inspector?

Right in his spe'tacles. I'd have gotten him earlier, but I'd to find jus' the right stone. I knew I couldn't miss."

"You did very well."

"I kept an eye on Madame Coudert, like you'd said. When I saw she was leavin' her home in a hackney, I jumped onto the back. It dropped her over there." He pointed in the direction of Place de la Révolution. "I almost thought I was too late to save her."

Blanche must have already reached her house on Rue de Babylone. It was no more than a fifteen-minute walk from the bottom of the Champs-Elysées. Roch, his hand still on Pépin's shoulder, headed for the Place de la Révolution. The familiar outline of the Statue of Liberty was no longer to be seen against the night sky. It had already been demolished to make way for a monumental tribute to Bonaparte. Roch remembered his conversation with Old Miquel on the night of the Rue Nicaise attack.

"So where're we goin', Sir?" asked Pépin.

"To my lodgings. I can't leave you to freeze on the streets after what you did for me. I want you to sleep in a warm bed tonight, with some soup in your stomach."

The boy grinned broadly. "Well, that's awful nice of you, and—"

"Believe me, you won't feel the least inclination to thank me once you set eyes on my maid. She is a redoubtable woman. She will scour every inch of your skin without mercy."

"Why, if she ever tries to—"

"Oh, it will take her but a moment to get the better of a shrimp like you."

Pépin sighed, apparently resigned to the prospect of a forced bath. "So long's it makes you happy. But, remember, Citizen Chief Inspector, you talked about a 'prenticeship th'other day . . ."

"I have changed my mind."

Pépin's lips formed a silent *Oh* of disappointment.

"I will send you to school instead," added Roch, "though it won't be easy to find a teacher brave enough to undertake your education."

Pépin breathed in sharply. "Ah, no, Sir, you can't do that! After I saved your life too! Don't you know they whip boys in schools?"

"They do, fiercely so. But better men than you have gone through that ordeal, and lived to tell the tale. I am afraid, my poor Pépin, that many changes are coming your way, like it or not."

They walked in silence until they reached Roch's lodgings twenty minutes later. He pulled his astonished maid from her bed and delivered Pépin to her care. The boy followed her with surprising meekness. She brought Roch a mug of honeyed tea. He seized a carafe on the sideboard and added a generous swig of plum spirits to the hot beverage. He needed to brace himself for the task ahead.

62

It was barely six in the morning when Roch was shown into the Minister's private apartment at the Juigné Mansion. He could not help staring at Fouché, the millionaire, the head of the Nation's police, the most powerful man in France after Bonaparte. Gray stubble made the Minister's face look still more cadaverous than usual. He wore a yellowed flannel waistcoat over his nightshirt. Its collar floated around his gaunt neck, where tendons pulled like ropes on wrinkled skin. Toes stuck out of the pierced slippers on his bare feet. A nightcap rested on the fireplace mantel, next to a box containing a bar of the cheapest shaving soap.

"Always good to see you, Miquel," said Fouché. "I gather that you are all for early visits. I am not adverse to them myself, but you will have to allow me to complete my ablutions in your presence." The Minister pointed at a chair. "Please make yourself comfortable."

Roch remained standing. "I saw Limoëlan last night."

Fouché took a deep breath. "Did you now? Did you arrest him?"

"Unfortunately not."

"Did you kill him?"

"He escaped."

The Minister seemed very thoughtful. "Escape, did he? That is most unfortunate."

"It depends on one's point of view, Citizen Minister."

Roch expected a valet to enter to shave Fouché, but the Minister seized a leather strap and proceeded to sharpen a horn-handled razor himself.

"And where would you have seen Limoëlan?"

"At the bottom of the Champs-Elysées, by the pier."

"Are you sure that the man you saw was Limoëlan? I doubt it, because I believe the scoundrel is dead. He died on the 3rd of Nivose, on the very night of the attack. Do you remember that man who owns the bathing establishment next to the Liberty Bridge? A Citizen Viger, or Vigier. He heard someone jumping into the Seine on the night of the attack. That must have been Limoëlan, driven to suicide by remorse over the horror of his crime."

"The man I saw last night, Citizen Minister, looked very much alive for someone who had drowned over a month ago. But you know that. You have always protected him. You met with him before the attack, you knew of his plans. Yet you did nothing to stop him, and nothing to put me on his track afterwards."

Fouché was lathering his cheeks. "And what about you, Miquel? Have you been forthcoming lately? You have known for some time of fair Madame Coudert's involvement in the conspiracy, and yet you have said nothing. Love, I suppose."

Roch started. Fouché was better informed than he had expected. The Minister smiled with indulgence through the lather that covered his face. "Ah, it is a fine thing to be young, Miquel. Enjoy it while you can."

Fouché walked to a small mirror hanging from a nail on the wall, under a sconce. He began to shave one of his cheeks, then paused. "I know Madame Coudert's husband fairly well, and have met her on a few occasions. So young, so charming. Very reckless too, very unwise in her choice of friends. No flattery intended, Miquel, but I believe the only occasion in which she showed any taste in men is in her choice of you as a lover."

Roch was furious with himself. Of course Fouché had known all about his liaison with Blanche. "And what, Citizen Minister, do you intend to do with regard to Madame Coudert?"

"She has been extremely fortunate, in that none of those arrested so far have mentioned her name. Frankly, under these circumstances, I see no need to press charges against her. Is this the face the First Consul wishes to give his enemies? Why make a Royalist martyr of one of the beauties of our age, the flower of Paris society? Carbon, with his brutish face, that cold-bloodied killer Saint-Régent, even a dour old maid like Mademoiselle de Cicé, these will do very well for the trial."

Roch held his breath, overcome by relief. So at least Blanche would escape the guillotine.

"But this does not mean," continued Fouché, "that her grave imprudence will be forgotten. I believe her husband owns a château in some remote valley in the Alps. She will be invited, for the sake of her health, to retire there permanently. You will agree, I believe, that she has a rather easy escape."

"Indeed, but so do others. You have not responded to what I said of your awareness of the plot to assassinate the First Consul. You did nothing to stop it."

Fouché turned around and pointed his razor in Roch's direction. "Now, this is a rather shocking accusation. A false one as well. I am not at all worried on that point, for I did my duty. Indeed I was well apprised, through several of my informers in the West, of the conspiracy. So I wrote a detailed report to the First Consul, setting forth all I had learned about the clandestine arrival in Paris of several notorious Chouan leaders, in particular Limoëlan and Saint-Régent. I omitted nothing of importance to warn General Bonaparte of the impending attempt against his life. Of course, I also mentioned that some of his new friends, such as the Count de Bourmont and his lovely wife, and many other *ci-devant* aristocrats, were linked to the plot. The First Consul treated my report as I had expected: with anger and contempt. He did not even forward it to General Duroc, who is in charge of his personal safety, or to the Prefect."

"The Prefect! What part has he played in this affair?"

"Dubois? *Play a part?* You give the poor man too much credit. Oh, he is capable of some awkward scheming on occasion, but in essentials he is pretty much what he appears to be, and we both know what that is."

The Minister, his face half lathered, half shaven, wiped his razor on a towel. "To go back to the First Consul, he is very desirous of gathering a new Court around himself and charming Madame Bonaparte. That is why so many names have been erased from the lists of the émigrés lately. He wants to attract those *ci-devant* nobles to Paris, to tame them, to shower them with favors. It will give him some legitimacy as France's new sovereign, and it also flatters his vanity. The last thing he wanted to hear was that his newly found courtiers were conspiring to assassinate him. He ordered me to drop that line of investigation altogether."

Roch posted himself behind Fouché, a foot away from the Minister's back. "You were content to write your report, while certain that it would be disregarded? You did *nothing*?"

"Well, the First Consul himself instructed me, in no uncertain terms, to do nothing. I am only the Minister of Police, after all. He is the glorious leader of the Nation. I obeyed."

"Yet when it suits you, you do not hesitate to provoke the First Consul. You had Bourmont arrested at his doorstep."

"Ah, yes." Fouché chuckled. "I indulged in some juvenile fun there. The best part of it was that the First Consul had to admit that I had been right, once I explained to him the close relationship between Carbon and Bourmont during the months leading up to the attack. Quite entertaining, and it also allowed me to make the point that those who disregard my warnings do so at their own peril."

"But Bourmont, though compromised by association, never played any active part in the plot. Limoëlan, on the contrary, is our main suspect, and should be our main concern. I am sure that he cannot have gone far. He is still in Paris, within our reach."

Roch looked straight into Fouché's eyes. "And Limoëlan, once arrested, would have many interesting tales to tell. He might, for instance, reveal his dealings with a high official, a member of the government no less, who has established contacts with George and

the Royalist government in London. Someone who has been scheming for the King's restoration, and his own future of course, in case the
attempt on the First Consul's life was successful."

Fouché put down his razor on the fireplace mantel. "My dear
Miquel, you are carried away by misguided zeal. These are wild
suppositions."

"Quite the contrary, Citizen Minister. I have proof of this. I was
able to seize from Limoëlan, before he escaped, some correspondence
between him and George discussing said Minister's offers of service.
I have entrusted these letters to a friend, with instructions to bring
them to the Prefect should anything untoward happen to my father
or me. And I am sure that the Prefect, despite his limitations, will
understand their import and know what to do with them."

Fouché was staring into the bright fire in the hearth.

"Well, of course, your father," he said after a while. "There is no
compelling reason to keep him in jail any longer, is there? I will speak
to the First Consul about it. Today, in fact. You may count on his release this evening."

Fouché was wiping his cheeks with the towel. "There is only one
thing, Miquel. The First Consul believes that vociferous Jacobins have
no place in his good city of Paris. I am sorry, but it will not be in my
power to change his mind on this point. Your father's rants have been
zealously reported by Dubois. There was barely a night when one of
the Prefect's *mouchards* did not patronize the Mighty Barrel. It fol-
lows that the First Consul is well informed of your father's opinions
and will not tolerate his presence in Paris any longer than necessary,
let us say beyond a few hours. Your father will have to leave by the
next stagecoach to his birthplace of Lavigerie, and remain there."

Roch glared at Fouché. "This means that my father will not be
allowed to stir from Lavigerie? But he has not set foot in Auvergne
in thirteen years, since my mother's death. His entire life, all of his
friends, are in Paris."

"That may be, but there is nothing you or I can do about it at this
point. Perhaps in a few years your father may be allowed to return to

Paris. It all depends on his behavior. In the meantime, no one, not even I, can undo the effect of the Prefect's reports."

Fouché put his hand on Roch's shoulder. "Come, Miquel. Your father will go back to the old country. Of course, in the beginning, people will be wary of associating with man exiled by the government. But after a while some of his acquaintances may be willing to renew old friendships. He will be the richest man around. He can afford to buy the best house in town. He will hire a peasant girl as a maid, and hopefully he will choose her pleasant and comely. Certainly, after the bustle of Paris, small-town life will seem tedious to him. Besides, he is not much over fifty, is he? The unavoidable will happen, that little maid will be with child, and, because your father is a decent man, he will marry her. Now, is this so terrible?"

Fouché removed his flannel waistcoat. "With your permission, I would now like to dress outside your presence."

"Can I fetch my father from the Temple?"

"I suggest that you go home and enjoy a well-deserved rest. I will let you know in the course of the day when the time comes."

Roch bowed and left. He had some trouble believing the good news, and still more trusting Fouché. Yet as soon as he reached his lodgings and lay down on his bed, he fell into a dreamless sleep.

63

Roch did not awaken until midafternoon, when his maid shook him forcefully to hand him a note from Fouché. He cursed his own laziness and tore it open. It announced that Old Miquel would be released at six o'clock that evening, in time to depart by the next stagecoach for Auvergne, which left from Sceaux a few hours later.

It had been exactly one month since Roch had seen his father. He had hoped to return to the Mighty Barrel for friendly evening chats in the Roman language, with Old Miquel restored to his rightful place at the helm of the tavern. That was not to be. Things would never be the same. The two men would be apart now, for the first time in many years. Roch could not imagine his father exiled from Paris, or Paris without Old Miquel's presence.

When Roch was shown into the clerk's office at the Temple, he had the surprise to find his father already there, sharing a pint of wine with Citizen Fauconnier.

"Yes, I received my orders in the afternoon," said the man. "I, for one, am sorry to see Citizen Miquel *père* leave. And I won't be alone, let me tell you."

"God, I missed you, son," said Old Miquel, wrapping his arm around Roch's shoulders. "But then I guess I'll have to become used to seeing you not so often as before."

Roch had dreaded making this announcement. "You . . . you know, Father?"

"About being exiled from Paris?" Old Miquel pointed at the clerk. "Oh, yes, Citizen Fauconnier was kind enough to tell me when he gave me the good news. Now I've settled everything that needed settling, so we can be on our way. We'll have a bit of time to talk before the stagecoach leaves."

Roch took his father to the hackney that waited outside the prison doors. He held the door open for Old Miquel and climbed in after him.

"We still have time to stop by the Mighty Barrel, Father," he said.

The older man shook his head. "I've thought about it. You see, Roch, I'm leaving Paris for good, and the Barrel'll be sold, so there's no point in looking back. That part of my life's over." He paused for a minute. "Tell Alexandrine I won't be able to thank her in person, and that I don't want to compromise her by writing her either. All of my letters'll be opened now. So please tell her that I'll never forget her kindness."

"I will, Father."

Old Miquel patted Roch on the thigh. "I know I must've pestered you to death about her."

Roch opened his mouth to protest.

"Well, Roch, I was wrong. You're such a dutiful, respectful son, you never told me to mind my own business. Now I've had plenty of time to think about that in jail. If Alexandrine's not to your taste, there's no arguing about it. Maybe you're not ready to marry anyway. And maybe she's not fancy enough for you. You're Chief Inspector, you're an important man at the Prefecture."

"I have realized over the past month how unimportant I am, Father."

"Don't say that. Look at what you've managed to do. You arrested the scoundrels who killed those poor innocents, you kept me from being deported and now you're pulling me out of jail. And you'll go higher than Chief Inspector yet. When it comes to men, nowadays people look at what you are yourself, not at your father. But for a woman, it's not the same. People still ask: *And who's her father?* And then what'd you say if you married Alexandrine? That your wife's the daughter of an old rogue of a wine merchant who can't even read or write?" Old Miquel shrugged. "People'd say you married her just for her money. You'd grow ashamed of her."

"That's not true, Father. No man in his right mind would be ashamed of Alexandrine."

"Oh, you'd try to hide it, of course, but she'd know it. She understands things, Alexandrine. A girl like her deserves better. What's sure is that you shouldn't marry her just to make me happy, now that I'm going away. So choose a girl to your liking, and choose carefully. Think of your mother."

"I will, Father, and of you too. And I will visit you in Lavigerie as soon as I can."

"Keep your own situation in mind first. Things might stay a bit shaky for a while at the Prefecture. Don't worry about me opening my big mouth down there in Lavigerie. I'll be as quiet as can be. I won't talk about Bonaparte, about Fouché, about politics, specially to my friends, if I still have any. They'd be the first to report me, I know that. I won't even complain about the weather. I don't want to cause trouble for you. Those things, the ideals of the Revolution, it's all done now. People want Bonaparte, so let them have Bonaparte, and see all the good that comes out of it."

Old Miquel shook his head. "It's a sad thing to watch a great nation sink into idiocy. They're all enamored of Bonaparte, of his victories, of his glory. Oh, someday they'll realize he only cares about himself, not about the good of the country. But it's too soon just yet." Old Miquel poked Roch's chest with his index finger. "So obey the government. Don't create trouble for yourself, but try to remain a decent man. Serve the First Consul, as he calls himself, and serve his valets, but only as long as it suits you. I don't think Bonaparte'll outlast his first defeat. When that time comes, and it will, mind you, don't waste your loyalty on a fellow like that. He isn't worth it."

Old Miquel stared straight ahead. "Anyway, I'll have other things to do in Auvergne than talking politics. I'll go to your mother's tomb, or what's left of it. I'm ashamed of myself. All these years've passed, and I've never gone back there to pay my respects and keep it in good repair. It'd have hurt too much. I'll go visit, and I'll have a proper cross put on it, with an inscription, like for rich people. It'll say what a good wife she was, and how much I've missed her. Something about the poor little ones too. And I'll put a few words about you. I know she'd have liked that. You always were her favorite child. But you already knew that, I guess. She'd be so proud of you if she could see you. In fact, I'm sure she can from where she is now."

Roch felt that old sorrow gripping his throat, choking him.

"Now I've said all I needed to say," added Old Miquel, patting Roch's arm. "I should stop talking, because I'm only causing you pain."

Both remained silent until the hackney arrived in Sceaux. There, in front of the Inn of the Silver Bell, they embraced a long time, like men who might not see each other again. At last Old Miquel gently pushed Roch away and walked in the direction of the waiting stagecoach. He turned around and waved one last time at his son.

64

Think of your mother. Those had been Old Miquel's words. Indeed Roch often thought of his mother, of the last time he had seen her, of that September farewell. She had kept him huddled in her arms so long. How he regretted to have fought his tears then, out of mistaken pride and bravery.

He also remembered the last time he had gone to Auvergne, at the age of twelve, with his father, the following June. During the final days of their journey home, Old Miquel's mood changed. He seemed absentminded, preoccupied, and barely answered any of Roch's questions. Roch guessed that his father was thinking of his mother and of their reunion behind the bed curtains. Old Miquel quickened their pace as they approached the village of Lavigerie, and they ran and cried with joy at the sight of its first houses.

That year they realized that something had gone wrong. The Miquel cottage was still there, with its thatched roof and walls made of huge black stones, mortared in white, but the shutter of the only window was closed, in spite of the fine weather. So was the door. It was locked. Old Miquel banged on it with both fists.

"Augalio!" he shouted.

Daval, one of the neighbors, walked slowly out of the next cottage. "She isn't home," he said under his breath.

Old Miquel walked to the man in a menacing manner. "Where did she go? When's she coming back?"

"She isn't coming back, Antonin. The *eicir* took her."

"The *eicir*..." said Old Miquel, as though in a trance.

The *eicirs* are the snowstorms of the high country, eddies of blinding whiteness.

"The priest wanted to write you," continued Daval, "but no one knew where you lived in Paris."

Old Miquel remained still, staring at the sunlit fields in the distance.

"It happened in April, the last *eicir* we had this year," continued Daval. "We found her the next morning, frozen, poor thing, just yards from your cottage. She must have lost her way."

"Why did she go out in the *eicir*? She knew better."

"The door to your cottage must've slipped loose during the night, and two of your sheep were missing. She went out in search of them. I told her not to go, to wait another day. The air smelled of snow. But she wouldn't listen. You owed seven sheep as rent to the Baron de Peyre, half of your flock, and she said she couldn't survive with only five left."

"And the children? Where are my children?" A vein was throbbing on Old Miquel's forehead. His voice had become shrill.

"The little ones went out with her, to help her find those sheep. They died together, Antonin. We found them like that, her holding them tight in her arms. So tight that we couldn't separate them, frozen as they were. So we buried them in the same grave, the three of them."

Roch pictured his mother caught in the twirling white sheets of the *eicir*. She had gone deaf from the howls of the wind and become disoriented. She had walked in circles for hours, so close to home and so hopelessly lost. Finally, exhausted, she had stopped to make a nest in the snow. She had gathered her children close. Then the *eicir* had lulled them all to sleep.

They said in the high country that, after one stopped fighting, it was a slow yet painless, merciful agony. One even felt warm and comfortable in the snow and simply went to sleep. Roch had prayed that it was true. Who could tell really? No one had ever awakened from the embrace of the *eicir*.

Old Miquel pushed open the gate to the Lavigerie graveyard. It squeaked on its rusty hinges. They looked for the fresher, unfamiliar graves. In a far corner, they saw a swelling in the dirt, a mound adorned with two gray planks nailed together to form a cross. As they drew near, they saw that it bore an inscription in black paint, half erased:

Eulalie, wife of Antonin Miquel
Anna and Pierre Miquel, their children

Both man and boy took off their hats and knelt before the tomb. Someone had tied a ribbon, yellow and red, already faded, to the cross. The sharp mountain wind that pierced Roch to the bone played with it. He recognized the trinket. His mother had treasured it and worn it, shiny then and brightly colored, on her bonnet on all holidays and the few festive occasions of her life.

Old Miquel wiped his eyes with the back of his hand. "I gave it to her as a wedding present," he said.

Roch reached for the ribbon, the last memento of his mother. It seemed alive, ready to fly away, fluttering in the wind like the wings of a butterfly. His father stopped him before he could touch it.

"Leave it," he said. "It should stay here, with her, till nothing's left of it."

That night, they accepted the Davals' hospitality for dinner. Old Miquel decided to sleep one last night in the dead cottage. Then they left for Paris before dawn, like thieves, without saying good-bye to anyone in Lavigerie. They had never returned to Auvergne.

65

Roch was startled when the hackney stopped in front of his lodgings. He realized all of a sudden that this was not home, it was not where he wanted to be. He shouted to the driver to whip his horse and drive as fast as he could to the Mighty Barrel, Rue Croix-des-Petits-Champs. He pulled his watch. It was eleven now, and the tavern had just closed. Though he barely knew how to pray, or to whom, he prayed ardently that Alexandrine had not left for her father's house yet. He breathed a sigh of relief when he reached the Barrel. Light still filtered between the cracks of the closed shutters. He jumped off the hackney and threw the driver a silver coin.

He ran to the door. He pulled a key from his pocket and let himself into the common room. It was tidy, the benches and chairs pushed against the tables, the floor swept. Alexandrine was standing in the middle of the room, adjusting her kerchief around her neck, when she saw him. Neither of them uttered a word. He dropped onto the nearest chair. He rested his elbows on the table and pressed his fists into the sockets of his eyes in an effort to stop the flow of tears. Fortunately he had been able to control himself in front of his father. But now sobs came from deep within his chest, suffocating him. The only way to breathe was to let out a long wail, a howl of pain over Old Miquel's exile, over the loss of Blanche, over his mother's death, so faraway and yet so fresh.

The next thing he remembered was breathing again, and a light scent of lavender. His face was buried in the folds of Alexandrine's dress, and he felt her fingers running through the short curls of his hair. She uttered indistinct sounds of comfort, like a wordless lullaby. He clasped his arms tight around her waist. What was so comforting was that there was no need to explain. Old Miquel was right. She understood things.

How long they remained thus he could not tell, but they were startled by a knock at the door. At this time it could only be Vidalenc's manservant coming to take Alexandrine home. Roch could not let the man see him weep. He let go of Alexandrine and ran up the stairs to his father's apartment. He collapsed on the bed in the dark and tried to bring his breathing under control. She would go now. It was only proper, of course, yet he wanted to cry to her to stay. He would not even touch her, he only wanted to feel her close to him through the night. He heard a man's voice coming from the common room, and then Alexandrine's answer.

"No, Fraysse, I can't come now," she said in her clear, poised voice. "I have not finished the day's accounts yet. You needn't wait for me, I will sleep here tonight in Citizen Miquel's apartment."

The man spoke again.

"But yes, of course," she added, "I will be fine here by myself. Please tell Father not to worry."

Roch breathed in deeply. Alexandrine would spend the night there with him, out of love, out of pity, out of the kindness of her heart, because she knew he could not do without her. Her words stirred within him such need as he had never felt for anyone.

He heard the clang of the front door being closed and locked. A minute later she appeared, carrying a candle. He did not rise from the bed, nor she did she look in his direction. His eyes followed her as she knelt in front of the hearth. She lit kindling and stoked the fire until flames danced merrily between the logs and cast an orange glow on her delicate profile. He realized how cold the room had been.

She rose and walked to him. She seized his hands and made him sit up to remove his coat, then pushed him back gently until his head rested on the pillow again. Standing by the bed, she pulled his boots.

He watched her as she deliberately stepped out of her shoes, then removed her bonnet and kerchief. She lay by his side, as though it were the most natural thing in the world, as though she were his wife. He did not want to move away from her, nor did he dare reach for her.

But now her fingers were caressing his cheek. He caught both of her hands in his. "Let us stay like this, Alexandrine. Please don't move. You don't understand how desperately I want you."

"I do understand," she whispered.

He pulled her to him. "It is all very simple now, dearest. I know what to do. I will go to your father in the morning and ask for your hand."

She closed her eyes and drew him to her breast. The skin there felt warm and soft, and he could hear her heart beating fast, as fast, he imagined, as a heart could beat without breaking.

Historical Note

Joseph-Pierre Picot de Limoëlan, Pierre Robinault de Saint-Régent and François Carbon are historical characters. They attempted to assassinate Bonaparte on Christmas Eve 1800 by detonating an infernal machine on a busy Paris street. Carbon did sleep with his sister and niece, Saint-Régent acquired a pug for his *lady*, whose identity was never discovered, and Limoëlan paid a little street vendor by the name of Marianne Peusol twelve *sols* to hold the bridle of their horse.

However, many accomplices are not mentioned in this novel. Their inclusion would have made for a cumbersome narrative. The code name *Pour le Roy*, "For the King," was actually one of Limoëlan's aliases, but I liked it so much that I decided to give it to my fictional heroine, and used it as the title of this novel.

My retelling of the search for the assassins, often considered the first modern police investigation, is based upon the archives of the Ministry and Prefecture of Police in Paris. Fouché was indeed in contact with Limoëlan and his mother in the months leading to the attack. In my opinion the Minister of Police was aware of the plot to assassinate Bonaparte, and did little to thwart it. I have no proof of direct contacts at the time between he and Cadoudal or the King's government in exile, but they would have been consistent with the man's character and the circumstances of the conspiracy.

The deportations of Jacobins who had nothing to do with the attack and the lamentable outcome of the alleged Conspiracy of Daggers are historical facts. Most of the characters in this story, including the painters David, Topino-Lebrun and Mulard, are real, though Roch, his father, Blanche and Alexandrine are fictional.

The trial of Carbon and Saint-Régent began in April of 1801. Among the other accused were Mother Duquesne, Mademoiselle de Cicé, Basile Collin, the medical student who had treated Saint-Régent on the night of the explosion, Catherine Vallon, the Guillou family, in whose lodgings Saint-Régent had been hidden, and many minor figures in the Rue Nicaise conspiracy. Limoëlan was tried *in absentia*. None of the accused acknowledged his or her guilt.

For days witnesses filed before the judges and jury, pointing accusatory fingers at Carbon and Saint-Régent. Captain Platel was not available to testify. Gangrene had settled in his thigh after the amputation of his leg, and he had now joined his landlady, pretty Widow Lystère, for all eternity. Then it was the turn of the victims, the blind, the maimed, the bereft. The audience cried during the testimony of Widow Peusol, whose little Marianne had been sacrificed in cold blood.

The final tally of the attack was twenty-two dead and fifty-six permanently maimed. Those would receive a lifetime pension from the Nation. Forty-six houses on Rue Nicaise had been destroyed, many more damaged. The entire street was condemned to make way for a wider, more handsome thoroughfare, with a new name, one that would not evoke the slaughter of innocents.

Carbon and Saint-Régent were found guilty of conspiracy to assassinate the First Consul and sentenced to death. So was Limoëlan, still missing. Saint-Régent, when advised by the presiding judge of his right to appeal, rose proudly, his hand to his breast, and demanded to be executed forthright. The other defendants were sentenced to various terms of imprisonment.

Yet Saint-Régent changed his mind, for both he and Carbon filed appeals, without success. On the 20th of April 1801, less than four months after the Rue Nicaise attack, the two men were led to the guillotine. The cart made its way through an unruly crowd that howled *Assassins of the people!* Carbon climbed the steps to the scaffold first and, before being strapped to the plank, cried *For the King!* Saint-Régent, waiting for his turn at the foot of the machine, lost his composure when the triangular blade, dripping with the blood of his companion, was raised again for him. His legs wobbled and the executioner's aides had to assist him up the stairs.

The executions of Carbon and Saint-Régent did not help the deported Jacobins falsely accused of the Rue Nicaise attack. They remained overseas, where most died of tropical fevers and exhaustion.

Georges Cadoudal returned to London after the arrest of his accomplices. In the ensuing years, he kept sailing back and forth between France and England, and conspiring to assassinate the First Consul. In 1804, he was arrested in Paris after killing two police officers. He too perished on the guillotine.

As for the course of the war that was tearing Europe apart, short-lived peace treaties were signed on more than one occasion, more glorious campaigns followed, victories were won and celebrated, millions died on battlefields. Napoléon Bonaparte, after crowning himself Emperor of the French and conquering most of the continent, was finally defeated and had to abdicate the throne. He would die an exile, in British custody, on the faraway island of St. Helena in 1821.

Fouché was twice dismissed by Bonaparte from his position of Minister of Police, each time to return, more powerful, more indispensable, more distrusted than ever. He was made Duc d'Otrante in recognition of his services.

In 1815 Fouché played a determining role in the final ouster of Napoléon and the restoration of Louis XVIII, which allowed him to remain Minister of Police under the new regime. For a while. A year later, the King exiled him from France as a *régicide*.

Dubois, Prefect of Police, kept his position until 1810, when he was dismissed. He still held various public positions and rallied to the restored Bourbons but, despite all of his hopes and efforts, despite the vagaries of Fouché's fortunes, he was never appointed Minister of Police.

Father de Clorivière, Limoëlan's uncle, remained in hiding following the Rue Nicaise trial. He was finally arrested in 1804 and jailed at the Temple without charges ever being brought against him. In 1808, he was released on account of his advanced years and the Latin verses he had written in honor of Napoléon. He died in 1820, at the age of eighty-five.

As for Limoëlan himself, sentenced to death *in absentia*, he left Paris for his native Brittany. He spent a few months in the family château that bore his name and had become the home of his newly wedded sister Marie-Thérèse. She had at last married her suitor, who had come into a large estate in America.

Limoëlan was not as fortunate as his sister. He had hoped to wed his fiancée, Mademoiselle Julie d'Albert, but fate had decided otherwise. Julie, during a tearful last meeting, informed him that, at the time of his greatest danger, she had vowed to forsake him forever if by some miracle he escaped unharmed. Now that her prayers had been answered, she intended to keep her pledge and take the veil. She gently suggested that Limoëlan too open his heart to God.

Soon his sister Marie-Thérèse's husband, Monsieur de Chapdelaine, had to travel to America with his bride to take possession of his fortune. He offered a passage on the same ship to Limoëlan, disguised as his valet.

Once in America, Limoëlan became a painter of miniature portraits under various names. He settled for a while in Savannah, then in Baltimore. Yet something was still missing from his life. At last, in 1812, like his former fiancée eleven years earlier, he received God's call. "The angel who was the instrument of my conversion showed me the way," he wrote.

He was ordained a priest in Charleston, South Carolina, under the name of Joseph-Pierre de Clorivière, adopted in honor of Father de Clorivière, his uncle. Perhaps the new cleric also felt that the name *Limoëlan*, even across an ocean and after the passage of twelve years, might still carry unfortunate associations with the Rue Nicaise atrocity. Whatever the reasons for the adoption of this name, Father de Clorivière, who became a curate in Charleston, was noted for his piety. He would fast on the holiday of Christmas, which he spent prostrated in prayers at the foot of the altar.

In 1814, he was overwhelmed with joy at the news of the fall of Bonaparte and the restoration of Louis XVIII. He forgot his usual reserve and was seen running through the streets of Charleston crying *Long Live the King!* He celebrated a *Te Deum* mass of thanksgiving in honor of the usurper's fall, which angered some of his parishioners. He paid those no heed, for he was already planning his return home.

In France, his past efforts were acknowledged by the King, but some of his old friends, from whom he had expected an enthusiastic welcome, hinted that his ministry was more needed in America than in his native country.

He chose to return to his functions as a curate in Charleston. There he faced the resentment of those of his flock who did not share his political opinions. Furthermore, his life was marked by many disagreements with his superior, Father Gallagher. The enmity between the two clerics and their respective supporters escalated into a bitter pamphlet war.

Under these circumstances, Father de Clorivière accepted with relief and gratitude the function of spiritual director of the Convent of the Sisters of the Visitation of Mary in Georgetown. He devoted his life, and the 30,000 francs he had received from King Louis XVIII as damages for assets lost by his family during the Revolution, to this community.

He designed himself the Convent's Chapel and oversaw its construction. It was dedicated it to the Sacred-Heart-of-Jesus, a symbol of the Visitation Order, and also the battle sign of the Catholic and Royal Army. The memory of all the Chouans who had died fighting with this emblem close to their own hearts never left him.

In 1826, Father de Clorivière tripped and fell after celebrating mass. He never recovered and passed away a few months later, at the age of fifty-six, attended to his last moment by the Sisters of the Visitation. He was laid to rest in his beloved Chapel, beneath the altar.

Acknowledgments

This novel was written thanks to my mother. For a year her spare bedroom became my office as I typed away on my laptop. She listened to my ideas, and offered support and advice.

Stephanie Cabot, of The Gernert Company, was everything an agent should be, and then some. It is truly a joy to work with her.

Erika Imranyi, my editor, took over the project midway, adopted it and brought it to fruition. My thanks go to her and the whole team at Dutton.

Last but not least, my son, William, offered to review the final drafts of my manuscript. He made insightful suggestions, which I followed. Congratulations on your very first editing job, William, and welcome to the literary world!